Fiona's Gift

The Fourth of
Mercy's Children

Katy Huth Jones

Fiona's Gift

ISBN-13: 979-8842319251

Published in the United States of America

First print edition: July 2022 by Quinlan Creek Press

Dedication

This book is dedicated to the memory of
Allie Sikes, my precious sister in Christ,
who loved visiting Levathia as much as I do.

Thanks

I want to thank my patient readers yet again. This book took longer to write than anticipated for a completely different reason than any of the other books: Fiona, being quite headstrong, changed the plot and wouldn't take "no" for an answer! Also, this book is officially the longest in both series. Authors only "think" they have control of their novels; after all, the characters are living, breathing people to them, and they can "hear" the characters' voices. Why wouldn't the characters have strong opinions about what happens to them???

Thanks as always to my husband Keith for his encouragement, moral support, and selfless love for almost 44 years;

My long-time critique partner, Pamela, for her fantastic content editing skills;

My beta readers, Barbara, Robin, Faith, and Nanette, for their encouragement and enthusiasm and understanding of my sometimes stubborn characters;

Julie C. Gilbert, a.k.a. the "Blurb Queen" for her help on my blurb;

Joshua Smolders for taking my pitiful hand-drawn map of Levathia and creating a work of art with dragons; I hope someday you can make my map of Moor Point look as cool;

And for you, Dear Reader, for adventuring with me in Levathia! Tristam's story is next, the last in this series. However, something unexpected occurred in Fiona's book, and it may be necessary to write a THIRD series about Mercy's grandchildren, so I can find out what happens.... For that is how every story begins: What happens? And what happens *next*?

For more about the author visit www.katyhuthjones.blogspot.com

Stories set in Levathia:

Mercy's Children Series

Dolan's Bride
Joy's Sorrow
Valerian's Flight
Fiona's Gift

He Who Finds Mercy Series

Mercy's Prince
Mercy's Gift
Mercy's Battle
Mercy's King
Mercy's Joy

KATY HUTH JONES

Chapter 1

For wisdom is better than rubies;
and all the things that may be desired are not to be compared to it.

Fiona MacLachlan stood at the landing of the Keep, gazing out over the nearly empty castle yard. The sun had barely risen, and she hadn't appreciated before how peaceful it was this time of day. She should rise early more often.

Smoothing her riding skirt, she lightly tripped down the stairs and hurried to the stables, anxious to be riding with her older brother Val this morning. When she entered her favorite place in the sprawling castle complex, Conrad the stablemaster met her with a concerned frown.

"Good morrow, Lady Fiona." He inclined his head.

"What is wrong, Conrad?" Her wariness turned to apprehension. "Nothing has happened to Firestorm, has it?" Her spirited mare could be accident-prone.

"No, my lady. Firestorm is well. But Prince Val left a message for you, that he and King Dolan had business in the Highlands today, and so he cannot ride with you until he returns." The stablemaster twisted his hands together and looked as if he'd rather be elsewhere.

"He left already?" Fiona glanced around, as if she might catch Val anyway.

"Not ten minutes ago, my lady. Both your brothers flew away astride their dragons." He grimaced, and Fiona couldn't stand to look at him any longer.

"Fine, thank you." She pressed her lips together before she vented her anger on Conrad, who was after all only the messenger, not the source of bad news. "I'd like to ride Firestorm anyway."

With obvious relief, the stablemaster bowed again. "I'll have her ready for you right away." He turned and called to the nearest stable hand.

Fiona saw with interest that it was Darby. Though he was not handsome, like her friend Roland Campignon, he was kind to the horses and to her, and when he smiled, his light blue eyes lit from within, making him very appealing. He pulled on his forelock, part of his long tangled yellow curls, and hurried to Firestorm's stall. Fiona followed.

She entered the stall and quietly watched Darby saddle and bridle her mare with his usual efficiency. Firestorm must have scented her, but she showed no notice, and so Darby hadn't either. He murmured to the horse in his calm, pleasant voice, and Fiona decided she could listen to him all day. When he grasped the reins and turned Firestorm toward the stall door, he startled, making the mare shy away too.

"My, my lady." Darby gulped and made an awkward bow. "Forgive me, but I did not see ye standing there." He bit his full bottom lip, drawing Fiona's gaze to his mouth. Had he ever kissed a girl?

"There is nothing to beg forgiveness for." Fiona smiled at him, hoping he would smile back. "I am the one who should apologize to you. I did not mean to startle you or Firestorm." She patted the mare, who ducked her head and snorted.

"Would my lady like to mount here, or wait until I lead Firestorm to the yard?" Darby still sounded flustered, and Fiona enjoyed watching the effect she had on him.

"Here is fine." She placed her hand on his arm, and his eyes widened. "Will you boost me to the saddle?"

Darby blinked several times and swallowed noisily. "Of course, my lady." He dropped the reins and positioned himself at Firestorm's side, cupping his hands for Fiona's foot. His head was down, so she couldn't see his eyes.

Fiona reached up to grab hold of the saddle, placed her left foot in Darby's hands, and let him lift her up while she swung her right leg around to straddle the mare. After settling into the saddle, she took the reins from him with a nod of thanks and urged Firestorm to the main door.

Then she put the stable boy out of her mind and focused on riding her mare out the dragon gates and into the town's narrow streets. Already townspeople were about, but she gave them only the attention necessary to keep from colliding with them. Once they exited the town gates, Fiona gave Firestorm her head, and the mare galloped along the road south of the Keep.

After a little while, Fiona turned the horse off the road, and they raced across the fields toward the lake. The rising sun illuminated the walls and towers of the Keep, making the stone appear gilded. Fiona had never noticed that color before, how it warmed the cold stone of the structure.

Then they were nearing the lake, and Fiona pulled up Firestorm to a walk. As soon as they reached her favorite meadow, Fiona halted the mare and slid down, letting her graze.

She walked to a fallen tree and sat upon it with a sigh. How like her eldest brother to steal Val away again. Since Val's return, they had only been riding four times. Four! Even though he was no longer the king's royal squire, he seemed as busy as ever doing Dolan's bidding.

Though he was not thirty years old, Dolan had been King of Levathia for eighteen years, longer than Fiona had been alive. Since he'd ascended the throne at age eleven, Fiona had heard others talk about how his reign might be the longest of any king in history, should he live to a ripe old age.

Perhaps it was because they were only half brother and sister, but Fiona had never felt especially close to Dolan. And she felt sure Dolan's wife, Queen Rhianna, had never truly liked her. Dolan himself seemed more cool and distant than usual, especially in the last year. Well no matter, Fiona had never cared for her brother's high and mighty ways, how he sided with Papa and Mama whenever she displeased them. Which was happening more and more often.

She'd tried to please them, she really had! But her parents had forgotten how it was to be young and unsure of oneself, especially since Fiona was the only one in the family without one of the Most High's gifts. The few times she'd tried to talk to them about it, Papa and Mama did not even *try* to understand how humiliating it was to be the only ordinary member of the royal family. And not just because they were royalty, but as so many referred to them: the most gifted family in the history of Levathia.

Fiona leaned over and plucked a yellow wildflower, twirling it between her hands. She used to dream of having Mama's gift of listening to plants, which was part of her Healing gift. Even Tristam, her younger brother, had that gift! He was good at everything, and Fiona hated being so jealous of her only full sibling.

At least her sister Joy, as well as Val, loved her for who she was and never made her ashamed of her lack of gifts. They also accepted her as if she were their full sister and never made her feel like an unwanted stepchild. Maybe Dolan didn't mean to act that way, but his feelings were clear, to Fiona's mind.

A bird sang in a nearby tree, and Fiona stopped her musings to listen. She rose from the fallen tree and walked closer, imagining the tones of the bird's song as written notation. With that image in mind, since she could not see the bird, Fiona began to sing along, not with words but with whatever syllables seemed best to match the birdsong.

In the last year, her voice had strengthened in range and quality, though she rarely had anything to sing about, at least when she had an audience. Here there was only Firestorm and the bird and the meadow and the sky, so Fiona poured out all the longing of her heart and sang until her throat became dry.

The notes of the song dissipated in the breeze, and Fiona noticed the bird had stopped too. She collected Firestorm's reins and walked to the nearest stream so the both of them could quench their thirst before returning to the Keep.

After she mounted Firestorm, Fiona sat unmoving while she scanned the few clouds in the clear morning sky. She wished Roland could have been here for her sixteenth birthday last week, but of course, he lived far away and had many obligations as Sir Thomas Cornwall's squire. At least the annual court and tournament would begin in less than a fortnight, and Fiona hoped Roland would have a little time of his own, at least.

She blushed when she recalled his most recent letter, not because of its contents but because it was yet another reminder she had only written him one time in the last eleven months. It wasn't that she didn't *want* to write to Roland, but whenever she sat down, it was too difficult to put her feelings into words on parchment. It was much easier for her to say them out loud, so she could read his facial expression and know what his reaction would be.

With a sigh, Fiona signaled Firestorm to head back to the Keep. She had thought to ride the long way around the castle complex and look for wildflowers, but without Val to accompany her, the beauty of the morning had quickly faded. Why did her life have to be so uneventful and—dull?

* * *

In the yard of the MacRorie fortress, Val d'Alden stood patiently with his brother the king while they waited for Cephalorix and Regnatorix—or Reggie as Val called his dragon friend—to examine six eager young people of the clan. The "examination" to this point had merely been for the two dragons to speak to each young person's mind, and if he or she could hear their thoughts, to *See* if they were of good character. Once it was determined they were suitable, the plan was for each candidate for dragon rider to be interviewed by King Dolan and himself before meeting the younger dragons. Thankfully several of Reggie's siblings were also willing to become part of Dolan's new Royal Dragon Couriers.

These six Highlanders were the first to be contacted, after preliminary messages had gone out to all the provinces earlier in the summer. Val felt it was cutting things close to visit everyone who had applied, but Dolan was determined to have it done by the time his annual court and tournament began.

Since Val would officially be made Lord of the Sky at the beginning of court and take oversight of the flying couriers, both the dragons and their riders would have to take an oath to him as well as to Dolan. This would hopefully ensure their willingness to submit to his authority, even though he was now only seventeen years old.

That part of the plan concerned Val not a little, but Dolan had been working with him, to help him learn ways to project confidence and strength.

"You have those qualities in abundance," Dolan had cheerfully said again this morning. "You merely need to wear them outwardly for all to see."

Much easier spoken than accomplished! But Val was determined to do his part to the best of his ability. It helped that Reggie was now his constant companion since returning from the far north. They had learned much and grown up together on their recent adventure beyond the boundaries of Levathia.

Now, however, his attention was distracted by his ever-present thoughts of Emma MacRorie, a young woman from this clan and one of Kieran's cousins on his mother's side. Val's stepfather had accompanied him last month to meet Emma, so she wouldn't be overwhelmed meeting all his family at one time. Val smiled, remembering how happy Emma and Kieran had been in their reminiscing about family members, though their Highland accents had broadened so thickly, Val could scarcely understand them.

He and Emma had written one another regularly since their first encounter in April. Back then, she had told him there were six months left in her apprenticeship with a midwife. She had just two months more to fulfill her obligation, and then Val planned to ask her to marry him. But first, he hoped to find someone else in the Highlands who could speak to dragons. That way, after he convinced Emma to become a courier, she would not have to be assigned here. Assuming she was willing, which was assuming quite a lot, Val planned for Emma to share his duties as a "roamer," flying wherever the need was greatest for a fast courier.

Sometimes his stomach clenched at the possibility she would reject both his marriage proposal and the invitation to join the Royal Dragon Couriers. Emma had already proven she could speak to dragons, and Val and Kieran were convinced of her impeccable character, but she was under no obligation, either to him or the couriers.

His only hope was the growing affection he read between the lines of her letters. Truly they did seem compatible in every way, and Val looked forward to the day when Emma and his mother could finally meet. He felt strongly they would get along very well, and the thought of it always brought a smile to his face.

Val? His attention was drawn to Reggie, since he could tell his friend was speaking only to his mind, not also to Dolan or Cephalorix.

Yes? He considered moving closer to the dragon, but Dolan might prefer that he remain where he was. They did look more official, or as Dolan might say, imposing, standing side-by-side like a pair of matching castle towers. Now that Val had attained his brother's height, he was noticing how few people in Levathia were as tall.

Two of these humans can speak easily to us, but the others cannot.

6

Val wanted to react outwardly to his great relief, but it might not be appropriate. He was, however, extremely grateful to know there were other Highlanders besides Emma who could speak to dragons. Before he could reply to Reggie, Cephalorix addressed both brothers.

My king, and Prince Val. The chief dragon used his most formal voice. *One male and one female of these six are acceptable to be considered as dragon riders.* Now he spoke to the Highlanders. *If you are hearing my voice, step forward.*

Two of the MacRories walked closer to Cephalorix, and both showed surprise when the others did not. Dolan spoke to the four unsuccessful candidates first.

"We thank you all for your interest in the Royal Dragon Couriers. Lord Cephalorix has determined that Kentigern and Caesg are the ones who will continue on as candidates." Val heard the young woman's name pronounced as "cask."

After the others bowed to Dolan and Cephalorix, they murmured congratulations to their fellows and wandered away. Before Dolan spoke again, he stared into Kentigern's eyes, sharing what he *Saw* with Val.

This young man is impeccably honest now, though in his younger years he was a prankster. I believe he will do well, if one of the dragons will bond with him. Then he turned his Sight on Caesg. *She is even younger than she appears, though she has a maturity and steadiness I believe the dragons will appreciate. Do you have any questions for them?*

Just two. Val cleared his throat, drawing the attention of both candidates. "How old are you?"

Caesg glanced anxiously at Kentigern, and he answered first.

"I be nineteen, Your Highness." He nodded at Caesg. "And me cousin be fifteen."

"Are either of you directly related to Fiona MacRorie, who was the wife of Lachlan MacLachlan? They were the parents of Kieran MacLachlan." Val stared pointedly at Caesg. She wouldn't always let Kentigern do the talking, would she? To his relief, she answered for herself this time.

"Lady Fiona was my grandsire's sister, Your Highness." Caesg's voice was soft but sure.

Kentigern shook his head. "Me Da and Caesg's be brothers, Your Highness, so Lady Fiona was only me distant cousin."

Val nodded once. His theory that at least one branch of the MacRorie clan had distant royal blood might never be proven, but he would keep searching for clues whenever there was an opportunity. "Thank you," he murmured, not knowing what else to say. Thankfully Dolan was never at a loss for words.

"We are both glad to identify others who can hear the dragons." The king smiled, trying to put the two cousins at ease, but Dolan did not understand the awe in which most of the people of Levathia held him. At least, that's how it appeared to Val.

"Pardon me, Your Majesty," Kentigern said. *Bravely*, Val thought. "What happens next for Caesg and me?"

"A good question, Kentigern." Dolan indicated them both. "In a few days, my annual court and tournament begins, so the choosing of riders will wait until the day after the tournament ends. On the last day of the month, an escort will arrive here to bring you both to the Keep, where all the candidates for dragon rider will have the opportunity to meet with the dragons who have indicated their willingness to bond with a sensitive human and become one of the new couriers."

"And if we are not chosen? What then, Sire?" Kentigern frowned, but Val sensed he was not unhappy, merely eager to ride a dragon.

"Obviously not all of the candidates can be chosen, but there will still be ways to help, either by contacting a dragon in an emergency or being receptive to receiving messages on behalf of the dragon riders." Now Dolan's smile was sympathetic. "I hope, for your sake, that one of the dragons will choose you."

"Thank you, Your Majesty," Caesg said with a grin and a curtsy. She elbowed Kentigern, and he murmured his thanks also.

"Watch for my letter, and I will see you soon." Dolan nodded gravely. Val knew it was a dismissal but wasn't sure the others did.

After a moment of silence, Caesg tugged on her cousin's tunic, and both hurried away. Once they were out of hearing, Dolan spoke to Val.

"That went well, I think. What is the next place on our list?" He gazed at Val as if he had all the time in the world.

"There are three at Northland later today, and you wanted to test Sean Hendry also, didn't you?" Val wondered if he would have time before then to see Emma briefly.

"I do. I think it likely Sean will be able to hear the dragons." A sad smile briefly appeared. "I sometimes regret never discussing the possibility with his father." He shook off the mood. "But it does not matter now."

"Dolan?"

"Yes, Val?" He gave him his full attention.

"Do you need to speak to anyone else in the Highlands while we're here?"

Dolan smirked. "Why do you ask? Is there someone else *you* wish to speak with?"

Val's face warmed. "You know there is."

Dolan laughed and clapped his hand on Val's shoulder. "Go see Emma, then. We can meet at Castle Northland mid-afternoon. That will give me the opportunity to confer with Dougal MacLachlan today."

His relief and anticipation were so great, Val couldn't hold back a wide grin. "I'll go now and see you later at Castle Northland."

"I really must be introduced to this young woman who has stolen your heart."

"You will. Soon." Val certainly hoped to keep that promise.

"Away with you, then." Dolan made a shooing motion.

"You don't have to tell me twice." With another grin, Val strode away, calling for Reggie.

* * *

With clenched fists and gritted teeth, Tammeron d'Jean stormed from the stables of Lord Henry Cornwall's manor. It was becoming more and more difficult for him to play the willing, subservient squire to the man, especially when his knight treated him like a slave. Tam could rarely find a minute all his own since moving here six months ago!

True, Lord Henry ran a disciplined, efficient manor, but why wouldn't he, after so many years as Guardian to the present Lord of Southmoor, Pascar Gowen? And, Tam had to admit, he had a more comfortable bed and much better food than when he squired for Sir Artemis Villeroy.

But Sir Artemis was so scatterbrained, Tam had found ample free time to indulge in his two favorite occupations, women and games of chance. Now he rarely had a chance to steal as much as a kiss from a chambermaid, and he'd had no opportunity at all to play at dice with the men in the manor's town. He knew they played every Friday and Saturday at midnight, but Lord Henry had set his captain of the guard to watch Tam like a hawk. Even after half a year, Tam had not yet earned either man's trust.

He was ready to burst from all the pent-up frustration! Hadn't Lord Henry and Captain Bronson been seventeen once upon a time? Did they not remember how it was to be a young man? Or had both grown so old they no longer felt the urge to prove themselves?

While he neared the broad manor door of oiled wood banded with gleaming metal, Tam slowed his stride and forced his hands to relax. He had to wipe the frown from his face and replace his smile before encountering Lady Helena. She could be even more perceptive than Henry. Tam had decided she was trying to protect her female servants from his advances, but she could have a more cynical motive, too.

Old Martina the laundress had whispered to him about a time years ago when the now deceased sister of young Lord Gowen had been rumored to be a witch. She had allegedly poisoned Lady Helena, as well as King Dolan. It couldn't have been deadly poison, though, since both the king and Helena had appeared to enjoy excellent health as long as Tam had known them. The incident had made the lady of the manor a bit paranoid, to say the least, and Tam contrived to stay out of her way as much as possible.

Today, that would not be possible.

Taking a deep breath to steady himself, Tam pushed open the door and made his way to the private suite of Lord and Lady Cornwall. As Lord Henry's squire, he of course resided in an adjacent room, within hearing of his temporary lord and master. Unfortunately, he shared that room with Henry's page, Prince Edward, who was the younger son of King Dolan.

When the young prince had first arrived, Tam had taken the boy under his wing, thinking the king would look favorably upon a squire who treated his son well. But already at the tender age of eight, Edward was arrogant, conniving, and vindictive. So Tam began more and more to see him as a possible ally. In what, Tam wasn't completely sure. Yet. But someone else had recently crossed his path who had already powerfully influenced Tam by stoking his discontent.

Chapter 2

Keep thy heart with all diligence; for out of it are the issues of life.

When Fiona walked Firestorm into the stables, Darby was still there. He glanced around him before approaching her. Surely he hadn't been hoping another groom would attend her, had he?

"Hello, Darby." She gave him her most sincere smile. To her surprise, he did not smile back, but kept his eyes lowered.

"My lady." He bowed stiffly before taking Firestorm's reins and leading her the rest of the way to her stall.

Fiona followed, puzzled. Did the young groom not find her attractive? She'd caught other young men around the Keep staring at her and smiling roguishly when she met their gaze. What was different about Darby? She felt unaccountably bold this morning.

"Darby?" She moved closer to him. Firestorm snorted and stamped a hoof.

"My lady?" He glanced up at her briefly before lowering his gaze again. "Was there something else you needed?"

"Yes, Darby. I need to know something."

He raised his head, startled. "What, my lady?"

"Have you ever kissed a girl before?" Fiona smiled when his cheeks flamed red. He really was quite appealing.

"N-no, my lady." He gulped, and his gaze darted to her lips. That was all the invitation Fiona needed.

"Then let me be the first." She moved closer to him, and he backed into Firestorm, who sidestepped.

"But, my lady, I be just a stable hand, and you—"

"And I am just a girl about your age." She smiled again to reassure him. "Don't worry, I won't tell anyone. I like you, Darby, and I would never wish for you to get in trouble."

He licked his lips, still nervous but obviously interested. "You won't tell?"

Fiona made the sign of a cross over her heart. "I promise. Just one kiss, nothing more."

Darby swallowed audibly again and nodded, but he did not move. Fiona stepped closer to him and leaned in. They were about the same height, so this shouldn't be too awkward.

Thankfully, he met her halfway, and their lips touched.

Fiona closed her eyes, savoring the sensation.

* * *

Mercy left the bed curtains open when she awakened, but Kieran didn't stir, making her smile. It had always amazed her how soundly he could sleep. She quite envied him that ability.

She pulled her work apron over her kirtle, intending to repot several herbs before cleaning up and then dressing for the day. When she entered the common room, to her surprise Tristam was seated there.

"Good morning, Tristam. Is anything wrong?" Her youngest son rarely got up so early, since he typically studied late every night.

"Fiona tried so hard to stay quiet, she made more noise than usual and woke me up." He yawned and scratched the side of his head. His thick dark curls looked just like his father's had before the white hairs began to conquer the black.

"Fiona? Where has she gone?" Mercy frowned. Fiona usually slept even later than Tristam.

"She was going riding early with Val." A bigger yawn gripped him, making Mercy feel the urge to do likewise.

Then she remembered what Dolan had said yesterday.

"That's not true; Dolan said he and Val were leaving early for the Highlands." Her frown deepened. "Did Fiona not remember?" *Or had she lied to Tristam? If so, why would she do that?*

"I suppose not." Tristam bit his lip, and Mercy felt compelled to reassure him.

"It's not your fault. Fiona knows what she is and isn't allowed to do." Mercy's mind raced ahead, wondering where her daughter might be. "Since you are dressed, please run down to the stables and see if she's already left. If so, one of the grooms might better know what her plans were." There, she'd managed to sound calm and collected.

"Yes, Mother." Tristam rubbed his eyes while he made his way to the door.

* * *

The long trek down to the stables helped Tristam come more fully awake, though it did not improve his mood. Why must he always be the one to fetch Fiona when she insisted on being where she was not supposed to be? He loved his sister, he truly did, but more and more he found himself completely exasperated with her. Didn't she understand how much easier and more peaceful her life would be if she would just cooperate?

When he entered the long building, the odors of manure and hay warred within his nose, threatening to make him sneeze. He didn't see a groom, but he knew which stall housed Fiona's horse and walked directly there. The door was open, and the horse's tail was visible. He stepped into the stall and found Fiona *kissing* one of the stable boys!

"Fiona!" His surprise made his voice much louder than usual.

She jumped back from the boy, who, Tristam saw, was Darby. What was he doing, kissing Fiona? Before he could speak, Darby dropped to his knees in the straw, and Fiona put herself between them.

"Forgive me, my lord," Darby said.

"It wasn't his fault," Fiona said. Her eyes flashed daggers at Tristam, making him angrier.

"Don't tell me it was *your* idea?" He balled his fists on his hips.

"Yes, it was all my idea." She mimicked his stance.

"So you lied to me and told me you were riding with Val today so you could come down here and kiss Darby? Fiona!" Didn't she realize he would have to tell Mother and Father now? Why must she always put him in such an awkward position with their parents?

"No, I did not lie to you." Fiona glowered at him. "Val told me last night we could ride today. When I got here, he had already left with Dolan, but I would not assume he had lied to me. When have I ever lied to *you*, Tristam MacLachlan?" Her eyes filled with angry tears, and Tristam felt wretched.

"I'm sorry, Fiona, I was too harsh." He pointed at Darby. "But why on earth were you kissing him? Darby isn't a suitable potential husband for you, and you know it."

Fiona drew herself up in that proud stance Tristam hated. "Of course, he isn't a suitable potential husband. We were just having a little fun, nothing more. You have no right to make more of it than that. And you certainly have no reason to tell anyone about it."

Tristam bit his lip, holding back angry words. It would be like trying to put out a fire with, well, fire.

"I will only keep this to myself I you promise it will never happen again." He stared pointedly at his sister. Thankfully she knew he could be insistent when he needed to be, and she relaxed her stance.

"I can definitely promise you, I will never kiss Darby again." She looked down when the stable boy peered around her skirt.

"I promise, my lord, I will never ever kiss your sister again." Darby looked as if he expected to be beaten any moment.

Tristam gestured to him. "Oh, come out now, Darby. I am not going to hurt you."

Darby scooted out from the corner and gave Tristam a profound bow. "Thank you, my lord." He kept his head lowered while he hurried around to Firestorm's other side and began to remove the horse's saddle.

Tristam jerked his chin at Fiona. "Let's go. Mother wishes to see you." He turned and left the stall, hoping Fiona would follow. To his relief, she did, so he slowed his pace to walk with her.

"What does Mother want?" Her voice was sullen.

"To know that you're well and safe." He glanced around, but there was no one close by, so he stopped to face her. "Believe it or not, we all care about you, Fiona." He flung out his hand toward the stables. "You really need to stop your dalliances with stable boys and guards. You're going to get a reputation as a flirtatious woman. Or worse."

Fiona's jaw tightened, and her brows came together, making her unattractive. Did she even realize that?

"Dalliances, are they? You're growing this tiny anthill into a granite mountain. There's nothing wrong with a harmless little kiss."

"Don't you see? You're sending those young men the wrong message, giving them the wrong impression. You're a lady, Fiona, not a loose woman." He wanted to shake some sense into her!

"Of course I'm a lady. Everyone knows that." Fiona stamped her foot. "Why can't you let me be, Tristam?"

He slowly shook his head. "I can't 'let you be' because I need to protect you from yourself."

"Well, stop it. Stop it, right now!" She whirled away and ran toward the castle steps.

Tristam took off running after her, but he didn't catch up until they reached the door of their family's suite.

* * *

Val shivered with anticipation when he and Reggie came near the village in which Emma temporarily lived. It had been a month since he'd seen her, though within that time they had exchanged four letters each. Val grinned, remembering his mother's surprise when he'd told her he had written to Emma at least once a week since he had met her. She more than anyone knew what a reluctant writer he was.

"I believe this means you like Emma a lot," Mercy had said. Her pleased smile made him smile wider.

"I do indeed." He'd taken a deep breath, fearing to say the words aloud, but he had wanted his mother to know how serious he was. "I am hoping she will consent to be my wife someday."

The fierce hug his mother had given him said louder than words how much she shared in his happiness.

Reggie made a show of circling low over the village, to the delight of several children.

We're here. Val called out to Emma, in case she wasn't busy and could hear his mental voice. She had told him during a previous visit that she did not hear him whenever she was fully concentrating on a patient. At first Val had been surprised, but he later admitted it was a good thing for Emma's laboring patients that she was so single-minded in her focus on their needs during childbirth.

I wondered if I might see you today, came her happy reply. Then she emerged from her cottage, bringing a smile to Val's entire face. The moment Reggie landed in front of the cottage, Val slid down.

Thank you, friend, he remembered to say.

You are welcome. Greetings, friend Emma.

'Tis good tae see you, friend Reggie. I thank ye for bringing Val.

15

I am happy to bring him, always. Then Reggie lumbered closer to the children, who eagerly gathered around him.

Val gave all his attention to Emma, who gazed up at him with her lopsided smile. Someday, Val hoped to work up the courage to kiss her sweet mouth. For now, he was content for their affection to grow at its own pace. He did move close enough to give her a hug, which she fiercely returned.

"I've missed you, so I have." Emma pulled back first and met his gaze again.

"Not as much as I've missed you." He kept staring at her until she took his hand and led him to the bench by the front door. They sat close together, still holding hands.

"So, what brings ye here today?" She stared up at him, waiting patiently.

"Dolan and I finished with the MacRorie dragon rider candidates early enough that I had a free hour before needing to leave to meet him at Castle Northland. He went to speak with Dougal MacLachlan about something."

"How did it go with the MacRories?" Emma's eyes sparkled with interest.

"Two of them could hear the dragons." Val grinned. "Kentigern and Caesg."

Emma gasped. "Why, they both be my cousins."

Val nodded. "I know. Isn't it great?"

Emma looked thoughtful. "If they be chosen as riders, you will have tae work closely with them, will ye not?"

Hadn't he explained it all to her? "Once Dolan officially makes me Lord of the Sky in a couple weeks, yes, I will be responsible for all the dragon riders." He cocked his head. "What are you thinking?"

She shrugged. "I would be surprised for a dragon tae choose Kentigern; he has grown up a lot but still tends tae be a bit reckless. Caesg, though. . . ." She ducked her head.

Val bent his head closer, trying to see Emma's face. Was she blushing? "What about Caesg?"

Emma did not look up. "She be perfect for a dragon courier— dependable, loyal, fearless, and— and lovely in every way."

Val gently lifted her chin with his finger. To his shock, there were tears in Emma's eyes. *What's wrong, love?*

She shut her eyes, and a tear escaped down her cheek. *My sweet cousin is sure tae fall in love with you.*

So, what if she does? It would never change how I feel about you, Emma MacRorie.

When she remained silent, he couldn't bear to see the sadness in her face. This wasn't how he'd thought to kiss her for the first time, but he leaned down and lightly brushed her lips. Though he'd only meant to comfort her, the brief contact was electrifying.

She opened her eyes and gazed at him in wonder, yet with that lingering sadness. *I be honored tae know you and be your friend, but you will need someone tae share in your life's work.*

Val squeezed her hand and gently cupped her face with his other hand. "You can share in it too, if you desire. You can also speak to dragons."

"But I will be a full-fledged midwife in two months." More tears welled in her eyes. "I canna give that up, not e'en for the chance tae be with you."

Val pulled her into an embrace and kissed her head. "I would never ask you to give it up. I know how much it means to you." After a moment he pulled back. "Emma, I wasn't going to ask you yet, but since it has come up, let me ask you now." He smiled. "Have you considered that you can do both? Be a dragon courier *and* a midwife?"

Her brows came together in a puzzled frown. "How, may I ask, can that be?"

"My mother is a Healer, yes, but she has also helped deliver many babies. She has often remarked that she believes more laboring women could be saved if there was a faster way to get help to them." He wagged his brows, encouraging her to make the connection.

She gasped. "If I were chosen as a dragon rider, we could fly tae where'er a midwife was needed?"

He slowly nodded, but her gaze was miles away. It gave him pleasure to watch her thinking, along with the spectrum of emotions that passed across her lovely face. *Please, God Most High, let her say yes.*

Finally she regarded him with a fond smile. "Me heart wants so badly tae say yes, but I still canna help but think Caesg would be a better match for you."

"A better match? Impossible!" He tried to keep his voice light, though inwardly a growing fear intruded that she would not accept his marriage proposal when he was finally able to offer it.

17

Can she not speak tae your mind, as we do? The sadness had returned to Emma's eyes.

As a matter of fact, no, she cannot. Only you and Dolan, and the dragons, of course. He watched with growing happiness as her blue eyes brightened.

And then he nearly fell off the bench when she threw her arms around his neck and soundly kissed him, curling his toes and making his heart ready to burst with joy.

* * *

Tammeron took a deep breath and knocked on the door to Lady Helena's sitting room. Her maid answered with a curtsy and went to call her lady. In spite of himself, Tam flinched before forcing himself to relax. Helena was just another aging lady of self-importance. He merely had to remain polite in her presence and hope this errand wouldn't take too long.

The maid returned and gestured for him to enter. Lady Helena glided into the room, staring at him. She held herself aloof with a stiff posture, her modest gown surprisingly not as dowdy as usual.

Tam bowed to her. "My lady."

"Good of you to be punctual, Tammeron." Even her voice was stiffly formal. She pointed to a basket on the floor beside the nearest chair. "I need your young legs to carry this basket to the inn in town and deliver it to Lady Honora d'Evrow."

Tam cringed at the name. Did Helena have no idea the connection to him?

"Yes, my lady." He picked up the covered basket and bowed again. When a pretty young maid entered the room, Tam had to squelch his instinct to smile at her. He already felt Lady Helena's stare boring into him, waiting for some infraction upon which to pounce.

Resolving to find another occasion to smile at the lovely girl, Tam quietly left the room. He took the stairs down two at a time, anxious to leave Helena's stifling presence. Once in the manor yard, he shifted the heavy basket to his other arm and strode out the gate.

The edge of town was only a stone's throw from the manor, down the tree-lined lane. Normally, Tam enjoyed the shady walk and the opportunity to visit with the townspeople. Today's errand made everything odious now, and he wasn't even curious about the contents of the basket.

Honora d'Evrow. His aunt, though she did not know it and surely would never claim him as a nephew. Tam had only in the last year discovered that Slade d'Jean was not his real father. The man who'd sired him had been a traitorous knight named Mortimer d'Evrow, slain by King Dolan himself before Tam was born.

All his life he'd heard about the unlawful king of Levathia and his unlawful Regency Council, on which Mortimer served as Lord High Constable. Tam's mother Aleia had briefly been married to that unlawful king, though the marriage was never consummated, during which time Mortimer had apparently raped and impregnated her.

He was the result of that violent act.

Tam slowed his pace as he approached the Boar's Head Inn. The weathered sign moved a little in the breeze, making a faint creaking sound. A dog barked in the distance, and the unmistakable sounds of clopping hooves and wagon wheels moved behind him as one of the farmers entered the town.

When he reached the rough wooden door, Tam stopped and set his jaw before entering the inn. The darkened room was empty of customers at this early hour. A lad half-heartedly wiping a rag over one of the trestle tables looked up at Tam's approach. The boy's gaze went to the basket.

"We ain't open yet," he mumbled.

"I'm not here to order anything." Tam's voice sounded harsh, but he couldn't let his guard down. "I have a delivery for Lady d'Evrow." He lifted the basket and adjusted the cover.

The boy dropped the rag on the table and gestured for Tam to follow him. "She's waiting for you in back."

"Can you not take it to her?" Tam would rather avoid seeing the woman, if it were possible.

"Naw, I was told to bring you back." He pushed open an interior door, and Tam had to follow.

He was expecting to see the kitchen, but there was another room, furnished as a small sitting room with a heavy wooden desk in one corner. The innkeeper, whom Tam recognized, sat at the desk, and a woman he'd never met sat in another chair beside the desk. When she noticed Tam, she rose, staring at the basket.

Tam studied her. She was tall for a woman and too thin for her frame. Her expensive gown, much too ornate for the setting, was frayed at the edges and ill-fitting. When she finally met his gaze, her dark eyes had a fevered look, and all the bones in her face jutted out. After a moment, her eyes widened.

"This is from Lady Cornwall, my lady." He held out the basket to her.

She took the basket with one thin claw, and for a moment they both gripped it. Tam wasn't sure she was strong enough to hold onto it.

"May I carry it for you, my lady?" he reluctantly asked, glancing over at the innkeeper, who nodded approval.

The claw let go of the basket, and the woman folded her hands together. "Yes, thank you." She dipped her head to the innkeeper. "And I thank you also."

"My pleasure, Lady d'Evrow." The innkeeper briefly smiled before returning to his figures. Tam thought it odd that he did not stand when the woman had, and he did not even stand when she took her leave of him. What was going on here?

"Come," she said to Tam and shuffled out the back door.

Curious now, he followed, closing the door behind them. Lady d'Evrow made her way across the dirt yard to a cottage adjacent to a large chicken coop. They both had to stoop to enter the small door under the eaves of the thatched roof. The single room was dark until the lady opened the shutters of a large window, revealing a small table, chair, and bed as the room's only furnishings.

"Set the basket on the table." She gestured to it while she seated herself in the chair.

He did so and then stepped back from the table. Though he wanted to bolt out the door, he knew Lady Cornwall would expect a detailed accounting of the visit, so he stayed where he was.

The obviously impoverished, once grand Lady d'Evrow eagerly lifted the cover and began pulling out the items inside the basket. Tam had expected it to be full of food, but there was only a loaf of bread and a few pieces of fruit. The rest of the contents included a leather-bound book, colored scarves, a carefully folded dress made of fine fabric, an embroidery hoop and many lengths of colored threads, and even several pieces of jewelry. Was Lady Cornwall trying to help this woman pretend to be a rich noblewoman again?

Lady d'Evrow studied each item with a wistful look on her face, apparently forgetting Tam was still there. But as soon as she emptied the basket, she stared up at him with tears in her eyes.

"Thank you for bringing this basket to me." She dabbed her eyes with the corner of a blue scarf.

"You are welcome, my lady." He dipped his head and prepared to leave, but she was replacing the cover inside the basket. Sure enough, she handed it to him, so he came closer and reached out for it.

With her other hand, she snatched his and gripped it tightly, making him gasp.

"What is your name?" Her gaze bore into him.

"Tammeron d'Jean, my lady." The sensation of her bony hand in his was most unpleasant.

Lady d'Evrow bit her lip. "You greatly resemble someone I knew long ago. But there is no way you could be related to him, I suppose." She let go of his hand, and he relieved her of the basket.

"Who was that, my lady?" Tam knew he shouldn't ask, but his curiosity was pricked.

"My departed husband's brother, Mortimer d'Evrow. He died nearly twenty years ago, long before you were born." She continued to study him.

Tam almost blurted out that it wasn't long before he was born, that it was less than nine months. But he suddenly realized he did not want this woman to know he was Mortimer's offspring.

Lady d'Evrow frowned in concentration. "It is uncanny that you are the very image of Mortimer when he was a squire." Her brows relaxed and her gaze unfocused. "How very proud their parents were that he was chosen to be King Orland's own royal squire."

Then she shook her head and straightened in the chair, folding her hands on the table. Tam knew he should leave, but he asked one more bold question.

"How did your brother-in-law die, my lady?" He expected her to dismiss him, at the very least berate him for his impertinence, but she seemed eager to talk to someone.

"I do not know all the details, but King Dolan had him killed." Her face hardened. "Some say Mortimer was a traitor, and others think the king himself murdered him, though I do not know how he would have accomplished that. He was only a boy when he became king, and Mortimer was a big, powerful man, skilled in fighting." Though her expression did not soften, her gaze had drifted again, as if she were lost in faraway memories.

Tam gritted his teeth, for this information confirmed what he had suspected for several months, ever since the foundation of his life shifted upon learning the truth of his birth. Why had his mother never told him? Did she think she could hide the knowledge forever?

He opened his mouth to ask more about Mortimer, but Lady d'Evrow came to herself and straightened in her chair.

"You are dismissed, squire. Give my regards to Lady Cornwall." She stared down her nose at him, and the anger he barely kept beneath the surface threatened to spill over. His grip on the basket tightened while he bit back the sharp words on his tongue.

Then Tam bowed and backed to the door, watching the pathetic woman sitting in the gloomy room. Apparently the entire d'Evrow family had fallen into ruin or disfavor. Though he felt the pull of blood, he was glad he had a different surname. After all, he intended to rise above the ill luck which had plagued his birth father's relations and forge a better path for himself.

But he did very much want to know why his mother and stepfather had kept the truth from him, that he was the son of Mortimer d'Evrow.

Chapter 3

Enter not into the path of the wicked, and go not in the way of evil men.

Fiona and Tristam arrived together at the door of their family's suite of rooms. Before Tristam could open the door, she grabbed his hand.

"You're not going to tell them that I kissed Darby, are you?" She managed to keep the panic out of her voice. If Papa knew, he would probably lock her in her room indefinitely.

"It's not fair of you to expect me to hide such things from them." Tristam frowned at her, though she could tell he was relenting.

She made tears well in her eyes, and thankfully they still worked on her brother, for Tristam held up his hands in a warding gesture.

"All right, all right. I won't tell them. But, Fiona, you must not do that again!"

"Yes, Fa—" She stopped before the word "father" slipped out. But honestly, sometimes her little brother acted as if he was her third parent! "Yes, *frater.*" She smiled sweetly, knowing how much he loved studying Latin.

She opened the door, and her parents turned toward the sound from their seat at the table. Papa looked worried, but Mama was frowning. Fiona didn't give them a chance to ask questions first.

"Val agreed last night to go riding early this morning, but when I got to the stables, Conrad gave me a message from him, that he and

Dolan went to the Highlands." Fiona folded her arms as if she were the wounded party. "I guess he forgot about that part."

"Apparently so." Mama sounded suspicious. "So why didn't you come back after you'd received Val's message?"

Fiona's ire rose. Why did Mama insist on treating her like a child?

"I was already dressed for riding, so I took Firestorm to the lake for a little while. Do I need permission for that, too?"

Mama kept staring, her mouth tightened in annoyance. "Not usually, no," she finally answered.

"Usually? What does that mean?" Fiona struggled to keep from stamping her foot. Her parents would never see her as an adult if she didn't make sure she acted like one.

"I think your Mum means tae say that you'd only need permission if ye were under restriction for some reason, say for being deceptive about sommat." Papa's gaze bore into Fiona, making her squirm. "There's no deception about this morning, is there?"

For an instant, Fiona panicked, but then she realized there was no way Papa could have known about her kissing Darby. She had better conceal her guilty conscience, though. With her sweetest smile, she approached her father and slipped her arm through his.

"Of course, there's no deception, Papa. Firestorm was ready for a ride, so she and I went to my favorite meadow by the lake. I sang along with a bird, and then we returned." Out of the corner of her eye, Tristam shifted his stance, but he kept his peace.

"Sang with a bird, did you?" Papa's smile was tired. It made Fiona sad to see how he'd aged in the last year. But he *was* almost fifty, nearly an old man.

"Yes, it was a marvelous duet. I think you would have approved." She leaned down and kissed Papa's cheek.

Mama sighed, but she didn't look as pleased as Papa did. "Well, have a seat, dearest, and break your fast with us."

With a smile at her brother, Fiona took the seat beside their father, and Tristam took the remaining chair. Before he sat down, he rolled his eyes, and Fiona knew she'd have to be extra nice to him, at least until he forgot about the kiss.

* * *

Val and Reggie flew south along the coast of the Highlands. It put him in mind of their recent months-long adventure to the north and all the marvelous sights they'd seen along the rugged coastline.

24

Normally he would delight in the vastness of the sea and scan the waves for a glimpse of a whale or other sea creature, but today all he could think about was Emma's kiss.

She had been worried he might fall in love with Caesg! Wasn't that a kind of proof of how much she cared for him? And yet, she had seemed willing to give up their special friendship for her cousin. Or *was* she willing? He'd never seen tears in her eyes before, and strangely, that was the greatest proof of all.

It still made him nervous that by the time he was able to propose marriage to her, she might say no anyway. At this point in his life, it was his greatest fear.

He inhaled deeply of the salty air and let it out slowly. How was the fear of rejection greater for him than the real dangers he and Reggie had faced in the last year? *God Most High, please forgive my lack of faith, and help me not to fear the future. I know You hold it in your hands.*

At last the walls and towers of Castle Northland came into view. This place was as familiar to him as the Keep, since he and his family had lived here during the time the Keep was being repaired more than eight years ago. Val considered Sean Hendry, the young lord of Northland, a friend of sorts, though not a close one, since he was only twelve, two years older than his nephew, Prince William. Like William, Sean was serious-minded and so seemed older than his years.

Cephalorix is already here, Reggie said, angling down for his approach to landing in the castle yard.

Val glanced up at the sun's position. Were they late? *How long ago did they arrive?*

Minutes only. Your brother the king is standing beside my father, waiting for us.

With a sigh, Val relaxed until Reggie gracefully landed close to the larger Cephalorix. A few men-at-arms in the yard stood back, their eyes wide at the unaccustomed sight of two dragons within the walls.

Before dismounting, Val noticed Sean and his new Guardian, Lord Geren Wyldwood striding toward Dolan. Sean waved at Val, and Lord Geren stopped and bowed to Dolan, his face pleasant yet troubled. Surely Geren was not having any trouble with Sean?

No, not Sean, he thought as he slid down Reggie's scaly side. That Blythe fellow, Sean's new stepfather, would be a thorn in the side of the most patient man. Lord Geren had proven to be not only patient but fair and firm, everything Dolan could wish for the Guardian of Northland.

After Val greeted Lord Geren, he turned his attention to Sean.

"I am so glad to see you, Val." Sean's genuine smile made his face relax. "I've been hoping we might have a chance to visit, since I've been anxious to hear more about your travels to the north country." As soon as Dolan and Geren ambled toward the castle door, Val and Sean fell in behind them.

"Do you know, my parents have been encouraging me to write down the account in a book?" Val shrugged self-consciously.

Sean's eyes widened. "That's a wonderful idea! I want to read it when you're finished." His excitement was contagious.

"Then you shall be the first to read it," Val promised. "I'm trying to make illustrations of some of the creatures and places Reggie and I saw, but I have a difficult time taking the image out of my head and making an exact image on parchment." He shrugged again. "I never would have believed it, but I think I'm better at writing than illustration."

They had entered the great hall, where refreshments were laid out. Val had scarcely time to take a sip of cold water before Lord Geren called for a servant to fetch the other candidates for dragon rider.

"I guess we won't have time to visit this trip," Val said to Sean. "I know my brother won't have much free time before his annual court begins, so I must stay on his schedule."

Sean nodded, though obviously disappointed. "Then I'll look forward to when we do find free time in the future." His face grew tense. "But is there anything you can tell me about this examination we're about to do with the dragons? It won't hurt, will it?"

Val managed not to laugh and make light of his friend's fear. "I can promise you, it will not hurt at all. And it won't take very long, either."

Sean let out an exaggerated sigh. "That's good to know."

*

Less than an hour later, they had returned to the castle yard. Val tried hard not to stare at Sean while Cephalorix and Reggie were speaking to all the candidates. It was difficult to rein in his impatience, for the silence seemed interminable. All four young people, three boys and a girl, stood in their places with eyes closed, as Dolan had instructed. But Val couldn't tell from the facial expressions if they were hearing the dragons or not.

At last both Cephalorix and Reggie sat back on their haunches, and Cephalorix spoke formally to Dolan.

My king, there is only one who is able to hear us clearly enough to be a dragon rider.

Dolan inclined his head and shared a glance with Val. *Ask that one to step forward, then.*

When Cephalorix gave the command, Val was not surprised to see Sean Hendry begin to walk toward Dolan. The young lord looked back, surprised when he realized he was alone. Val smiled to reassure him.

"The chief dragon Cephalorix tells me that you alone can hear their mental voices." Dolan remained calm, but Val could tell he was disappointed—not that Sean could be a dragon rider, but that it might complicate matters in Northland, since he was the province's minor lord.

Dolan held up his hands and addressed the others, all of whom wore their disappointment openly.

"Thank you for coming today, and for your interest in the dragons, but unfortunately they were unable to speak to your minds. You are dismissed. Go in peace."

The three bowed to Dolan and shuffled away. One boy kept glancing over his shoulder, as if hoping there had been a mistake, and his fellow had to pull him along.

"Well, my lord, how does it feel to be an acceptable candidate for dragon rider?" Dolan warmly clasped Sean's shoulder.

The young man grinned at both brothers. "Exciting, to be sure, Sire. What happens next?"

"Directly after the royal court and tournament, those from all the provinces who were able to hear Cephalorix and Regnatorix will meet with the rest of the dragons to determine which will become an actual rider and which will fill supporting roles with the dragon couriers." Dolan indicated Val. "And then you will answer directly to Prince Val, who will be in charge of the couriers." He stared at Sean. "That won't be a problem for you, will it?"

Sean solemnly shook his head, and Val held in a smile. He looked forward to working more closely with young Sean. Perhaps they could have their own adventure someday.

* * *

Tam took the long way back to Lord Henry's manor, a wooded path he'd recently discovered that meandered alongside a rippling brook. Sometimes the sound of the water helped to calm him, but today his agitation increased with each step. He wanted to fling the basket into the brook, but reason stayed his hand. With the horrid image of Lady d'Evrow in his mind, he strode along the path unseeing until a voice startled him from his thoughts.

"Mornin', Tam. What's wrong, friend?"

He jerked up his head and stopped. His new friend from the village, Jevan, stood leaning against a tree with his arms folded. Jevan was twenty years old, living with his widowed mother, who, Tam had recently discovered, had been a friend of Lady Mercy MacLachlan in their youth. Jevan's mother appeared much older than Lady Mercy, though. In fact, Tam had first thought the woman was Jevan's grandmother, so worn did she appear.

"Nothing is wrong, and—everything." Tam let out a huff of air, but he still felt as if he needed to break something.

When Jevan beckoned to Tam, he followed through the trees and brambles until they came out behind the blacksmith's stables, where Jevan worked. Before speaking, Tam glanced around to make sure none of the spies who worked for Lord Henry and Captain Bronson were nearby.

"I have news for you." Jevan's gold-flecked eyes pierced Tam's gaze. When he didn't continue, Tam's irritation grew.

"Well? What is your news?" His mouth twisted in annoyance. Why must Jevan be so dramatic?

Jevan smirked. "Our dice games continue on Fridays and Saturdays, but a new one has been added, beginning Tuesday."

"I see." Tam bit his lip. If he couldn't participate on the usual days, there was no reason he'd be able to on another day. "Same time?"

Jevan wagged his brows. "That's the beauty of this game, friend. 'Twill be at three o' the clock, when everyone is abed, or asleep on watch."

Tam's mind leaped ahead to Tuesday. Would it be possible to sneak out of the manor at that hour? Captain Bronson would surely not suspect a dice game on that day and time.

"Same place?"

Jevan shook his head. "Naw. Since we want you to join us, we'll do it under the nose of the manor guard." He grinned at Tam's suspicion.

"What do you mean?" Tam's brows furrowed. "Where could a dice game take place 'under their nose' without being discovered? Captain Bronson has the nose of a bloody hound."

"The good captain knows about the secret tunnel to the kitchen, but he does not know about the one leading to the base of the lookout tower."

"A second tunnel? How did I not know about it? Lord Henry has shown me every secret door and entrance in the entire manor." As he spoke the words, Tam realized the manor house was older and bigger than most he'd seen before. Was it possible there were secrets even Henry hadn't discovered?

"The second one exits here." Jevan gestured to the stables. "I discovered it by accident and followed it until the cave-in." He straightened and puffed out his chest. "The lads and I dug it out, bucket by bucket, until it led to the tower base."

"You can get into the manor through this tunnel?"

Jevan shook his head. "It was meant for escape *from* the manor, because the trap door is locked from the inside. You should be able to find it and unlock it, and then you can finally join us at dice."

Tam had only been inside the manor's tower a few times. He'd always been focused on going up, to spy out the land from above. Never had he considered there might be more to the tower by going *down*.

"Then I will look for this trap door before Tuesday and hope to see you at three o' the clock." If he was careful, he should be able to look later today.

"Good!" Jevan leaned closer and lowered his voice. "Don't forget to bring lots of coins. We play for keeps."

Tam nodded, shifting the basket to his other hand. "That's the only way I play."

They parted then, and Tam returned to the manor in a better frame of mind, now that he had a goal to accomplish.

Chapter 4

The light of the eyes rejoiceth the heart: and a good report maketh the bones fat.

Fiona adjusted the bodice of her new green gown and then ran her hands along the soft fabric of the full skirts. They rustled as she came closer to the mirror. She turned first one way and then the other, checking the fit.

"It's beautiful, Oleta." She whirled around to test how the skirts would look while dancing.

"Don't give me any credit, my lady." The faithful lady's maid smiled sweetly. "This one came from the new dressmaker in town, Widow Agnes."

"I shall give credit where credit is due." Fiona stopped and faced Oleta, whom she'd known all her life, and who had been patient with her almost all the time. More patient than anyone else in her life, certainly. "You took my measurements and gave the dressmaker instructions." She twirled in a full circle. "Agnes could not have done so well without your help."

Oleta curtsied, her cheeks turning pink. "Then I thank you, my lady."

"And I thank you. For more than the dress." Fiona came near and embraced her. "For everything."

After Oleta helped her step out of the gown and laced up her plain work dress, a courier arrived with letters for the family. Fiona thanked the young man while Oleta took them from his hand.

"Any for me?" she asked with interest, because the stack seemed larger than usual.

"As a matter of fact, yes." Oleta sorted through them, careful not to damage the seals. "There are two. And if I'm not mistaken, at least one is from a certain young squire in Southmoor." She grinned impishly, and Fiona snatched them from her, pretending to be displeased.

With a giggle, Oleta took the others to Mama's small writing desk, while Fiona settled in the window seat.

She stared at the two letters in her hands, one from Roland Campignon and the other from his sister Iris, who in June had finally become Lady Fitzhugh, wife of Sir Aidan Fitzhugh of Moor Point. Though Fiona had received a letter almost weekly from Roland, this was the first letter Iris had written since her marriage. She fingered the sealed parchment, admiring her friend's neat handwriting.

"I would never take the time to write so beautifully," she murmured. Only one of many differences between herself and Iris, though they'd been close friends as long as Fiona could remember. She decided to read this letter first.

She slid her fingers under the fold and broke the wax seal. To her surprise, the message was brief.

Dearest Fiona,

I apologize for not writing sooner, but Aidan and I have been busy settling in at his new manor not far from Castle Moor Point. King Dolan will officially make him a lord at the upcoming court, and I look forward to spending time with you and catching up in person. I also hope you will come visit me soon. Aidan and I will give you a royal welcome.
May you someday be as blissfully happy with your husband as I am with mine.

Always,
Iris

She read it through twice. It surprised her that instead of being happy for her friend, Fiona felt a twinge of envy that Iris was happily married, and she was not. Not yet, anyway.

After dropping Iris' letter in her lap, she picked up Roland's and studied his writing in comparison to his sister's. Roland had a fair hand, for a busy young man, but he was obviously not trying to impress by the style of his letters. No matter; he wrote to her regularly, and that was all she cared about.

The seal he used was Sir Thomas' since he did not have one of his own yet. As she often pondered, she imagined what he might choose at his knighting, which was still *two* long years away. With a groan of frustration, Fiona broke the seal and began to read Roland's longer letter.

My dear Fiona,

You may be surprised that I am writing again so soon after my last letter, especially since I will see you in less than a fortnight at your brother's court and tournament. I look forward to spending time with you then, as Sir Thomas assures me he will grant us the time. In truth, I am counting the days and hours until we meet again. I know I have no right to feel the way I do, but sometimes I despair that I must wait so long to become a knight, since you must have many admirers, now that you are sixteen. There is something particular I would like to ask you when I am able to come to you, though I know I have no right to hope. The only thing which gives my hope wings is the knowledge that my mother waited for my father, in a similar situation.

If the reason for your lack of letters is that you have given your heart to another, then I have prepared my own heart to accept it. But if you have simply been too busy to write, then I ask only that you please allow me to share my idea with you in a few days, so you can tell me what you think of it.

This will be my last letter before I see you face-to-face. May the Most High guard and keep you until that day, which will come very soon now.

Your loving friend,
Roland Campignon

Fiona read this letter three times, and her heart swelled with anticipation. Was Roland going to ask for her hand? If so, what would she tell him? Two years was an eternity, after all. Did she have the patience to wait that long to marry him? Waiting, and having to forego flirting with all other handsome young men and the possible kisses that might result in the meantime?

She leaned her head against the stone wall with a sigh. What was that saying Papa always used? "A bird in the bag is worth a dozen in the field." Did she dare risk losing Roland on the slim chance she might find another to love her sooner? Hadn't Mama told her that marriage was a commitment through good and bad, and that trials could strengthen a bond, as long as both parties were determined to work through the hard times together?

That was all well and good after marriage, but how did one find patience *before* the marriage?

She did love Roland, didn't she? Of course she did, but she sometimes wondered if she truly felt more for him than she would a beloved brother or cousin. They had never kissed before, after all. How could she marry someone if she wasn't absolutely sure he would excel at kissing?

A smile came to her lips. There was one way to find out, wasn't there? When Sir Thomas granted Roland time off from his duties during the court, she would just have to find a quiet place, preferably in a garden where fragrant flowers bloomed. Oh, and a comfortable bench would be essential. This was their future at stake, hers and Roland's. It was imperative they have the opportunity to find out if they were truly compatible, wasn't it?

With a giggle of anticipation, Fiona jumped up from the window seat, put the letters in her special wooden box, and went to find Mama. Today she would be a model daughter and help her mother at whatever task was needed.

* * *

It was two days before Dolan could get away with Val to visit the hopeful dragon riders at Castle Frankland. There were only three young men, including the minor lord Hamelin de Grignon, who had been Bennet's heir before Robard had been born. Val had been surprised at Hamelin's interest in the dragons and was even more surprised when he turned out to be the only one able to speak with Reggie and Cephalorix.

The one disappointment was not seeing Joy during their brief visit, since she was Healing at a nearby village.

The following day, Val and Dolan were scheduled to visit Westmoor and Moor Point. Thanks to a Privy Council meeting that went longer than planned, they were late arriving at Castle Westmoor. Duke Nowles Meverel greeted them with some anxiety, and Dolan was quick to reassure his father-in-law.

To Val's astonishment, not one of the six candidates could speak to the dragons. And as soon as that was determined, Reggie grew distracted, lashing his tail in a way that startled some of those who had hoped to be a dragon rider.

What's wrong? Val asked, coming nearer to his friend.

There is someone who can speak to dragons, but he is not one of these. Reggie turned his head, cocking it as if to hear better.

Do you know who it is? Val closed his eyes, hoping for a revelation of some sort.

No, but he is near.

A he? Not a she?

He is definitely male.

"Lord Nowles." Val spoke softly, as the disappointed young people were only now leaving the castle yard.

"Yes, Your Highness?" Westmoor's duke approached Val.

"Regnatorix says there is someone here who can speak to dragons. Whoever it is, he is nearby."

When Nowles' eyes widened, Val couldn't hold back a smile. The duke was not easily startled, and it felt like a small kind of accomplishment to perturb his composure just a little.

"Then we shall discover who is nearby and bring them all to the dragons." Nowles explained to Edelbert what was needed, and the young steward marshalled several servants to round up all the nearby men, young and old.

After more than two dozen entered the castle yard, a few reluctant to come so near the great dragons, Reggie turned to Val in distress.

None of these is the one, either. But I still feel him nearby.

Before Val could speak to Nowles, the duke's youngest son, Fletcher, strode toward his father from the stables, and Val remembered that he was supposed to be installed as Dolan's squire at the upcoming court. Now sixteen and as handsome as his sister Queen

Rhianna was fair, Fletcher bowed to Dolan and grinned up at the dragons.

This is the one. Reggie's voice rang in Val's head.

What is your name? Cephalorix added, making Fletcher's eyes widen.

I can hear you. He looked from Cephalorix to Reggie and back again. *Are you speaking to me?*

Yes, Cephalorix answered. *Tell us your name, please.*

Fletcher Meverel, my lord. How am I able to hear you?

Val wondered the same thing. He also wondered how he was able to hear Fletcher also.

You have the gift, Cephalorix continued. *There are few humans who can speak with us. Are you willing to become a dragon courier?*

Fletcher's wide-eyed gaze flew to Dolan. *My lord dragon, I am supposed to become the king's squire a few days from now.*

When Dolan spoke to Fletcher, he gasped, and the young man's eyes grew even wider.

It appears you will serve me in a different manner, if you are willing to use your gift in a way you did not expect. Dolan smiled, his eyes sparkling.

Your Majesty? Fletcher dropped to one knee, overcome with emotion. *I don't know how this happened. I'm not sure what to say.*

You can still be a knight, but instead of being merely a royal squire, you can be a dragon rider in my Royal Dragon Couriers. Dolan raised up Fletcher, whose face was still filled with awe.

"You mean, Sire, that I might *ride* on a dragon?"

Val grinned at his friend's combined wonder and excitement. "Not just take a ride on a dragon."

"No, indeed." Dolan included Nowles in the conversation. "If one of the dragons chooses you, then you will bond with that new friend and fly around the realm, delivering messages that cannot wait for the regular courier riders."

Fletcher stared at Dolan while he thought through the possibilities of his statement. Then his face began to glow until Val thought he would burst with joy.

"Your Majesty, Your Highness, and Father." Fletcher opened his arms wide. "I would like to be a dragon rider and serve Levathia with this incredible gift."

*

It was late afternoon before Val and Dolan landed in the courtyard of Castle Moor Point. Lord Dracen rushed over to meet them, as anxious as Duke Nowles had been at the delay. Val knew that was one of the important reasons to form the dragon couriers, so messages could be delivered in a more timely fashion.

There were only two candidates, a young squire of one of Dracen's knights, and a young peasant girl. Val was surprised there was not more interest from the people of Moor Point. He remembered Mother telling him about the time Joy had been kidnapped, and she along with Kieran, Dolan, and Drew had ridden on the dragons to rescue her. Kieran and Dorricia had been badly burned, and the dragon had spent a few weeks being pampered by those in a fishing village along the coast. Surely the people had favorable memories of her during that time?

As had happened in Westmoor, neither of the candidates could answer Cephalorix's questions, and Reggie again became distracted, listening beyond the small gathering in the courtyard.

Val, he finally said. *There is another here in the castle who I am sure can speak to us.*

Nearby?

Reggie turned his head, scanning the castle complex. Finally he stopped and focused on one of the towers. *He is there, in the tallest tower.*

Val spoke to Dolan mind-to-mind, since the two failed candidates were still present. *Reggie has found another hidden candidate.*

Where? Dolan gazed at the dragon, who was still listening intently.

In the lookout tower. Val nodded in that direction.

Dolan turned to Lord Dracen, startling the man. "Pardon me, my lord, but I need for you to send someone to fetch all who are currently inside the lookout tower."

Dracen's brows raised. "That is an unusual request, Sire, but it shall be done." He signaled to a servant nearby. "Run to the lookout tower and have all the men inside report to me at once."

The servant pulled his forelock and sprinted away. Dolan took the opportunity to thank the two young people and dismiss them. Once they were beyond hearing, Dracen cleared his throat.

"Are you at liberty to explain what is going on, Sire?" The Lord of Moor Point sounded curious, not irritated, to Val's relief.

Dolan gestured to Val. "My brother can better explain, my lord."

Val was glad to point out Reggie's new ability. "Regnatorix here, as we have learned today, can sense when someone is able to speak with dragons. He discovered a potential dragon rider in Lord Nowles' son Fletcher, and now he has sniffed out one of your men." Val held back a smile, since he didn't think Reggie would appreciate being compared to a hunting dog.

The servant ran back, leading a handful of guards, who trotted behind him. They all stopped a respectful distance away and bowed.

"Come forward, all of you," Lord Dracen said. "The dragons will not harm you." At his words Val noticed how nervous a couple of the men appeared. To their credit, they did not hesitate to obey Lord Dracen.

Reggie? Can you tell which one? Val scanned the faces of the men, most of whom were fairly young.

Cephalorix took over then. *There is a simple way to find out. Those of you who can hear my voice, step forward.*

Only one of the men began moving, but he stopped once he realized he was alone.

Fear not. We wish to know your name. Cephalorix arched his long neck, causing one of the other men to gasp.

I am Erian. He frowned in puzzlement. *I do not understand how this is possible.*

The king will explain.

Dolan spoke in an aside to Lord Dracen. "The rest of the men can go."

Dracen raised his hand and spoke to the others. "All but Erian may return to your duties." The chosen guard watched his comrades leave and then gave Dolan his full attention.

"Erian." A thoughtful smile lit Dolan's face, making Val's curiosity burn. "Do you have a sister named Elvina?"

The young guard's mouth dropped open. "Yes, Your Majesty. How did you know?"

"We have met before, though it has been many years and you would not recognize me from the boy I was then."

Erian studied Dolan. "I am at a loss, Sire."

"Then let me enlighten you." Dolan smiled at Val before continuing. "When I was twelve years old and you a little younger, my stepfather was burned by a rogue dragon and took shelter with a kind widow of your village. You visited him, having known him by a different name, and I first saw you there when I came to check on his condition. Later, once Lord Dracen had him moved to the castle here, you boldly came to visit my stepfather once more before he started his long journey back to the Keep in the north." He tapped his finger against his chin. "What was that name you called him? Flynn? Finn?"

Erian smiled then. "You mean Finn MacRorie, Sire. And I did know that he married your lady mother, Healer Mercy. They saved me from the dreaded fever some years ago." His smile faded. "But please, Your Majesty, how is it I can speak to the dragons?"

Dolan nodded to Val before continuing. "My brother suspected there were others in the kingdom who could speak mind-to-mind with the great dragons as he and I do, and he is right. We are forming the Royal Dragon Couriers, separate from the regular couriers on horseback, to send and receive urgent messages between provinces, either by dragonback or mind-to-mind. Since we will need at least one courier in each province, we have been searching out potential dragon riders, and Regnatorix here believes you to be one." He gestured to Reggie.

Erian's brow wrinkled even more in puzzlement. "But, Your Majesty, I am only a guard. How can I be a dragon rider?"

"Because, Erian of Moor Point, the dragons have deemed you acceptable, and I *See* that you are loyal and utterly trustworthy. Is there anything that would hinder you from serving Levathia in this manner?" Dolan raised his brows in a subtle challenge, and Val focused on Erian to hear his answer.

"Nothing, Your Majesty." Erian made a graceful bow. "I am grateful for the chance to better serve you and the kingdom."

When Erian straightened and met Dolan's gaze, they stared at one another for a long moment.

"Why did you never apply to the path of knighthood as a boy? For I *See* you once desired that life, and that Lord Kieran, or Finn as you call him, encouraged you to do so."

"I could not leave my family, Sire. My sister needed me then." The young man shrugged, and Val liked him better and better for his humility as well as his quiet strength.

Erian has known tragedy, Val. He lost his wife and baby daughter last year to a fever. Being a dragon rider will give him new purpose.

Then I am especially grateful Reggie was able to find him. Val smiled at his dragon friend while Dolan explained what would happen in the next few weeks. Then he and Val bade Lord Dracen and Erian farewell and headed back to the Keep.

*

It was full dark before they made it home. Val said goodnight to Dolan and walked wearily to his small room in the new tower. Hopefully he could avoid his family until morning. Not that he didn't enjoy their company, but he was tired and wanted to spend some time alone to think about what had happened today.

That Reggie was able to sense humans with the ability to speak to dragons was incredible! Now that this ability had awakened, Val could see its great benefit to the dragon couriers. Wherever they went in Levathia, Reggie need only keep his senses attuned and would be able to find others to help intercept important messages. How, exactly, Val would figure out later.

He ate a leftover half loaf of bread and still felt hungry. He didn't feel like going down to the kitchen to find more, though. Knowing he would probably regret his decision in the middle of the night, he pulled off his riding clothes and readied himself to turn in early by pulling on his long nightshirt.

Then he noticed a letter on the table. How had he not seen it earlier? As soon as he saw the seal, his heart leaped. It was from Emma!

Wide awake now, he fell into his chair and propped his bare feet on a stool. Eagerly he broke the seal and smiled at Emma's distinctive handwriting. Though a hurried script, it was readable, and it made him miss her even more.

Dear Val,

I have been thinking about what you said and praying to know God's will. The very idea of having the means to reach laboring women in such a timely way appeals to me greatly. I do not know if I can learn to ride on a dragon, but I am willing to try, if the dragons will allow me.

I do like being able to speak to your mind, and to Reggie's. You say this ability should only get stronger with time, and I believe you. I don't understand why the Most High God has chosen to give this gift to me, a lowly midwife, but I have learned not to question His will.

So consider this letter my answer to your question: Yes, I want to be a dragon rider!

Affectionately yours,
Emma

Val pressed the letter to his heart, wishing only that he could speak with her right now, either in person or mind-to-mind. Emma's ability to stay calm and sensible when faced with entirely unfamiliar situations, along with her courage, made him love her all the more. She *wanted* to be a dragon rider! Maybe now they had a real chance at a future together.

He leaned his head back in the chair and closed his eyes, breathing a silent prayer of thanks. Just a few minutes ago, he was ready to fall asleep. But with his heart beating so strongly from anticipation and hope, there was no way he could sleep now.

Val jumped up from the chair, carefully folded Emma's letter, and tucked it into his tunic. Then he pulled on a pair of trews, tucked in his nightshirt, and strode from the room in his bare feet, headed for the kitchen.

* * *

Tam woke early Tuesday from excitement and anticipation. He heard the watch sound two bells, so he knew the dice game would begin in another hour. It would be better to leave now and wait on the others than to risk dozing off and being late. Or worse, missing the game altogether.

He lay still, listening intently. Prince Edward slept nearby, wrapped in a blanket on his cot. His audible breathing revealed that the page was deeply asleep. Silence came from Lord Henry's bedchamber, also indicating he and Lady Helena were asleep.

As noiselessly as possible, Tam rose from his cot and arranged his pillow and blanket to appear, at least in the dark, that he was still lying there. Then he picked up his boots and tiptoed in his stockinged feet to a small closet beside the garderobe shaft in the wall, which he now knew was not merely a closet. Over the past few days, he had oiled the door's hinges and opened and shut the door several times to be absolutely sure it would not squeak.

To his relief, the door opened silently, and he carefully stepped inside, avoiding the broom and spare sleeping furs stored within. The side wall was a false panel, which he'd also reworked to make sure it opened silently. Tam slid inside the lightless passageway, feeling for the latch to make sure it did not lock him out for the return trip.

Then by feel, because he knew the way by exploration earlier with a candle, he slowly made his way down past ground level to the base of Lord Henry's tower. Now he had another hidden panel to open, which led into a short passageway between the two towers. Before he stepped out, he peered into the darkness, searching for any hint of light. Seeing none, he committed himself and traveled as fast as he dared to the base of the lookout tower.

Above in the tower, a faint murmur of voices could be heard. Tam imagined the two guards trying to keep one another awake in the dead of night. And since they were focused on their conversation, he used the opportunity to slip a purloined key into an unusual and unobtrusive lock. Turning the tumblers sounded loud to Tam's ears, but no footsteps came running to investigate, so he slipped inside this last passageway, down to the hidden room one level below.

As he'd surmised, the others had not yet arrived. If they did not come, Tam would be sure to berate Jevan royally. For the first time, he wondered if he were being played for a fool. Jevan was not his favorite person in the world, for all that he claimed he was his friend; Tam could have remained happily ignorant of the circumstances of his birth, had he never met the young man. He considered leaving. But no, he'd come this far; he could wait half an hour or so.

Just as he settled himself in a corner, he heard the noise of muffled footsteps. The closer they came, whispered conversation could be heard, too. Was it Jevan and the others? Or was it the guard?

Tam hunched down, making himself as small as possible. The door swung open, and light spilled into the room. Hardly daring to breathe, Tam watched to see who was there.

To his relief, Jevan stepped inside first, holding a fat candle. Three others slipped in behind him.

"Tam? Are you here?" Jevan placed the candle in the center of the rough wooden table. Its light did not reach the corner where Tam had hidden, so he stood up.

"Yes, I'm here." He walked into the light so Jevan could see him. The man's eyes glittered, and an unpleasant smile stretched across his face. Unpleasant? Or just the deep shadows from the dim light?

"Good. Let's get started while we have the darkness to hide us, then." Jevan pulled a pouch from his tunic and poured out a set of hand-carved dice, larger than Tam was used to using.

Tam never learned the names of the other three players, though he'd seen two of them in the village before. The oldest man was the stranger. He never smiled and acted nervous, often licking his lips. One of the younger ones, who had long stringy hair, worked at the stable with Jevan, and Tam had seen the third young man working in the smithy, though he didn't think he was an apprentice. He had a barrel chest and strong arms, so he looked the part, anyway.

After Jevan explained the rules of the game, they began in relative silence, speaking as little as possible, even betting by placing their coins directly in front of them, so all could see. When it was finally Tam's turn to throw the dice, he hefted them with a frown. They felt odd in his hand, but perhaps it was their size. When he rolled them, they landed in his favor.

In fact, they rolled the right combination more times than not. By the end of the game, he had won more than the others, but only by a little.

When four bells sounded, Tam jerked up his head, surprised that an hour had already passed. He was even more surprised when the others picked up their coins and the dice and prepared to leave.

"Are we finished so soon?" Tam whispered to Jevan.

"We can't risk staying later than four bells," he whispered back.

Tam stuffed his coins into his pouch and stood. He wanted to ask why they didn't meet at two, but he'd find the opportunity later to discuss the time with Jevan. His small taste of winning definitely made him want to return next week.

Jevan picked up the candle, and the five of them exited the room. Without a word, Tam went one way, and Jevan and his friends the other direction.

Carefully, so as not to stumble in the now complete darkness, Tam made his way back up to his cot, feeling smug about his clandestine adventure. There was something quite satisfying about pulling off such a feat without being caught. It gave Tam a sense of power. It was such a delicious feeling, he looked forward to securing a greater portion of it in the near future.

Chapter 5

The heart knoweth his own bitterness;
and a stranger doth not intermeddle with his joy.

The next morning, Fiona was on her way to the stables when she saw Val in the castle yard talking to one of the couriers. Val noticed her and beckoned her to him, while he finished his instructions to the young man, who, Fiona decided, was not very handsome. Still, he glanced her way before he bowed to Val and strode away.

"Good morning, Sis. How are you this fine day?" Val's face shone with contentment.

"I am well, but apparently not quite as well as you." She stretched up and kissed his cheek, and he briefly hugged her.

"Then I am sorry to hear that, for I wish everyone was as well contented as I am."

"Let me guess." Fiona pretended to be thinking deeply. "You have received a letter from Emma?"

Val nodded. "That is one reason for happiness."

"And you have already sent a reply?" A pang of guilt struck her for her lack of letters to Roland.

"Yes, I have. But that is not all that is well." He winked at her.

She crossed her arms. "Are you going to tell me? Or must I continue to guess?"

He laughed and took her arm. "Come and walk with me, for I must meet with Dolan and his Privy Council in a few minutes."

"All right." She slipped her hand in his. "I am still hoping we can go for a ride soon."

"We will. I promise." He waited until they climbed the steps to the landing before speaking again. But first he stopped and faced her. "You know I have been going with Dolan to choose candidates for the dragon courier riders?"

"Yes." She pursed her lips, holding back more words to encourage him to continue.

"Yesterday we went to Westmoor and Moor Point. And, Fiona, something unexpected happened." His eyes shone.

"What?" The word came out more impatiently than she intended, but he didn't even notice.

"At both places, none of the candidates could hear the dragons. But each time Reggie found someone who *could* hear them: Fletcher Meverel at Westmoor, and Erian at Moor Point. Isn't that amazing?"

"Amazing that Fletcher and this Erian person can hear mind speech, or amazing that Reggie discovered them?" An unpleasant sensation roiled Fiona's belly. It felt suspiciously like envy.

"Both! I know for a fact that neither Fletcher nor Erian knew they had this gift, and none of us knew about Reggie's unique ability. Even him!" Val chuckled, obviously delighted.

"So, how many candidates are there now who have the gift to speak with dragons?" It scared Fiona how close her temper was to erupting upon her favorite brother.

"Let's see, counting Emma, there are now seven, including two others from Clan MacRorie, Sean Hendry, Hamelin de Grignon, and the two newest ones." His gaze grew distant. "We only have two more southern provinces to visit, where we will fly in the morning."

Bitter words rose to Fiona's mouth. "And none of those seven have royal blood. Have you discovered *how* those without the d'Alden blood can hear the dragons?" Tears pricked her eyes.

Val shrugged, oblivious to Fiona's distress. "Not yet. But I suspect they might have some connection to the royal family, even if it was several generations in the past."

Well, didn't that rub nettle weed into Fiona's open wound? All the current generations of the d'Alden family had one or more gifts except her. And now even commoners were gifted to speak to dragons! It was *so* unfair!

"Fiona? Are you all right?" Val bent down to peer into her face, and she rubbed her eyes and took a step back.

"I'm fine. Just got something in my eyes. Probably dust." She threw back her shoulders and pasted on a smile. It certainly wasn't Val's fault she had no gift.

He studied her a moment and then straightened. "Well, if you're sure—"

"I'm fine, Val. You should go to your meeting. You know how snippy Dolan gets if you're late."

"Snippy, eh?" He chuckled again. "That's a good description." With a fond smile he leaned down and kissed her head. "I'll see you soon. And we will take that ride, hopefully before the annual court begins." With a little wave, he strode into the castle, leaving Fiona alone on the landing.

She let out a sigh of frustration and thought about sitting on the steps. But here someone was sure to notice her, and the possibility of an annoyingly banal conversation did not interest her in her troubled frame of mind.

Lifting her skirts, she entered the castle and trod through the empty great hall to the stairs leading to the royal tower. She hadn't been to the gardens in several days, and there she could always think in peace. The bench was even more comfortable than the one on the new tower, where her family had their rooms.

To her relief, no one was about, not even a guard. Fiona went straight to the bench and slumped down, feeling like a failure.

Why were commoners given gifts and not her? What was special about them?

She snorted and crossed her arms. What was not special about *her?*

And then she remembered the strong feelings she used to have a few years ago that maybe she'd been a foundling and didn't even have any royal blood. That would certainly explain the lack of a supernatural gift.

Except even commoners had gifts, these days!

Fiona let out a moan and covered her face with her hands. She couldn't go on like this, filled with frustration and jealousy and despair. Even she had sense to realize it would only fester and transform her into a bitter person. She'd known a few bitter people, and they were absolutely miserable. In fact, no one wanted to be around them.

She gasped and jerked up her head. Was she already a bitter person? Had she been driving people away and didn't realize it?

Surely someone would notice and point it out to her? Auntie Gwen, if no one else.

Fiona stood and began to pace along the flagstones. Her skirt swirled at her feet, knocking against the leaves of smaller plants. A yellow butterfly darted close enough to touch before it changed direction and flew away.

For some reason, the butterfly reminded her of Joy, and the hint of a smile came to Fiona's lips. Mama had told her yesterday that Joy was planning to come early this year, several days before the court began. Something about Bennet needing to do—something, but that wasn't important.

Joy was coming. That *was* important. She always had time for Fiona, and talking to her always made Fiona feel better. It was Joy's gift, after all. And maybe, just maybe, Joy could help Fiona accept her fate, if it was her destiny to remain without a gift. She only wished Joy could help her *discover* a gift, but perhaps that was beyond even Joy's ability.

* * *

Before Joy rode under the Keep's portcullis with Bennet and Robard, she wondered if Dolan and Rhianna would be waiting to greet them. After all, they were several days early for the beginning of Dolan's annual court, so he really didn't need to give the formal welcome. Bennet had felt the need to arrive early to settle in everyone from Frankland, as well as meet privately with Dolan and Jambray. Sir Hamelin would participate in the joust this year, along with Sir Aubrey Durandal, and Bennet's squire, Arthur d'Jean, planned to enter the squire's races. The only ones not in their party who planned to arrive later were Slade and Aleia and their daughter, since Slade had to make sure Castle Frankland was well-cared for in his and Bennet's absence.

When the castle landing came into view, Joy smiled at the sight of her brother and sister-in-law standing there. William and Matilda stood to either side.

Robard's pony must have felt his rider's excitement, for he surged ahead and reached the landing first. William hurried down the steps to meet him, and the two cousins began to chatter excitedly.

Joy wouldn't have minded urging her horse to leap ahead, but she held back for Bennet's sake. They halted only a few minutes after Robard had, and Dolan and Rhianna came forward to greet them with hugs and kisses. Rhianna pulled her aside with Matilda, who curtsied.

"Welcome, Auntie Joy." Now five years old, Matilda was a serious little princess in public.

"Thank you, Your Highness." Joy curtsied in return, for she knew Matilda appreciated the effort.

The formalities completed, Matilda grinned up at her. "Mama has news for you."

"Oh?" Joy met Rhianna's shining blue eyes.

"I was going to wait to tell you, since we just found out ourselves last night, but I think I'll burst if I don't tell someone." Rhianna's cheeks turned a pretty shade of pink.

"What is it?" Joy gripped her sister-in-law's hands.

"I am with child, already eight weeks along, and Mercy is certain it's a girl."

With both Rhianna and Matilda staring at her, Joy squelched her initial reaction, which was envy. She even managed to feel genuine happiness for the chance to hold another infant niece someday.

"Why, that is wonderful! Congratulations!" Joy kissed Rhianna's cheek and hugged Matilda. "You will have a sister," she told the girl. "A sister is special; a forever friend."

Rhianna spoke softly to Dolan, and he and Bennet headed toward the stables.

"Come, let's retire to my sitting room. I'm anxious to show you the tapestry I'm working on."

Matilda slipped her hand in Joy's, and the three of them made their way to the royal tower.

*

Once they settled themselves in the sitting room of the queen's suite, Rhianna bade her maid serve the refreshments. While Joy sipped the tart, freshly squeezed pomegranate juice, to which a little honey and cloves had been added, Rhianna went to her press and took out a rolled-up cloth.

"I'm almost halfway finished. This is the first time I've managed to work so diligently on a piece like this." She sat beside Joy and placed the cloth roll in her lap. Slowly she unrolled it, revealing threads of shimmering colors, mainly shades of green and blue.

"Why, it's a dragon." Joy admired Rhianna's even stitching. "You even delineated the individual scales. I am in awe of your skill." She looked up and met Rhianna's pleased gaze.

"There are tapestries of men fighting dragons, but I wanted to make one specially for Dolan." Rhianna continued to unroll the cloth so the unstitched portion was visible. "The lines are faint here, but I am planning to seat Dolan upon Cephalorix's back." She shrugged. "I'm sure it won't look anything like him, but I'll know who it is."

"If anyone can stitch my brother's likeness, it will be you." Joy couldn't help but smile when Rhianna blushed again.

"Please reserve judgment until I actually complete the picture." Rhianna carefully rolled up the cloth. "Only then will we know if I am able to capture Dolan's likeness."

"Where will you hang it?" Joy glanced around the room, but didn't see a place for it.

"I'd like to hang it in our bedchamber, or at least the sitting room in the king's suite. That way he can see it whenever he likes." Rhianna replaced the cloth in her press and resumed her seat.

Their conversation was easy, as always. Being lifelong friends, it was simple to resume where they left off a few months ago and catch up with one another's lives. Joy especially loved to hear stories about Dolan from Rhianna's point of view. It made her miss her brother a little less, knowing his wife never failed to supply the details Joy craved to know.

Matilda listened with interest, too, not the kind of girl to put herself forward in a conversation. Joy tried to draw her out, but she showed little interest in talking about her own activities. She was, however, enthusiastic about what William was doing.

"He can shoot the bow almost as good as Mama and Papa, and Papa just gave him a real horse instead of a pony." The girl's eyes shone. "It's a black gelding named Coal, but he's not as pretty as Papa's horse."

"What about you?" Joy set down her cup. "Do you shoot a bow? Or ride a pony?"

Matilda solemnly shook her head. "I do not wish to shoot a bow, and I prefer to ride with Mama or Papa. Papa says I will have my own pony when I am six years old."

"Are you looking forward to having a pony of your own?"

With a little sigh, Matilda met her mother's gaze. This was apparently an old disagreement.

"I promised I would try to like riding. And I will. Try, I mean."

Rhianna nodded and leaned over to squeeze her daughter's hand. "That is all we ask, dearest, that you try new things before you decide you do not like them."

Joy stared at their joined hands. How she'd longed for a daughter! When she and Bennet had married, Joy had hoped for at least ten children. But it had taken years for her to become pregnant with Robard, just before Bennet had broken his neck, and Mama had told her that Bennet's accident had probably guaranteed she would not have another child.

She held back a sigh and chastised herself. Hadn't she learned long ago that dwelling on what she *couldn't* have only fostered melancholy and even bitterness? Counting her blessings, of which there were many, was the secret to contentment.

Rhianna and Matilda looked up at Joy at the same moment, as if they were hearing her thoughts. Thankfully, Joy was able to give them a genuine smile, filled with all the love she felt for them both.

* * *

Tam could not fall asleep the following Tuesday. His belt pouch was heavy, full of coins from last week's win, and his daydreams were filled with the possibility of winning even more. Lord Henry intended to leave for the Keep early in the morning, planning to arrive the day before King Dolan's annual court began, so it was imperative Tam get a little sleep, at least. Otherwise, he might fall off his horse.

He finally dozed off sometime after midnight, but he came fully awake when the watch sounded two of the clock. Carefully he left his cot, though the coins sounded loud when he picked up his belt pouch. He paused, listening, but all was quiet, so he pulled on his cloak.

He had just started for the hidden door when Edward stirred behind him. Tam froze, but it was too late.

"Tam? What are you doing?" Edward sat up, rubbing his eyes.

"Nothing. Go back to sleep." Tam couldn't keep the annoyance out of his voice.

Edward stood and came closer. "It's not nothing. Are you going somewhere?" His childish voice sounded imperious, which always rankled Tam.

"Yes, I am going somewhere, but you don't need to worry your head about it. I will return in an hour or so. You should go back to sleep. We have a long day ahead of us."

Edward folded his arms. Though Tam couldn't see his face in the shadows, he could imagine the boy's frown. "If you don't tell me where you're going, I'll tell Lord Henry you were sneaking out. You know what he said about that."

Tam fisted his hands. He wanted nothing more than to teach the little snitch a lesson. But Edward was a prince, not just a page he could abuse, and Tam could not afford any more black marks with Lord Henry. He let out a sigh and lifted the pouch full of coins so Edward could hear them clinking.

"While I was in the village yesterday, I found these coins, which someone had obviously lost. Not knowing who they belonged to, I brought them back here for safekeeping." He paused, trying to make the lie as plausible as he could.

"That doesn't explain why you're sneaking out in the middle of the night." For a child, Edward's voice was aggravatingly stern.

"Let me finish my tale." For it was a tale, wasn't it? "After careful thought, I decided I would take these coins to the church and leave them in the box with a note, asking the priest to find the owner, and if he couldn't, to use the money for the poor." The words nearly caught in Tam's throat, and for a moment he wondered if lightning would strike him.

"Why now? Why not in the morning before we leave?"

Tam decided Edward was miscast as a page; he should have been made a magistrate, even at his tender age.

"Because Lord Henry wants to leave at first light, and I thought it would be easier to remain anonymous under cover of darkness." Tam squirmed, but it was the best he could come up with.

"Hmph." Edward didn't have an answer to that, and Tam hoped it meant the discussion was at an end. "If you're lying to me, I will tell Lord Henry that, too."

Tam pictured twisting Edward's scrawny neck like a bird's and had to banish the image before answering him. "You won't need to tell Lord Henry anything, because I am not lying." He gestured to the cot, even though Edward probably couldn't see his hand. "You ought to get some sleep. I promise, I'll be back as quickly as I can."

Edward mumbled something Tam couldn't make out, but he did flop back onto the cot and settle down. Though he knew he'd probably have to show Edward the secret passageway when they returned from the court and tournament, at least Tam had managed to talk his way out of this confrontation. Unfortunately, he had lost quite a bit of time and would need to hurry to make it to the tower room by three o'clock.

He moved through the dark tunnel faster than he liked. Every sound was magnified to his ears. Would the sleepy guards hear him?

At last he arrived at the door of the little-used room. He heard low voices behind the door and slowly opened it. Jevan and the others were already seated, ready to play.

"Sorry I'm late," Tam whispered while silently closing the door. "My lord's page woke and saw me leaving. I had to tell him a lie to make him go back to sleep."

Four stony faces stared at him. Jevan finally spoke.

"We only just arrived. You're not late." He gestured to the place beside him, and Tam dropped to the dirt floor, folding his long legs. "Did you bring your coins?" Jevan's eyes glittered in the dim candlelight.

Tam pulled out his belt pouch and hefted it. "Right here." He held back a grin, but he felt like winning some more tonight.

"Good." Jevan held out the wooden dice. "You roll first."

Tam took the dice and rubbed them between his hands. "Are these the same dice we used last week?" He anticipated the lucky dice would bring him luck once more.

"Of course." Jevan gave him a toothy smile. "What do you think we are, cheaters?"

"Well, no." But Tam's belly fluttered, and he felt unaccountably nervous.

"Then roll the dice," one of the others said.

Tam rolled.

*

In less than an hour, Tam had already lost most of the coins in his pouch. He grew more and more anxious, even though what he'd lost was only the same amount he'd won last week. Should he drop out now? Cut his losses and turn his attention to being a model squire on the trip north? Or should he try one more time to retrieve some of the coins? They would come in handy on the journey, after all.

Even though he didn't have enough to cover the bet if he lost, Tam wagered all he had, double or nothing.

He took a fortifying breath, rubbed the dice, and spat on them for luck before rolling.

It was the worst possible numbers. The worst! Jevan smiled, and one of the others snickered.

Tam turned his pouch upside-down and emptied it. The remaining coins rained down atop the pile.

"That's not all of it," the gruff one said. "You owe a lot more than that."

"I don't have any more with me," Tam grumbled. "I'll get it." His mind grasped for ideas on how to come up with the amount owed within a short time, but the only easy way would be to steal it.

"When?" The gruff one's glower matched his voice. "You won't even be here next week."

"I'll get it." Tam glowered back. "I'll bring it in two weeks."

Faster than a striking snake, the big man pulled out a knife and knocked Tam to his back. The man sat on top of him, holding the knife to his throat. "If you try to cheat us, I'll kill you."

Tam couldn't answer right away. His heart pounded so frantically, he thought it would leap from his chest. Why was Jevan letting this man treat him like this?

"I'll get it," he croaked. "I swear by all that's holy."

With a grunt, the man slowly backed away. Tam glanced at Jevan, but he sat still. No emotion showed on his friend's face.

"You'd better get it and be here in two weeks, or else." The man jammed the knife into the dirt and glared.

Tam rose on unsteady legs and picked up his empty belt pouch. Without a word, he fled from the room and made his way back to his quarters, shaking all the way.

Chapter 6

Counsel in the heart of man is like deep water;
but a man of understanding will draw it out.

Fiona raced down the stairs of the tower and didn't slow her pace until she met Lady Arella Richmund in the ground floor hallway. With a murmured greeting and a quick curtsy, she hurried on to Joy and Bennet's guest room near the great hall.

After knocking loudly enough to make her knuckles smart, Fiona smoothed her hair and her skirts and waited impatiently.

Robard opened the door instead of one of the servants.

"Hello, Auntie Fiona. Here to see Mother?" He gave her an impish grin.

"Of course. But, Rob, where are your servants?" She entered the empty sitting room.

Robard shrugged. "Oh, Father sent them to the kitchen to get their breakfast. He lets them have a holiday as often as possible, especially when we're here."

Fiona frowned. This was the first she'd heard of such a practice. Was it common? Or had she simply not been paying attention?

Joy entered from the bedchamber and held open her arms. "Fiona! I'm so glad to see you, Sis."

Fiona happily hugged her dear sister. "I'm even more glad to see you." She pulled back after Joy kissed her cheek, though she didn't let go of her hands. A frown wrinkled her brow. "No one thought to tell me you had arrived yesterday until it was too late to see you."

"I'm sorry, I should have sent you a note. We traveled more quickly than we anticipated and arrived a day early." Joy's smile faded. "Is something else troubling you?" She gazed into Fiona's eyes and mirrored her frown. "You may confide in me, you know."

Fiona shrugged, breaking eye contact. "I know."

Joy let go of one hand and lifted her chin with a finger. "Fiona." She waited until Fiona looked up again. "Please, tell me what's causing your heart unrest."

Fiona let out a sigh and glanced at Robard, who was looking out the window. Joy noticed.

"Robard? Why don't you see if William is free this morning?"

"Yes, Mother." With a bounce in his step, Robard headed out the door, leaving the two of them alone.

"Now, let's have a seat so we can make ourselves comfortable." Joy led Fiona to the nearest chairs and sat beside her. Fiona sucked in a fortifying breath.

"I am troubled by more than one thing," she admitted, twisting her hands in her lap. Joy reached over and placed a hand on her arm.

"Why don't you begin with the most troubling thing?" Her smile was filled with sympathy.

"Honestly? The worst thing is being the only member of our family without a supernatural gift." To her dismay, frustrated tears sprang to her eyes, and she wiped them away.

Joy stroked her arm, nodding. "That must be especially trying for you, since you feel things so keenly. But our gifts only appear when the Most High needs them to. They are from Him, for His purposes. Have you prayed about it?"

With a sinking feeling in her belly, Fiona shook her head. "No, I have not prayed about it, I am ashamed to admit." Her cheeks felt warm, and she looked down at her clasped hands.

Joy gently squeezed Fiona's arm, and Fiona was relieved to note her sister did not condemn her like she was condemning herself. "What else?"

Fiona squirmed a little but made herself answer. "I think Roland is going to ask me to marry him."

"How is that a troubling thing to you?" Joy's question was a simple one, lacking the undercurrent of frustration that most people revealed when asking such questions.

"Because I don't know if I love him enough to wait two years, when he will be knighted." Fiona shrugged, embarrassed at her honest answer.

"I didn't know if I loved Bennet enough to wait three years to marry him, but I was sure that I loved him. And more importantly, I trusted him utterly."

"I trust Roland." Fiona was certain of that. "I would trust him with my life."

"Do you trust him with your heart?" Joy smiled again, and this time Fiona could feel the sisterly love in the air between them.

"Yes." She said the word slowly. "I think I do."

Joy reached up to caress Fiona's hair. "If Roland does ask you, talk to him openly and honestly about your fears. You will know the answer to your question when you hear his response to that honest concern. From what I know of Roland Campignon, I am certain of that."

Fiona pictured his handsome face and smiled when she remembered his earnestness, his industry, his devotion to his family and to his duty. She felt she already knew what he would say to persuade her of his trustworthiness, and she would believe him. He had never lied to her, not once.

"Thank you, I will." Though she still felt nervous about their meeting, she realized she did not have to dread it.

"Anything else?" Joy's gentle voice made Fiona drop her guard.

"I wish Papa would stop treating me like his 'wee lass' and realize I'm a woman grown." Fiona huffed, and then realized she was pouting like a child. She straightened in order to look and sound like an adult.

To her surprise, Joy laughed. "Oh, poor Kieran."

"What?" Fiona blurted out the word, surprised and a little angry that Joy would sympathize with him.

"Try to understand his point of view." Joy gave her a sad smile. "It's always difficult for a father to accept that his daughter is old enough to marry and leave his household. He felt the same about me, and I'm not his blood relation."

Fiona opened her mouth to deny Joy's words, but instead sat back, thinking hard. Was *that* why Papa had looked so old and sad lately?

Was he anticipating her marrying and leaving the Keep, perhaps to live in a far corner of the kingdom? Joy was as near as Frankland, and yet their families only visited a few times a year. Fiona had not truly considered how much her life would change once she did marry.

"If he's melancholy because I might move away soon, then why does he try so hard to anger me, keeping me under his thumb with such strict rules?" Fiona's frown returned, and she had to consciously keep it from turning into a scowl.

"Dear, dear Fiona, do you not realize what a lovely young woman you have become?" Joy's eyes filled with emotion. "Papa wants only to protect you from young men who might try to take advantage of your inexperience. He's been your protector since the day you were born. It's how fathers demonstrate their love." She leaned over to kiss Fiona's cheek. "My father, Valerian, was the same, and Kieran was always my second protector even before he became my stepfather. You should be so blessed to have two men who love you so well." Joy laughed, a sparkling sound. "Actually, I have had three protectors in my life, for Bennet shows his love for me in a similar way."

"Truly?" Fiona's eyes widened. Was that how Roland saw himself regarding her? She would have to notice his actions more closely.

"Truly." Joy rose, pulling away from Fiona. "Is there anything else?"

Fiona shook her head, still pondering Joy's unexpected words.

"Then come with me to the kitchen, for I have not yet broken my fast, and my stomach is letting me know of that neglect." She covered a giggle with her hand, as if she were a much younger woman.

Fiona couldn't hold back a smile. Was that why Mother had named her Joy? It was impossible to stay in a foul mood around her, after all.

"I have not eaten either, but my stomach has not yet informed me." She laughed, and it felt good to laugh.

They went to the kitchen together, still laughing.

* * *

Since there was no Privy Council meeting that day, Val and Dolan were able to leave early for the last two southern provinces. Dolan wanted to stop first at the Southern Woodlands. When the dragons approached the castle to land in the yard, Val saw Lord Rudyard MacNeil and his son, Sir Nathan waiting to greet them.

As soon as Reggie and Cephalorix landed, Val and Dolan slid down at the same time. Both MacNeils approached and bowed before giving the brothers a hearty welcome.

"I would ask if ye'd like tae refresh yourselves before examining the candidates, Sire, but I know ye have tae visit Southmoor also on this trip." Lord Rudyard grinned beneath his still-red mustaches, though they like his hair were streaked with white. Otherwise, it was difficult to remember how old the Lord of the Southern Woodlands was, for his posture was that of a younger man, and he walked briskly upon his wooden leg, not needing a cane.

"Thankfully we will see more of one another at court," Dolan said with a genuine smile.

"Aye, Sire, 'tis that, for sure." Rudyard turned and gestured to several people nearby, who cautiously approached, bowing to Dolan.

Val studied the group, the largest they'd encountered so far. There were eight, six men and two women. He only knew one of the group, Oswald Cornwall, Lord Henry's youngest son, who was exactly his age. A couple of the young men had a swagger about them that made Val distrust their motives for wanting to be part of the dragon couriers, but the others had honest faces, at least.

He had them line up across the yard. One of the arrogant men sneered at Val, which validated his instinct to dislike him.

"His Majesty will explain the process now," Val said in a mild voice, though he kept his eye on the two haughty ones.

I don't like them either, Reggie said. *They won't be able to speak to us, anyway.*

That's a relief! Though, even if they were able, I would not accept them as part of the couriers.

After Dolan finished describing what would happen next, Reggie and Cephalorix concentrated on reaching out to the eight humans. Dolan, Val presumed, was *Seeing* each of them, to determine their character or lack of it. After only a few minutes, Cephalorix spoke.

Those who can hear my voice, step forward.

Only two heard the chief dragon, Oswald and the shorter young woman. Oswald grinned at Val, but the young woman's eyes widened, and she looked back at the others in amazement.

"The rest of you are free to go," Dolan said. "Thank you for your interest in the Royal Dragon Couriers, but Cephalorix the chief dragon has chosen."

"Excuse me, Your Majesty, but how did we fail?" It was the man who'd sneered at Val, daring to question his king.

Dolan straightened and used his sternest voice. "You failed not only because you could not hear the dragon speaking to your mind, but because your character is lacking in judgment and humility. Consider this a warning to change your ways before you entrench yourself in attitudes and activities that will require me to take action." He stared down at the young man, who suddenly lost his cocky swagger and whose face went pale.

"Y-yes, Your Majesty." He and his friend both bowed more respectfully this time before they fled. The others who'd been dismissed were already leaving.

What are your names? Cephalorix asked the two candidates.

Oswald took a step closer, though he was somewhat timid and pale. *I am Oswald Cornwall, my lord.* He glanced at Val and whispered, "Was I supposed to answer like the dragon spoke? In my mind?"

"Cephalorix can only understand your mind speech, though my brother and I can hear you either way." Val gave his friend a reassuring smile.

And I am Oriana, my lord. She ducked her head. *I am but a laundress here in the castle. It was my brother who urged me to come today.*

"Who is your brother, Oriana?" Dolan asked in a gentle voice.

The laundress jerked up her head, startled. Then she curtsied with a blush that made her freckles stand out. "Your Majesty, he was one of those who did not hear the dragon and had to leave. His name is Arnulf. He works in Lord Rudyard's stables." Her gaze went to the castle's lord, and she curtsied again.

"Her brother does not only work in the stables, Sire. He is my stable master." Rudyard grinned, making Val smile too. "And no, he was nae one o' the cheeky ones. Arnulf and his sister are both loyal and dependable, hard-working, too."

At Rudyard's praise, Oriana's face turned bright red. Val took pity on the poor girl.

"Oswald I know, and I know he is eager to ride on a dragon." Val winked at his stockier and somewhat shorter friend. "But what about you, Oriana? If a dragon chooses you, are you willing to be its rider?"

Val felt better about Oriana when she didn't answer right away. She studied Cephalorix and Reggie with interest, not fear.

I might ride on a dragon's back? She sounded wistful speaking to Cephalorix.

Yes, if one of my children chooses you. The great dragon lowered his head, and Oriana reached out a hand as if she wanted to touch him. *Go ahead,* he urged her.

When she touched the scales between his nostrils, her face glowed.

Even if you are not chosen in a few days' time, Cephalorix said, *you will still be able to hear the dragons and speak to them, and we will still need you to help send and receive messages.*

And in the future, when there are more dragons, you would have another chance to be chosen as a rider, Reggie added.

Val smirked when Cephalorix's eyes widened, and he wondered if Dorricia and Mathairia would lay eggs soon. Surely they would let him and Dolan know?

Have you noticed, Val said in a private message to Reggie, *how much Cephalorix seems to be enjoying his interaction with the candidates for dragon rider?*

Yes, I have. Reggie sounded surprised. *I would not have expected him to enjoy this part at all.*

Though Val would have liked to stay and speak more with both candidates, he had to say his goodbyes as soon as Dolan explained that he would send for them when it was time for the selection. *How* was he going to remain patient through the long days of the king's court and tournament, when this much more important event was pending?

He waved to Oswald and Oriana while Reggie launched them into the air for the short journey to Castle Southmoor.

*

When they landed in Southmoor less than half an hour later, the young Lord Pascar Gowen came eagerly to meet them in the castle yard.

"I am glad to see you, Your Majesty and Your Highness," he said with a bow. When he straightened he grinned at the dragons. "I'm sorry, but there are only two candidates. I confess, I am curious as to whether I can hear the dragons, though I know I cannot be a dragon rider."

"Sean Hendry can hear them," Val said.

"Truly?" Pascar's face glowed. "Will he ride a dragon, then?"

Dolan spoke up. "That will be the dragons' choice. We are only to offer them suitable candidates."

Val shivered, for Dolan's choice of words made him remember how Aasvogel the witch planned to offer him as a sacrifice to a volcano. He was thankful the dragons would never expect a human sacrifice!

"Please, my lord," Val answered Pascar belatedly, "present yourself with the other two and find out if you can hear the mind speech of dragons. Even if you aren't chosen by one of them, it will be of great benefit to you if you are able to send messages directly to a dragon courier."

Dolan nodded, meeting his gaze. "Val is correct, as usual." He smiled before speaking to Pascar. "And he will head the new Royal Dragon Couriers once I make him Lord of the Sky at the opening of court next week."

"Is that so?" Pascar bowed to Val. "Then I offer my congratulations, Your Highness, and will try not to be envious."

"Thank you." Val squirmed, feeling a bit self-conscious. He needed to conquer those feelings before the court began so he wouldn't embarrass himself or his family when Dolan singled him out in front of everyone.

"Are you and the other two candidates ready, Lord Pascar?" Dolan steered the conversation back to the task at hand.

"Yes, Sire, they are merely waiting for my signal to approach." Pascar turned toward the castle, where several people stood on the landing. He lifted his hand, and two of the group made their way down the steps and across the yard. Both were young men about Val's age. They bowed when they came near.

"Line up with Lord Pascar," Dolan instructed them before explaining what was about to happen. None of them appeared anxious, and Val found himself hoping all three could hear the dragons.

While Dolan, Reggie, and Cephalorix communed with one another and studied the hopeful men before them, Val thought about all the others who had been discovered with the ability to speak to dragons. There were only nine dragons available to choose a rider, since four of Reggie's generation had chosen to live north of the Highlands and breed more of their kind. Even if Dorricia and Mathairia hatched eggs by the end of the year, it would be several years before that generation was ready to join the couriers.

Which of them would the dragons choose? For Val fervently hoped Emma would be one of the nine, and he found himself growing more impatient as the day approached.

Cephalorix spoke then, asking those who could hear him to step forward. Pascar and only one of the others did so. The Lord of Southmoor grinned.

I can hear you, my lord! I am honored. Pascar bowed to Cephalorix, and the younger man beside him did also.

You are lord of this province, are you not?

Yes, my lord. I am Pascar Gowen.

And what is your name? Cephalorix spoke to the other candidate.

I am Norman, my lord. I am an apprentice to Lord Pascar's falconer.

Dolan spoke to the one who was unable to hear the mind speech. "Thank you for your interest. You are dismissed."

At the disappointed look on the young man's face when he bowed, Val felt sorry for him and watched him trudge back to the castle.

"If you will plan to stay at the Keep an extra day or two after the tournament, Lord Pascar," Dolan was saying, "Prince Val and I will arrange for all the candidates to be presented at one time to the dragons."

"Of course, Sire." Pascar sounded so eager, Val couldn't decide if he wanted him to be chosen or not. It seemed that it could complicate matters regarding the rule of Southmoor, if he was. "May I bring Norman with me?"

Dolan glanced at Val. They had been telling all the other candidates they would send an escort. Because the Keep was always overcrowded during the week of the annual court, it hadn't seemed practical to add all the candidates, especially since they would not have the choosing until the day after most of the guests had left. Val nodded at his brother. It wouldn't hurt for Norman to come as one of Lord Pascar's party, would it?

"Certainly, my lord." Dolan folded his hands, seemingly unaware of the awe he inspired in the young falconer. "Norman, you are welcome to accompany Lord Pascar to the court and tournament."

"Y-your Majesty, I thank you for this great honor." Norman bowed, first to Dolan and then to Pascar. "My lord, is it possible I will be given leave for so many days?"

"Of course." Pascar waved his hand in a magnanimous gesture. "I will speak to your master right away."

Norman's gaze returned to Cephalorix and Reggie, and he bowed gravely. Val watched him stride across the yard with a spring in his step, and he smiled in understanding.

He had not anticipated how this process of discovering others who shared in the great blessing of hearing the dragons would affect him so profoundly. Val prayed it was the beginning of something extraordinary and life-changing, for more than just the future dragon riders.

* * *

Tam waited with Edward outside the manor's main door, each holding the reins of their mount, and Tam also held Lord Henry's horse. What was taking him so long? Henry Cornwall was never late.

Then Tam realized it was probably his nerves combined with lack of sleep making him less patient than usual. He stifled a yawn, but Edward noticed and snickered.

"Do you regret your midnight errand of charity now?" The page's voice was smug.

"Yes, actually I do." Tam sounded irritable to himself. He'd better gather his wits before Lord Henry appeared.

"Maybe you should have found another way to donate the coins." Edward's smirk made Tam wish he dared slap him.

"Maybe I should have, but it's too late for that now." Tam held back a groan. Where was he going to get the money needed to pay his debt? Would his father—stepfather, he'd learned since becoming Lord Henry's squire—be willing to loan it to him? Even if he did, how would Tam pay him back?

At that moment, the manor doors opened, and Lord Henry stepped out, followed by Lady Helena. Tam was grateful she would remain here at the manor; he would not have to be on his guard against her, at least.

The only downside meant there would be no female servants in their party with whom he could flirt. There was only Lord Henry, Edward, Captain Bronson, and two men-at-arms, but later today Lord Henry's two older sons would join them as they passed their manor houses. Both intended to compete in the tournament this year. Sir Henry, the eldest, was aloof and didn't bother Tam, but Sir Thomas had been a squire when Tam was a new page to a traitorous knight of

Northland, and the experience had been so traumatic, they had not gotten along since.

Lord Henry's horse shifted while the big man mounted, and Tam held the animal steady. When he handed up the reins to Henry's gloved hand, their eyes met briefly. Tam shivered and broke contact first, for it felt almost as if the lord had *Seen* his thoughts. He'd only had that experience once as a lad, when King Dolan had made sure the unlamented traitorous knight had not unduly influenced Tam, who'd been his page for less than a year. A few months was more than long enough to change the course of one's life, as Tam had recently experienced.

He moved stiffly to his own horse and pulled himself into the saddle. If only he'd never met Jevan, he would have remained ignorant of who his real sire had been. Jevan had been happy to relate all kinds of sordid tales about Sir Mortimer d'Evrow, as if he and his friends held the man in high esteem.

Bad enough he could no longer see Slade d'Jean as his father, Tam now lived with the knowledge that he and his mother had both lied to him for seventeen years. How could he ever trust them again?

When he once more became aware of his surroundings, Tam was startled to note they had traveled several miles along the road leading to Moor Point. Lord Henry and Captain Bronson rode ahead, discussing something in quiet voices. Edward rode in silence beside him, and the two men-at-arms brought up the rear. The morning was already hot and humid. That was one thing Tam looked forward to at the Keep—milder weather.

Without warning, Lord Henry pulled up his horse and dropped back to ride beside Tam. Captain Bronson beckoned Edward forward to take Henry's place.

"What troubles you today, Tammeron?" Henry's gaze pierced him again, though he sounded more concerned than suspicious.

Tam shrugged, surprised at the man's unexpected attention. "I'm fine, sir. Just didn't sleep well." He tried in vain to suppress a yawn.

"Are you sure that's all?" When Tam didn't answer immediately, Henry ordered Captain Bronson to stop for a rest.

Once the horses were grazing and the other four riders seated themselves under a large shaggy oak tree, Henry beckoned Tam to walk with him. They came upon a large rock near a stream, and Henry sat facing him.

"Hovering at the cusp of manhood is an awkward and frustrating place to be, Tammeron. I know how disappointed you were at not being chosen by Lord Jambray last year, and it must pain you to return to the Keep as squire of a minor lord instead."

Tam squirmed inside but tried to remain calm and not look away. Did Henry expect him to comment on that? Fortunately not, for he continued speaking.

"I'm sure you've felt like an exile these last several months, but I want to commend you, squire, on your conscientious attention to your duties, even those which are dull and tedious. Even my lady wife can find no fault, and she is quite particular about these matters." The stern lord actually smiled. "And I know my reputation as an exacting taskmaster." He grew somber again. "But you have dealt with all these new situations in an admirable way, and I intend to inform Lord Jambray about your exemplary attitude and service, should you wish to apply to squire for him or another great lord."

Tam was so shocked at the compliment, he couldn't answer right away. Now he felt even more wretched about his deception with the dice game. Could that cursed event pain him any more than it already had? He bowed to break eye contact and tried to make his voice sound pleased. It wasn't too difficult, considering the possibility of leaving Southmoor and not having to deal with Jevan and his friends.

"I thank you, my lord." He straightened and forced a smile. "I am happy to serve, either you or another lord, if the opportunity presents itself."

Henry's gaze pierced him once more. "But there is yet something troubling you, is there not?"

The man's compassion coupled with his exhaustion and desperation made Tam lower his guard.

"Just one question, my lord. Did you know Mortimer d'Evrow?"

Henry's brows raised, and his jaw dropped. Tam had never seen Lord Henry Cornwall surprised before.

"Yes, I did know him. Why do you ask?" His open manner vanished, replaced with stiff formality. Did Lord Henry know the truth of Tam's birth?

Lack of sleep was making him light-headed and more unguarded than he could ever remember.

"I was told by a reliable source that I am the son of Mortimer d'Evrow, not Slade d'Jean. Is it true, my lord?" Though Tam desperately wanted him to contradict it, he could see in Lord Henry's eyes that it *was* true.

He didn't question the "reliable source," nor did he deny the charge. "Mortimer was killed before you were born. Slade d'Jean has been your legal father in every sense of the word." Henry's eyes were sad, and Tam's anger erupted.

"He raped my mother! Why would he *do* that?" What kind of animal had sired him? And why hadn't his mother and Slade ever told him the truth?

"It matters not the circumstances of your birth, Tammeron. What matters is what you have made of your life, with the guidance of your parents and mentors who greatly care about you." Now Lord Henry was back to his usual lecturing tone. It was as if their brief rapport had never existed.

"Yes, my lord. Thank you." Tam bowed, hoping the conversation was over now. He wished he had never asked the question. Under normal circumstances he wouldn't have.

"You're welcome. Let's resume our journey now. We have a long way to travel." Without glancing at Tam, Henry led the way back to the horses.

Tam had never felt so desolate. He was truly alone in the world, after all.

Chapter 7

Wrath is cruel, anger is overwhelming, but who can stand before jealousy?

Fiona let Firestorm have her head as soon as she and Val crested the hill north of the Keep. She leaned over the mare's neck and urged her to a gallop. As fast as Firestorm was, Alydar was faster, even carrying Fiona's much taller brother. He passed them once they reached the next hill, and Val slowed Alydar an instant before Fiona did the same with Firestorm.

"All right, I admit it; Alydar is faster." Fiona grinned at Val. "But he's the only one."

"I believe that! We were hard-pressed to catch up with you." Val patted his horse's neck. "I think he smelled the challenge and rose to the occasion."

Her brother's easy smile made Fiona sad, for she knew this might be their last ride together for some time. Once Val was made Lord of the Sky, his life would change, and his responsibilities would keep him away from her more than ever.

"Fiona? Is something wrong?" He dismounted and let Alydar graze while coming closer to her.

She forced cheerfulness into her voice. "Oh, nothing much." She also slid down from Firestorm's saddle and caught Val's hand. "I do hope you will introduce me to Emma when she comes to the Keep.

I'm anxious to meet the woman who has stolen my favorite brother's heart."

Val blushed furiously, but he couldn't hold back a grin. "You'll like her, Fiona, I'm sure you will."

Fiona took his other hand and gazed up at him. "Why isn't she coming for court? Won't you need an escort for the opening ceremony and banquet?"

He lowered his gaze. "I did not ask her to come for court because I thought she might be overwhelmed with all the people and the spectacle." He shrugged. "I don't want to frighten her away. She is used to a quiet life; I'll have to ease her into this one more gently."

Fiona frowned. "She does know you're a prince, doesn't she?"

Val straightened and met her gaze again. "Of course she does." His smile returned. "And even knowing that, she has agreed to come and be presented to the dragons as a possible rider. I can't ask anything more of her right now."

Though she managed to hold back a smirk, Fiona couldn't help herself. "Are you planning to ask her something else soon?"

He blushed again, and the look in his eyes made her stomach clench. "Yes, I am, and I hope Emma will agree to be my wife in the not-too-distant future."

Fiona wanted to be happy for him, she truly did. But his happiness, like that of Iris and Aidan, only underscored that she had not yet found it for herself. Instead of jerking away from him, though, she forced herself to squeeze his hands and smile up at him.

"I wish you and Emma all the joy in the world." She tried to pull away, but Val didn't let her.

"Thank you, Sis, and there's something I want to ask you, too." He sounded unsure now, and she gave him her full attention.

"What is it?" She only hoped he wasn't asking something she could not promise, for she hated to disappoint him.

"Would you be my escort for the opening ceremony and banquet? There's no one else with whom I'd rather share the day's life-changing events." Though his voice was earnest, his face had some of his old shyness, and Fiona hurried to reassure him.

"I would be honored to share the day with you, dear brother." Now she could give him a genuine smile, for her heart felt light indeed.

"Thank you, dear sister." Val kissed her hands, one at a time. "Shall we return to the Keep? For by the position of the sun and the rumbling in my belly, it must be close to time for the noon meal." He wagged his brows and then winked at her, something he hadn't done in a long time.

"Heaven forbid you miss a meal." Fiona collected Firestorm's reins and pulled herself up to the saddle while Val mounted Alydar.

"Aye, 'twould be a tragedy all around," Val replied in a Highland accent, making Fiona laugh.

They rode back at a slower pace, and Fiona savored every moment.

* * *

Roland Campignon climbed the lookout tower of Sir Thomas Cornwall's manor house for the third time in an hour. Sir Thomas' father should be arriving any minute, and then he and his knight would join the party heading north to the Keep for the king's annual court and tournament. They were all planning to spend the night at the eldest son's estate a few miles north of here, and at first light would press on to Moor Point.

His wish had been for the Cornwalls to travel the most direct route, along the road through the pass in the Dragon's Backbone, but apparently Lord Henry had business in Westmoor before continuing along the eastern road. Roland hoped this business would not take long; he was anxious to see Fiona and speak with her the moment Sir Thomas released him from his duties. He patted the small pocket tucked inside his tunic where he kept the simple gold ring for safekeeping. It had taken him two years to save enough to buy it for Fiona. His only fear was that it was too plain for her tastes.

What would she say when he asked her to marry him? Roland did not expect her to say yes outright; he knew two years was a long time to wait, and Fiona was not always the most patient person. He did not assume she loved him as well as he loved her. It was his hope, certainly, and he knew she was fond of him, at least. But was that enough for her to consider his marriage proposal? She was so beautiful, he felt certain half the kingdom was in love with her. Certainly she could have her pick of eligible men. He sighed. What was special about him, anyway?

Then Roland straightened when a cloud of dust appeared, and Lord Henry's party came into view. Perhaps he wasn't special, but he had worked hard to be a good squire, and even more important, had striven to grow in his faith and virtue so he could become a good and gentle husband someday.

And right now, he was praying Fiona would come to realize they were especially suited for one another, and that a marriage like theirs was sure to be worth waiting for.

The riders neared the manor, and Roland could pick out individuals. Lord Henry was in good spirits, laughing at something one of his men-at-arms said. The others smiled with good humor, all but one.

Tammeron d'Jean, who had been Lord Henry's squire for several months now, had a black look upon him, as if he were angry or exceedingly troubled.

Roland sighed. They had encountered one another on several occasions, usually at Henry's manor when Sir Thomas had visited his father. Tammeron had been cool and distant to Roland, but at least he had always been polite. Though not his choice of traveling companion on a journey of several days, Roland did not expect any problems.

He would treat his fellow squire the way he would wish himself to be treated—with kindness and by not forcing a friendship upon him, even though it went against his upbringing to avoid being friendly with a peer. Most of the squires Roland knew were grateful at his overtures of friendship, for being a squire was a difficult, sometimes lonely job.

In fact, he reflected while hurrying down the tower stairs, Tammeron was the only squire to rebuff his friendliness so thoroughly. Perhaps Roland should see Tam as a challenge for the duration of their journey. Could he befriend the aloof squire before they reached the Keep? It was worth a try.

"Roland, there you are." Sir Thomas brushed at his tunic, always self-conscious when in his father's presence. His young page Serle followed at a hurried pace, with his short legs pumping.

"I've been watching for Lord Henry and his party, sir." Roland came to stand beside his knight with an encouraging smile. Lord Henry Cornwall had a reputation for being strict and exacting, but Roland had always found him to be a good listener and genuinely interested in others.

"Good man." Thomas gave Roland an anxious smile. "I can always count on you to be prepared."

"Thank you, Sir Thomas." Roland inclined his head as the horses entered the manor yard.

"Welcome, Father!" While the head groom and his two stable boys hurried to take the horses, Thomas approached Lord Henry. As soon as Henry dismounted, he and Thomas embraced. "Come inside and refresh yourselves before we set off for the Scarecrow's lair."

Roland chuckled as he and young Serle moved nearer to Captain Bronson and the others. Sir Thomas often referred to his elder brother, also named Henry, as a scarecrow because he was noticeably leaner than Thomas. Both were tall like their father, though.

He turned at the sound of Lady Lidia's voice. Sir Thomas' overly emotional wife stood in the doorway with her hands resting upon her pregnant belly.

"So good to see you, Father." Her pained smile did not match the brightness of her voice.

Roland shook his head. He needed to grant Lady Lidia a little more grace. His mother had once told him that expecting women were hardly ever their best selves.

"Good day, Captain Bronson." Roland smiled up at Lord Henry's stern but good-hearted captain of the guard. "I trust the first leg of your journey was uneventful?"

"Yes, Roland, thank you. I can only hope the rest of our journey will be likewise." Bronson handed his reins to the older stable boy and followed Lord Henry.

Roland checked to make sure the two guards were taking care of their own horses and turned his attention to Tammeron and Lord Henry's new page, Prince Edward. Sir Thomas had cautioned Roland to treat Edward as he would any other page; Lord Henry was not allowing the young prince to identify his rank or claim privilege because of it.

"Hello, Tammeron. And greetings to you, Edward." Roland's smile was less easy with these two.

"Roland." Tam coolly nodded before staring at Lord Henry's departing back. "Are we to stay here with the horses, then?"

"Oh, no." Roland beckoned to them both. "Bring them into the stables, and they'll be cared for while we all eat the noon meal."

Tam nodded without comment and went with Roland. Edward followed, leading his own mount. Roland gestured to the two empty stalls near the entrance and waited while squire and page shut them in, first making sure they had water. Serle hovered nearby, wanting to help, but Roland shook his head. Then the two squires and two pages made their way to the manor.

The silence of the newcomers made Roland uneasy, but he was at a loss to know how to begin a conversation with them. While the others had an animated discussion at one end of the trestle table, Roland sat at the other end with his two sullen companions. Serle had managed to escape when Sir Thomas called for him, but Roland had had no such luck.

And then one of the female kitchen workers came bearing a tray of bread and cheese. Though she was not especially pretty, Tammeron perked up, even smiling at the girl when she served him, making her giggle. All the way back to the kitchen, she kept glancing back at him. When Tam winked, she collided with the door frame, changed course, and disappeared inside.

The squire dug into his food with renewed enthusiasm. "A shame we aren't spending the night here," he remarked.

Roland had to measure his words. "If you did, it would make our journey to the Keep that much longer. I feel certain Lord Henry has planned the itinerary carefully." He took a sip from his cup, but he watched Tam over the rim.

He shrugged. "Well, no matter. There will be other stops along the way and other opportunities."

"Opportunities for what?" Roland asked innocently, glancing at Edward.

Edward stopped chewing, waiting for Tam's answer.

"Oh, you know, the usual. Making new friends." Was that a hint of a blush in Tammeron's cheeks?

"Playing games with new friends?" Edward smirked.

Roland choked and began coughing. What did the young prince know about such matters? Had Tammeron been a bad influence on him already? That was only one problem with having a reputation of immoral behavior. True, Roland did not know Tam well enough to confirm or deny the rumors, but even if all he did was flirt with the servant girls, it was a poor example to set for the young impressionable prince.

"Not at all, Edward." Tam brushed a crumb from his tunic before turning what Roland saw as a proper squire's gaze upon his lord's page. "There won't be any time to play games with friends, either new or old. We have work to do."

"Quite right," Roland agreed, apparently with too much fervor, because both Tam and Edward stared at him.

After a moment, Tam sat back and folded his arms. He kept his gaze on Lord Henry without speaking again, and the minute his lord finished his meal and rose from the table, Tam stood also.

With a sigh, Roland prepared to leave on what might prove to be a tortuous journey.

*

The situation did not improve once they left the manor to travel to Sir Henry's larger estate near the border of Moor Point. Edward ignored poor Serle, but was willing to talk with Roland. Tammeron remained silent, lost in his own thoughts.

"I'm sure my Aunt Fiona will be glad to see you, Roland." He smirked, and Roland chose not to be irritated by the young prince's tone of voice.

"I hope so, Edward, for I am very fond of her." He glanced at Tammeron, but the squire didn't appear to be listening.

"So when are you going to marry her?" Thankfully the smirk disappeared, and Edward sounded genuinely curious.

Painfully aware of the traveling party all around, Roland lowered his voice. "I can't even think about marriage until after I am knighted, which is two years from now." That only reminded him of Fiona's lack of letters and his concern that she had fallen in love with another.

Edward frowned in thought. "So, if she agrees to marry you, she would have to wait two whole years? That's a long time."

"Yes, it is." Roland let out a sigh. Then he chastised himself and straightened in the saddle. "But, Edward, all good things are worth waiting for. In the Holy Writ is a narrative about a man named Jacob who had to work for seven years before he could marry the woman he loved. And it says those years felt like only a few days, because of the great love he had for her." Personally, Roland could not understand how Jacob could say that about waiting *seven* years, because a mere two years was going to feel like an eternity!

Edward grunted and looked as skeptical as Roland felt. "Father read that story to us, and I did not understand how it could be true. A few days feels like seven years to me, when you have to wait for something you really want." Then the young prince's smirk reappeared. "I also remember how Jacob was cheated later in that story and ended up with a wife he didn't really want."

"Yes, that is true." Roland didn't want to think about that part of the story, though. "If your aunt agrees to marry me, you will be one of the first to know." He forced a smile he didn't feel.

"Why are you asking Fiona? Isn't she of higher rank than you?" Edward's frown was deeper this time, as if in disapproval.

Roland tried to remember the exact wording of his father's recent letter, after Roland had written to him on this very point. "Though Lady Mercy was a princess and does indeed have royal blood, she is no longer styled 'Highness' and so Fiona's title is Lady, not Princess. Her father and mine are equal peers of the realm." When he glanced Tam's way, the squire had apparently been listening.

Edward bit his lip, thinking it through, and then his face relaxed. "I didn't think Grandmother could go lower in rank, but now that I think about it, I have never heard anyone call her 'Highness.' So I suppose you can ask Aunt Fiona to marry you."

It sounded as if Edward was giving his *permission*, and Roland stiffened when Tam laughed. Roland had to force himself to let go of his indignation and his embarrassment, for Sir Henry's manor came into view.

The party entered the manor yard, and Lord Henry and Sir Thomas were enthusiastically greeted by Sir Henry and his lady wife, Luella, who had once been Queen Rhianna's maid. Their two small sons toddled out and held up their hands for "Grampa" to pick them up. Lord Henry obliged, holding one child in each arm.

The rest of them dismounted, and Sir Henry's people came to take the horses. Roland removed his pack as well as that of Sir Thomas, and Tammeron took charge of Lord Henry's.

Roland followed Tam's gaze up to a second story window. Two female servants peered out, staring at Tam, and he gave them a smile and a wink, making them giggle. For the first time since he'd known Tammeron, Roland realized his fellow squire had a type of charisma he'd never noticed before—the ability to summon his charm in a moment, for a particular person or persons, and then as quickly hide it. As if by magic.

Should he be alarmed about this? Or was he merely envious?

Then Sir Thomas beckoned to him, and Roland turned all his attention to his knight and his duty.

* * *

The following morning, it grew more and more difficult for Tam to hide his growing frustration. It appeared he would have to travel the entire distance alongside Roland Campignon. Lord Henry and his sons were having an animated discussion ahead of them, followed by the three pages, and the several men-at-arms took up the rear. Sir Henry's squire Manard was to be knighted at the court, so a new squire would be assigned Sir Henry then. Perhaps it was his sober reflection of impending knighthood, but Manard ignored both Tam and Roland and rode alone ahead of them.

That left him trapped into riding beside Roland. It was bad enough Tam had to work with a spoiled prince for a page, the insufferable Roland was going to marry a princess, or at least as good as one, since Fiona was the king's sister.

Tam acknowledged to himself that he was jealous of Roland's plan to marry into the royal family. Roland, the son of the realm's Lord High Steward, would be set for life while he, the lowly son of a provincial steward, had little hope of improving his status in such a spectacular way. With two marks against him already, Tam wasn't even sure of attaining knighthood, especially if Lord Henry discovered his gambling debt.

The journey from Southmoor to the Keep took three days, even taking the most direct route. But they were not going directly to the Keep. Lord Henry had business with Sir Aidan Fitzhugh in Moor Point, and so the party was to stop there first. Did Sir Aidan have any idea how many were to spend the night at his estate? Surely Lord Henry had given him warning?

"Did you ever have opportunity to meet Sir Aidan while you were in Moor Point?" It took Tam a moment to realize Roland was speaking to him.

"Yes, several times. Sir Aidan and Sir Artemis, my former knight, often hunted together." Tam hoped the answer satisfactory enough to keep Roland from continuing the conversation.

For several minutes, it appeared he had dissuaded Roland. Tam wanted only to savor the memory of last night's stolen kisses with Clarinda in a dark corner of the great hall. For a servant, she was especially enthusiastic, and he promised, as he always did, to return and continue what they had begun.

"Are you entering the archery contest this year?" It was Roland's high and mighty voice again, which Tam was coming to despise.

"Yes." He bit off the word.

"Which kind of bow do you prefer?" Others might consider Roland's questions friendly, but to Tam they felt more like an interrogation.

"I have a recurve yew bow." How could he get the squire to shut up without being reprimanded by Lord Henry in front of everyone?

"As do I. Perhaps we can practice together when we arrive at the Keep." When Tam didn't reply, Roland opened his mouth to continue, but Lord Henry held up a hand, signaling a halt.

"There is a flock of pheasants ahead. All who wish to, string your bows and we'll bring a gift to Sir Aidan's table tonight." Henry smiled in anticipation.

Reluctantly, Tam strung his bow, and Roland did likewise. While the men-at-arms held the horses, the three Cornwalls and their squires approached the nearby meadow. In unison, six bows aimed and released. Four of the pheasants did not lift from the ground. Tam's arrow was one of those that missed the mark. Manard nocked another arrow and shot a fifth pheasant from the sky. Lord Henry directed Tam and Roland to collect the game.

While they did so, Tam found his arrow and retrieved it. Fortunately, he was not required to field dress the dead birds. That job, he was pleased to note, went to the pages. It gave Tam great pleasure to watch Edward's revulsion at disemboweling his one bird, which took him as long as it did the others to dress two.

They tied the carcasses to Captain Bronson's saddle and continued along the road. It was near sunset when they reached Sir Aidan's manor.

It had been several months since Tam had seen the man, and the difference in his appearance was striking. After Aidan had lost his wife and child, he'd aged years in his grief, but now that he'd remarried, it was as if he'd been brought to life again.

And then Aidan's new wife appeared at his side, smiling up at him with obvious devotion. The beautiful woman was familiar to him. Where had he seen her before?

Of course! She was Iris Campignon, who, Tam remembered, was a great friend of Fiona MacLachlan. His gaze slid to Roland, Iris' brother. Fiona, who this bumbling idiot wished to marry. As if Fiona would have such a self-righteous little marsh fly!

Tam thought back to his brief encounter with Fiona at last year's court. She had certainly become a lovely and desirable young woman. And he had sensed in her a playfulness and passion that would never be satisfied by someone so stiffly formal as Roland.

If, as Tam suspected, Fiona craved adventure and excitement, Tam felt confident he could better satisfy her than Roland. He was even more sure she could satisfy all *his* desires, the most important being a sizeable dowry.

The warm feeling that filled his chest faded. Tam would not be able to offer a marriage proposal for three years, and he needed money *now*.

He would have to approach his father. No, his stepfather. Tam scowled. It was going to be incredibly difficult to even speak to the man, knowing the truth of his birth now. But who else would be willing to loan him the sum he needed to pay off his debt?

With a growl in his throat, he forced himself to push down that anxiety before Lord Henry noticed. How Tam wished he could sneak away in the night and find a place where no one knew him and he could live in peace.

Instead, he was trapped as surely as if he were locked inside a cage. Why did everything have to be so *unfair*?

Chapter 8

Deceive not with thy lips.

Val stood nervously in the front row of nobles watching Dolan receive the renewed vows of fealty from the seven provincial lords. Beside him Fiona clutched his arm, trying to reassure him, and he patted her hand to let her know how much he appreciated the gesture.

At least Dolan hadn't insisted on installing him first, though Val knew his brother had wanted to open the court with that ceremony. As a compromise, he would have the seven lords come forward first, a subtle way to publicly demonstrate their importance to him, before giving a new title to his young brother, the prince.

The final lord, Dougal MacLachlan, who was the Highland's High Chieftain this year, stepped down and met Val's gaze with a nod and a knowing look. Val nodded in return and then gave all his attention to Dolan, who signaled the herald.

"Will His Highness, Prince Valerian d'Alden, now approach the king?" The man's rich voice compelled Val to rise from his seat. Fiona squeezed his hand, and he gave her a brief smile before approaching the throne by stepping up to the dais in front of him.

Breathing deeply to ward off his nervousness, Val knelt on the cushion and tried not to think about all the people packed into the throne room this day. Instead, he focused on his brother's pleased expression.

"For generations, Levathia's courier system has served the communication needs of the realm through its efficient routes between provinces, fast horses, and dedicated couriers. Flint Mallory has been the loyal head of the couriers for many years, and we have every confidence in him to continue to lead these able messengers." Dolan found Mallory in the crowd and inclined his head to him.

"In some circumstances," he continued, "notably times of emergency, even the fastest relay teams are not able to bring timely word or assistance over great distances. From time to time, the great dragons have carried myself and others to those in need, since their powerful wings can fly much faster than our valiant horses, but even that method has its inefficiencies and shortcomings.

"Therefore, after consultation with Cephalorix the lord of the dragons, we are forming a new courier system, in addition to the current one, which we will call the Royal Dragon Couriers. As Prince Valerian has proven with the dragon Regnatorix, it is possible for a dragon and a human to form a close bond by speaking mind-to-mind. After I install him as Lord of the Sky, Prince Valerian will enable the willing dragons to each bond with a human able to speak to his or her mind, and one will be assigned to each of the seven provinces so that the most important messages can be sent mind-to-mind, and help and assistance can be given via dragon back." Dolan grinned at the excited murmuring of the audience.

Then Dolan met Val's gaze. "Prince Valerian." His eyes shone with his inner joy. "It is with great pleasure that I confer upon you the title of 'Lord of the Sky' and entrust you with the authority to form and oversee the Royal Dragon Couriers." He placed a chain with an emblem of a man riding upon a dragon around Val's neck. Then he waited for Val to hold up his joined hands, which Dolan warmly clasped between his own.

"And I, Prince Valerian, Lord of the Sky, gladly accept the authority you have given me and pledge to you my loyalty. I will faithfully execute the duties you have entrusted to me, so help me God."

With a smile, Dolan released their hands. "Rise, Prince Valerian, Lord of the Sky."

Val rose to stand before his brother and returned the smile. He had no words to express his feelings, not even mind-to-mind. When Dolan bade him turn around, everyone in the crowded throne room burst into applause and cheers, and Val's cheeks grew warm.

*

After the opening ceremonies concluded with the presentation of the candidates for knighthood, Val escorted Fiona to the feast. He wasn't able to converse with his sister, since so many individuals wanted to congratulate him and ask questions about the dragon couriers. When he glanced at Fiona, she barely held in her irritation, making Val feel guilty for neglecting her. As soon as they reached the head table and took their seats, he ignored the approaching Lord Tavis to speak to Fiona.

"If I neglected to tell you earlier, you look especially radiant today, Sis." Val lifted her hand and kissed it. Her peeved look vanished, and she gave him a genuine smile.

"Thank you, Val." She gestured to his new tunic. "And you look especially handsome today." She leaned closer to examine the medallion on his chain. "That dragon looks almost exactly like Reggie."

Val lifted it and turned the image to better see it. "I was told the goldsmith used Reggie as the model." He dropped it and chuckled. "It must have been difficult for him to create such a tiny likeness from an enormous original."

Fiona nodded. "That shows the skill of the goldsmith."

"Indeed." He took her hand and clasped it between both of his. "So, are you going to dance with me after the meal tonight? Or do you have your sights set on someone else present?" Val scanned the crowded hall, which was still buzzing with activity while people seated themselves.

"Oh, I will surely take pity on you and be your dance partner." Fiona tried to hold a haughty pose, but she giggled instead.

"Then I am especially honored to be favored with my lady's pity." Val couldn't keep a bored face, either, and burst into laughter.

"Are you two going to share your private joke with us, or must we guess?" Dolan said from Val's other side, and Rhianna leaned forward to better see them.

Val winked at Fiona before turning to answer Dolan. "Sorry, brother, but chivalry prevents me from revealing a secret where a lady is concerned."

"And rightly so." Dolan nodded to him and gave Fiona a tight smile.

Val wondered at that, but he kept his peace. It was time for Dolan to give his usual speech, though Val didn't listen to his words. He could only think that there appeared to be some strain between Dolan and Fiona. How had he never noticed that before? Was there anything he could do about it?

* * *

Fiona's lightness of heart vanished at the look Dolan gave her before standing to give his usual welcome speech. Was he displeased that Val had chosen her to be his escort, and therefore she had to sit at the head table? Would Dolan always be so strict and unyielding that she would never find favor in his eyes?

He was even worse than Papa!

Though she wanted to yank her hand away from Val and storm from the hall, Fiona made herself breathe deeply. When her fingers convulsed, Val squeezed and briefly met her gaze with an encouraging smile. She knew he was not comfortable at being singled out tonight, but he was making the best of an uncomfortable situation. If Val could do it, then so could she.

While the first course was being served, Fiona picked at the unidentifiable objects on her trencher without immediately tasting them. The head cook had apparently decided the entire meal would be dragon-themed, and had chopped meats and vegetables into fine pieces in order to shape them into dragons or wings or eggs. She did eat an actual boiled egg when it arrived with the second course.

By the third course, Fiona remembered to look for Roland. She hadn't noticed him earlier, and it took quite a while to find him, for he was stuck serving the lower tables farthest from the head table. Of all the bad luck! They hadn't been close enough to even greet one another since he arrived with Lord Henry Cornwall's party the day before yesterday.

Then she remembered Roland's last letter, and her heart thumped. Was he truly going to ask for her hand? She still didn't know how she would answer. With a sigh, she sat back in her seat and dabbed her mouth with her napkin. Best she wait and hear what he had to say.

"Fiona? Are you well?" Val turned his attention from Dolan and stared at her with concern.

"Oh yes, I am well." She made herself smile brightly. No matter what, she did not want to dampen any of Val's triumph tonight.

When the confection was paraded through the hall on its journey to the head table, people murmured with delight at the blue dragon with a long-legged rider upon it. The kitchen servant placed it on the head table between Dolan and Val and made an exaggerated bow. Dolan spoke loudly, to be heard over the general hubbub.

"On behalf of my brother, the Lord of the Sky, we thank you for Robin's skill in creating this representation of what we hope to accomplish with the new Royal Dragon Couriers." Then Dolan gestured for the servant to cut the confection and serve it.

Fiona cringed when the man pulled out a long knife and made precise slices of the castle base upon which the dragon and rider perched. She could only eat a small portion of hers, for it was just a little too sweet for her taste.

Then the music changed in volume and tempo from quiet background tunes to the opening chords of the king's traditional first dance. After the lower tables were moved to the edges of the room, Val gave her his hand.

"Shall we?" His eyes pleaded with her, for she knew how uncomfortable he was about dancing in front of others, and this first dance would be just the two of them along with Dolan and Rhianna.

"Of course." Fiona squeezed his hand in reassurance, for this was the easy part of the day, for her.

While the four of them performed the stately dance to the hushed crowd, Fiona focused on her brother's face, letting him know that as far as she was concerned, they were the only two in the room. Whatever she did, it worked as well as if they could speak mind-to-mind, for Val did not miss a step, and he managed to keep a pleasant look on his face the entire time.

At the end of the final chord, they bowed to one another in unison with the king and queen, and the crowd warmly applauded the royal siblings.

Though Fiona could have continued dancing, she sensed that Val wanted to return to the table for now, and so she held his hand and joined him. He grabbed his goblet and drained it.

"Thank you for helping me stay calm." He wiped the corner of his mouth and smiled sheepishly.

"It was my pleasure. I love to dance and I love you, so it was no trouble at all." She patted his arm and was about to say more when a man she did not know approached the table with a bow.

"Your Majesties, Your Highness. Pardon my boldness, but I am Sir Artemis Villeroy of Moor Point. Might I have this dance, Lady Fiona?"

Her eyes widened, and she wanted to say no. But Val lightly elbowed her and whispered, "Go on." So she rose slowly, reluctant to leave him.

"I thank you, Sir Artemis." There, that was polite without being encouraging, wasn't it? The man wasn't terribly old, only about ten years her senior, but he seemed scrawny for a knight. Once the dance began, she changed her mind about not trying to converse with him.

"I am wondering, Sir Artemis, why you chose to ask me to dance with you?" They were facing one another, so she stared into his slightly bulging eyes. He cleared his throat.

"You are the most beautiful lady in the room, and I knew if I wanted an opportunity to dance with you, I would have to be bold and take the initiative, for I suspect you will have no lack of partners tonight." His nervous smile matched his clammy hands.

"I thank you for the compliment, but it is not necessary to flatter me." Instinctively she straightened, trying to project a detached aloofness. This was not a man she would wish to know better. He put her in mind of a fish with his eyes and his moist lips. Most unpleasant!

It was a relief when the song ended, and Sir Artemis escorted her back to the head table. She nodded a cool thanks to the knight, dismissing him, and waited for Val to return from speaking to Lord Jambray. At the sound of a faster dance, her feet tapped under the table in anticipation.

To her disappointment, Val and Rhianna partnered for the next dance, and Fiona's heart sank. Dolan, she was thankful to note, was in conversation with Papa, so she would not be forced to dance with either of them. Though she'd rather have Val's company, it was far better to sit alone and sip from her goblet, watching Val and Rhianna dance together, than to have to dance with someone like Sir Artemis.

While she listened to the song, Fiona's gaze traveled to the other end of the cavernous room, searching for Roland's golden hair. Instead, a tall, dark-haired young man turned in her direction. He was so handsome, Fiona gasped. Who was he? Had she seen him before? Surely she would have noticed him.

He must be a squire and not merely a servant, for he wore a fine russet tunic, one of the new sleeveless kind worn by the younger knights and lords, so they could wear elaborate linen shirts underneath with large embroidered sleeves. The contrast of colors accentuated his hair, which framed his striking face.

Across the table from the tall squire, Roland came into view, handing a goblet from a tray to a smiling lady. His hair seemed less golden, his tunic plain and unremarkable. Fiona's gaze returned to the dark-haired young man.

When a servant approached the head table to refill goblets, Fiona beckoned to him.

"Y-yes, my lady?" The young man stammered while he bowed to her.

"Do you see that squire with the russet tunic serving Lord Jambray?" She pointed in the general direction while trying not to be obvious to anyone else.

The servant followed her finger and squinted. "Aye, my lady."

"What is his name?" She reined in her impatience with difficulty.

"That is Tammeron d'Jean, my lady, the son of the steward of Frankland." He shifted his stance, obviously in a hurry to be off.

"Thank you." Fiona dismissed him with a smile and turned her attention back to the handsome squire. Tammeron d'Jean. Tam. Of course! She should have remembered, even though she hadn't seen him in a whole year. He'd been good-looking then, but he'd grown positively beautiful. Watching him interacting with the lords and ladies at Jambray's table, Fiona guessed Tam was nearly as tall as Val and Dolan now. How could she contrive to move closer to him and get a better look?

Providence intervened, and Sir Alfred Meverel came striding toward the head table. His hair was darker than Roland's, but the knight had a physical resemblance to his younger cousin. Alfred was much more outgoing and flirtatious than Roland ever could be, though.

"Hello, Lady Fiona." When she held out her hand, he brushed it with his lips. "What a pleasure to see you again."

"Hello, Sir Alfred. Still unmarried, I presume?" Fiona arched her brows, making Alfred laugh.

"My lady is perceptive as ever." He shrugged, feigning innocence. "I have yet to find one special lady with whom to give my heart."

"And so you tease us all by pretending to share the smallest portion of it." She had to bite her lip to keep from laughing. Rhianna's brother was so predictable. Sure enough, he pressed his hand over his heart and screwed up his face in pretended pain.

"Ah, my beautiful lady, you surely wound me! I might pretend with others, but never you." He winked and gave her a mocking bow. "After that well-placed arrow, you must repent of your misdeed by agreeing to dance the next one with me."

Fiona tapped her chin and looked up at the ceiling. "I suppose I could deign to dance with you, Sir Alfred." Then she lowered her hand and gave him her most serene smile.

"Then I would be honored indeed." He held out his hand, and she let him assist her down from the dais.

They stood hand-in-hand until the current dance ended, and then Alfred led her to take their places for the Highland reel. Once the song began, Fiona had to concentrate on the steps and had no attention to spare Tammeron. Only toward the end, when her feet moved of their own volition did she glance toward the place where she'd last seen him.

He was standing near the wall, holding a wineskin and staring at her. When she met his gaze, he smiled, making Fiona's heart thump painfully. She turned away to finish the dance with Alfred, but the butterflies dancing inside her would not be ignored.

* * *

All during the banquet, Tam's annoyance grew at having to serve the same table as Roland. With all the people at the Keep during court, surely Lord Drew could have assigned his own son elsewhere? Fortunately the hall was so crowded and chaotic, Tam rarely had to interact with Roland.

Once the confection was served, Tam hoped to have a few free minutes to speak with his stepfather. Perhaps he could get away while the other squires were eating and before they would be required to refill goblets during the dancing. How he wished squires were allowed to dance; there were several uncommonly pretty girls present tonight.

Then his gaze traveled to the head table, where Fiona MacLachlan sat with her brothers. She had grown even prettier in the last year. It wasn't fair that someone like Roland Campignon had all the luck to someday marry a wealthy woman of high rank, who also happened to be a beauty.

Lord Drew met him and several other squires when they returned empty trays and trenchers.

"You now have half an hour free time before returning to duty. There is a table with food in the back, by the oven." Then the Lord High Steward left them, expecting their obedience.

The other squires headed toward the food, but Tam hung back, waiting until Lord Drew was out of sight to slip back into the great hall and speak with the man he'd always called his father.

He found Slade in conversation with an older knight of Frankland. Fortunately, Tam's mother was nowhere nearby. He was not ready to face her yet. Slade looked up at his approach.

"Tam." He smiled brightly, and the knight nodded to him and left them alone.

"Father." Tam had to force out the word. It tasted bitter on his tongue.

"You're looking well. Is your situation in Southmoor a better one than you had in Moor Point?" Though Slade's question was an innocent one, Tam heard the true question he was asking.

"Yes, sir. Lord Henry is a firm yet fair lord, and I am learning much from him." That, at least, was true.

The relief on Slade's face was palpable. "I am very glad to hear that, Son."

Tam's gut twisted, and he almost blurted out the truth he had learned in Southmoor, that he was not Slade's real son. He had to calm himself before asking his most pressing question.

"I have, however, found myself in a bit of trouble. May I borrow from you and repay you as soon as I am able?" Tam knew he would not be able to get away with such a vague request.

"What kind of trouble?" Slade's eyes narrowed. "You haven't been gambling again, have you?"

In the past, Tam would have dropped his gaze and backed off. But he was feeling too desperate—about the truth of his birth, about feeling trapped squiring for Lord Henry, and about his debt with Jevan's "friends." He set his jaw and forced himself not to look away.

"It was just a dice game. No one was hurt." *Except me, if I don't pay my debt to those rotten cheats.*

"Tam." Slade lowered his voice and made sure no one else was listening. "Even a simple dice game has unintended consequences and can lead to greed, lack of self-control, and even a life of crime. We've talked about this before." His frown deepened.

"I know." Tam clipped off the word before he automatically added "father" to it. "You don't need to treat me like a child."

Slade clenched his teeth, and Tam knew he was going to say, "Then stop acting like one." But he didn't. Did that mean he was finally seeing Tam as an adult? Or near enough to one?

"I will not loan you money to pay off a gambling debt. And I feel obligated to mention this to Lord Henry, if you have not already." Slade's gaze bore into Tam's. It felt as if he were looking for more evidence of wrongdoing.

"Fine. I apologize for asking you." Tam tried to sound as if he didn't care, but the trembling of his voice betrayed him. "And there is no need to tell Lord Henry anything. I will tell him myself." He turned and started to walk away, but Slade gripped his arm.

"Tam. You know I love you, but this is a serious situation, especially coming after the other two incidents while you served Sir Artemis. Your profession as a knight is in jeopardy."

He shook off his stepfather's hand and whirled to face him. "Maybe I'm not destined to be a knight, but I will take that up with Lord Henry. I only asked you because I thought you would want to help me."

"I do want to help you, but I will not encourage your penchant for gambling. If Lord Henry releases you from squiring, I will help you find a job more suited to your abilities." The hurt in Slade's eyes pricked Tam's conscience, but he pushed away that uncomfortable feeling.

"I am sorry to have bothered you. I must return to my squiring duties now." Tam straightened, blinked back angry tears, and stormed to a table against the far wall. Its occupants had moved closer to the dancing, leaving behind the remains of their meal.

The act of stacking leftovers on the table's tray helped calm him a little. He had to regain a clear head, for now he needed another way to pay his debt. His gaze traveled back to the head table. Fiona was no longer sitting there. He found her dancing with Sir Artemis, of all people! And then he chuckled. Of course; Artemis was looking for a rich bride, the same as other knights and minor lords. Though Tam did not know Fiona well, he suspected that she would never be satisfied with his weak-minded former knight.

A rich bride. His thoughts about Fiona from a few days ago caught up with him, along with what he'd overheard between Roland and Edward on the journey here. Even though Roland planned to ask for Fiona's hand, it was by no means certain she would accept him. As the king's sister, she could have her pick of any eligible man in the realm. Indeed the word "unattainable" came into his head, but he shook it away. Nothing was unattainable; there was always a way.

Lady Fiona MacLachlan would be quite a prize, indeed. Enough to pay off his debt and plenty to spare. He didn't need to be a knight. If he could marry her, he could use her dowry to buy his own land, or even a shop, if he decided he wanted to be a merchant of some kind.

He picked up the laden tray and carried it back to the kitchen. The other squires were still eating in the back, laughing as if they didn't have a care in the world. Tam snorted. Let them have their fun. He had more important considerations.

There was a full wineskin near the entrance, so Tam picked it up, intending to work his way closer to the head table. Fiona would have to sit down sometime, and he intended to speak to her before the evening ended.

Fate intervened. After refilling a lord's goblet, Tam looked up, and Fiona appeared in the crowd, staring directly at him. He gave her one of the smiles that always drew young women to him and felt great satisfaction at her obvious response. When she moved in his direction, he made his way to the end of the long table.

* * *

Since Sir Alfred asked Fiona to dance the next one also, she consented only because it was one of her favorites, and Alfred happened to be an excellent dancer. Tammeron's presence nearby distracted her from enjoying the dance, and when it ended, Fiona thanked Alfred and begged to take her leave of him. Instead of returning to her seat, she looked again for Tammeron. He was refilling goblets for two minor lords, so she waited for him to finish. She had to step behind a tall man to hide from Auntie Gwen. After she passed, Fiona peered around the man, and Tammeron was free, scanning the room in search of something, or someone. She stepped into view, and their eyes met.

Truly, she had never seen a young man so beautiful. She felt something like a bolt of lightning leap between them in the crowded room. Was that the "love at first sight" the bards sometimes sang about? It wasn't her first sight of him, after all. They'd known one another as children. But Tammeron d'Jean was no longer a child. Her feet moved in his direction, and Fiona felt as if she were floating.

"Hello, Tam." Up close he was even more handsome. It almost took her breath away.

"Lady Fiona." His smile sent shivers down her spine. And his lips—so full and sensuous. What would it be like to kiss him?

The opening chords for the next dance sounded, and Fiona impulsively grabbed Tam's hand.

"Come, let us find a quiet place, away from all this noise." She didn't even wait for his reaction, just pulled him along through the press of bodies and out into the hallway.

A few people strolled along, and two guards stood to either side of the doors. Fiona remembered a secluded alcove nearby, away from prying eyes, and led Tam there. It wasn't the bench in the gardens, but it would have to do.

Once they were out of sight of those in the hallway, Fiona let go of his hand and looked up into his beautiful eyes. She could drown in those eyes. And his thick hair curled around his collar, tempting her to comb her fingers through it, as she could never do with Roland's shorter hair. Tam shifted the wineskin to his left arm.

"Lady Fiona, I am glad to see you are still spontaneous and quick-minded." His smile was so bright, it made his eyes sparkle in the dim light.

"I think you will find me ever as I was." She held back a smirk. "Just a little older, and hopefully a little wiser." Coyly she clasped her hands and batted her eyelashes, making him laugh.

Then his expression grew more intense. "I think you have become the most beautiful lady in the entire kingdom, and I am honored to be singled out by you, for I am but a humble squire." He gently took her hand, bent down, and lightly kissed it, staring into her eyes all the while.

Fiona shivered again, enough for him to notice.

"Are you cold, Fiona?" Tam moved closer, still holding her hand.

"Not at all." Her voice was breathy, and she could not stop staring at his full lips. "The sight of you has made me warm all over."

With a thud, Tam dropped the wineskin and took Fiona in his arms. She stretched up to meet him until their lips touched, and she let him cover her mouth with his own. Her fingers rested on his tunic, feeling the hard muscles of his chest. When he gathered her closer, she moaned with pleasure.

"Fiona! What are ye doing?" Papa's voice penetrated the haze of Fiona's thoughts.

Papa?!

She pulled away from Tam, out of breath, and turned toward her father.

"What are you doing here? Did you follow us?" Fiona knew she was not speaking respectfully, but she was angry at Papa for treating her like a child, and most of all, for interrupting what she and Tam were doing.

"I saw you leave the hall and wanted tae find out what ye were up to." Papa glowered at Tam. "It appears I was right tae be suspicious."

Tam opened his mouth to say something, but Fiona spoke first. "Suspicious? What did you suspect I was up to, *Father*?" She spoke the last word with the full force of her anger.

Papa continued to frown, but Fiona saw the hurt in his eyes. Under other circumstances, she would have begged him to forgive her, but this time she *wanted* to wound him. He was being completely unfair to accuse her of anything wrong!

"When a squire who is supposed tae be on duty leaves that duty tae seduce me daughter, I can only think the worst." Kieran glared at Tam.

"Lord Kieran—" he began, but Papa cut him off.

"I'm glad ye know who I am, Tammeron d'Jean." He gestured to the wineskin. "Take that back tae the hall and then confine yourself tae Lord Henry's guest rooms. He and I shall speak with you later."

Tam bowed before looking squarely at Kieran. "My lord, I apologize if I have offended either you or Lady Fiona. Truly, this is all my fault, and Lady Fiona deserves neither censure nor punishment." He bowed again, snatched up the wineskin, and gave Fiona a look of regret.

In that moment, Fiona's heart swelled with admiration. Tam was defending her, even though she had been the one to instigate this encounter. How chivalrous of him! She stared at him until he strode away from her sight, his boots loud on the stone. Kieran crossed his arms, not relenting one bit.

"What do ye have tae say for yourself, Fiona MacLachlan?" His gaze, though still tinged with sadness, did not waver.

"All I have to say to you is that I am a grown woman, and who I choose to spend my time with is no longer any concern of yours." She crossed her arms, matching his determination.

"As long as you live in my household, under my authority, then your actions *are* my concern. I am responsible for you, whether you like it or not, and until you marry and have your own household, you will respect my guidance, as one who loves you and wants tae protect you."

"You don't have to protect me from Tam." Fiona threw out her arms in frustration. "We've known him and his family all my life. He's no criminal, Papa, so stop treating him as if he were."

"Whether he be a criminal or no is yet tae be determined. He was already on restriction, but I'm sure he didna tell ye that, did he?"

"Restriction?" For the first time, Fiona felt unsure. Had she gotten Tam in trouble?

"Aye, and he already had committed two offenses against the code of chivalry, so a third will be the end o' his continuing as a squire and becoming a knight someday."

Fiona's heart sank. Was she going to be the cause of Tam losing his status as a future knight of the realm?

"How could a simple kiss be against the code of chivalry? That's not fair, either to Tam or to me. We did nothing wrong. I thought squires were allowed free time once the banquet ended?"

"Squires do have free time, but Tammeron was not allowed tae leave the hall. Did he not tell ye that?" Papa had not softened, not even a little.

"No, he did not." Fiona frowned, unwilling to bend, and certainly not willing to apologize.

"If ye wanted tae spend time with a squire, why did ye not seek out Roland Campignon? Haven't ye been complaining about not having a chance tae speak with him?"

Fiona blinked, caught off guard. Roland had flown out of her head at the sight of Tam. She felt only a small twinge of guilt when she decided to ignore Papa's question. "Are you finished with your inquisition?"

"Aye, finished for now." Still that sadness in his eyes but hardness in his face and posture, more than she could ever remember seeing before. "Just one more thing, Fiona."

She blinked, having expected him to react to her harsh word. "What is it?"

"Have ye considered the shame ye bring tae your brother Val by abandoning him 'ere the night is o'er? He chose you tae be his companion on his special evening, after all."

Now Fiona felt like sinking into the stone. It didn't bother her that Roland had gone completely out of her thoughts, but to forget Val was unforgiveable. What had she done? She couldn't bear it if Val was disappointed in her too!

Papa's voice did not soften. "Return tae the feast now and comport yourself as the sister o' the king. Be the lady you were brought up tae be."

"Yes, Papa." She hated that her voice sounded so meek, but she was so choked up she could barely hold back tears. She would *not* cry in front of Papa, though.

Without a backward glance, she lifted her skirts and hurried away, heading straight for the doors to the hall. She paused and calmed herself. All she could think about was the unfairness of Papa's reaction, but she had to give Val her undivided attention for a little longer.

Smoothing her skirts, she lifted her chin and walked as calmly as she could around the edge of the room to the head table. Val was dancing with Mother, and Dolan and Rhianna had made their way to the other side of the room to speak to someone, so Fiona would have a little time to herself.

She finished the dregs in her goblet and set it down. A smile came to her lips when she closed her eyes and relived Tam's exquisite kiss, swaying to the music.

Then the most unexpected voice shattered her reverie.

"Hello, Fiona." Roland stepped up to the table, holding an ewer with both hands. "May I refill your goblet?"

She stared into his earnest face with dismay. "No, thank you."

Then she rose and hurried around the table to join those surrounding the dancers.

* * *

When Kieran returned to the hall, he went straight to Lord Henry, who sat in conversation with Lord Dracen. Though reluctant to interrupt them, he caught Henry's attention, and the man was astute enough to understand Kieran needed to speak with him alone.

"Excuse me, Lord Dracen. We can continue this discussion later." Henry inclined his head and stepped over the bench. He stood almost a head taller than Kieran, a broad-shouldered, powerful man.

"Pardon me, Lord Dracen, for taking Lord Henry away." Kieran tried to force a smile at Moor Point's lord, but it would not reach his lips.

"Not to worry, Lord Kieran." Dracen's voice was more cheerful than usual. "Go and solve the problem, whatever it is. There is no one more capable than the two of you."

Henry stepped into the hallway with Kieran, who walked several paces away from the guards at the doors before turning to his old friend.

"I sent your squire tae your guest room, and I must tell ye why." Kieran rubbed his temples.

Henry let out a sigh. "What has Tammeron done this time?"

"I found him in the hallway with a discarded wineskin, locking lips with my daughter." Kieran gestured in the direction of the nearby alcove.

Henry briefly shut his eyes. "I'm sorry, Kieran. The last I saw him, he was serving wine."

"I noticed Fiona leaving the hall with a young man in tow, but I didn't know 'twas young d'Jean until I came upon them. So he hadn't been gone but a few minutes." Kieran shook his head.

"Thank you for letting me know, and for sending him to my room." The unflappable Henry Cornwall seemed at a loss. "I think I shall retire now, so I can speak to Tammeron and decide what happens next." He shook his head. "Please do not speak of this to anyone until I can consult with Lord Jambray, especially since the young man's parents are present this week."

"Of course." Kieran started to reach out to grip Henry's arm in sympathy, but something stayed his hand. "You have my word."

Henry met his gaze. "Your word means more than most men's." He gave Kieran a slight smile and then slowly walked away.

Kieran didn't return to the hall right away. Lord Dracen's earlier comment mocked him in a way the man would never have meant; perhaps Kieran was capable in other matters, but not where it concerned his daughter. *What* was he going to tell Mercy?

Chapter 9

If a wise man contendeth with a foolish man,
whether he rage or laugh, there is no rest.

Kieran slowly entered the great hall, his black mood contrasting sharply with the gaiety all around. He scanned the room, searching among the dancers as well as those sitting or standing along the perimeter. There was Mercy, sitting with an older lady of Southmoor. Kieran couldn't remember her name, but he remembered she could talk the ears off the most patient person. From the expression on Mercy's face, Kieran felt sure she would not mind being rescued, even to hear the news Kieran had to tell her.

He carefully made his way around the enthusiastic dancers until he stood beside Mercy. The lady looked up with a puzzled frown, until she recognized Kieran.

"My lord, pardon me. I was passing the time with your lady wife." She rose and stiffly curtsied before moving away.

Mercy let out a sigh. "Thank you, love. I thought she would never take a breath."

"You're welcome." He held out his hand. "Will you come with me? I have something tae tell you, and 'tis far too noisy here."

She looked curious and gave him a hesitant smile before allowing him to help her to her feet. He let go of her hand, though, anxious to move quickly through the press of the crowd. He nodded to those who

93

greeted him, but he did not pause for conversation. Surely the scowl on his face would repel even the most garrulous person at the banquet.

At last they reached the door, and Kieran kept walking. He assumed Mercy was following, but he didn't dare slow down, lest his troubled emotions spill over. His hands were clenched so tightly, he did not notice until they began to cramp, and he forced them open.

Without being aware of his surroundings, he made his way to the Keep's newest tower, in which their suite took up the entire top floor. Instead of going to their sitting room, Kieran kept climbing the spiral staircase to the roof. He did not stop until he reached the bench in Mercy's gardens. Finally, he turned. To his relief, Mercy had followed him and came to stand within arm's length. He gestured to the bench.

"Let's sit here." He waited until she seated herself before planting himself on the other end. How did he begin to tell her what happened?

He stared up at the moon between the crenels on the wall. There was no easy way to say this.

"Earlier, I came upon Fiona and Tammeron d'Jean kissing passionately in an alcove." His jaw tightened.

"Tammeron?" Mercy's eyes widened in surprise. "Did she explain herself?"

"What was there tae explain?" Kieran blurted out. "A kiss like that should only happen between married couples." He clenched his fists again. "Fiona shows not the slightest bit o' shame at her behavior."

"Did you send her to her room?" Mercy wrung her hands.

"I couldn't do that tae Val, since she was his escort, but I sent Tammeron tae *his* room." He frowned at the memory.

"Shall I speak to her?" She leaned over and placed her hand on his arm.

"If you think 'twill do any good." He stood and walked a few paces away from the bench, unable to sit still any longer. "I'm inclined tae lock her in her room until she proves she has grown out of the need tae throw herself at young men."

"Well, that's a bit harsh, don't you think?" Mercy kept her voice mild, but still the words rankled.

"No, I dinna think so at all." He turned to face her. "We are fast running out o' time tae curb her rebellious ways." With effort, he lowered his voice. "It may already be too late."

Mercy slowly rose. "I don't believe it's too late. She just needs to be reminded to comport herself as a lady."

"Mercy! 'Tis much worse than the need for a simple reminder. She abandoned Val and found a private place tae allow a young man not her husband tae take liberties with her body."

"You said they were kissing." Mercy clasped her hands with a frown.

"Passionately. Pressed as close together as they could be." He threw up his hands. "I know I've taught her tae save herself for marriage."

"So have I." Mercy's voice came out strained.

"Then you must see she has become completely intractable."

"Not completely. She will listen to me." Though her words were confident, the look on Mercy's face said otherwise.

"I wish I could say I hope she will listen tae what ye have tae tell her, but after tonight I fear I have lost that hope." He could taste and hear the bitterness in his words.

"We can't give up on our daughter, Kieran." Mercy sounded desperate.

"No, we should not," he agreed. "But I have no idea how tae help her keep herself pure when daily she is surrounded by temptations for her obvious weakness."

"Weakness?"

Kieran huffed in frustration. "Are ye so blind, Mercy? Do ye not see how Fiona flirts with every young man she sees?"

Mercy's hurt was evident, and he felt a twinge of guilt, but he *had* to make her see this painful truth about Fiona, a truth he had not wanted to admit until the irrefutable evidence had been thrown in his face earlier. When she didn't answer, he tried to continue in a more reasonable tone.

"I know you were not like that when you were Fiona's age, so mayhap ye do not recognize what I have come tae see in her. And I accept my share o' the blame in being too lenient with the lass. But Mercy!" He held out his hands in entreaty. "We have got tae do something swiftly and firmly now."

Mercy's voice was stiff and formal. "It is too late to determine punishment tonight; the banquet is almost over. Fiona will retire to her room the moment Dolan dismisses everyone, and I will speak to her as soon as she wakes on the morrow. Is that acceptable?" She clenched her teeth, and he gave her a curt nod.

"Aye, that it is." He should have embraced her then. It was what he would have done in the past. But he didn't. "We should return now."

Without waiting for her reply, he headed back down the tower stairs.

* * *

After a mostly sleepless night, with the barrier of hurt and anger between her and Kieran, Mercy said yet another quick prayer for wisdom before knocking on Fiona's bedroom door. When it opened, Fiona peered out, her eyes red-rimmed.

"Good morning, love. I'd like to talk to you." Mercy clasped her hands, more nervous than she wanted to admit.

Without a word, Fiona opened the door wider and moved back. Mercy stepped inside and closed it behind her. She gestured to the window seat. "Come, sit with me."

Fiona shuffled alongside her and plopped down on the seat, folding her arms defensively. Mercy sat on the other end, leaving space between them.

"Your father told me what happened last night, but I'd like to hear the account from you."

Fiona looked up, and her misery turned to defiance. "We weren't doing anything wrong! Tam kissed me, and Papa came upon us. That's all there was to it."

Mercy inhaled deeply. She chose her words carefully.

"The kiss is not what concerns us, dearest. It's where this kiss might lead." She bit her lip before continuing.

"There are kisses of affection between friends or family members, and there are kisses which are a prelude to the intimacy which should only be enjoyed within marriage." Mercy's heart squeezed painfully, remembering Kieran's description of what he'd come upon. She had also recalled Tam's reputation for dalliances with servant girls. How could she help Fiona see that Tam was someone she should stay well away from?

"Yes, I know the difference, Mother." Fiona frowned.

"The kiss your father saw was no mere token of affection, but the intimate kind which has led to the ruin of many a reputation." Was she being too vague? If she explained her concerns about Tam, would Fiona refuse to see that he could lead her down the wrong path?

"All we did was kiss. We did nothing wrong. How does that ruin anyone's reputation?" Fiona threw up her hands.

"You're right; one kiss does not a reputation ruin." Mercy tried to smile, but she was too concerned about her daughter. "What I'm trying to tell you is that there are young men who do not hold young women in esteem, but see them only as playthings. Virginity is a treasure which can only be given once, and that treasure should be saved for one's husband."

"I know all this, Mother; you've told me a thousand times. What did you think Tam and I would do? Steal away and make love, without thinking about the consequences?" She jumped up, and tears sprang to her eyes. "Do you and Papa have so little confidence in me?"

Mercy held out her hand. "We have every confidence in you, dearest. But we were both young once and know the great temptation that comes with strong feelings of desire."

"Do you still think I'm too young to be married?"

"Well, I—" Mercy paused, not wanting to voice aloud her true opinion of Fiona's maturity.

"Weren't you fourteen when you married Val's father?" Fiona's eyes narrowed.

"Yes, but—"

"Didn't you once tell me you and your first husband had a strong connection from almost the instant you met?" She balled her fists on her hips.

"A connection of minds, yes, but our love took time to develop." Mercy frowned when she realized it hadn't taken long at all for their love to blossom, less than a month. She felt desperate to reach Fiona before it was too late.

"I felt a connection with Tam last night in the hall, and I'm sure he felt it too." Fiona closed her eyes, and a silly smile came to her face. "There *is* something powerful between us." Her eyes flew open, and she set her jaw with new determination. "If that's not love, I don't know what else it could be."

Mercy's panic rose. Surely Fiona didn't believe herself in *love* with Tammeron d'Jean?

"Love is so much more than physical attraction, especially when one is considering marriage. Your father and I want you to stay away from Tammeron. His reputation—"

Fiona's eyes widened with her own kind of desperation. "You can't keep us apart! The true connection of our souls cannot be denied!"

"Lust is not love!" As soon as the words left her mouth, Mercy wished she could take them back.

"Mother! How dare you cheapen what we feel for one another? You have grown so old, you have forgotten what it is to feel this way about a man! No matter what you say, you cannot take away what is in my heart!" Fiona stormed to her bed and threw herself upon it, weeping.

Mercy rose, angry at herself as well as Fiona. "No, I cannot take away what is in your heart, but I can protect you from yourself. You are confined to your room until the tournament has ended and all the guests have gone home." When Fiona didn't answer but continued sobbing, Mercy strode out of the room, shutting the door behind her.

Now she had to explain to Kieran what she had done.

* * *

The second morning of her imprisonment, Fiona waited until she was sure her parents were long gone to the castle yard. She put her ear to the door one more time, listening, but she could hear no voices. After opening her door a crack and peering out, she slipped out and raced up the spiral staircase from her family's suite to the tower, her heart pounding in time with her bare feet on the stone steps. She nearly stumbled on the last one as she burst into the sunlight. Her mother's garden did not distract her today; she was too focused on getting to the crenelated wall in time.

In the yard below, horsemen paraded before her brother, the king, all mounted knights. Standing at attention four abreast were the squires and men-at-arms. Would Tam be among them? Surely Lord Henry wouldn't confine him to *his* room, just because Papa had sent him there? Even if he was down on the field, Fiona knew it might be difficult to spot him from this angle, and from this height.

Though she scanned each row of squires holding a spear bearing their knight's pennon, she did not see the one tall squire she desired most to see. On the front row, however, Roland Campignon stood ramrod straight, his squire's surcoat blazoned with Sir Thomas Cornwall of Southmoor's griffin. To Fiona's surprise, Roland appeared to be taller than many of the other squires. He was not nearly as tall as

Tam, though. And though Roland could be considered handsome, he could not compare to Tam in any way.

She sighed, leaning her chin upon her folded hands. Tam was not down on the field in the colorful parade of squires and their knights, so he must be locked in his room, punished as she was. It didn't appear likely she'd even have a chance to speak with him before he had to return to Southmoor. Both Mother and Papa were adamant she would have to stay confined to her room until after all the guests left the Keep. How utterly unfair!

Tammeron. If he was standing with the other squires, he would tower over them all, including Roland. She closed her eyes, savoring as she often had over the last two days Tam's passionate kiss. What an unexpected delight! But had it been worth this solitary confinement?

Yes, she decided, *it had*. She would kiss him again, if she ever had the opportunity. Even Roland could not possibly kiss her with more fervor than Tam had! No one could!

With a start, her eyes flew open. How long had she been day-dreaming? The opening ceremony of the tournament was nearing the end, the knights parading before Dolan, where he and Rhianna sat under a purple canopy. Shading her eyes, Fiona scanned the rows of spectators. She found Val sitting with their parents, and Joy and Bennet below them, on the front row.

Sighing again, Fiona leaned against the crenel. Why did *everything* have to be so unfair?

"Fiona? Are you up here?" It was Tristam. What was he doing *here*? Why wasn't he down in the stands with the rest of their family?

For a moment, Fiona thought of trying to hide from him, but she'd chosen this portion of the tower wall because it had the best view of the castle yard. She was too far from the garden's fruit trees. If she tried to run in that direction, he'd be sure to see her. Maybe if she ignored him, he would overlook her standing here.

"There you are." He trudged between the rows of late summer vegetables, headed toward her with a purpose. "Mother and Father both said you had to stay in your room." With his curly black hair falling into his eyes and his linen shirt collar askew, it was difficult to take her distracted brother seriously.

"Oh, Tristam, why must you be such a tattler? Are you hoping to attain sainthood someday?" If Fiona hadn't been so aggravated with him, she would have laughed. "I should call you Saint Tristam."

Tristam balled his fists on his hips. "I'm not a saint, but I overheard Mother tell Father she plans to check on you during the break in the ceremony. You had better be in your room by then."

Fiona groaned. Why did he have to be so serious about everything? Didn't he understand she had to catch a glimpse of some part of the tournament or she would simply die of boredom?

"Don't let your indignation twist your bowels in knots." She pushed away from the wall without a backward glance. "I'm going to my room now, *frater*. You won't have to bother Mother about anything because I didn't do anything wrong."

"This time," Tristam muttered, and Fiona glared at him.

She managed to hold back a biting comment about his unsocial behavior in avoiding the ceremony, but he sorely tempted her to wound him!

Irritated that he was following her, Fiona quickened her steps and reached her room before Tristam had exited the stairwell. Then she firmly shut her door, shutting out the sight and sound of him.

With a huff, Fiona went to her window seat and peered out. It was no use; none of the castle yard was visible from here. She could hear but not see that the tournament events were beginning. Tomorrow would be the joust, and she would not get to see any of it!

Wiping away angry tears, she snatched up the embroidery hoop on the seat and stitched with more than her usual ferocity.

* * *

Tam paced in the tiny room he and Edward were sharing for the week. He felt like a wolf or feral cat that had been captured and locked in an airless box.

If only Lord Henry had released him from being a squire, then Tam might have choices about what to do next. Instead, Henry had explained to Tam that, although he had been exceedingly unwise in stealing away with Lady Fiona, his action was not strictly against the code of chivalry, and so he did not feel obligated to dismiss him. To Tam's utter shock, Henry hadn't even told Lord Jambray about the incident! If Tam had known that, he would not have been so quick to take the blame after Lord Kieran had caught them.

Under ordinary circumstances, Tam might have felt relieved that he'd been given another chance. But his debt to Jevan and his friends still hung over his head like an executioner's ax, and so all he could feel was trapped.

The door opened, and Tam stopped pacing. Edward burst into the room, startling him.

"What are you doing here? Does Lord Henry know where you are?"

Edward snorted. "That's rich, coming from a squire under house arrest. Oh, I mean under disciplinary restriction." The boy smirked, and Tam clenched his fists.

"You don't want to join me, do you?" Tam said mockingly.

Now Edward looked annoyed. "Of course not. I'm just looking for something I forgot to give Lord Henry."

Though Tam's curiosity was aroused, he had something more important to ask Edward, since the annoying page always managed to find out what was going on. Either he had arcane powers, or more likely, he was good at sneaking around and overhearing what was not meant for his ears.

"Is Lady Fiona still restricted to her room?"

Edward stopped searching his pile of discarded clothing and stood. "Yes, she is." The smirk returned. "Wanting another kiss from her, are you?"

"If I did, I wouldn't tell you." Tam crossed his arms, but he didn't let the jab dissuade his own questions. He still didn't know how Edward had found out about the kiss. "Fiona's room is in the newest tower, isn't it?"

Edward nodded and resumed his search. "Yes, but telling you which room it is won't do you any good."

"True." Tam tried to sound bored. "But I had hoped you might pass along a message from me to your aunt."

With a sigh of relief, Edward held up what looked like an embroidered handkerchief and stuffed it in his tunic.

"Why would I take her a message from you? That would get you both in even more trouble." Edward wiped a stray lock from his forehead. His eyes narrowed. "And I would probably get in trouble, too."

Tam shook his head. "You would never get in trouble, because you would never let yourself get caught." He returned Edward's smirk when he saw the boy's eyes light up. The young prince did enjoy a challenge.

"Of course I never let myself get caught." He frowned at Tam. "What kind of message? Written or verbal?"

"Verbal, of course. A written note is too easily discovered." He beckoned to Edward, and the boy came closer. "If you see her, tell her I wish to speak with her."

Edward laughed. "You'd never get out of this room, and even if you did, you'd never get past the guard to get into her tower." He stared at Tam as if he was out of his mind for even considering it. "True, it's not as heavily guarded as the royal tower, but there's still a guard at the entrance to the stairs." Then he frowned. "Hmm, I just realized that tower is closer to us than I thought. But it's still impossible for you to get to her room."

"No secret passageways, I'm sure." Tam stared at Edward sidelong, hoping he would take the bait.

"As a matter of fact, yes, there is one!" The boy returned Tam's sideways stare. "But why would I tell you where it is?"

"If you're looking for a bribe from me, you know I have nothing of value." Tam turned away, disgusted. "Go on, and don't waste my time."

Edward took a step in Tam's direction. "There is nothing of value you *own* that I want. But you could teach me how to win at dice."

Tam held back a bitter laugh. "Dice is a game of chance." Then he thought angrily about what had to have happened with Jevan and his friends. "The only way to guarantee a win is to cheat."

"Then show me how to cheat." Edward's gaze narrowed. "If you do, I'll tell you how to get to Fiona's room."

What other way was there to cheat besides weighted dice? That was obviously how Jevan's friends had cheated him. He himself didn't know how to do it, but he could still promise to teach Edward.

"All right, I'll show you how." Tam gritted his teeth.

"When?" Edward's stare bore into Tam, as if he were sizing him up.

"If you find a pair of dice, I'll show you as soon as we get back to Southmoor." Tam returned the stare and finally, Edward nodded.

"I can find the dice." He glanced over his shoulder before continuing, and Tam leaned closer to better hear him. "I discovered the secret passageway last year when I was in Tristam's room. It opens near his bed but comes out under the stairs down the hallway." Edward pointed to the right. "No, wait, it's in the new tower, so it would be the stairs to the left of here."

"Tristam's room, eh? Not Fiona's?" Tam sounded disappointed.

"Of course not Fiona's room. Granddad—Lord Kieran to you— would never allow that." Edward snorted in disgust. "In an emergency, Fiona can access the tunnel, because her room adjoins Tristam's." Now he headed toward the door. "So, as you can see, it would do you no good for me to deliver your message to Fiona."

Tam let his shoulders droop. "I can see that. Well, you can't blame me for trying."

"No, I don't blame you at all. Lots of men want to kiss Aunt Fiona." With an impish grin, Edward left the room.

Tam sat on his cot, staring at the door and waiting until the boy's footsteps receded.

"Thank you, Edward. Now I only need decide if I have the nerve to go to her tonight."

Chapter 10

The wicked worketh a deceitful work.

Fiona went to sleep that night with difficulty, for her thoughts would not be still. She awakened several times and then fell back into a fitful doze. The last time she started to waken, she heard a small sound like footsteps. And when she opened her eyes—

A figure loomed beside her tall bed where he'd pushed back the curtains. Fiona was so startled, she did not scream right away. But when the figure climbed upon the bed, she sucked in a deep breath, and a large hand clamped over her mouth.

"Fiona, it's me." The man's voice was breathy. "Tam."

Her eyes widened, but it was too dark to make out his features. She nodded, and he dropped his hand. "Tam?" She kept her voice low. "What are you doing here? How did you find me?"

"I used the passage into your brother's room. I'm sorry for startling you." Tam's voice was so contrite, Fiona wished she could see his face.

Of course! She had a candle.

She pushed open the bedcurtain on the other side and slid down in her nightdress, fumbling for the bedside candle. It took her a few moments to light it, her hands were trembling so much. Once the flame burned steadily, she beckoned to Tam to join her in the window seat, making sure the shutters to the outside were completely closed.

He sat down beside her, and she held up the candle between them. The harsh shadows distorted his handsome face, so she focused on his glittering eyes.

"First, I want to apologize for getting you in trouble with your father." He sounded so humble, she wanted to hug him.

"It wasn't all your fault, you know. I'm the one who dragged you out of the hall and into that alcove in the first place."

He smiled, making his eyes shine even more. "I offered no resistance."

She smiled back. "And I'm glad you did not." Her smile faded. "But if we are discovered here, we will both be in far more trouble."

"I know, and I will make this as brief as I can." He swallowed noisily. "First, I have heard you are already promised to another. Is that true?"

An image of Roland filled Fiona's thoughts, but she pushed it aside, gently but firmly. "No. I am not promised to another." Her gaze did not waver. "Why?"

Tam licked his lips, and she stared at them briefly.

"I wondered if you felt, as I did during our brief encounter, that there is some connection between us."

"Yes," she breathed, glad for the candle between them, or else she might throw herself into his arms, nightdress and all.

"I have had a lot of time to think the past three days—"

"As have I."

"And, my lady." His gaze traveled over her face, lingering on her mouth. "Fiona." He smiled and stared into her eyes. "I know I am unworthy to even ask, yet I can't but think we are destined to be together."

Fiona's breath quickened, making the candle flame twitch. "What do you want to ask me, Tam?"

His eyes became a bit wild, but that only made him more attractive to her. Slowly he took the candle from her and stood to set it down on a nearby table. Fiona rose, her gaze never leaving his face. Smiling, he pulled her to him and kissed her soundly, making her swoon.

She could lose herself in his kisses. He stirred such longing within her, she wanted to meld herself to him, body and soul. But a nagging voice in her head intruded with a warning, and reluctantly she pulled her lips away from his. It gave her physical pain to step back. Was that proof that she loved him? She had never felt this way about anyone before.

"I adore you, Fiona." Tam's voice was husky, seductive. "I want you with me always." His presence drew her to him as if a golden thread now bound their hearts together. But the ever-present sense of duty to which she had been trained for sixteen years dispelled some of the heady emotions.

"I feel the same." Her voice sounded hoarse, so she swallowed. "How long until you are knighted?"

"Three more years. I am seventeen, a year older than you, I believe."

Fiona's heart sank. It would take him even longer to be knighted than Roland! Three years was a long time to wait. Practically an eternity!

Tam inhaled and briefly shut his eyes. "I have decided I am not suited for knighthood, my lady. I am better suited to be a merchant of some kind. I hope that does not disappoint you."

"Not at all." Fiona thought about Val coming to the same conclusion. "Not every nobleman needs to follow the path of knighthood." She gazed into his eyes, which now appeared troubled. "Where would you want to set up a shop?"

"South. In Moor Point." His gaze softened. "We can be married and make our own life together."

"Married?" A bolt of lightning jolted through her. "So you do want to marry me?"

"Of course, my dear Fiona." Tam pulled her even closer this time, taking her breath away. "I know you feel as trapped as I do. Come with me, and we can be free to be ourselves, to live as we choose, not the life others have chosen for us."

He kissed her temple and then her ear, making it impossible to think clearly. She had to pull back before she completely lost herself in his kisses.

"I have friends in Moor Point—" He gently pulled her closer. "There is an opportunity waiting for me, if I take advantage of it quickly, and then we can be married there."

"Married there?" When Tam started to kiss her again, she stepped away, forcing him to look at her and, hopefully, listen. "My family would be hurt if I was not married here, where they could all attend."

Tam let go of her and visibly wilted. "I understand. It was an impossible dream to hope I could convince you to come with me." He turned to leave, and she grabbed his sleeve.

"Tam! Why do you say that?" Fiona twisted her fingers in the fabric of his linen shirt, desperate to keep him with her. "Can you not go there ahead of me and prepare a place for us? Then I can tell my family we are to be married in Moor Point, so they can arrange to join us." That was a reasonable compromise, wasn't it?

He gave her a sad smile. "I feel certain that if I leave without you, your family will never allow you to marry me, a lowly merchant."

Fiona frowned. He was right; her parents might accept Tam's suit as a knight, but never would they agree to him otherwise. This was her only chance to marry him, or he was lost to her forever.

He stood there, looking so hopeful and yet prepared to have all his hopes dashed. A surge of love and pity compelled her to take a step closer. She could find happiness as a merchant's wife, couldn't she?

"I had better go before someone finds me here and your reputation is unjustly tarnished." Tam swallowed as if holding back tears, and she couldn't stand to hurt him any longer. She seized his hand.

"Do you love me, Tam?" She kept her voice low, but she compelled him to answer her.

"Yes, I do." He went down on his knees and pressed his free hand into a fist over his breast. "You are the lady of my heart."

His sincere declaration brought tears to her eyes. Before she could think of what to say next, he spoke again.

"I need you to know, that we will struggle in the beginning, while I am establishing my trade." The sorrowful look returned. "I won't be able to support you in the manner to which you have been accustomed."

She shook her head and smiled. "That does not matter to me, as long as you love me for myself and not for who my family happens to be."

Tam reached out and took her hand, pressing it to his warm lips. "I would love you, Fiona, if you were a shepherdess. It is your kind heart and your exuberance for life that I love, not your position."

She smiled. "I believe you." Taking a deep breath, she made her decision. "I accept your offer, Tammeron d'Jean. I will go with you to Moor Point." He started to rise, but she held up her free hand. "And to pledge my heart to you, I will bring a dowry to help us as you begin your new profession and we begin our life together."

He cocked his head, as though puzzled. "A dowry? I don't understand."

As quietly as she could, Fiona went to her press and took out a hand-carved wooden box. Tam rose and helped her carry it closer to the candle, where she opened it.

Inside lay her accumulation of jewels, necklaces, bracelets, hair clasps, and a golden circlet, all bedecked with precious stones. It was the extent of her personal wealth, though she knew Papa had planned to offer more as a dowry, had someone like Roland asked for her hand.

She tightened her jaw. Time to forget about Roland Campignon. Tam would be her husband, and she would be his partner in business as well as in marriage. "This belongs to both of us now."

Tam embraced her then without kissing her again, for which she was grateful. When he kissed her, it was impossible to think about anything else.

"Oh, Fiona, you have made me the happiest man in the kingdom!" When Tam pulled back, his eyes shimmered with tears, and she reached up to gently wipe them away.

"When will we go? Tonight?" Her breath caught with the excitement of this new adventure.

"Tomorrow. I must get everything in place for our departure." He cupped her cheek.

"I'll be ready. What time will you come for me?" She trembled at his touch.

"Same time. Three of the clock. Everyone should be asleep by then, since it will be after the final banquet of the tournament." His hand shifted to the back of her neck. "Bring what you need," he whispered near her ear, making her shiver. "But pack as little as you can so we can travel light. We'll have to ride double."

"Yes," she breathed, and her lips parted to receive one more kiss from him. How could she bear to be separated from him for an entire day?

This time, Tam let go first, and a little moan escaped her.

"Until tomorrow, my love." His joyous smile melted her heart.

She felt bereft watching him head toward the door. He opened it carefully, blew her a kiss, and vanished from her sight.

*

108

The rest of the night and all the following day, Fiona alternated between nervous excitement and fear that she and Tam would be discovered and prevented from leaving. She packed her jewels in the carry sack with her clothing, picking out her two most sensible dresses from the heavy trunk, along with her nightdress and a few other small items. For traveling, she would wear her sturdiest riding skirt and matching tunic. Even though the weather wouldn't turn cold for several weeks, especially in the south, Fiona decided to bring the lightest of her cloaks, which she could also use as a blanket.

Whenever she went out riding for an afternoon, she always brought water and a little food. Was Tam going to take care of that? Or should she bring some food, at least? From all three of the meals Oleta brought her, Fiona saved her bread and tied it in a kerchief. She knew there were edible berries and seeds this time of year. Perhaps Tam had planned for them to stop at an inn each night, and they could eat there, at least for their evening meal.

One question intruded several times during that long day: *What will I tell my parents?* More than once, she started to write them a letter, but in the end decided not to. If she explained that she was eloping, they would not accept it and try to bring her back. But if she waited until after she and Tam were married and sent word from Moor Point, they would have to accept what she had done.

Even though Fiona could hear the sounds of the joust outside her window, for the first time in her life, she had no interest in learning which knight would become the tournament champion. There was only one who interested her now, and he was the champion of her heart.

When Fiona settled on the window seat, she leaned back her head and closed her eyes, replaying Tam's kiss and declaration of love. A smile relaxed her face.

But then others whom she loved intruded into her thoughts, and Fiona's conscience briefly pained her. She knew her family, and Papa in particular, would be hurt and not understand her decision. Fiona only hoped that someday, once she and Tam were established, her family would come to see how happy she was and be happy for her. Until then, she knew she was choosing estrangement, and that realization did mar her happiness somewhat.

Then she shook off the melancholy and looked ahead, to the great adventure awaiting her and her handsome husband-to-be. Perhaps this was what needed to happen to finally make Papa accept that she was not his little girl anymore.

* * *

Thanks to a compliant servant girl with whom Tam had a history, he managed to get word to a stable boy who owed him a favor, and the lad demonstrated he had received the message and would do as Tam asked. His horse would be tied to the rowan tree near the Keep's hidden entrance by the third hour of the night watch. Now all that remained for Tam was to keep his thoughts and emotions under control, lest Lord Henry or one of his sons stop by to check on him, and to pack the fewest items he needed to escape.

While Tam placed a change of clothing and his cloak in the sack, he brought to mind Fiona's jewels and estimated how much each piece would be worth. He knew selling them in Moor Point would not bring their full price, but it should be enough to pay his debt and have a little left over with which to make a living—somehow.

He was counting on Sir Artemis and Rodney Folville to help him find a place to live and work. And with any luck, once he and Fiona married, surely Lord Kieran and maybe even King Dolan would be willing to help support them. His future was looking more optimistic than it had in a very long time.

After he arranged his belongings in the sack, Tam was glad to note there was still room. A full waterskin would be too heavy, especially since his old nag would have to carry two riders. It was a long journey to Moor Point, but the weather was mild, and there would be plenty of water along the way. This time of year, they should also be able to find food near the streams and rivers. Although, without a bow, they'd have to eat what they could forage in the fields and under the forest canopies.

He wondered if Fiona would remember to pack her jewelry, but then he chuckled at himself. Of course she would; Fiona was quick-witted and more practical than he had expected. The one thing Tam feared was thieves, but if they stayed off the roads as much as possible, perhaps those who would rob them could be avoided.

After the tournament ended, Lord Henry returned to their guest room and had Tam help him into his finery for the final banquet. While Henry opened a wooden box to retrieve his signet ring, Tam wondered if he could get away with taking something from there, too.

"Are you not going to wear your chain, my lord?" While he was Guardian of Southmoor, he had taken to wearing a gold chain studded with amethysts.

Henry eyed Tam, as if wondering why he asked such a question. "I think not." He gestured to his tunic embroidered with gold thread. "This is ornate enough." Then he stared intently at Tam.

"Yes, my lord?" Tam made his face as innocent as possible.

"We leave in the morning. Be ready then, and this evening prepare yourself to resume all your squiring duties." Henry's face was grim.

Tam bowed to break eye contact. "Yes, my lord."

"I hope this time of solitude has been one of reflection for you, so you may go forward with a heart of service and an attitude of determination."

Tam straightened. "I believe it has, my lord. Thank you."

Henry opened the door and turned back once more. "Don't wait up for me, for I shall be late tonight."

"As you will, my lord." Tam forced himself not to grit his teeth, and finally Henry left.

How late did he mean? Would Tam have to worry about encountering him while he was making his way to Fiona's room?

He paced the length of the room, and each time he passed the place where Henry's box lay hidden, Tam slowed, wanting more and more to open it.

After the fifth circuit, he gave in and took the box from the inside pocket of Henry's cloak. With sweaty palms, Tam lifted the lid. The heavy chain with its amethysts winked at him, but he realized that not only would it be immediately obvious to Henry if Tam took it, few would be willing or able to buy it, making it almost useless to him. Under the chain, however, was a clasp made of gold that Tam had only seen Henry wear once. The lord preferred his sturdier bronze clasp to secure his cloak, which was the reason he kept it pinned on the garment.

Without hesitation, Tam removed the golden clasp. He needed it far worse than Henry ever would, for it would be easy to sell and even easier to conceal in his carry sack. Satisfied, Tam closed the box and returned it to Henry's cloak. By the time the man discovered the missing clasp, Tam would be long gone, so he need never be connected with its loss.

He wished he had the opportunity to find more small objects of value to sell in Moor Point, but he needed to focus all his stealth on his actual escape with Fiona.

*

After darkness fell, Tam became restless again. The solitude was maddening, but it would only be for a few hours more. The music and laughter and exuberance of the banquet carried up to his room as a faint reminder of all the opportunities Tam had lost and would never have again.

Then he reminded himself that being a knight was not the only way to find success. He would forge his path in the world in his own way, by his own rules. No one was going to stop him now!

He would not have to be alone, either. Fiona had agreed to come with him. She had chosen him over the insufferable Roland. That was an accomplishment, indeed!

Just a few more hours, and he would finally be free.

*

When the watch sounded two bells, Tam opened his eyes. He listened, hearing faint sounds coming from the great hall. Was Lord Henry still down there?

Tam turned his head and made sure Edward was sound asleep on his cot, wrapped in a blanket. Slowly Tam rose and pulled on his boots. Then he collected his carry sack and walked silently to the door. He'd just grasped the handle when rustling sounded behind him.

"Where are you going?" Edward hissed.

"Nowhere that concerns you," Tam whispered back. "Go back to sleep."

Edward padded over to him, barefooted. "Not until you tell me where you're going." He rubbed his eyes. "You're running away, aren't you?"

Tam clenched his teeth. He hadn't planned for Edward to wake up. What could he say?

"You can't run away. You'd be in big trouble with Lord Henry. And you haven't shown me how to win at dice yet." Edward balled his fists on his hips.

"I have to go. I'll keep my promise to you about winning at dice, but it will have to be later."

"No! I won't wait until later because you'll forget all about it. I'm going to tell Lord Henry if you step through that door."

Tam panicked. He grabbed Edward and clamped his hand over the boy's mouth. Edward tried to bite his hand, so Tam had to squeeze harder. The boy thrashed around so much, Tam could hardly hold him. Surely Lord Henry would hear the commotion!

Desperate, Tam punched Edward in the jaw and successfully knocked him unconscious. He stared down at him for a moment, thinking of what to do with him. First, he made sure Edward was still breathing, and then he tore the boy's blanket into strips, binding his hands and feet and tying a gag across his mouth. Then he lifted his dead weight with effort and stuffed him in the wardrobe.

Panting, Tam stood in the middle of the room to catch his breath. After a few minutes, he opened the door and peered out. Thankfully Lord Henry had not returned from the banquet yet. He nabbed his carry sack and slipped out into the hall. Good, the guard was asleep.

Before anything else could stop him, Tam made his way to the stairs and found the hidden door to the passageway leading to Tristam's room.

Chapter 11

The light of the eyes rejoiceth the heart.

Tam had only one anxious moment on the way to Fiona's room. He pressed his ear against the door leading into her brother's bedchamber, and when he heard nothing after a full minute, he peered out before stepping into the room.

To his horror, Tristam was not asleep. He sat hunched over a desk on the other side of the canopied bed, poring over a scroll by candlelight. Tam froze with his hand still holding open the door of paneled wood. The door to exit the room lay on the other side, in plain sight. It would be impossible to cross the room without being seen. His only option was to return to the passageway and wait for Tristam to fall asleep. But how long would that be?

He had just decided to turn around when Tristam's head bobbed once, twice, and came to rest upon his arms. His thick curly hair was too near the candle, but Tam was not about to get any closer to move it away from the lad's head.

As soon as Tristam's breathing changed to indicate he was sound asleep, Tam carefully pushed the paneled door partially closed and tread softly to the bedchamber door. Though he was anxious to leave the room, he listened again, lest Lord Kieran and Lady Mercy were returning late from the banquet. All was quiet.

Trembling with anticipation, Tam made his way to Fiona's door. When he pushed it open, the room was dark. Was she asleep?

"Tam? Is that you?" Her whisper came from the bed.

"Yes, it's me." He stepped up to the bed just as she opened the curtains. She climbed down, fully dressed, and slung an overstuffed carry sack across her chest.

"I pretended to be asleep, in case one of my parents came in to check on me after the banquet, and they did. They only went to sleep an hour ago, since they're usually out late the last night of the tournament." In the near darkness, her eyes shone as they gazed up at him.

Impulsively, he leaned down to kiss her, and she flung her arms around his neck. No doubt about it, she was exuberant and would bring him many pleasant hours! With reluctance, he pulled away. Now was not the place or time to become distracted by Fiona's kisses. He grasped her hand.

"Are you ready to leave?"

She smiled up at him. "Yes, I am ready."

"Then let's go." He opened her door slowly and silently, and they padded over to Tristam's door, which Tam had left open a slit. He paused and listened to make sure Fiona's brother was still soundly asleep at his desk, and then he pushed open the door just enough for them to squeeze through. Tam pointed to the door of the passageway, which he'd also left ajar.

While hardly daring to breathe, Tam started across the floor, assuming Fiona was still behind him. When he turned his head, she had glided over to the desk where her brother lay slumped upon it. Tam waved his arms, trying to get her attention, but she didn't see him.

To his dismay, she moved the candle away from Tristam's head and stood there staring down at him. Tam kept making gestures to get her attention, but she never turned around. Was she going to kiss him goodbye? And what would he do if Tristam woke up? He was sure Fiona wouldn't like him to knock out her brother and stuff him in the wardrobe, as he'd been forced to do with her nephew.

Finally, she turned back and joined him at the passageway. With a smile, she stepped inside first and led the way. After closing the door behind them, he felt for each step, staying close behind her. When they reached a junction, Fiona turned right, and Tam reached out to stop her.

"I came from the other direction," he started to explain, but Fiona leaned in close. The scent of lavender reached his nostrils while she whispered.

"If we go right, it will lead down to the sublevel and connect to the tunnel which exits at the rear of the Keep."

"How do you know?" he whispered back.

"Iris and I used it more than once to gather wildflowers." Tam could imagine the grin on her face. This castle was her home, after all.

"Lead the way, then." And he followed her down.

* * *

Fiona shivered with anticipation as well as dread at being caught. Surely the guards would be too exhausted to be fully alert? With any luck, they would have nodded off to sleep.

She and Tam exited the secret passage under the stairwell at the beginning of the tunnel. There were no sounds within, so she took Tam's hand while they made their way along the tunnel's wall toward the outside door.

It had been at least a year since she'd come this way, but she knew it was still a functioning entrance. Over the years it had been discussed as an unacceptable weakness in the Keep's defense, but rather than seal up the door, Dolan left it for emergency egress. Instead, pains had been taken to disguise it from the outside and make it difficult to use.

As long as she and Tam could get out without being caught, that was all that mattered to Fiona.

They reached the end of the tunnel without encountering a single guard. That seemed odd, as there hadn't been any lit torches, either. But it was the last night of the tournament, and Dolan was always very generous to the guards, allowing them to partake in the feast. Perhaps some of them had partaken too liberally of the ale.

"There's a bar on the door," Tam whispered. "It feels heavy."

"It is, but together we should be able to lift it." Fiona slung her carry sack around to her back, out of the way, and went to one end of the stout wooden bar.

With much effort and barely subdued grunts on her part, she and Tam were able to push the bar up and out of its brackets. Fiona intended to keep hold of it so they could lower it quietly to the stone, but it slipped from her hands and landed with a loud thud. She gasped and froze, expecting the entire guard to descend upon them. But nothing happened.

Tam grabbed her hand, startling her.

"Come, Fiona. The door will be discovered eventually, so we should be far away when it is."

She nodded and followed him out into the night. Insects called from the trees across the open section of grass and rocks. By the starlight, Tam scanned the wall above before pulling Fiona along in a run toward the trees. Her carry sack bounced against her back, but she waited until they stopped beneath the dark canopy of branches to adjust it.

"My horse should be nearby, tied to a rowan tree." He looked both ways and started toward the right. Fiona hurried to keep up with his long strides. She nearly tripped over roots and walked more carefully after that.

Finally, a horse nickered ahead. When Fiona and Tam came upon it, he immediately untied the animal from the branch.

"There's a stream nearby. Your horse looks thirsty. What's his name?" Fiona reached out to stroke him, and he pushed his muzzle against her hand, snuffling.

"This is Basil." Tam handed her his reins. "Please, lead on to the stream."

Fiona gladly complied. "Basil," she murmured, and the horse snorted. "Interesting name."

"I didn't name him. Lord Henry let me ride him when I became his squire. Basil is an old fellow, but he's dependable." He sighed. "Squires are never given the best of anything. That's part of the training."

"Well, he may not be Lord Henry's best horse, but I can tell he's a good one." Fiona pushed aside a clump of tall grass, and the stream sparkled below them in the dim light. Basil surged ahead, and Fiona let him go.

While the horse drank, Fiona and Tam went upstream and quenched their thirst, too. Then Tam took a small waterskin from the saddle and filled it. He secured it behind the saddle with a long piece of leather.

"Ready?" he asked.

"For anything," she answered with a smile.

Tam mounted and held out a hand for her. She pulled herself up behind him and slipped her arms around his slender waist, trembling at his nearness. Though she had rued having to leave Firestorm behind, she would not have had the opportunity to ride so close to Tam if she'd had her own horse.

"Is Basil strong enough to carry us both?" She did not want the horse to suffer, and it was too dark to check his legs and hooves. Tomorrow she would find the time to do that.

"Of course he is. We'll pace ourselves so we don't overtire him." Tam glanced over his shoulder before urging Basil to move forward.

For the rest of the night, they traveled southwest. Basil picked a path through the trees, though it would have been easier to leave their shelter and ride in the open. They skirted the lake, and by the time the sun began to lighten the eastern sky, the Keep had grown smaller in the distance. Not small enough to make Fiona easy, though. They were still close enough that Papa could find them, if he really wanted to.

They crossed the main road leading south from the Keep just before the sun burst above the hills. With any luck, they'd be out of sight before people began to travel along it. The looming peaks of the Dragon's Backbone stood between them and their destination.

Fiona leaned her head against Tam's warm back. What an adventure lay ahead for them! She did not fear the unknown future, since she had Tam to share in the journey.

* * *

Val woke early, even though he hadn't slept long. Today all the candidates for dragon rider would arrive, at least those who weren't already at the Keep. He and Reggie would leave soon to collect Emma from the Highlands. He could hardly wait to see her again, and he was eager to know which dragon would choose her to be its rider. For there was no doubt in Val's mind that she *would* be one of the chosen.

Customarily, the lords of all the provinces left for home the day after the king's tournament ended. Dolan had mentioned they all wanted to stay one more day so they could find out which dragon and their rider would be assigned to them as part of the Royal Dragon Couriers. That was fine with Val, but he was concerned that Emma would balk at being under the scrutiny of the seven lords, as well as the king of Levathia.

Could he bring her directly to the royal tower first, and introduce her to the rest of the family before so many nobles and other strangers were thrust upon her? He was sure none of his family would mind, but he would have to hurry to accomplish the meeting before the scheduled time of the Choosing, which was two in the afternoon.

Reggie? Are you ready to leave in a few minutes to pick up Emma?

How many minutes is a few?

Val chuckled at the dragon's sleepy voice. *I'll meet you on the royal tower in half an hour. That is thirty minutes. Is it enough?*

Yes, I will be there.

Thank you, my friend. Val pulled on his boots and slipped a leather jerkin over his linen shirt. He draped his cloak over his arm and headed down the stairs of his parents' tower, on his way to the royal tower.

When he had first returned after his adventure in the north country, he and Tristam had shared a room. But his brother's nocturnal study habits proved too much for Val, so he moved into an empty servant's room on the floor beneath the family suite and was well content. That is, until the time came for him to marry, and then he and his bride would need someplace a bit larger.

The sun rose, brightening the sky with a cheery glow. Val hoped Dolan was already awake. He knew his brother had stayed up even later than he had. But he also knew Dolan would do his duty to the provincial lords, as long as they were guests at the Keep.

Val trotted up the spiral steps leading to the king's and queen's rooms. He knocked lightly on Dolan's door, and was met by his sleepy page Christopher Decourt, with whom Val had served when he'd been Dolan's squire.

"Good morning, Christopher. Is the king awake?" Val smiled when the page rubbed his eyes.

"Yes, my lord. Please, come in."

Before Christopher could leave to announce him to Dolan, Val clapped his shoulder. "You don't need to call me 'lord' when it's just the two of us. It's just me; I haven't changed."

Christopher's eyes widened. "But you have changed. You're all grown up, and you have an important title now."

Val stepped closer to a tall-backed chair in the king's sitting room and gripped it with both hands. "By all means, use my title when we're in public, but here, please let us be friends, as we were before."

For a moment, Val thought Christopher would refuse him. But he finally smiled and nodded.

"All right, Val. I can do that. I'll tell the king you're here."

"Thank you." He watched until Christopher knocked upon the bedchamber door and was admitted. Then he laughed to himself and sat in the chair. "I am just me, just Val. The title is something I have to wear, but it is not me."

"Good morning, Val." Dolan came out of the bedchamber, bareheaded and wearing a dressing gown over his nightshirt. "What brings you here so early?"

Val rose and went to greet his brother. "I realized Emma has only met Kieran, and I'd really like for her to meet you and the rest of the family before she has to face the nobles and the choosing ceremony."

"Hmm, that is a good idea. When did you want to do this?" Dolan ran a hand through his disheveled hair.

"I plan to leave with Reggie in a few minutes and can have her back here by late midmorning. The Choosing begins at two, so perhaps she can dine with us?" Val clasped and unclasped his hands. He wasn't very good at planning unexpected things, if they involved other people.

Dolan nodded. "That's a good plan. I'll speak to Rhianna, and we'll put together a simple family luncheon at eleven."

Val gave Dolan a relieved smile. "Thank you. I'm anxious for everyone to meet Emma."

Dolan smirked. "I know you are. That is why I'm willing to help you."

Val's smile widened so much, he couldn't think of anything to say. He knew he must appear ridiculous, but he was too happy to care.

"Go on, then." Dolan made a shooing gesture. "Hurry up and fetch Emma before your face freezes like that."

They laughed together, and then Val left with a wave.

*

He felt certain Reggie was flying as swiftly as usual, but it seemed to take twice as long to reach Emma's village near the coast of the MacDonald's land in the far north corner of the Highlands. As always happened when Reggie was expected, the village children came eagerly to greet him. Val chuckled while he dismounted and left the dragon to his admirers. The children hardly spared him a glance, but he didn't mind. There was only one person in this village whose attentions mattered to him.

Emma stepped out of her cottage before he reached the door. She smiled nervously and pulled the door shut behind her. With her hair bound and covered with a tightly knotted scarf, she wore a riding skirt and a vest over a long-sleeved tunic as well as soft leather boots that laced up to her knees. Slung across her chest was a bulging carry sack.

"Good morning, Emma. You're ready, I see." Val leaned down and kissed her cheek.

"I decided ye might come early, and I was too anxious tae dawdle much." She adjusted her carry sack.

"That's a good thing, for I'd like you to meet the rest of my family before the dragons make their choices." He smiled to reassure her, for he hated seeing her so unsure of herself.

"All o' them?" Her eyes widened.

He nodded. "They're all at the Keep right now, so it would be a good time."

"How big be your family, anyway?" Emma gulped. "Me cousins fill MacRorie lands, but in me family there be only four."

"And I hope to meet your parents and your brother soon." Val was anxious to do so, but today it was her turn to meet his. "I have two brothers and two sisters. Dolan's wife is Rhianna, and they have three children, William, Edward, and Matilda." He paused when he remembered something. "You might not meet Edward, though, since he is a page for a knight in the south. And my sister Joy is married to Bennet, and they have one son, Robard." He smiled. "And Fiona and Tristam are not married yet. So you see, counting my parents only twelve in all."

"Only twelve, he says," she muttered. "Very well. But I would nae agree tae this for anyone else, dinna ye ken."

"Oh, I do ken, Emma, and I appreciate your willingness to meet so many strangers." He gently clasped her hand. "Hopefully you will like them as much as I do."

Her anxiety melted away for a moment, and she gave him a pleased smile. "If they be anything like you, they're sure tae be bonnie fowk."

Val cocked his head. "Fowk?"

Emma bit her lip. "People, I think you lowlanders say."

"Lowlanders?" Val laughed. "I have never heard you say that before."

"Weel, 'tis true, is it not? Up here be the Highlands, down in Levathia be the Lowlands."

Val took both of Emma's hands in his own. "You have never seen the rest of Levathia, have you?" He supposed he knew that on some level, but they had not discussed it before.

She bit her lip and shook her head. "Until I came here tae train as a midwife, I had ne'er left me village in the MacRorie lands."

"No wonder you were reluctant to accept the offer of being a dragon rider." He bent down and kissed each of her hands, his gaze never leaving hers. *Come, Emma, and I will show you what else is in the world.*

To his relief, she did not hesitate. *I trust you.*

Hand-in-hand, they walked over to Reggie. Several of the children had climbed on his tail, and he was turning in a slow circle, dragging his tail along in the grass. Their laughter made Val smile.

I am sorry to interrupt your game, friend Reggie, but we really must return to the Keep.

The dragon stopped, and the children all made disappointed sounds. Reggie also looked reluctant to leave.

"Go on wi' ye, now." Emma made a shooing motion. "Ye've had yer fun, and now the beastie must fly tae his home."

One by one, the little ones backed away, but they would not leave until after Reggie had flown out of sight. He crouched down so Val and Emma could mount him.

"I'm going to climb on first, so you can watch how I do it. I will sit between those back ridges." He pointed them out, though he wasn't sure Emma would know which two he meant. "I want you to sit in front of me, between the next two ridges."

She nodded, and he slowly placed his hands and feet along the scales and crevices of Reggie's joints until he grabbed hold of the back ridge and positioned himself to straddle the dragon's backbone. Then he held out his hand to her. "Your turn."

Emma took a deep breath and then carefully placed her foot on Reggie's arm, though she didn't lean against him. *I dinna want tae hurt ye, friend Reggie.*

You cannot hurt me, friend Emma. He turned his head to face her. *Go on. I am ready.*

Emma's face tightened with determination, and she copied Val's handholds and footholds all the way up. Deftly she took her seat astride the dragon before looking over her shoulder.

"Well done. Now all you have to do is hold onto the ridge in front of you and grip with your knees. Reggie is a smooth flier and will take no chances with acrobatics in the air."

I will take good care of you, friend Emma.

I trust you, friend Reggie. Emma faced forward and did as Val suggested.

Are you ready, Emma? Val's heart leaped within his chest, anticipating how exhilarated Emma would be at takeoff.

Aye, as ready as I'll e'er be.

Then please take us to the Keep, friend Reggie.

The dragon opened his wings to the exclamations of the children and sprang into the air. Emma gasped once, but she did not scream, to Val's relief.

She did not speak to him right away either, so Val scanned the ground below, trying to see it through Emma's eyes. He was thankful for the cloudless day, so there was nothing to impede her view of the Highlands from aloft.

Her village receded in the distance before she spoke to his mind.

It takes me breath away. Ye ne'er did say how large the world looks from up here. 'Tis what the birds see, I imagine.

I'm so glad you aren't afraid. And I never told you, because it's difficult to express in words.

I ne'er said I weren't afraid, but the fear be worth the view. I dinna think I could describe what I'm seeing in mere words, either.

Val chuckled, thankful the wind noise kept Emma from hearing him, lest she think he was laughing at her. He was just so happy she was enjoying the experience despite her fear. Riding a dragon was always exhilarating but not without its dangers.

Until they reached the MacRorie lands, Val pointed out landmarks that might be familiar to her. To his delight, she recognized the MacRorie fortress from the air, exclaiming her amazement that it looked so small.

That's because we are flying so high above it, he explained.

Aye, everything looks so tiny, as if the whole world has shrunk.

After a few minutes, Val heard her gasp, and she briefly pointed. *There! 'Tis me Da's land, and there be our cottage!*

Val looked in the direction she'd indicated and found a patchwork of planted fields. At the edge was a small structure with a thatched roof and a barn nearby. Sheep grazed in a meadow, and a small figure walked behind a team of oxen, plowing a furrow. *Is that your father?*

Aye, 'tis him. I wish I could call tae him. Can he see us, do ye ken?

If he looked up, he would see a dragon in flight, but he might not be able to tell that we're on Reggie's back.

Oh, weel, that does make sense. I shall tell him later.

Val had a thought that if Reggie roared, Emma's father would look up, and she could wave to him. But not being able to see her well enough to know it was his daughter, having a great dragon roar overhead might startle him as well as his oxen. He hoped that soon he and Emma could visit her family together, each riding on their own dragon friend.

That thought pleased him immensely.

Emma marveled at the distant peaks of the Dragon's Backbone, but when the Keep came into view, she sounded dismayed.

I did nae ken 'twould be so monstrous big! How many fowk live within?

I have never counted, but I would estimate one hundred and fifty, at least. Right now the population is more than double that because of the annual court and tournament, so people from all over Levathia have been within the castle walls.

So many?

It takes many to take care of all that needs doing in the stables, the armory, the kitchens, including the castle servants, plus the several knights and guards who live there, as well as the lords of the king's privy council and their families.

And twelve in your family.

Only twelve. That's not such a large family, is it?

I suppose not. Dinna worry, I will nae retreat from meeting them, nor from the dragon choosing.

Val glanced over his shoulder. *Oh, I know you would never retreat.* Instinctively, he sent Emma a mental caress, which made him long to give her a hug.

Reggie approached the Keep. There was some activity in the yard. Probably some of the tournament attendees leaving for home.

Please land on the royal tower, Reggie.

The dragon did so with an economy of motion and deftly folded his wings. He crouched down so Val could slide off. Then he stood beside Reggie in case Emma needed help. She managed to imitate Val and slid into his waiting arms.

'Twas a most bonnie experience. I thank ye, friend Reggie. Emma's eyes never left Val's gaze.

You are very welcome, friend Emma.

Before Val could answer, running footsteps approached, and he pulled away from Emma.

"Uncle Val!" It was William. The young prince came near and stopped, looking from Val to Emma. "Hello, you must be Emma. I'm William." He gave her a brilliant smile.

"'Tis good tae meet you." Emma dropped in a little curtsy while speaking to Val's mind. *What do I call him? What be his title?*

You don't have to call him anything right now, but in formal situations he would be addressed Your Highness, since he is the crown prince.

Before they could continue, William spoke again to Val.

"Father asked me to watch for you. The family is gathered in his sitting room, except for Aunt Fiona. She's missing." He turned to leave. "Granddad thinks she may have run away."

"What?" Val's mouth hung open, but he couldn't seem to close it. Emma clasped his hand.

William shrugged and looked back. "That's all I know. But come on, someone may have learned more since I came to find you."

Val hurried to follow him down the spiral stairs, his concern growing by the minute.

Chapter 12

Who leave the paths of uprightness, to walk in the ways of darkness.

Mercy awakened before the sun and rolled over. Though she hadn't heard Kieran come to bed, she had been hoping he would sleep beside her, at least. With a sigh, she climbed down from the bed. He wasn't on the cot he'd set up the night before, either. Without waiting for Oleta, Mercy pulled on a simple dress without back lacings and entered the common room.

Kieran sat at the table with his head bowed, though he didn't appear to be praying. He was so deep in thought, he didn't hear her approach. But before she could speak to him, someone rapped on the door. Kieran pushed himself from the table to answer it. Christopher Decourt, Dolan's page, stood outside.

"My lord," he said with a bow. "The king requests the honor of your family's presence at a luncheon in their sitting room to meet Emma MacRorie before the meeting with the dragons and the candidates for courier riders in the afternoon."

Kieran hesitated only a moment. "Tell His Majesty we will be there." His voice was wooden.

"Thank you, my lord." Then Christopher noticed Mercy. "And my lady." With another bow, he pivoted and strode away.

After Kieran shut the door, he slowly turned to her, and Mercy tried in vain to smile.

"I will be glad to meet Emma at last."

"You will like her very much." Kieran's face twisted in pain. "She is a bonnie lass."

"She must be, since she is related to you." Mercy winced when he didn't react. "And since Val is so smitten with her."

"Aye, he is besotted." Kieran returned to his chair and leaned his forehead against one hand. "I confess I am hoping their attachment becomes permanent someday."

"How could it not, since they can speak mind-to-mind?" Mercy shook her head in amazement. "That Val should find a young woman with that ability is an incredible blessing." She continued to stare at Kieran, but he never once glanced her way.

"What do you think about letting Fiona come with us tae meet Emma, even though not all the visitors have left the Keep?" Kieran still did not meet her gaze.

"I think it would be good for her to be there. I know it would mean a lot to Val for him to be able to introduce Emma to her." *After all, if we four go to Dolan's suite together, there is little chance of Fiona encountering Tammeron d'Jean.* But she did not say the thought aloud, and she was too far away to touch him and speak it to his mind.

Kieran rose again, even more slowly this time. "Shall I tell her, then?"

Mercy started to nod, but his gaze was far away. "Yes, please. And while you do, I'll make sure Tristam is awake." Holding back a sharp remark, because she knew her hurt feelings would come out as anger, she headed to Tristam's door.

Gritting her teeth, Mercy lightly rapped on the door. She didn't expect her youngest son to be awake yet, so she opened the door and peered inside. Sure enough, Tristam was asleep at his desk. His head with its mop of dark curls lay cushioned on his folded arms. How could he sleep in that position?

She came closer and saw that he'd been studying from an old scroll written by a physician who'd lived two hundred years ago. The messy fat candle on the edge of the desk had thankfully burned itself out, else Tristam might have accidentally knocked it over. It was so near the edge that some of the wax had dripped onto the floor.

Mercy gently stroked his head. "Tristam, it's time to wake up. Dolan has asked that we come to his suite this morning."

Tristam groaned and stirred, and his eyelashes fluttered, but he did not wake up. Mercy shook him firmly but gently.

"Tristam. You must wake up now. We are needed elsewhere."

Finally he lifted his head and slowly blinked. "Mother?" He rubbed his eyes and then ran his hand through his tangled curls. "Is someone ill?"

"Not this time. Dolan has sent a message requesting our presence in the king's suite. There is someone Val would like for us all to meet." Mercy smiled at how much Tristam resembled a young Kieran when he was half-asleep.

"Who?" Tristam held up his hand to cover a wide yawn.

"Her name is Emma MacRorie."

Tristam pushed himself out of his chair. "She's that girl he's always talking about."

"Yes, that's the one." Mercy patted Tristam's shoulder. "I'll leave you to clean up. We need to leave in half an hour."

"I'll be ready." Tristam rubbed his eyes again and headed straight for the water basin.

Holding back a chuckle, Mercy left Tristam's room. Kieran opened Fiona's door at the same time, his face twisted in distress.

"What is it, love?" She hurried to his side, her hurt feelings forgotten.

"Fiona's gone."

* * *

Kieran waited until Mercy was inside Tristam's room before going to Fiona's door. He had a hunch his daughter would not wish to see him. She did not answer his knock, so he opened the door and called to her. Still no answer.

The room was dark, and the bed curtains were closed. Was she still in bed? Sometimes Fiona liked to wake early and greet the dawn. Perhaps she'd had trouble sleeping.

He came near the bed and called her name again, but she remained silent. Taking a deep breath, Kieran pushed back the curtain.

The bed was empty. Kieran whirled around.

"Fiona? Are ye here, lass?" He strode to the window seat, opened the shutters, and peered out, half-expecting there to be a rope dangling from the window. If she had gone out riding, disobeying her parents' orders yet again, the stables were not visible from this position. He'd have to check with the guard and find out what time she left.

He met Mercy in the sitting room which adjoined all three bedchambers. "Fiona's gone."

"Gone?"

"Aye. I suspect she has disobeyed us yet again and gone riding."

Mercy entered her room, and Kieran followed. "Did you notice if any of her things are missing?"

"No. What would be missing if she's gone out riding?"

Mercy stared past him, her brows knitted together. Had Kieran overlooked something? Finally, Mercy spoke. "Why don't you ask the guard if he saw Fiona leave, and I'll look for clues here."

"I will." Frowning at Mercy's strange statement, Kieran hurried down the spiral stairs. The guard straightened at his approach.

"Good morrow, Parkin."

"Good morrow, m'lord." The young man dipped his head.

"How long ago did Lady Fiona leave this morning?" Kieran kept his tone neutral.

Parkin cocked his head. "Lady Fiona has not left the tower, m'lord."

"But she's not in her room." Kieran's throat constricted. Where had the lass gone *this* time?

Parkin's eyes widened. "M'lord, I've been 'ere all night an' I swear Lady Fiona never left the tower."

Kieran's gut tightened. "I believe you. Thank you, Parkin." He took the steps two at a time to return to Fiona's room. Mercy was bent over, searching inside Fiona's wardrobe.

"She did nae leave the tower, at least not by the stairs," he reported. His voice still sounded strangled. Mercy straightened and turned to him.

"Her box of jewels is missing, as well as a few other items."

Her words felt like a gut punch. This was too like what had happened a year ago, when Val had run away.

Mercy's eyes narrowed. "We should ask Lord Henry if Tammeron is in his room."

"Do ye think she would run away with him?" Now his earlier image of a rope out the window seemed more plausible, especially when he said the words aloud.

"I do." She closed the wardrobe. "As soon as Tristam is ready, we should go to Lord Henry on the way to Dolan's rooms."

A pain spiked in Kieran's head, and he clapped his free hand over the place.

"Headache?" When he nodded, Mercy raised both hands to his head and massaged it while calling on the Healing power. The pain subsided in moments, and Kieran caught her hand as if to anchor himself.

Thank you. But Mercy didn't answer, and he released her.

The door opened behind them, and Tristam came in.

"Father? What's wrong?"

Kieran met his son's concerned gaze.

"A wee headache, which yer mum has taken away. We're leaving a bit early so we can meet with Lord Henry." He grimaced. "Your sister is not in her room."

"What has that got to do with Lord Henry?" Tristam frowned in confusion.

Mercy spoke first. "We want to know if Lord Henry's squire is still in the Keep. If he is also missing, it's possible he and your sister ran away together."

"Fiona ran away like Val did, without telling us?" Tristam's frown deepened. "Do you mean she went with Tam?"

Kieran's throat tightened and he could barely squeak out the word. "Aye." Then he cleared his throat. "Did Fiona, by chance, mention anything about him?"

Tristam shook his head, but concern filled his features. "I thought she liked Roland Campignon?"

"We thought so too, until three days ago." Kieran beckoned to Tristam. "Come, hopefully we'll know more after speaking to Lord Henry."

The three of them left together.

*

After exiting the tower, they headed for the nearby barracks, where Lord Henry had been given one of the larger guest rooms. To Kieran's surprise, they met Henry and Edward coming toward them. Both looked angry.

"Henry? What happened?" Kieran strode ahead and gripped the lord's arm. Mercy and Tristam remained silent, and thankfully so did Edward.

"My squire has run away." Henry's mouth was grim, and Kieran nodded in resignation.

"So has Fiona. They must have gone together."

Edward spoke then. "And Tam knocked me out and tied me up and gagged me and locked me in the wardrobe!" He drew himself up in indignation. "Granddad, you need to arrest Tam and hang him!"

Kieran and Mercy shared a troubled glance. Could this situation become any worse?

Mercy bent down to examine Edward. "Where does it hurt?"

"Tam hit me in the jaw." He fingered the large bruise there. "It only hurts a little." The boy's frown deepened.

"Let me *See* it to make sure." Mercy cupped her hand over the place, and the Healing glow briefly appeared before she let go.

"Thank you, Grandmother. The pain is gone." Edward felt his jaw and moved it from side to side.

"I was on my way to see King Dolan," Henry said.

"We need to see him, too." Kieran's jaw tightened. With the evidence of Tammeron's willingness to use violence, Kieran felt even more frantic with worry. He wouldn't hurt Fiona, would he? He'd better not!

"Then let us report this to the king." Henry gestured for Kieran to lead the way.

* * *

Tam urged his horse into the foothills of the Dragon's Backbone. He felt an urgency to be in Moor Point as quickly as possible, but he knew riding double would tire the animal sooner. And since he would rather not walk all the way, he took care to conserve its strength, stopping often for water and grass. At least they were well away from any road.

When they halted at midday in a shady place beside a spring, Fiona slid down and cupped her hands in the clear water. Tam climbed an outcropping of rocks to get his bearing. When he returned to the spring, Fiona sat beside it, nibbling on a piece of bread. She looked up at him expectantly.

"We're making good time. With the weather so fine, we can sleep under the stars tonight at a level place higher up." He smiled with relief. There was no way anyone from the Keep could follow them.

"Are you sure you know where you're going?" Fiona appeared distressed. "We are nowhere near any road."

"Yes, that's the point, my love. And I do know where we're going, for I have traveled this route with Sir Artemis twice." He turned and pointed southwest. "We continue as straight as possible in that direction, and we will arrive in Moor Point in four days."

"Four days?" Fiona gracefully rose, dusting off her riding skirt. "I thought we would ride through towns and villages, spend the night at inns along the way. I don't mind sleeping out of doors, but what will we eat?"

Tam moved closer to her. "The mountain streams are full of fish, and we'll be able to find berries and other edible plants." He pointed near the place where she'd been sitting. "That is sorrel. I've eaten it before." To demonstrate, he bent down and plucked a handful, which he shared with Fiona. He folded his portion and stuffed it in his mouth.

"How will we catch fish?" Fiona nibbled on her sorrel.

"If we look for a thorny plant among the rocks and vines, we can make fishing lines." He patted the sheath on his belt. "And I'll clean them with my knife."

"How will we light a fire?" Fiona ate the last of her sorrel and wrung her hands together. "I have never started one before."

Tam patted his carry sack. "I have flint with me. I know how to start one using my knife. Don't worry, Fiona; I'll make sure you have food and water and warmth." He wagged his brows, making her smile.

They traveled a few more miles that afternoon before stopping at a stream beside a flat grassy bank. Tam proclaimed it their inn for the night. He had managed to find a large thorn and a tough vine, but it took a while to find a locust for bait. The first fish, a large suckermouth, took the bait so quickly, Tam thought luck must be with him. But it turned out to be the only fish he caught. After half an hour, he left off drowning locusts and worked at starting a fire instead. Fiona collected several armloads of dead wood while Tam made several unsuccessful attempts to light his pile of kindling.

When he was about to give up, he finally made a good spark which caught on the twigs and dried leaves. He gently blew as Sir Artemis had shown him, and after several minutes had a tiny fire going. With difficulty, he made himself sit still to feed it with larger and larger twigs, and at last he was sure the flame was not going out.

Fiona took over tending the fire while Tam prepared the fish to cook. He gutted it and scraped off the scales, and then he washed it in the stream and skewered it onto a stick he'd prepared. Fiona gathered some water cress, and they had a respectable meal, though not as filling as he'd hoped it would be.

The sun was setting by the time they'd finished. Fiona laid her cloak upon the grass, and Tam laid his next to hers. They lay side-by-side and watched the stars. The fire crackled, occasionally sending up sparks. Insects made music in the background. Tam reached over and took Fiona's hand.

"It's beautiful," Fiona said. "There seem to be more stars in the sky here in the mountains."

"I have noticed that, too. Perhaps the sky is clearer." He turned and watched her until she looked at him. Then he leaned over and kissed her.

When she returned his kiss, he moved closer. They were all alone here, many miles from any town or farm. What a perfect place, with only the stars to bear distant witness—

"Tam, please." Fiona pulled away, breathless. "We have to be careful until we find a priest to marry us."

"Yes, of course." He held back his impatience. "We'll find one soon, I promise."

"We should sleep now so we can get an early start." Fiona smoothed out her cloak. "Goodnight, Tam." Then she laid down, turning her back to him.

Tam clenched his fists, fighting the unbearable tension. "Goodnight, Fiona." He slowly unclenched his fists and flopped down on his cloak, turning toward the fire and trying to forget that a desirable young woman lay inches away.

That, he decided, was going to be impossible.

Chapter 13

A good name is rather to be chosen than great riches,
and loving favour rather than silver and gold.

When Mercy entered Dolan's sitting room with Kieran, Tristam, Edward, and Lord Henry, Dolan and Rhianna's smiles changed to puzzlement when they saw the looks on their faces. William and Matilda stopped what they were doing and came to join the group.

"Mother, what's wrong?" Dolan bade everyone take a seat. "Joy and Bennet and Robard will be here shortly."

"There's no need to wait until they arrive to tell you that Fiona is gone." Mercy gestured to Henry. "It appears she may have run away with Lord Henry's squire, Tammeron."

"What?" Dolan looked from Mercy to Kieran to Lord Henry, and back to Mercy. "Why would she do that?"

Because she was standing close to Kieran, Mercy reached out and gripped his hand. "I had told you Fiona was confined to her room, but I didn't tell you why." She gulped, ashamed to say the words aloud. "Kieran discovered her kissing Tammeron when he was supposed to be on duty. She believes herself in love with him, so I do not doubt they have run away to be married." She tightened her grip and spoke to Kieran's mind. *And she must have run away with him because she knew we would be reluctant to give our permission.* When he didn't answer her, she frowned. Was he so angry with her, he refused to speak to her mind?

"Tam wanted me to give Aunt Fiona a message," Edward said sullenly from his place near Henry's chair. "He tricked me into telling him about the secret passageway into Uncle Tris's room."

"I didn't hear anything." Tristam scratched his head. "And I was up late studying."

"I know," Mercy said, her voice choked. "I found you asleep on your desk again."

"If Fiona and Tammeron came into my room, I would have heard them, wouldn't I?"

"No," Kieran said, pulling away from Mercy's grasp. "Ye sleep much too soundly tae hear those who would be trying tae move quietly."

"If Fiona eloped with Tammeron, then surely she will contact you once she's married and settled, won't she?" Rhianna's gentle voice caused Mercy's throat to tighten. Trust her sweet daughter-in-law to see the most optimistic version of the situation.

"I wish it were that simple, dear." Mercy let out a sigh.

Kieran and Henry shared a look, and Henry nodded.

"Tammeron must be arrested and returned tae the Keep." Kieran clenched his jaw.

"I can't arrest him for eloping with Fiona," Dolan explained, looking from Kieran to Henry.

"But he knocked me out, Father," Edward piped up.

Rhianna gasped. "What?" Edward nodded at his mother and continued.

"He also tied me up, and gagged me, and locked me in the wardrobe." He glared at Dolan. "You must arrest Tam for punching me, Father."

"Why on earth would he do that, Edward?" Dolan gripped the arms of his chair.

"So I wouldn't stop him from running away by telling Lord Henry what he was planning to do." Edward crossed his arms.

"Did you know about Fiona leaving too?" Mercy asked.

"No, Grandmother." Edward, thankfully, sounded sincere this time.

Before anyone else could speak, Joy, Bennet, and Robard arrived, and the entire story had to be repeated for them.

"I should have gone to see Fiona while she was confined to her room." Joy's face filled with regret. "Maybe I could have convinced her not to run away."

Mercy sadly shook her head. "I don't think anyone could have done that, dearest. Your sister believes herself in love, and no one would have been able to reason with her." She held back tears, for the sake of all her family. What was done, was done, and crying would only make everyone feel worse. But it was even more difficult to hide her emotion, knowing that Kieran's resentment was so strong, he'd felt the need to refrain from speaking mind-to-mind.

"Can we not send men to arrest Tammeron and return your sister, Sire?" Henry avoided Mercy's gaze and focused on Dolan instead.

"Yes, Lord Henry, we can," Dolan said with a decisive nod. "Do you have any idea where they might be headed?"

"I assume they would be traveling south," Henry said with a shrug, "though I do not know precisely where. He has lived in both Southmoor and Moor Point and would be more familiar with those two provinces."

"Then I will send men to both places." Dolan rose and bade his page send for Captain Hodor.

Mercy took a deep breath. "When Val and Emma arrive, should we tell him? I'd hate for the news to overshadow our introduction to Emma, and hers to us."

"Val will notice Fiona missing and ask about her," Joy pointed out. "We can't lie to him."

"Of course not." Tears pricked Mercy's eyes, and she struggled to keep them at bay. "It's so unfair to Emma."

"While all o' ye are getting acquainted with the lass, I'll take Val aside and let him know." Though Kieran sounded uncharacteristically gruff, Mercy could be grateful he was able to come up with a sensible solution.

"William," Dolan said, interrupting his son's quiet conversation with Robard.

"Yes, Father?"

"It's almost time for your Uncle Val and his guest to arrive. Please run up to the tower and watch for them."

"Can Robard come, too?" William's gaze upon his father was hopeful rather than pleading.

"I think Robard had better wait here. You won't be gone long." Dolan's smile was grim.

"Yes, Father." William's posture slumped a little, but he obeyed and exited quickly.

Captain Hodor arrived almost at the same moment. Lord Henry spoke up.

"Sire, permission to leave and inform Captain Hodor so you and your family, including Edward, can have some privacy with Prince Val when he arrives?" Henry was so thoughtful, Mercy felt the urge to hug him, but she wisely refrained.

"Thank you, Lord Henry." Dolan nodded to Hodor, and both men quit the room.

"Now, we wait," Bennet said softly.

"Aye." In Kieran's single word, Mercy heard quiet anguish.

*

It wasn't long before William's running footsteps could be heard approaching the door, and Dolan's page opened it. Everyone rose, and Mercy moved closer to catch her first glimpse of Val and his young lady. He met her gaze and grinned. How she hated to mar this meeting with the news about Fiona!

Val held Emma's hand while they stepped into the room. She was pretty with her striking green eyes, the same shade as Kieran's, and her shy lopsided smile. When Mercy met her gaze, Emma's smile widened, and Mercy stepped forward to greet her first. She knew Dolan would understand and not make a fuss about protocol.

"I am so glad to finally meet you, Emma. I'm Mercy MacLachlan, Val's mother." She held out her hand, and Emma lightly gripped it, dipping in a curtsy.

"And I have wanted tae meet you since the day I first learned Val be your son." She glanced back up at Val, who looked so pleased, Mercy wanted to hug him.

"'Tis good tae see ye again, Emma." Kieran gestured to the rest of the family. "As ye can see, there be many eager tae make your acquaintance." Then he took Val aside, presumably to tell him about Fiona and Tammeron d'Jean.

Mercy was grateful Emma hadn't noticed Kieran's diminished enthusiasm in the press of other family members anxious to speak with the girl who had captured Val's heart. While she met each one, Mercy watched her gradually relax. She seemed especially comfortable with

Joy and Rhianna, but Mercy wasn't surprised, since both young women had that effect on most people.

Even after they all sat down at the table prepared for their luncheon and began eating, conversation flowed freely. Emma seemed amused at a longstanding disagreement between William and Robard over something Val had done with them on a camping trip. Something about a fish.

When she noticed that Kieran hadn't eaten anything but was absently pushing food around his trencher, Mercy gripped his hand under the table. *You were right about Emma. She's a lovely young woman.* As before, he didn't answer her. Was he not listening? Or was he so despondent, he didn't care?

She let go of his hand and straightened, trying to pretend it didn't hurt to be ignored. And then her gaze met Edward's sullen one farther down the table. For the first time, Mercy wished she could speak to *his* mind in that moment. She didn't trust her grandson to refrain from blurting out to Val what Tammeron had done to him.

But the moment passed, and Edward said nothing. Mercy's relief wasn't enough to offset the sadness she felt, though. Nothing should have marred the joy of this first meeting with Emma. Between the missing Fiona and Kieran's dark mood, Mercy wished she were elsewhere.

* * *

Val gratefully led the way to the castle yard after the family luncheon. He'd been so pleased Emma had seemed comfortable with his family! And though the news about Fiona and Tammeron was unfortunate, Val was not entirely surprised. His sister had always been strong-willed. Perhaps that determination would help her make the best of her marriage with Tam. Though Val had not spent much time with him in recent years, he knew from past experience that Tam could be personable and conscientious. He would hope that Fiona could bring out the best in him.

Emma squeezed his hand. *Should we let go now, so tae show your impartiality tae the others?*

Val stopped so Dolan and Kieran could catch up with them. *I suppose it would be best, though I dislike having to stand apart from you on this momentous day.*

'Tis only for a little while. Emma gave him a tight smile. *You're not nervous, are you?*

A wee bit, but not tae worry.

While Dolan and Kieran came nearer, the other dragon candidates approached from the barracks. Some had been present for part or all of the tournament, and others had arrived last night.

I see Caesg. Emma squeezed his fingers once more and pulled away. *I'll go stand with her.*

All right. Val sent her a mental caress while she gave him a quick wave. Then he pulled his attention away from her.

"Looks like everyone has arrived with time to spare." Dolan nodded to the candidates, who gathered in a loose circle.

"Before the dragons arrive, we should have them all line up nearer to the wall, to give the dragons room to land." Val glanced around the yard. Though workers had finished taking down the temporary grandstand, there were more people about than he'd anticipated.

"I'll clear the area," Kieran said, as if he'd read Val's mind. He strode toward a group of ladies and explained the situation, herding them back toward the castle steps.

Val and Dolan placed the hopeful candidates in order by province, beginning with the Highlands.. By the time the last one was in position, the dragons arrived.

Greetings, King Dolan and Prince Val, Cephalorix called out while he circled to land closest to them. Reggie and most of his siblings landed behind their sire.

Welcome, my lord, and all of you as well. As they'd agreed upon, Dolan spoke first. *We thank you for participating with us in the formation of the Royal Dragon Couriers.*

It is our pleasure. When Cephalorix signaled the other dragons, they partially opened their wings and dipped their heads in a salute.

Since everyone is present, we shall begin. Dolan turned to the candidates. "It is not necessary for the dragons to choose one rider at a time. As Lord Cephalorix and I have determined, based on the initial bonding between Prince Val and Regnatorix, all that is necessary is for the dragon and bonded rider to hear one another, now that we have brought you all together in one place." He nodded at Val, who cleared his throat before speaking.

"Please, all of you, close your eyes and quiet your minds. When you hear a single dragon calling to you, reach out with your mind and answer." A smile came unbidden, remembering that first time he and

Reggie had spoken to one another. "You will know without a doubt that you have been chosen."

While all the candidates closed their eyes, Val's gaze trained on Emma. He held back his mind speech from her, so all she would hear was one of the dragons. For he was convinced that one of them would choose her.

Hardly daring to breathe, Val waited with anticipation. As he'd hoped, the Choosing only took a few minutes. Slowly, as if they were sleepwalking, the candidates moved closer to the dragons. One by one, they came to stand before their new friends.

Emma stopped before Veynaria, who lowered her head to nuzzle her chosen rider. With awe shining in her eyes, Emma reached up to gently stroke the dragon's eye ridge.

Val tore his gaze away to see who had been chosen by whom. When he noted that Lord Pascar and Oswald Cornwall were the only two not chosen, he walked straight toward the Lord of Southmoor, feeling badly for him. Oswald stood nearby, trying bravely not to appear as dejected as he must feel.

"I'm sorry, my lord, that you were not chosen, truly I am." Val caught Oswald's gaze. "And I'm also sorry you weren't chosen this time."

"It's probably for the best, Your Highness." Pascar's gaze at the others was wistful, but he quickly pulled himself together. "I would not wish to be distracted from ruling my province."

"You can still speak to the dragons directly," Val reminded both of them. "*Any* of the dragons. That will never change. You will have an advantage in being able to call to them when you need to send a message, or hear them when they send a message to you."

A smile quirked Pascar's lips. "Yes, that will be an amazing help. And I pledge to work closely with Southmoor's dragon rider." He nodded to the beaming Norman who stood beside Alleluia.

Oswald dipped his head. "And I will pledge to Lord Rudyard to always listen for the dragons." A pained look crossed his face before he added in a mumble, "and to work closely with the Southern Woodlands' dragon rider."

"Thank you, Oswald." Val wanted to continue the conversation, but Lord Henry's youngest son drifted away from the dragons and their new partners.

"Your Highness." Pascar lowered his voice, so Val leaned in closer. "I would caution you to keep a close eye on Northland, now that young Sean Hendry is a dragon rider. Geren Wyldwood, his Guardian, is an able leader, but his stepfather Hugh Blythe is an ambitious man, as your brother well knows."

Val nodded, aware of the situation with Sean and Hugh Blythe. "I thank you for the reminder, my lord." He inclined his head to him, and Pascar bowed in return. "I'd best set the tone for these young riders now." With a smile, he pivoted and strode to Dolan's side.

Shall we show them how to mount their dragons now and lead them on their first flight together?

That is an excellent idea, Val. Choose a memorable place nearby where the riders can pledge their fealty to you, while I inform the provincial lords, and then Cephalorix and I will meet you there. He nodded at Val before speaking to the others.

"The Lord of the Sky will now instruct you in mounting your dragon. Once you land in another location nearby, I will join you." Dolan strode toward the crowd of onlookers in the distance. Val presumed the lords were there as well; he hadn't noticed them because he'd been so absorbed in what the dragons were doing. Now he spoke to the new riders.

"I'm grateful for each of you here, and I look forward to working with you. Today is your first lesson: how to climb upon a dragon and prepare to go aloft." He grinned at them, and all of them smiled back, though most revealed at least a little apprehension.

While he approached Reggie, the dragon crouched and instructed the others to imitate him.

"As you can see, the dragons will make it as easy as possible for you to ride them. Their hide is thick and tough, so don't worry about hurting them." He stepped on Reggie's forearm to demonstrate. "You want to sit between the ridges directly above the shoulder, so look for handholds and footrests on your way up." With grace born of long practice, Val made his moves deliberate while he climbed upon his friend's back and swung his long leg over Reggie's backbone. "Now, it's your turn." He winked at Emma, who was the only one present to have ridden before.

Emma and Caesg had no trouble climbing and were seated first. Erian and Sean followed close behind. The others took a bit longer, but in minutes all the riders were in position.

"You'll want to grip with your legs, as if you were riding bareback," Val instructed. "Feel along the ridge in front of you for natural indentations. Those make good places to hold on tightly." He waited until every rider's hands were in position. "Does everyone feel secure?" All of them nodded.

"Since we're inside the castle walls, we will lift off one at a time, to make sure each dragon has plenty of wing room. Your dragon will spring into the air, so your stomach might lurch at first, but you'll soon settle down." He grinned at Kentigern's worried frown. "Regnatorix and I will go first, then Emma and Veynaria, and so on down the line. All right, here we go!" *Reggie, please show them how it's done.*

While he launched himself, Reggie pointed out subtleties of flying with an inexperienced human upon their backs, cautioning them against wild antics lest the riders fall off. Val glanced over his shoulder to make sure Emma and Veynaria were following. One by one the dragons leaped into the air, and the whole lot followed him and Reggie. What a sight to behold! Had there ever been so many humans riding dragonback at the same time?

As Cephalorix and Reggie had agreed upon beforehand, Val led the fledgling riders to the dragon's hidden glen north of the Keep. He wasn't sure, since he and Reggie were flying ahead of everyone, but Val thought he heard exclamations from some of the riders at what they were seeing aloft. Though the Dragon's Backbone lay behind them, their jagged peaks dominated the horizon, if one turned his head. Rivers and ponds and farms passed by beneath them. And of course, the Keep continued to be visible, though it grew smaller and smaller.

Val spied the hill with the northbound road winding along its slope, then the collection of trees sheltering the dragon's home beside a creek. *Reggie, please pass along the message that our destination is just ahead, a clearing within a stand of trees. As we went aloft one by one, so we shall land in the same order. Once you have dismounted your dragon, step aside to make room for those behind you.*

I will, and I have. Reggie sounded thrilled to have so many of his siblings join them in the Royal Dragon Couriers.

After Val and Reggie landed first, they demonstrated to the other riders how to quickly dismount and move out of the way. Once everyone had landed, the clearing seemed crowded, even though more dragons than these had lived here until recently. Val beckoned for the riders to join him within a circle of rocks and stumps off to one side while they waited for Dolan. Emma came to his side, her face glowing. The others conversed among themselves, clearly just as elated after their first flight.

Though Val wanted to hold Emma's hand, he tried to maintain a little distance for the sake of appearing an impartial leader. He could at least speak to her mind.

I take it you enjoyed your solo flight upon Veynaria? He smiled at the brilliance in her green eyes.

Oh, aye! 'Twas a flight o' magic, so it was. Then her eyes widened. *Not that our flight together on Reggie was nae magic also.*

Val gently gripped her arm. *I do understand, Emma. There's no freer feeling than to ride upon a dragon friend.* He grinned. *May you and Veynaria someday be as close as Reggie and I have grown.*

Before he could say more, a large shadow announced the arrival of Cephalorix and Dolan. As soon as the chief dragon landed, Dolan slid down and approached the new dragon riders. He spoke out loud as well as in his mind, so all the riders and their dragons could hear him.

"We welcome all the new dragon couriers and their riders as we begin a new journey together. This has been the dragons' home for several years, and they are always welcome here. But now each of you will have a new home with your new human friend, which your provincial lord will assist in providing for you.

"In a few minutes, you will each pledge your fealty to Prince Val, who as Lord of the Sky is the true head of the Royal Dragon Couriers and as such you must obey him as you would me, your sovereign king. No matter what your current rank or lack of it, as dragon riders all of you are equal because each of you was chosen by the dragons." His sharp gaze scanned each of the riders, and Val wondered if his brother was *Seeing* their thoughts again. They'd each proven to be loyal when they were first chosen as candidates.

With a satisfied nod, Dolan gestured first to Hamelin de Grignon.

"Hamelin, you and Frendatorix will return to Frankland, where you are assigned to Lord Bennet as the province's point of contact with all other dragons and their riders. And now you will swear fealty to Prince Val, who will become your liege lord in all things related to the Royal Dragon Couriers." Dolan beckoned Hamelin to approach Val, and the young lord dropped to his knees and held up his joined hands.

With only a slight bit of nervousness, Val grasped Hamelin's hands while the new dragon rider made his oath of obedience to the Lord of the Sky. Val managed not to wince, thinking about the huge responsibility he felt toward each of these young men and women, many of whom were older than his seventeen years.

As soon as Val accepted Hamelin's oath and raised up the young lord, Dolan recognized the second dragon rider.

"Sean Hendry, you and Damareia will return to Northland, where you are now assigned to Lord Geren Wyldwood your Guardian in your additional role as Royal Dragon Courier." Dolan gestured for Sean, the youngest rider but also the one of highest rank, to kneel before Val and swear his oath.

As Lemedorix's rider, Fletcher Meverel became Westmoor's courier, Erian and Amadorix became Moor Point's, Norman on Alleluia Southmoor's, and Oriana on Neleisia became courier for the Southern Woodlands.

To Val's great joy, both Caesg and her dragon Sacobeia and Kentigern with Malloreia were assigned to the sprawling Highlands, leaving Emma and Veynaria to be a roving pair like he and Reggie, going wherever the need was greatest. Val still hoped Emma would agree to marry him and come live with him at the Keep someday. For now, she could remain in the Highlands to complete her midwife apprenticeship.

Everything was falling into place so nicely, how could anything go awry?

* * *

On their second day in the mountains, Fiona surprised herself by tiring of the magnificent scenery. She had always supposed that if she had the opportunity to travel the wilderness, she would have delighted in the peace and quiet. But it was too quiet. She missed the sounds of civilization.

Even Tam was too quiet, wrapped up in his own thoughts. But to prove she would be a good wife, she did not nag him to pay attention to her. It was her noisy stomach growling from hunger that finally captured his attention midafternoon.

He peered over his shoulder at her. "Hungry? So am I. Let's stop here for the night and find something to eat." Tam gestured to the lovely meadow beside yet another mountain stream.

Fiona eagerly agreed, but let Tam dismount first. He held up his hands, and she slid down into his arms, thankful he didn't try to kiss her. She was sore from riding behind him, and she badly wanted a bath.

Once she'd quenched her thirst from the cold stream, Fiona spied some berry bushes and went to forage. Tam had taken out his makeshift fishing line and was trying to catch locusts for bait. Fiona could sense his presence nearby while she stripped off some berries and shoved them in her mouth, but she was so focused on filling her belly, she didn't spare him a glance.

After four handfuls, the pinching in her stomach eased. She was able to be more selective about the berries and collected only those that were full color. The green ones were too sour to enjoy, while the purple ones squirted juice in her mouth.

Using her blanket to hold the berries, Fiona decided to try her hand at weaving a container with the long wide grass blades growing near the stream. Tam gave her his belt knife so she could cut the grasses evenly. After that he occasionally glanced her way, bemused, in between casts of his fishing line.

First, Fiona sorted the blades on a bare patch of dirt. As she'd done before with strips of cloth, she threaded them over and under, over and under until a large square emerged. Fiona knelt, staring at the woven square, and wondered how she was going to sew the edges together without needle and thread.

Splashing from the creek seized her attention, and she rose to watch Tam land a large fish.

Fish bones! She remembered Papa saying that certain fish bones could be made into needles. But what about thread?

Tam's horse stamped a hoof and snorted, and Fiona remembered Papa also explaining how a long coarse hair from a horse's tail made excellent thread in a pinch.

The fish flopped about in the grass, and Fiona walked closer to see it. "What kind of fish is that?" The dying fish stopped thrashing and lay gasping for air. Tam hooked his fingers under its gills and lifted it up.

"This is a trout." He grinned. "They are good to eat." The fish writhed feebly.

Fiona cringed in empathy. "Will you please put it out of its misery?"

"The knife?" Tam held out his hand, and Fiona returned the blade. He deftly cut off the trout's head, making Fiona wince.

That evening, after Tam cooked the fish and they shared the succulent meat along with the berries, Fiona found a sharp bone with a hole in one end. Tam cut off a hair from Basil's tail, and Fiona was able to thread it through her makeshift needle. But when she tried to sew the edges of the woven grasses to make a container, they tore, making them ragged. Fiona threw down the ruined mat in disgust.

"Giving up so soon?" Tam scooted closer, and Fiona noticed it was now twilight.

"I had no choice. I've ruined it." She gestured to the bruised edges of the grass mat.

"Don't worry about it." Tam's voice was soothing. "We can try again tomorrow." He leaned over and kissed her head. "I'm proud of you for trying, Princess," he murmured. His warm lips were so close, Fiona turned her head to meet them.

With an urgency he'd not shown before, Tam pulled her close, and Fiona pried herself from him with a gasp. "Please stop," she said hoarsely. "We must wait until we are married."

His eyes gleamed in the low light. "I would marry you this instant, if I could, but there is no priest nearby."

"Then we'll ask the first one we find." Fiona trembled but thankfully her voice didn't reveal her turmoil. How was she going to keep from going too far until then?

Chapter 14

Which forsaketh the guide of her youth, and forgetteth the covenant of her God.

Val and Dolan spent another hour planning a weekly meeting with all the dragon riders for the foreseeable future. They would rotate meeting places throughout the width and breadth of the kingdom so that all the dragons and their riders would become comfortable with flying to any place in the realm as well as estimating how long it would take to get there.

One week from today, they would all meet at the newest garrison in the far northwest corner of the Highlands. Once everyone was confident they could fly alone with their dragon to their assigned castle, the other dragon couriers lifted off, one by one.

While he watched them all fly away, Val felt unaccountably anxious, as if he were watching hatchlings leaving the nest. Would they feel all alone and unsure? Especially those who would reach their provincial castles before their own lords arrived on horseback? Dolan had had the foresight to write out a royal order for the riders to carry with them, in case they were questioned by guards or stewards on their journeys. Val would never have thought to do that and now felt badly that he hadn't even considered how valuable it would be.

Now only he and Dolan and Emma remained with their three dragons.

"I hope we covered everything they'll need until next week." Val looked to Dolan for reassurance, and his brother smiled.

"Everything? I'm sure something will come up that we haven't anticipated, but that, after all, is the reason for the weekly meetings." He clapped his hand on Val's shoulder. "It will take a little time to work out all the details. As we think of them, all we have to do is implement them." He raised his brows, and his intense gaze bore into Val. "I am only taking a vocal part in this in the beginning, you know. The day will come when you will be well able to take complete charge on your own."

Val cringed. He couldn't imagine when that day would come. "I am grateful you are so involved right now, considering how busy your schedule is."

Dolan grinned. "I only wish I could always be so involved. Riding about the land with Cephalorix, even if just to meet with other dragon riders, is much more satisfying than meeting with the Privy Council or sitting in judgment or poring over dusty scrolls of obscure laws."

Val started. "Is being king really so full of tedious things?" He frowned, trying to remember Dolan's schedule from the time he was his brother's royal squire.

"You know it is." Dolan peered closely at him and then laughed. "You've forgotten, haven't you?"

Val shrugged, glancing at a puzzled Emma. "I guess I have. Quite a lot has happened since that time."

"I'll say." Now Dolan included Emma in his smiling gaze. "Why don't you two fly back together? I know you want to." He winked, making both of them blush.

"If you insist, Your Majesty." A grin stretched Val's face, and he didn't care how foolish he looked.

Emma dipped in a curtsy. "I thank ye, Your Majesty."

Dolan stepped closer to Emma with a fond smile. "There is no need to be so formal when we are out of the public eye, Emma. Only when others are about. Consider it royal dispensation."

With her lopsided smile, Emma looked from Dolan to Val. "So, are ye goin' tae be a gentleman and escort me home, or nae?"

"Aye, me bonnie lass." Val's attempt at a Highland brogue made Emma chuckle. He clasped Dolan's hand. "I'll see you back at the Keep this evening."

Dolan nodded before mounting Cephalorix. They left first, but Val and Emma weren't far behind.

*

For the first half hour, Val didn't have much to say, either to Emma or to Reggie. He was still feeling the weight of responsibility for the dragon couriers and hoped all of them made it home without incident.

Then they crossed the Highland border, and Emma couldn't contain her excited thoughts.

Look yonder, Val! There be a large herd o' sheep. They move o'er the heath like a flock o' wheelin' gannets.

I see them! Yes, it's enjoyable to watch their movement from above.

He made appropriate comments about all the sights Emma pointed out to him, though his mind was distracted. When they finally reached MacDonald lands and came near to Emma's village, he made himself put aside his concerns in order to give his attention fully to her. He might not see her for another week, after all.

Veynaria and Reggie landed side-by-side and stood patiently while Emma and Val climbed down. Val captured Emma's hand while they walked to her cottage, and the dragons stretched out in the sun.

When they reached the door of the cottage, Emma sat on the bench and Val sat beside her, still holding her hand. She gazed up at him with a concerned frown.

"What about Veynaria?"

"What do you mean? She will stay here with you." Val tried to sound reassuring. They had covered all the details about quartering a dragon in the meeting, hadn't they?

Emma gestured to the clearing where the two dragons napped together. "Be that a proper home for one o' the great dragons?"

"I would say so." Val glanced around. "In fact, I believe Veynaria will have the finest of dragon homes as long as you remain here."

"How so?" Emma cocked her head.

"Not only does she have that quiet meadow in which to rest, but the sea is a stone's throw away with all the fish she can eat."

Emma gasped. "I did nae e'en consider what she might eat. How oft will she need tae eat?"

"Emma." Val gently stroked her hand with his thumb. "The dragons are used to faring for themselves. They are not at all helpless or dependent, like a lady's lap dog." He smiled when he saw her relax.

"Our dragons need only be close enough to come when we need them. Otherwise, they are free to sleep where they find a suitable place and eat almost anything they desire."

"As long as 'tis wild food and not a shepherd's beloved lamb or a farmer's draft horse." Her eyes twinkled with her smile.

"Exactly." He pointed to a thistle plant growing alongside the dirt road. "Did you know dragons consider thistles a delicacy?"

Emma's eyes widened. "Are ye joshin' me?"

He slowly shook his head. "Not at all. Believe me, Veynaria will be very happy here."

She leaned her head against his shoulder and clasped his hand with both of hers. "I be glad tae ken that."

They sat in companionable silence for a little while, each knowing they wouldn't see the other for a week but enjoying the quiet moment together. Finally Emma straightened and looked up at him.

"Will ye have time tae come for me and Veynaria before next week's meeting? If not, I understand. There be no others what have a personal escort, so I should nae expect one."

Val couldn't stand to see her talk herself out of his "escort," so he leaned down and gently kissed her.

"Don't think of it as a privilege no other dragon riders have. It's a way for us to spend a little more time together when that time is difficult to come by—right now." His mouth went dry. He'd almost blurted out that he wanted to marry her. Surely she knew that already? And yet, he was still so afraid she would find a reason to say no when he did ask. Did every young man feel the same apprehension?

"Difficult, aye." Emma sighed. *Nigh impossible, is what it be.*

Nothing is impossible, love. Val drank in the sight of her, for he knew he had to leave soon. "Kieran used to say, 'Where there is a will, there is a way.'"

Emma gave him a lopsided smile. He loved how it made her eyes shine with life and love. "Weel, if cousin Kieran said it, then it must be so."

Laughing, Val rose and scooped up Emma, twirling her around. She put her arms around his neck, and he kissed her deeply. Could she tell he meant it as a promise? That he wanted to pledge his life to her happiness before year's end? If anyone could deduce all that from a kiss, it was Emma.

* * *

Near the end of their third day in the mountains, Fiona grew weary and heartily disgusted at having to wear the same clothes three days in a row. Bad enough she had to sleep in them, too! The afternoon had grown warmer as they climbed a narrow path, only wide enough to walk single file as Tam led the horse. If they came upon a clean pond or a big enough stream or, she could only hope, a waterfall, Fiona would insist on a bath. If she washed her clothes, could she wear her extra outfit while they dried?

To her relief, Tam called a halt for the day in a high meadow beside a spring-fed stream. There were only a few trees at this height, evergreens of some kind. Fiona knelt beside the stream to take a long drink. The water was sweet and cold, and so pure she could see the pebbly bottom.

Tam took their bedrolls from behind the saddle before removing it to let Basil graze. He beckoned to Fiona, and she came to his side.

"Look, Fiona. We're at the highest point. In the morning we begin our descent, and by the third day we'll reach Moor Point."

The view was stunning. Fiona had never seen the land from this height spread out so far before. Beyond the mountain peaks lay valleys and rivers and green clumps of trees. She'd never had the opportunity or desire to ride upon a dragon, but she imagined this was what Val saw all the time. A pang of grief stabbed her. When would she see her brother again?

"It feels as if we are on top of the world," she murmured, pushing away her sadness.

"That's because we are, my love." Tam gently turned her to face him and cupped the back of her head, pulling her closer. "What more do we need than one another?" When he bent his head to kiss her, Fiona encircled his waist and met his lips, intending to make the kiss a brief one. But Tam was so tender, she found she did not want to let him go. Instead, she lost herself in his arms, forgetting her troubles in the warmth of his embrace.

But when his kiss became more urgent, warning bells sounded in Fiona's head. She pulled away, breathless, and stepped back. Tam moaned, and Fiona had to look away from the anguish in his eyes.

"I must bathe and wash my clothes in the stream." She tried to keep the tremor out of her voice. "I'll hurry so I can help you find something to eat and fuel for a fire." When he didn't answer, Fiona pretended she wasn't bothered by his silence.

She collected her spare clothes, her cake of lavender soap, and her cloak to wrap herself in until she dried off. Then she followed the stream until she was out of sight of Tam and the horse. Her thoughts tumbled around inside her head as if she were wrestling with a dark angel.

How long would it be before they found a priest? Tam said they'd be in Moor Point in three days. Could they wait that long? And what if something happened to prevent them from making their vows of marriage? Did those vows really have to be made before a priest? Couldn't the Most High be their witness out here, where they were closer to heaven than Fiona had ever been before? Hadn't the first man and woman had the same Witness?

Glancing over her shoulder to make sure Tam wasn't near, Fiona stripped off her clothing, twisted her hair into a knot at the base of her skull, and stepped into the cold stream. She gritted her teeth while she knelt to immerse herself to the neck and then quickly cleaned herself with the soap. Before leaving the water, she also washed the soiled clothing.

When Fiona saw how she'd clouded the formerly clear stream, she felt a pang of guilt. But she just had to be clean and there was no other way to do it. She only hoped the stream would clear itself shortly. During heavy rains it would become clouded with mud, wouldn't it? So obviously the water had experience cleaning itself.

Feeling better about the water and herself and the question of marriage vows, Fiona rose from the stream and climbed out, wrapping herself in the cloak. First she wrung out her clothes to remove as much of the water as possible. Then she shook out the wet garments and laid them flat upon the nearby rocks to dry. And finally, she glanced toward the meadow to make sure Tam wasn't peeking before she removed the damp cloak and pulled on her spare clothes. Leaving the cloak spread on the rocks, Fiona made her way back to Tam, rehearsing what she would say to him.

* * *

Tam decided to fashion a couple of fishing lines before building a fire. After all, if he couldn't catch one of the fish he'd spied in this stream, a fire wouldn't be as urgent until nightfall, when the temperature would drop enough to need one. The lines he made from vines growing under a stand of gnarled pine trees, and he had two hooks already, but it took him quite a while to find two locusts for bait.

He had just tossed in both lines and made sure they were secure when Fiona returned, barefooted and wearing different clothing. She reached back and let down her luxurious auburn hair, all the while gazing at him intently.

"What is it?" he asked when she came near. She took his hand and led him to the grassy bank, where she pulled him down beside her.

"I have a question." Her eyes glowed with an inner fire, making Tam's heartbeat quicken.

"Yes?" He entwined his fingers in hers and leaned closer.

"Is it possible to make our vows to the Most High here, without a priest?" She licked her lips, drawing his gaze to her mouth.

Tam was so stunned he couldn't answer right away. "You mean, say them to one another *today*?" His heart threatened to leap from his chest, and he had to hold himself still with all the self-control he possessed.

"Yes." Fiona swallowed, obviously nervous, but her voice and purpose were sure. "Of course, we can repeat our vows before an altar later so there will be no question we are legally married."

"Of course!" Tam eagerly agreed. "We'll ask the first priest we can find."

Fiona rose to her knees. "Then I am ready now to become your wife."

Tam went to his knees also and faced her. Then he took both her hands in his. "I have no ring to give you."

Fiona shook her head impatiently. "I don't care about that; I care about you, about us."

Tam raised their joined hands and kissed each of hers. "Who shall go first?"

"I believe you are supposed to go first." Fiona smiled at him, and Tam cleared his throat, not sure he could remember everything he was expected to say in his promise.

"I, Tammeron d'Jean, take you, Fiona MacLachlan, to be my wife, to have and to hold from this day forward, in sickness and health, for better or for worse, um—"

"Rich or poor," she prompted.

"Whether rich or poor, to love and cherish until death parts us, and as the Most High is our witness, I do pledge you my faithfulness." He cringed a little at that word, because he wasn't at all certain he could remain faithful to one woman his entire life. At this moment, however, he was willing to promise anything, if it meant they didn't have to wait to consummate the marriage.

"I, Fiona MacLachlan, take you, Tammeron d'Jean, to be my husband, to have and to hold from this day forward, for better or for worse, in sickness and in health, for richer or poorer, to love, honor, and cherish until death parts us, and as the Most High is our witness, I do pledge to you my faithfulness in heart and soul and body." Tears shimmered in Fiona's eyes, and Tam did not dwell on the minor differences between their two vows.

"Is that all we need to say?" he asked in a quiet voice.

She nodded. "I think so. After all, the Most High won't pronounce us man and wife out loud, even though we are now married, here in the sight of heaven." When she lifted her gaze to the clear sky, Tam did likewise. The sun sank low in the west, hovering above the horizon. Soon the stars would appear on this, their wedding night.

"Then I think it is time I kissed the bride." Tam grinned when Fiona returned her gaze to him.

Laughing, she threw her arms around his neck, and he drank of her love until the moon rose hours later.

Chapter 15

For their calamity shall rise suddenly; and who knoweth the ruin of them both?

Fiona opened her eyes at the sound of sweet birdsong. The sun's rays peeked between two of the distant mountains, bathing the meadow with a golden hue.

She turned her head to gaze at the sleeping Tam. *My husband.* After last night, she felt such a tender connection with him, as if they were meant to be together for all time. Why had no one ever mentioned that part of becoming one in marriage was the profound joining of *souls*, not merely flesh?

Tam looked even more beautiful in peaceful sleep. His face was relaxed, his full lips turned up in a smile, and his long dark lashes quivered. Did he dream of her like she had dreamed of him?

She felt impatient for him to awaken, but she did not try to disturb him. Her stomach growled, and for the first time since they'd exchanged their vows, she recalled they had not eaten anything.

Fiona slowly rose from their makeshift bed—Tam's cloak—and pulled on her clothes. Then she picked her way to the stream to take a long drink of the cold water. A splash nearby drew her to investigate. It was a fish caught on one of Tam's lines. Had it been trapped there all night?

For a moment, Fiona felt sorry for the fish and considered releasing it, but her stomach rumbled so alarmingly, she changed her mind. This fish was large enough to feed them both. It would be exceedingly foolish of her to let it go. Especially since there were no berry bushes in this high meadow.

So she gathered the few dead branches and twigs she could find and stacked them on a bare patch of dirt. By that time, Tam had risen and dressed. He came to her, smiling.

"Good morrow, sweet Fiona." He pulled her to him and kissed her passionately. She had to break their contact before she lost herself to his caresses. They had more urgent tasks to accomplish right now, and she had to remind him.

"Should we not eat and continue on our journey while there is light?" At his crestfallen demeanor, she added coyly, "After all, night will fall again soon enough, when we can do naught else but keep one another warm."

Tam chuckled, and his eyes brightened. "You're right, of course." He stroked her cheek and then cupped her chin. "You are so bewitching, my love. I shall have difficulty thinking about anything other than your exquisite kisses until we stop again." He leaned forward and kissed her more gently. This time he was the one to pull away. "I heard the fish. Since you have provided the wood, I shall start the fire and cook our breakfast."

Though it was not as fully cooked as Fiona preferred, she ate ravenously in between shared glances and smiles. Then they packed the horse, and Tam led the way down the other side of the mountain.

*

By mid-afternoon, the clouds to the south had grown to an impressive height, darkening in a menacing way as they curled toward the mountain peaks. Then the wind began to gust, making Basil shy and snort, his eyes rolling and his nostrils flaring. Tam could hardly control him.

Fiona was especially glad they weren't riding the horse when a bolt of lightning split the air above their heads, followed immediately by a deafening crack of thunder. Basil whinnied and jerked the reins from Tam's hand. Then the horse reared and galloped away.

"No!" Fiona made as if to run after him, but Tam grabbed her waist.

"We'll find him later," he shouted in her ear over the howling wind. "We must find shelter."

Torrential rain began to pour down, soaking them. Tam led the way, and Fiona tried to keep hold of him, but the wind and the slippery path conspired to keep them apart.

Finally, after another startling crash of thunder, Tam grabbed Fiona's hand.

"Ahead is a traveler's cave I've slept in before," he cried out while pulling her along.

Trusting her husband to find the way, Fiona concentrated on placing her feet so she did not stumble. The next thing she knew, the rain stopped pelting her. They had entered a small rocky cave with a dirt floor littered with twigs and leaves. She'd heard of traveler's caves but expected more than this. Did an animal live here now?

She stood just inside the opening, shivering. While Tam went deeper into the cave, Fiona hugged herself, and her thoughts tumbled over one another. How long would they have to stay in this cave? What would they eat? If they couldn't find the horse, how would they walk all the way to Moor Point? And if they reached Moor Point, how would they live without her jewels, which were securely strapped to Basil's saddle?

"Are you cold?" Tam said, startling her.

"Y-yes." Fiona clenched her teeth to stop their chattering.

Tam held up a sleeping fur and shook out the leaf clutter. "If we hang up our wet clothes, they will be drier by morning, and then we can look for Basil."

Even though the cave was warmer than the stormy wind and rain outside, it was still cold. She nodded at the sleeping fur. "Is that large enough for both of us?"

Tam came nearer. "Of course it is, as long as we stay close and warm one another with our body heat." He spread out the sleeping fur on the dirt and began unlacing his sodden shirt.

Fiona stripped off her wet clothes and arranged them on the protrusions of rock. She pushed her wet hair behind her ears and took a deep breath. It would be difficult to put aside her worries, but she determined to do so, at least for this night.

Tam was right; the sleeping fur had plenty of room, and they were able to keep each other warm. However, there was nothing to be done about the utter darkness after night fell except wait for the sun to rise again.

* * *

While Dolan and Val were busy with the business of the new dragon couriers, Kieran met with Captain Hodor to see if any of the search parties had reported finding Fiona and Tammeron. When Dolan had first instructed Hodor to gather the best trackers, he'd impressed upon them how important it was not to injure either of the young people, even though they should regard young d'Jean as potentially violent. Kieran hated that it was even a possibility, but there was no doubt he had treated Edward abominably and had to be arrested.

Kieran had wanted to join the search, but Mercy had convinced him to wait at the Keep for news. Was she afraid he might lose control and vent his wrath upon Tammeron? Mercy surely knew he was capable of doing so, but did she realize he was angry enough to do the young man even worse harm than a black eye?

He was so thankful Slade and Aleia had left before dawn yesterday for Castle Frankland. They didn't yet know the news about their son, but they would discover it soon enough. Kieran knew they'd done their best to raise him to be morally upright and hard-working, but he was Mortimer's get, after all. Sometimes blood trumped good parenting, and it hadn't helped that Tammeron had been assigned to knights outside of Frankland. Kieran had argued against him serving Sir Ronan MacCallum as a page, and it appeared Sir Artemis Villeroy had not been the best choice when Tammeron had been his squire, either.

Wearily Kieran climbed the steps to his rooms. He had never felt so old, and he wouldn't turn fifty until next year. If he was this wrung out now, he'd be positively decrepit in a year or two.

He entered the empty sitting room and stood there dumbly, staring at Fiona's door. His wee lass had run off with a scoundrel, and their family would never be the same again. And—

And Fiona would never be his wee lass again.

"I dinna want him for a son-in-law," he muttered. "How could ye have chosen him, lass? O' all the young men in all the land, you had tae choose *that* one!"

Kieran sank into the nearest chair and dropped his head to his hands.

"Father?"

Kieran lifted his head and met his son's troubled gaze. "Hello, Tris."

Tristam studied him with a frown. "You look unwell. Let me *See* you, Father." He held up his hands. Strong hands. Hands that had saved lives and Healed many injuries and illnesses during his young life.

His son should have had more time to be a lad, go on adventures with young friends, not spend hours shut up in his room with stacks of scrolls. That was his fault too, surely. He could have made sure Tris had more of a carefree childhood and not grow up so quickly with adult responsibilities.

He wanted to *See* his old Da, did he? Kieran's first impulse was to refuse him. He and Mercy had learned long ago it was not possible to Heal a broken heart. But why not let him try?

"All right, son." He started to rise, but Tristam shook his head.

"Stay there, Father. And try to relax." He laid his hands on Kieran's head.

When Tristam's hands made contact, Kieran shut his eyes and made the effort to keep his breathing steady. Even with his eyes closed, he knew the moment Tristam called upon his gift, both from the sensation of warmth and through the mental connection he and his son had developed years ago.

While Tristam silently examined him, Kieran thought back to the day the boy's gift had manifested itself. He'd been only four years old. Four! But his powerful Healing gift had appeared full-grown in a time of desperate need when Bennet's life had hung in the balance after breaking his neck. During the past ten years of study and practice, Tristam's gift had surpassed Mercy's, at least in the essentials. He had not yet learned enough about human nature to know how best to deal with individual patients and their emotional needs. In time, after he lived a few more years and developed more common sense, Kieran felt he would grow to understand that part of his Healing gift better and better.

His *gift*. Kieran recalled something Fiona had said recently. Something about not having a gift of her own. Had he tried to reassure her? Or had he, like Tristam, not been attuned to her emotions when she'd revealed her despair? Why wouldn't the lass be grieved over not being gifted, especially when all four of her siblings did have one or more of the Most High's rare and special gifts?

Had he driven his daughter into the arms of a scoundrel because he'd dismissed her concerns? His eyes flew open, and Tristam withdrew the Healing gift.

"Your heart is strained, Father. The pressure in the blood vessels is elevated." Tristam's frown deepened. "You must find a way to calm yourself. Fiona's leaving is not your fault."

"Oh, but I fear it is. I have failed your sister." Kieran clenched his fists, and Tristam firmly pried the fingers apart.

"Here, place your hands in mine." Tristam held both hands palm up, and Kieran laid his across them. Instinctively he gripped them.

"No, not like that." Tristam pulled his hands away and again held them palm up. "Set them atop mine, lining up your fingers in the same direction, but don't grip them. Keep your hands, and especially your fingers, lightly resting on top."

With a frown of concentration, Kieran did as his son directed.

"Good. Now, close your eyes." Kieran did so. "And sit calmly while you concentrate on taking measured breaths."

Though it was difficult to quiet his mind, Kieran made himself breathe slowly while counting each inhalation and exhalation. It became his single thought.

Do you feel that, Father?

Kieran continued to count his breaths while opening his awareness. At some point, Tristam had called on the Healing power again. Was that what he felt? No, there was something else.

I feel peace between us, coming from your hands into mine. Is that through your gift?

In part, yes. But it is possible for one who is not a Healer to calm a distressed person, with this kind of touch and the right intention.

Kieran opened his eyes. Tristam's frown had relaxed, and he even smiled a little.

"Thank you, son. I do feel better." Though his heart was too heavy to smile back, he squeezed Tristam's hands before giving his precious son a MacLachlan bear hug like his brothers always gave him.

In spite of the heartaches, truly family was a wondrous blessing.

* * *

In their guest room, Joy had almost finished packing when Robard burst through the doorway.

"Mother, may Will sleep in my room tonight?" His eyes pleaded with her, making her frown in puzzlement.

"He's coming home with us in the morning, dear. Don't you think his family will want to spend the evening with him?"

Robard shrugged. "That's the problem; Edward is spending the night in the royal suite, since Lord Henry hasn't returned to Southmoor yet." He grimaced. "At least Edward is going back to Southmoor, now that Tammeron won't be there anymore."

"Oh? Who told you that?" Joy folded the last handkerchief and sat on the nearest chair, giving him her full attention.

"I heard Auntie Rhianna and Grandmother talking about it." He blushed and ducked his head.

"Robard! You know what your father and I have told you about eavesdropping." Joy pretended to be more stern than she felt when she remembered she'd been guilty of listening in on others' conversations herself.

"Yes, Mother. I suppose it is rude, but how else am I supposed to learn what's really going on around here?" He balled his fists on his hips, and Joy had to hold in a laugh.

"I concede your point," she finally said, holding up a finger to stop him from speaking. "But, you must tell William that Auntie Joy wants to remind him he will be spending a fortnight with you at Castle Frankland, and you can stay up all night once we get home, and not before."

Robard let out a sigh. "All right, I'll tell him." He started toward the door but turned back at the threshold. "We're leaving early, aren't we?"

"Yes, son. Directly after breakfast."

"Treble good!" He grinned when Joy chuckled.

"What in the world does that mean?" She smiled at his enthusiasm.

"Just something Will and I made up. It means that something is not merely good but very *very* good."

"Hence the 'treble'?" She smirked. "As long as you and Will stay out of *trouble*."

With a laugh, Robard left, and Joy heard his running feet.

The room became quiet. Too quiet.

Joy rose and went to the window seat, peering outside to the castle yard. So many had already gone home, including Aleia and Slade. She would see Aleia again the day after tomorrow. What would she say to her friend? Surely by now she had heard the news about Tam?

How was she supposed to comfort Aleia when she couldn't comfort herself? She blamed herself for not making time to speak with Fiona after she'd been confined to her room. There had never been a time that Joy couldn't coax Fiona into admitting what was troubling her, and even more importantly, Joy had always been able to encourage her strong-willed sister to do the right thing, even when no one else could reach her.

She would never forgive herself if anything happened to Fiona because Joy had filled her days during this visit with other people, none of whom needed her more than Fiona apparently had. She must have felt desperate indeed to elope with Tam. Knowing now what kind of character the young man had, Joy was convinced Fiona had not been thinking clearly at all to leave with him.

Or else, she'd known her family would not approve, and so had run away before any of them could prevent the elopement.

Joy bowed her head to pray, but she didn't know what to pray for. Should she ask that Fiona's eyes be opened in time to prevent the marriage? Or should she pray that both she and Tam would grow up quickly and make the best of it?

Or should she simply say, "Thy will be done," and ask forgiveness for her part in not reaching out to her sister?

She chose the third option, even knowing that after the Most High forgave her, she would still feel the guilt of her neglect.

* * *

The moment Kieran returned, Mercy met him in the sitting room. She should have prayed for serenity, to be still, to listen, and not blurt out her fears to him. But resentment at her daughter's foolish choice rose up within her.

"How did we fail Fiona so badly? She is the most headstrong person I have ever known." Mercy's gut twisted. "She has leaped headlong into disaster, and there's no way to stop her now." She lowered her voice. "Perhaps there never was a way to stop her."

"I always believed our lass had a good heart." The anguish on Kieran's face did not match his calm words. "I thought we needed only tae love her." He reached over to take Mercy's hand.

His refusal to see his contribution to the situation infuriated her.

"Why have you never accepted that you have been too lenient with Fiona *all* her life? Part of loving our children is disciplining them, to keep them from making the choices that will result in permanent,

162

life-destroying consequences." *Like running away with Mortimer's son. Oh, why can you not see that Fiona has bewitched you?*

But he seemed not to hear that last. *Kieran?* She squeezed his hand, and he lifted his head, but did not answer right away. With a puzzled look on his face, he finally spoke.

"Ye dinna understand, Mercy. Ye were a mum from the time ye were Fiona's age. I didna become a Da 'til I was much older. How could I be harsh with the lass I ne'er hoped tae have? I was sure if I only loved her enough, she would grow up tae be a loving, sensible woman, like her mother." He tried to smile, but his heart wasn't in it.

"But love is more than kind words and affection." Mercy fought to keep from shouting. "Love is doing what is best for our children, even when it is difficult, even when it's painful." *Kieran? How can you not see what is under your very nose?*

He looked up and met her gaze, but he acted like he hadn't heard her mind speech again. Then he frowned. "Did ye not hear me in your mind just now?"

Mercy shook her head. "I have been speaking to your mind, also, and you have not answered me once."

Kieran's frown deepened. He had never looked so old before. "What does it mean, that we can no longer hear one another's thoughts?"

Maybe it means our love has died. Years of conflict over our daughter has finally broken our bond. Half of Mercy's heart was devastated by the loss, and the other half was furious with Kieran and Fiona both.

"Since so few have had this ability, there is no way to know if it can be undone." She pulled her hand away.

"Then perhaps 'tis for the best we canna know one another's hearts, since apparently they no longer beat as one." His green eyes briefly flashed anger, which faded into misery and despair. He strode away without a backward glance.

Mercy's pride kept her from following him. She clenched her fists and walked to her chair by the fireplace, sinking onto it without relaxing.

Why was he so stubborn that he could not see how years of coddling Fiona had created a spoiled, ungrateful girl? She was sixteen. Sixteen! And still she had not matured enough to think about others more than she thought about her wants and desires. At sixteen, Mercy had been married more than a year and had given birth to a child.

But she could not compare her life to Fiona's. Mercy had had to become a mother to her infant brother when she was only ten. She'd had to grow up quickly, while Fiona had lived a sheltered life.

If Valerian had been Fiona's father—but no, she had vowed to herself long ago never to compare Kieran with her first husband. It was utterly unfair of her to do that, and it helped nothing. In her experience, there were some personalities much more difficult than others, and Fiona had always been challenging. She would test the patience of the most gentle person in the world!

Mercy hugged herself, and her head felt terribly heavy. The weight of this situation was more than she or Kieran could bear, obviously. They'd had disagreements and even arguments over Fiona many times, but they'd never had trouble speaking to one another mind-to-mind. Never!

She lifted her head, gazing into the empty fireplace without really seeing it. Had Fiona truly come between her and Kieran? She'd known other parents to whom that had happened, and she'd always thought it the most tragic and avoidable situation. With a sob, she fell to her knees and covered her face with her hands.

Oh, God Most High, please let us find a way to mend this rift, even if we lose our mind speech forever. Please, help me to see where I have contributed to the problem and humble myself enough to apologize.

Chapter 16

He that troubleth his own house shall inherit the wind.

When Fiona awakened, she found herself in Tam's arms and remembered they were in a cave. Sunlight made the cave entrance glow, so she pulled away from her husband's embrace, eager to go outside.

"What's the matter, love?" he murmured, slowly opening his eyes.

"It's morning. We must find Basil and leave these dreadful mountains." Fiona hurried to her clothes and found they were still damp. Shivering, she pulled them on anyway. Perhaps they'd fully dry in the sun.

Tam pushed himself to a sitting position and yawned. "Why the hurry? The morning is new."

Fiona collected his clothing and tossed it to him. "I'm hungry and thirsty, and I'd like to find an inn with a soft bed, which we can't pay for unless we find Basil." She stood with her hands on her hips until Tam dressed himself. Then he came to her and put his hands on her shoulders.

"I'm sorry, love. You're absolutely correct; we must find the horse before we can do anything else." He leaned down and kissed her, but she didn't let him linger. Instead, she took his hand and they exited the cave into a beautiful clear morning.

They headed down the mountain, stopping at the first stream to quench their thirst. There was no sign of Basil, but Fiona kept scanning the way ahead as well as the path, searching for hoof prints.

When they came to a switchback with a steep drop-off, on impulse Fiona carefully peered over the edge. With a gasp, she spied Basil's broken body on the rocks far below.

"Tam, look!" She pointed, and Tam came to see. He let out a growl.

"No! How will we reach Moor Point in time?" His eyes were wild, so Fiona gently grasped his arm.

"In time for what?"

"To get the offered job, of course." Tam's voice rose in agitation, so Fiona pointed down the cliff to distract him.

"Can we get down there and retrieve our things, at least?" She made her voice calm, as if he were a distressed horse in need of reassurance.

"I don't know how." Tam shook his head. "We're descending along this path, but it won't take us down there." He jabbed his finger. "It may not be possible to get to the body."

"We can try." Fiona turned and continued down the path, hoping Tam would soon follow.

*

Hours later, they found themselves in a broad valley at the base of the mountain. Fiona had lost her sense of direction with all the switchbacks.

"Which way to the place where Basil fell?" She gazed up at Tam, weary and with her belly pinching sharply.

Tam looked around and then up at the sun. "I have no idea, Fiona." When he met her gaze, she was alarmed to see defeat in his eyes. "We're lost."

"We're not lost," she said firmly. "You said we just needed to go south." She pointed to the sun. "Which way is south?"

Tam threw up his hands. "How should I know? It's midday. Until the sun lowers in the west, I won't be able to find south."

Fiona searched the valley, undaunted. "Then I'm going to find water and something to eat." Again, she set out, hopeful Tam would come along too.

She hadn't gone far before she heard the rushing of water ahead and quickened her pace. After struggling through the tall grasses, she came upon a fast-moving river and hurried down the bank to the water's edge, dropping to her knees. She filled her cupped hands with the cold water and sucked it greedily, wishing for a cup, or even a bucket. After the fourth handful, her attention was drawn to familiar plants growing at the water's edge. Was that sweet water grass?

Fiona plucked some of the long bright green leaves and rinsed them in the water before stuffing them in her face. The sweet juices soothed her hunger as much as the grass itself. After she'd eaten her fill, she gathered an armful for Tam.

"What have you got there?"

Fiona turned at the sound of his voice and hurried up the bank to offer him the sweet grass.

"Something to fill your belly and give you strength to continue on." She smiled, hoping to encourage him.

Tam frowned and broke off one of the leaves. "Are you certain this is edible?" He eyed it with distrust, making Fiona angry.

"Of course I'm certain! My mother, who is a Healer, taught me about plants, and I've just eaten about this much of the sweet grass." She glared at him. "Don't you trust me?"

He held up his hands. "No need to snap at me. I trust you." He took a bite of the grass, and his eyes widened. Without a word, he held out his hands, and Fiona gave him the entire bundle. Then she stormed away.

She was trying to be a supportive wife, she really was! Didn't Tam understand how difficult this situation was for her? They were lost in the Dragon's Backbone with nothing but the clothes on their backs. No horse, no supplies, and no way to purchase any even if they could find a town. She suspected the nearest people lived many miles from where they were.

Oh, why hadn't they taken the time to better plan this journey?

* * *

By the time Tam had eaten all of Fiona's sweet grass, he had managed to calm his panic and think more clearly. Obviously, he and Fiona were in a dire predicament. The loss of her jewels was devastating, and he had no immediate way to replace them. All he carried on his person was his belt knife and a pouch with his flint, a few small coins, and Lord Henry's cloak clasp. If he didn't reach the village attached to Sir Artemis' manor within three days, he would miss the opportunity his old gambling associate, Rodney Folville, had offered him.

Folville had been constable of Cawthorne Village until he'd discovered a more lucrative occupation, that of relieving foolish wealthy folk of their excess goods. He'd asked Tam to join him, but at the time he thought he'd wanted to continue on the path of knighthood and said no. Folville had said as long as Tam could return to Moor Point before Saint Adrian's Day, he could still accept the offer. After that, Folville had to move on to his hideout near Ravenford Village, and Tam might not be able to find him.

An image of his pathetic aunt came to mind, how she desperately clung to an illusion of her former wealth. For a moment Tam wondered if the d'Evrow family had fallen because of someone like Rodney Folville, but he didn't think so. Folville had assured him, he never took more than his due, for he never wanted anyone to go hungry. In fact, he often shared his spoils with the unfortunate.

Tam snorted. He wanted to believe that, but it seemed unlikely. His gaze traveled to Fiona's angry back, ramrod straight. Could they find a church and ask for alms? No, he wouldn't do that. Besides, Fiona would insist they say their vows to the priest right away, and he was having second thoughts about chaining himself to her for the rest of his life. She was beautiful, true, and passionate and exciting, but at heart she was a spoiled princess with a fiery temper. That aspect of her would grate on him until it became unbearable.

Better they find the quickest route to Moor Point. If he tired of Fiona by then, he could always leave her at Sir Aidan Fitzhugh's manor, as it was close to Cawthorne Village. Since their "marriage" was not legally binding, he would have no more obligation to her.

Meanwhile, she would make the journey bearable at night, every night they were together. And as long as he delivered her safely to Sir Aidan, no one could accuse him of wrongdoing.

With new resolve, he strode toward Fiona. It was not as easy as it had been to force tenderness into his voice.

"Fiona, love? I'm sorry for being irritable." He stepped in front of her and made his face sorrowful. "Will you please forgive me? I know you are as concerned as I am about our circumstances." He held out his hands, and to his surprise, she threw herself into his arms.

"Oh, Tam, I'm sorry for getting so angry. I'm frightened, and I let myself lose my temper instead of being supportive. Can you forgive me?" She stared up at him, and though she was disheveled, her eyes wide with fright, she had never been more appealing to him than in her helplessness.

He held her close and murmured in her ear. "Of course, I forgive you, my love. We will find a way, I promise you." Before she could answer, he kissed her, tasting her salty tears. He did not stop until he felt her tension ease. Good, she was more pliable now.

"Come, Fiona." He put all the confidence he had into the words. "We are young and strong, and we will make it to Moor Point."

She smiled timidly. "You're right. Together, we can accomplish anything we set our minds to do."

Hand-in-hand, they walked the length of the valley while the sun sank in the west. Now Tam was sure which direction to go.

* * *

Three days after the last of the tournament guests had departed the Keep, Mercy and Kieran ate a private breakfast in their suite. Though they sat at the same table, they might as well be in separate towers. Kieran had not spoken to her or even met her gaze since yesterday, and Mercy was at a loss to know how to open a conversation with him. That he sat here with her, even in silence, gave her hope that he wanted to reconcile, though he probably felt as reluctant as she to be the first one to speak.

At a knock on the door, Kieran jerked up his head. "Come," he called out.

A courier opened the door, but he carried no letter. The young man went down on one knee.

"My lord, one of Captain Hodor's trackers has sent word he found something in the Dragon's Backbone and wishes you to come and see for yourself. He will meet you at the southmost edge of Briarwood Village at noon today and lead you there."

Kieran jumped up from the table with the most energy Mercy had seen in him in a long time.

"Do ye know which tracker? Did he tell ye more details?"

"Talon Fowler, my lord. And he revealed no details, said he wanted to show you what he found."

"Thank you, I will be waiting for him at noon." Kieran fished a coin from his belt pouch, and the courier took it with a bow, shutting the door behind him.

"What do you think he found?" Mercy rose from her chair but did not approach him.

Kieran shook his head. "Impossible tae guess." He briefly met her gaze. "I will plan tae be gone for a while. But first, I need to let Dolan know."

Without another word, or even a peck on her cheek, Kieran quit the room, leaving Mercy standing there. A myriad of emotions warred within her—anxiety about Fiona's safety, anger at her foolishness, sadness about the effect her choice was making on her family, and a growing helpless despair that her relationship with Kieran might be forever strained because of this situation.

The childish part of her wanted him to feel the hurt his distance had caused her, but she struggled instead to understand his own despair and guilt. He *had* been too lenient with Fiona, but Mercy could not honestly blame his actions for Fiona's choices. She had made her own mistakes with Fiona. Their daughter had free will, and she had been taught right from wrong. In the end, the choice was hers, and she would suffer the worst consequences, if what Mercy feared most had come to pass.

She wiped the tears that spilled from her eyes and walked to the bedchamber. The canopied bed stood accusing her, and she wanted to shout that it wasn't her fault Kieran hadn't slept with her in several days. He'd used a cot in the sitting room, if he'd slept at all, and now he was going to the mountains with a tracker. How long would he be gone? There was no way to know.

She had missed her chance to apologize, to find a way to restore their mind speech. And if Fiona never returned, or God forbid, if she was dead, Mercy was convinced Kieran would be so devastated, she might never have the chance to make things right with him.

God Most High, please let Fiona be alive. And if she is, please let her come to her senses. Forgive me for my part in failing her and Kieran both, and if it be Your will, let Kieran and I rekindle our love so our marriage will not die.

With a sigh, Mercy pulled Kieran's sturdy saddle bag from the wardrobe and set it on the bed. Then she collected the extra clothing and supplies he usually took with him on journeys. It wasn't often she packed the bag for him, but she had done it often enough through the years and knew what he liked to take.

She started to tie down the flap, but a strong urging stopped her. Instead, she went to her desk and took out a small piece of parchment. On it she wrote:

My dearest husband, I am praying daily for your safety as well as Fiona's. May the Most High give you success in finding her, and may He give us the strength to love one another as we once did, not letting anyone or anything come between us.

Waiting anxiously for your return,
Mercy

She read it through twice. It was impossible to put into words what she was feeling right now, but hopefully when Kieran read the note, he would be in a frame of mind to see her honest desire to reconcile.

Not long after she carried the bulging bag into the sitting room and resumed her seat at the table, Kieran returned. Mercy rose, wanting more than anything to rush to his side and embrace him, but the look on his face stopped her. He noted the saddle bag and picked it up. Finally he met her gaze. Concern deepened the lines in his face.

"I suppose you packed all the usual?" There was no warmth in his voice.

"Yes, love. Everything you've taken before." She maintained eye contact with him, though it was painful. He looked away first.

"Thank you. I will send word if I can." He turned to leave, and she took a few steps closer.

"How long will you be gone?" She wrung her hands, feeling utterly helpless.

Kieran stopped but did not look back. "I have no idea. It depends on what I find." He hurried out the door as if he couldn't get away fast enough.

Mercy waited until his footsteps faded on the stairs before she sank back to her chair and wept.

Chapter 17

Confidence in an unfaithful man in time of trouble
is like a broken tooth, and a foot out of joint.

When night fell, Fiona and Tam had reached another valley. All they'd managed to find for food was more of the sweet grass along the river and a few handfuls of berries. Tam was now more interested in traveling as far and as quickly as possible than in catching a fish or building a fire. Although the night was not as cold as the previous two, and they kept one another warm in their makeshift nest of long grasses beneath the stars, Fiona sensed Tam's attention was elsewhere.

Well, of course your husband is distracted, she scolded herself. *The situation has not yet improved. Give him all the grace you have to give.*

So when the time came for them to sleep, Fiona did not insist he reassure her or tell her all his plans. Instead, she let him turn away and pillow his head upon his arms. She waited until his breathing told her he was asleep, and then Fiona scooted over beside him, close enough for warmth but not so close as to risk waking him up. It took her a long time to fall asleep, and then her dreams were not at all pleasant.

*

Fiona startled awake when she felt the absence of Tam's warmth. The glow of dawn slowly lightened the valley, and she pushed herself upright in a panic. Where was he? Had he left her here alone?

She scanned all around until she spied him walking back from the river. With a sigh of relief, she hurried toward him.

"Is anything wrong?" Her voice trembled more than she wanted it to.

"More than the obvious, you mean?" A frown creased his brow.

"Well, yes." She stepped aside and let him walk past her.

"Then, no, there is nothing wrong that hasn't already been wrong." He kept walking, and she followed him.

They trudged along, traveling south, Fiona presumed, with infrequent brief stops throughout the day. Fiona was tired and hungry and near despair, but she kept her peace. Tam surely felt the same, so voicing her concerns would do nothing to improve their situation.

By evening, Fiona's feet were sore. She was so hungry, she would have eaten an insect, could she have caught one. Papa had told her locusts had a nutty flavor when roasted over a fire. Her mouth watered, thinking about it.

When Tam stopped at the crest of a grassy hill, Fiona almost bumped into him. She turned and scanned the way they had come, pleased to note that the tallest mountain peaks lay behind them. Would they reach Moor Point sometime tomorrow? She opened her mouth to ask Tam, but he spoke first.

"There's smoke at the far end of that valley." He pointed ahead.

Fiona came to stand beside him. She narrowed her eyes and stared in the direction he pointed. Something moved, but in the waning light she couldn't tell for sure whether it was smoke.

"Does that mean someone is living there?" Her brief hope was dashed when she realized how long it would take to walk from here, and night was falling.

"Few people live in this region, but it looks like a place for a farm to me." Tam started walking down the other side of the hill.

"It will be long dark before we reach it," Fiona pointed out while scrambling to follow him. "Should we not wait until tomorrow, after the sun comes up?"

Tam spread his long arms. "There's not a good place to stop here. We've got to get water, and there's a river running toward the smoke, so we might as well keep going."

Fiona was too tired to argue. It wasn't long since they'd drunk from a spring higher up, but they would grow thirsty soon enough. The spark of hope rekindled, and Fiona imagined bedding down in a farmer's barn with, perhaps, a crust of bread or an egg, if his wife was kindly toward others who had suffered misfortunes.

She wouldn't hesitate to help others, so why wouldn't this farmer's wife?

Tam's pace increased, and he slowly pulled ahead of her while the last glow of sunlight faded. Fiona tried to speed up, but her legs felt as if they'd turned to iron.

"Tam, please! I can't go any faster."

He stopped, but she couldn't tell if he was facing her or not. "You must walk faster. We've got to reach the farmhouse before they go to sleep. It's our only chance at food and shelter for the night."

Thoughts of food pinched her belly with a sharp twisting pain, but they also propelled her forward. When she reached Tam, she thought he might take her hand and encourage her, but he simply began walking again. With a sigh, Fiona trudged after him, forcing herself to take one step after another at his pace. It wasn't fair, though; Tam's legs were longer than hers, so she had to take more strides.

When at last the sound of water rushing over rocks could be heard, it was the most beautiful music to Fiona's ears. She and Tam stumbled down the bank and drank of the water. Unlike the springs they'd found in the mountains, this river water tasted a little muddy. It didn't stop Fiona from quenching her thirst, and she marveled at how low she'd come in just a few days.

She must look a fright, but she did not care if the farmer and his wife saw her in this state. All she cared about was something to eat and a place to sleep where she wouldn't wake up damp from the night's dew. It was a predicament she never could have imagined.

After they climbed up the bank, Tam gave a cry of excitement. "Look! There's a light. A lantern, or a fire. Come on!" He strode forward, and Fiona forced herself to keep up with him.

They headed for the distant light, and it slowly grew closer and larger. Fiona kept expecting it to go out long before they reached it. Surely half the night had passed already?

To her surprise, they finally arrived at a small structure dimly lit by the rising moon. The light came from a fire inside, so the smoke Tam saw must have come from a chimney or vent in the thatched roof.

When they approached the house, for the door stood open, making the fire visible, Fiona felt an inkling of fear. Would the farmer think them intruders and turn them away? Did Tam have a plan for how to approach the inhabitants of this isolated homestead?

Wordlessly, Tam took Fiona's arm and pulled her with him to the open door. He lightly rapped on the door frame.

"Hello? Is anyone there? My wife and I have lost our horse and supplies in the mountains. Can you help us?" Tam's voice sounded friendly. Could the farmer hear his sincerity?

"Go away," a gruff voice barked. "No charity here."

"Please, sir, we've eaten nothing but grass and berries for days. We're willing to work."

"Don't have work for you. Get on with you now."

Fiona's anger rose, fueled by hunger and indignation. "What kind of person would turn away two unfortunate souls? Where is your heart?"

The light from the fire was suddenly blocked by the silhouette of an enormous man dressed in rough furs.

"I have no heart." He growled like a big dog, and Fiona inched backward.

"If you have no heart," Tam said, "then maybe we can appeal to other instincts." He gestured to Fiona. "This is the king's own sister. If you treat us well, he will be sure to reward you."

Fiona wanted to protest, but it was too late. The man stepped outside and leered at Fiona.

"Sister to the king?" He roared with laughter. "You must take me for a fool, boy." His mirth vanished. "She, I can use, but I can't risk you telling anyone I'm here."

The man lunged at Tam, who leaped back, jerking Fiona off balance. Mercifully she fell, for she heard the whoosh of an object in the man's hand pass by her head. Was he attacking them with a knife?

She tucked and rolled as she'd been taught when falling off a horse, while the man directed his attack at Tam. Horrified, Fiona climbed to her feet and looked for a weapon. She knew Tam only had his belt knife.

Nearby was a second structure. A barn? Fear propelled Fiona's legs while she ran toward it. Luck as much as sight helped her find a pitchfork, and she grabbed it and hurried back to the house, where

Tam was still dodging the big man's knife. The large blade flashed in the reflected firelight.

Gripping the pitchfork with both hands, Fiona aimed for the man's knife hand and managed to stab his forearm with two of the three metal tines. He roared and threw up his arm, yanking the pitchfork out of Fiona's hands and causing her to stumble to her knees.

Before she could stand, the man lifted the knife over her head, and Fiona screamed, covering her head with her hands.

Tam yelled, there was a thud, and the man fell backward. When Fiona lifted her head, a body lay on the ground, and Tam picked up the fallen knife, since his protruded from the man's chest.

Fiona sucked in a deep breath, but her shock at seeing Tam slash the fallen man's throat strangled the scream before it could leave her throat. She shut her eyes against the horror, but she would never be able to forget what she'd seen.

You didn't have to kill him. She stopped the words before they leaped from her mouth. Her husband had rescued her from certain death, had killed the man in self-defense, but all she could think was that he would be accused as a murderer.

The knife thumped to the dirt, and Fiona opened her eyes. Tam stood hunched over, pressing his arm against his body. Fiona came to herself and jumped up.

"Are you hurt?" She hurried over to him, averting her eyes from the bleeding body on the ground.

He nodded.

"Let's get closer to the light so I can see." She guided him into the house, which was one small room, and turned him toward the fire. The aroma of stew in the iron pot over the stove made her stomach growl.

When she pulled Tam's arm away, blood spurted from a deep gash just below his elbow. Instinctively she clamped her hand over the gash and tried to remember what her parents and Tristam had done for similar injuries.

Using her other hand, she felt along the underside of Tam's upper arm and then pressed her fingers against it. With the sleeve in the way it was more difficult to feel the pulse, but she finally found it and pressed harder.

"Tam?" She had to twist to see his face and was alarmed to see how pale and gaunt he appeared. "I need for you to hold this pressure point while I find something to bind your wound." To her relief, he nodded and was able to press his longer fingers against the artery so she could release hers.

Before she let go of the gash, Fiona scanned the room for any piece of cloth she could make into a bandage. There, draped over a roughly built stool near the fire was a long piece of homespun. It probably was not very clean, but she'd deal with that later. She waited until the pounding pulse under her fingers slowed, and then she leaped the few steps to the cloth, snatching it up and folding it lengthwise.

She pushed up Tam's blood-soaked sleeve in order to wrap the cloth directly over the wound. It looked deep enough to need stitches, but the priority was to bind it to slow the blood loss, which it did. If she could find a needle and thread in this man's house, for obviously a woman had never lived here, she would try to sew the gash, though it made her queasy to think too much about it.

"Sit here, love, and I'll look for food." She helped Tam sit in the room's only chair. "Keep holding pressure, and hopefully the blood will clot without the need for stitches."

He nodded and leaned his head back, closing his eyes. Fiona scanned him, wondering if he had another injury. Only his sleeve and the hand holding the pressure were bloody, though droplets had splashed on the front of his shirt. Fiona put the thought of whose blood that was out of her head so she could search the room.

She ladled stew into the only bowl and helped Tam eat first before refilling the bowl for herself. Then she spied two freshly cooked rounds of flatbread, and they each ate one. There was no water inside, not even a basin with some to wash the blood off her hands. She did find a half-full wineskin and a cup and first poured some for Tam. He made a face before settling back in the chair. Fiona drank a cup and discovered why; the wine was sour.

To her relief, the bleeding had almost stopped. If Tam didn't jar the arm, the wound should heal on its own, as long as infection didn't set in. Fiona wasn't sure what she'd do if that happened. When she looked up at Tam's face, he had relaxed, and she realized he'd fallen asleep in the chair. So she slowly stood and backed away, trying not to wake him.

The fire was big enough it would keep burning for a while. Fiona stared at the cot in the corner piled with furs, but the thought of sleeping where the dead man usually did turned her stomach. There might be a place to sleep in the barn, but she wasn't about to leave Tam or the warmth of the fire.

First she shut the door so she wouldn't have to be reminded of the dead body just outside, and then she found a wooden chest near the cot. Her hands hesitated, but, she reasoned, the man would never need what was inside again. Opening the lid, Fiona discovered a fairly clean blanket folded on top and gratefully took it without examining the rest of the contents. She spread the blanket on the dirt floor near the fire and curled up on it like one of the Keep's hounds. Pillowing her head upon her folded hands, she fell asleep almost immediately.

* * *

When Tam woke up, he couldn't remember where he was. His arm throbbed abominably, and his back was stiff from sleeping in a chair. The only light came from the embers of a fire and morning sunrays streaming through cracks in the wooden wall.

He sat up with a groan and recalled what had happened last night. Gingerly he moved his injured arm. It had stopped bleeding, at least. When his eyes adjusted to the dim light, he slowly rose and felt a little dizzy. He walked to the room's only cot, but Fiona wasn't in it.

Then he turned back toward the fire, noticing something on the floor. There lay Fiona on a blanket, sound asleep. Quite a difference from the beds the princess had grown accustomed to, wasn't it? He smirked until he remembered she hadn't complained or blamed him the last two days, as most women of his acquaintance would have done. Was Fiona not the pampered lady he'd assumed her to be? Was there more than met the eye to her character?

Lowering himself to one knee beside her, he stared down at her face. She looked even younger in sleep. And she had agreed to leave everything and everyone she knew to come with him. A twinge of conscience pricked his heart. He'd thought to leave her here and hope that someone would find her. Now the more he thought about what she'd done and how she'd comported herself, he realized he did want her with him after all.

She let out a little sigh and slowly opened her eyes. When she saw him, she smiled and sat up.

"How is your arm?" Her gaze darted to the bandage.

"The bleeding has stopped, thanks to you." He found he could smile back at her. "I think we need to find out if there's a horse in that barn."

Fiona nodded and gracefully rose. Despite her disheveled appearance, she was a lady through and through. "What about—the body?"

Tam shrugged. "We don't have time to bury it." He walked to the door and opened it to a brilliant morning. When he stepped outside, the body was gone. Drag marks suggested something had taken care of it for them.

Fiona followed him, carrying a blanket draped over one arm. "Where did he go? There's no way he could have survived."

"He didn't. Probably scavenger dragons came in the night."

Fiona gasped and covered her mouth with both hands. "Scavenger dragons live out here?"

"Of course." He cocked his head at her unexpected reaction.

"Will they attack us?"

He shook his head. "They're not like river dragons. They only eat dead things. Real scavengers."

Fiona slowly nodded and relaxed before glancing back at the cottage. "Shouldn't we see if there's anything we can use before we leave?"

"I was just going to suggest that." He gestured for her to go inside first.

It didn't take long to rummage through everything in the small room. Tam only found a few small coins, and Fiona found some dried meat. At least she had the blanket.

"Before we check the barn," Fiona said, holding up her sticky hands, "I would like to wash off and drink some water."

Tam pointed to the nearby stream, and they went together. After both washed their hands, Fiona removed the bandage on his arm and washed the healing gash, careful not to disturb the scab.

"This isn't very clean, but it will protect the cut," she said while securing the cloth on his arm again.

He then took one of her hands with his uninjured one and led her to the barn. Fiona had to help him lift the bar on the door, and a whinny greeted them. They glanced at one another with relief. Now if the horse would only let strangers ride upon it, they might make it to Sir Artemis' manor in time.

Fiona pulled ahead and reached the horse first. "He's beautiful," she murmured, and Tam had to agree.

This was no old nag of a plow horse though it was the size of most draft horses. By the powerful muscles and the good proportions, this could even be a retired knight's destrier. It had plenty of strength yet and could easily carry the two of them.

"There now," Fiona murmured while she stroked the horse's head. The gelding was a bay with three white socks. "We're your masters now, and we'll take good care of you. I'll call you Uncle."

"Uncle?" Tam laughed. "You'd call this magnificent animal such a mundane name?"

She lifted her chin in that proud way that appealed to him. "He looks like an Uncle to me, and I know he will be a good horse to ride, dependable like an uncle ought to be."

He cocked his head at her. "How do you know that?"

She stared into the gelding's large eyes. "I just know; it's as if he told me himself."

"Hmm." Tam made no further comment but looked about for a saddle and bridle and found them. He had to carry both with his uninjured arm. When he approached Uncle, the horse snorted and stamped one of his large front hooves.

"You had better let me put those on him." Fiona took the bridle first and replaced the horse's halter. Uncle chewed at the bit but didn't protest. But when she took the saddle, Tam stared up at the gelding's tall back and frowned.

"There's no way you can reach his back," he began, but she led the horse over to a block of wood, and he responded as if he'd known her always. And he stood still while she threw the saddle up to his back, positioned it, and tightened the girth.

When she pulled herself up to the horse's tall back, Tam had to admit, her confidence and tenacity impressed him more and more.

"You never told me what a little horsewoman you are." He gave her a little bow before approaching the horse.

"You never asked." Her eyes shone. "You haven't learned much at all about me yet."

While she held Uncle steady, Tam awkwardly climbed up behind her. Even using the block, he had trouble pulling up with only one arm. Once he seated himself, he held Fiona close with his good arm around her waist.

"I'm learning the best part of you," he whispered in her ear, smiling when she shivered.

Fiona slapped the reins, and Uncle stepped forward, leaving the barn. Once they were outside, Fiona turned her head. "Which way?"

Tam studied the sun's position and pointed to the southwest. "That way."

*

They rode at an easy pace, which was still somewhat faster than walking and certainly less tiring. Tam made sure they stopped whenever they found a good place to let the horse drink so they could drink too. While Uncle cropped grass, Tam and Fiona both foraged whatever they could find, whether sweet grass or berries or mushrooms.

By evening they were finally out of the mountains and into the rolling hills between the Dragon's Backbone and Moor Point. Though they spied the occasional farm in the distance, Fiona never mentioned a desire to stop at one of them. After their terrible experience last night, Tam would rather avoid isolated strangers. There was a reason they were isolated, after all, and not living near a village or town.

Twilight was falling, and they had to find a sheltered place for the night before all light was lost.

"Look ahead, Fiona. There's a stand of trees at the top of the next hill. We'll have shelter, and the location is defensible."

She stiffened. "Defensible from what?"

He shrugged to demonstrate less concern than he felt. "Mostly river dragons. They won't climb the hill."

She gasped. "River dragons?"

"They are common in the south. Didn't you know that?"

Uncle plodded steadily on, unconcerned about anything, except maybe his next meal.

Fiona hunched a little in the saddle, and Tam pulled her closer.

"I have only been in the south a handful of times," she admitted. "Usually only to Westmoor."

"We're following the border of Westmoor, which is to the right of us." It made him feel older and wiser to know things she did not. "In fact, we'd best stop here and all get a drink, because there won't be any water on top of that hill."

They did so, but Fiona was more skittish than Tam had yet seen her. He did spy the telltale bubbles of a submerged river dragon, but he did not mention it to her, since it was far downstream. Once all had their fill, he and Fiona mounted up again rather than lead the horse up the hill.

At Fiona's urging, the horse dug in his hooves to ascend, and Tam leaned forward in the saddle, pressing against Fiona's back. When they reached the top, Fiona halted Uncle, and Tam slid off first. While she unsaddled the horse, Tam scouted out the best place to bed down with a nearby tree having suitable branches upon which to tie their mount. He was not about to risk losing another horse.

Fiona fussed with the animal while Tam selected a level place between two trees, away from large roots. He brushed away leaves and twigs and then placed the blanket on top of the grass. Growing impatient, he sat on the blanket and waited for Fiona.

His arm burned a little, but he ignored the discomfort. Right now he was only interested in Fiona.

She approached at last, taking careful steps, for it was dark beneath the canopies of these large trees. Tam reached out and touched her leg, making her squeal.

"You startled me." She dropped to her knees beside him.

"I didn't mean to frighten you." He pulled her closer. "I'm also sorry for my irritation yesterday. It was unpardonable, and I treated you ill when you did not deserve it." He kissed her gently and then with more urgency.

She returned his kisses with such ardor, Tam assumed all was forgiven.

* * *

Kieran met the tracker Talon Fowler at the appointed time. Neither man dismounted but they did ride down the road to a secluded place under a copse of trees.

"What did ye find, Fowler?" Kieran rested his arms on the pommel of his saddle, steeling his heart for the worst.

"My lord, I found a dead horse that had fallen off a cliff. In its saddlebags I found both men's and women's clothing, as well as a broken box of jewels." The grim-faced man opened a carry sack and pulled out a handful of glittering items, which he held out.

Kieran reached over and picked up an item he recognized—Fiona's tiara studded with amethysts. "No sign o' their bodies?"

"No, my lord. They at least did not fall off the cliff." Fowler made to put away the carry sack, but Kieran nodded at him.

"If you will, please continue tae carry these for now." He returned the tiara, and the tracker replaced all in the sack.

"Are you wanting me to lead you to the place where I found these?" Fowler looked at Kieran expectantly.

"No need tae examine the dead horse, but I do want tae try and catch up with them, which seems possible if they are now on foot." Kieran gripped the reins, ready to leave. There was still hope Fiona was alive.

Fowler nodded. "I feel sure we can overtake them, my lord."

"Then, lead the way."

They set a fast pace for the first part of the journey, until the faint path ascended into the mountains. Kieran wondered why Tammeron would take them this way. Did he know he was in trouble? Or did he have other motives in mind?

Kieran set his jaw and tried not to think too far ahead. First, they had to find them. Once that goal was accomplished, he would have time to decide what to do next.

*

Fowler had tracked the two runaways to the places they'd camped their first and second nights. At each site, Kieran could see for himself the remains of campfires. The third night, which is when Fowler suspected the horse had been lost in a storm, had been more difficult to find, but he proved why he was Captain Hodor's best tracker when he showed Kieran the small cave where the two young people had sheltered.

After he examined the footprints outside the cave, Kieran entered, and a shudder gripped him. They had spent the night here. He could feel traces of their presence in the stale air. Fowler was still studying the floor of the cave, but Kieran had to leave and take a deep breath of fresher air. Once he recovered, he followed the footprints until he was sure which direction they'd headed. By that time, Fowler had emerged from the cave.

"The horse ran off before they slept in the cave, I'm sure of it." Then he glanced up at the sky. "We have less than two hours of daylight, my lord."

"Then let's continue for as long as we have light." Kieran mounted his horse and rode behind Fowler, for the path had become narrow and treacherous. It wasn't long before Fowler pointed out where the horse had gone over the side. Kieran was just glad Fiona hadn't fallen, too.

By the time the sun disappeared behind the mountains, they had reached a valley with a spring and plenty of grass for the horses. Kieran knew they were still far enough away from river dragons that they could safely let the horses loose. His reliable Burdock would not wander far.

Since the night was mild and they each had dried food to eat, they didn't bother making a fire. That was fine with Kieran, for he enjoyed looking at the stars on a clear night like this one. Fortunately, Fowler was not a talkative man, so Kieran didn't feel the need to engage him in conversation. Not long after they ate in companionable silence, each bedded down. Fowler had awakened before dawn yesterday, so Kieran wanted to be ready to leave at morning's first light. Maybe they could catch up with Fiona and Tammeron by tomorrow night.

He couldn't fall asleep right away, though. His thoughts were of Mercy, not Fiona. He hadn't really told her goodbye, and in truth, he hadn't been supportive of her since the evening he'd caught Fiona kissing Tammeron in the alcove.

Had he let their daughter come between them? If so, he hadn't meant to. But he supposed it didn't matter if it was unconsciously done; the result was the same, and he had never in his wildest dreams thought their marriage would be strained.

It had seemed to come on suddenly. He hadn't noticed there was any problem. They'd tried to work together as parents the last couple of years, hadn't they? In Fiona's case, however, it was probably too little, too late. Her stubborn willfulness had been set in stone from a young age.

Would Mercy ever forgive him for spoiling Fiona? He knew she tried hard not to resent him. It didn't help that he had never forgiven himself. So perhaps the fault was all his.

But how could he ever forgive himself, especially if Fiona had given herself without benefit of marriage to the scoundrel? Foolish lass! Would she e'en consider that she might become pregnant? Kieran didn't know Tammeron well, but he couldn't imagine him doing aught but abandoning Fiona. A young man who would elope with a young woman and travel through the wilderness without making it a priority to marry first could never be depended upon to make the sacrifices necessary to protect her and a babe.

Then he cringed, for he was casting stones. Criticizing a foolish young man for his lack of honorable behavior, when this foolish old man had made his share of mistakes. Such as, trying to be a friend to his daughter instead of the firm parent she had desperately needed.

And pretending that his lenient parenting had not affected his relationship with his beloved wife.

Kieran stared up at the winking stars, feeling a crushing weight upon his chest. *God Most High, forgive me for failing Mercy and Fiona both. Please, let it not be too late to make things right between us. Please, God, help me to be the man they need me to be.*

He was able to sleep fitfully and managed to rise when Fowler did. While repacking his saddle bag, he felt a scrap of parchment he'd not noticed before and pulled it out. Holding it up to the growing sunlight, he read Mercy's brief but heartfelt words. Knowing she was praying for him and wanted their marriage to be strong again gave him the resolve to make it happen.

Love was a choice, after all. It could grow again. It *would* grow again. What had Valerian told him all those years ago? That the Most High had given humans an unlimited capacity for love.

His heart swelled, and for the first time in days he no longer felt dead inside.

Tucking Mercy's note carefully into a corner of the saddle bag, Kieran jumped up, ready to find his daughter, arrest Tammeron d'Jean, and return to his wife as quickly as he could.

Chapter 18

All the brethren of the poor do hate him:
how much more do his friends go far from him?

After riding over rolling hills most of the day, Fiona saw a crossroads ahead. A wagon pulled by two draft horses headed away from them. It was the first sign of civilization since they'd left the farm in the hills. Fiona's stomach twisted painfully. Hunger pains? Could they pay for a meal at an inn with the coins Tam had taken from the dead man's cottage?

She urged Uncle to a faster walk. Tam tightened his hold around her waist.

"When we reach the crossroads, turn to the right."

Fiona nodded, wondering where the road would lead. She revived a little with hopeful anticipation.

Once she turned Uncle to follow the new road, Fiona scanned the way ahead, looking for indications that a village or town was nearby. It didn't take long for a village to appear, but Tam dashed her hopes.

"We won't stop here. There's a town further down the road where we can stop for the night."

She nodded again, and her weariness was such that she wasn't even bothered by the stares of the villagers, knowing how filthy and unkempt she must appear. Nobody knew who she was, and that suited her fine just now.

They passed a few people on this road, both walking and riding. A few nodded in greeting, but all of them seemed to be in a hurry to get to their destination before night fell. Fiona didn't blame them. There were enough tall trees that it would be difficult to travel at night, especially where the branches formed a canopy over the road.

Fiona heard the town before they came upon it. The townspeople had a celebration going, with rows of trestle tables laid out in the square, and booths with merchants hawking food and drink and other items all around. The aromas of roasting meat and bread made Fiona's mouth water and her belly growl.

"There on the right is the Crooked Tree Inn." Tam pointed out the sign, and Fiona guided Uncle toward it.

The building was indeed crooked. In fact, the second story looked as if it would topple over in a strong wind. But she refrained from comment when she pulled up Uncle to a halt in front of the door. Tam slid down and held up a hand.

"Wait here, and I'll see if there's a room for the night."

Fiona was glad she sat upon a tall horse. Two men stood nearby, staring at her, and she tried to ignore them. When Tam returned, she let out a breath in relief. He did not look happy, though.

"No rooms due to the festival. We can sleep in the hayloft of the stables, if we pay for the horse."

"Is there no other inn?" Fiona noted that the men were still staring.

Tam shook his head. "They're all full, too. It's the hayloft or nothing."

Fiona tried to hide her disappointment. "I suppose it's better than the bare ground."

In answer, he took the reins from her and led Uncle around the back. The stables were leaning, too, and Fiona didn't think they had built them that way on purpose.

She and Tam settled the horse in his stall, and then he grasped her hand, leading her back to the inn. "At least we can eat a real meal tonight."

"They're serving food, even during a festival?" Fiona hadn't been to many such celebrations in her life.

"The innkeeper strikes me as one who will do anything to make an extra coin." Tam set his jaw, and with his height, Fiona thought he looked imposing.

They entered the Crooked Tree, and more aromas assaulted Fiona's nostrils, not all of them pleasant. Four men sat at a table in the corner. Their stares made Fiona's skin crawl. She was glad when Tam found a place at the far end of the room. Right away the innkeeper himself brought them mugs of ale and two wooden trenchers with chunks of meat and a few small potatoes in greasy gravy. Even though Fiona was starving, her lip curled in revulsion. At least there was a loaf of bread to soak up the gravy.

Tam tore the loaf in half and gave a portion to Fiona. She ate ravenously, and would have licked the trencher when she'd finished, but there were dried slivers of meat from a previous meal, and her stomach threatened to revolt.

"I shouldn't have eaten so fast," she groaned, but Tam hadn't heard her. He was watching an old man enter the room from the back. He walked with a pronounced limp, yet he wore the gaudy costume of a traveling bard and carried an old lute.

Fiona forgot her discomfort when she realized he was going to sing. First he perched upon a stool near the center of the room, and then he plucked on his strings, tuning them. Finally, he scanned his small audience before strumming the opening chords of a song Fiona had never heard before.

The bard's voice was no longer sure, though Fiona felt certain in his younger days it had been pleasant and true. The tune was simple, but the words were unfamiliar, so she could not sing along.

But then his second song was an old ballad, a love song Papa had taught her long ago. She hummed at first but soon joined in, keeping her volume low. He must have heard her, though. At the end of the second verse, he beckoned for her to join him.

"Go on, sing with him." Tam held up his mug for a refill, and Fiona hurried over to the old bard.

"So you can sing, can you?" the old man said gruffly.

"Yes, I can sing very well." Fiona smiled at him, for he looked even older and more tired up close.

"Well then, help me finish the last two verses." He strummed the bridging chord, and Fiona sucked in a breath.

This time, she sang louder to make the song a duet. Having someone to sing with gave the bard new energy, and they finished to the sound of applause, both within and without the room.

"What other songs d'ye sing, girl?" The bard's eyes glittered when more than one person dropped a coin in his hat on the floor, so Fiona named one she thought he might know.

They sang one song after another, soon attracting such a large crowd, the innkeeper was hard-pressed to keep the ale and food flowing. He grinned hugely, and so did most of the audience.

Normally, Fiona could have kept singing for hours. But the exhaustion of the journey soon manifested itself, and she had to excuse herself, despite all the pleas for her to sing "just one more." After Tam spoke with the bard, and the old man handed something to him, he took Fiona's hand. She gratefully let Tam lead her to the stables, and she waited below while he climbed up to the loft first to check it out.

"We'll need the blanket," he called down, and she went to Uncle's stall to collect it from the saddle. Then she wearily climbed the rungs of the creaky ladder one by one. Tam helped her pull herself up to the platform.

"Where's the hay in this hayloft?" she asked, glancing around.

"There's enough for a bed in this back corner." Tam took the blanket from her and arranged a bed for them. Then he went back to the ladder and pulled it up, setting it on the platform.

"Why did you do that?" She struggled to hold back a yawn.

"We don't want anyone climbing up here, do we?" He gathered her in his arms, making her frown.

"Aren't you tired?" she said with another yawn.

"I'll never be too tired for your kisses." He bent down and kissed her soundly before scooping her in his arms and carrying her to their bed in the hay.

Later, when she was trying to fall asleep, despite the festival goers still making merry outside, Tam sat up, wide awake.

"The bard shared some of his coins with us," he said happily. "Maybe you can sing again sometime, Fiona. You have a beautiful voice, and obviously everyone there thought so, too. Can you play the lute?"

"Yes," she answered sleepily, unable to keep her eyes open.

"Then I'll find a way to buy one for you. Between the job waiting for me and your singing, we should make enough coins to fill our bellies and put a roof over our heads."

"Mmm." Fiona drifted off to sleep and dreamed about strumming on a new lute.

*

A rooster crowed so loudly, Fiona startled awake. It was still dark. Was it near dawn? Roosters only crowed at the beginning of a new day, didn't they? Tam still slept, and she was reluctant to wake him.

She was grateful they'd found this inn, even though they hadn't had a proper bed. At least with full bellies and a few unexpected coins, Tam's mood was happier, which made Fiona happy. And now that they had left the wilderness, she was feeling more optimistic about this adventure of theirs. Sometime today, she would insist on getting a bath. And then, she would insist they find a priest to legally marry them.

The rooster crowed again, and Fiona decided he must be standing on the roof above their heads. This time Tam heard him, too, for he sat up with a yawn.

"Good morrow, love," Fiona said, moving closer. "Are we leaving soon?"

Tam raked his fingers through his hair. "As soon as we break our fast."

"I am hungry." Fiona studied Tam's sleepy face and decided she'd better wait to present her two greatest desires for the day. He'd be more receptive after he ate something.

Tam replaced the ladder, and they climbed down from the loft. Fiona made sure to bring their blanket. She rolled it up and tied it to Uncle's saddle. Then she hurried to catch up with Tam's long strides.

There was no one else inside the inn except for a yawning servant boy who brought them two bowls of gruel and a loaf of stale bread. Fiona was so hungry she refrained from commenting on the quality of the meal, and they left as soon as they finished eating to saddle Uncle.

While they rode through the quiet town, the sun appeared over the rooftops. The stalls and tables remained from last evening's festival, but there were few people milling about. Fiona gazed longingly at the church, but its doors were shut, and she doubted Tam would want to take the time to look for the priest.

Once they left the town, Fiona let Uncle have his head, and he cantered for a short while. Soon a fork in the road came into view, and Fiona pulled the horse back to a walk.

"Which way?" She turned her head toward her silent, brooding husband.

"The right fork ends at Port Town. We'll take the left to Ravenford."

They continued on in silence, though Fiona wanted to ask about Port Town. Now she wished she had paid attention to Papa's maps. How could she have known she'd ever end up living in Moor Point?

When the crenelated wall of a large manor house came into view, Fiona admired the cultivated lands surrounding it and enhancing its pleasing lines. She would be happy to be mistress of such a holding someday.

"Should we not stop and let Uncle graze?" Fiona hoped Tam would agree so she could have more time to admire the manor. The river running parallel with the road grew wider as they traveled, and Fiona had spied more than one ideal place to stop and rest beneath the trees.

"Not yet. There's a place a mile or two down the road from here." Tam's voice sounded strained.

"Is something the matter?" Fiona looked over her shoulder, wishing she could read his face.

"Only an unpleasant memory." He pointed at the manor. "That is the home of Sir Aidan Fitzhugh."

Fiona gasped. "Iris lives there?" Her heart sank, remembering her friend's invitation to visit. How long might it be before she saw Iris again? Could she and Tam be successful enough on their own to meet Iris and Aidan on equal terms again? "Have you been there before?"

Tam nodded. "With Lord Henry. And yes, Lady Iris lives there."

"Then how could it be an unpleasant memory?" Fiona's pride warred with a sudden urge to ask Iris for help.

"I know Lady Iris is a great friend of yours. And no, she was not the cause of any unpleasantness." He forced a smile. "I'm sorry, I should not have brought it up."

Fiona had presence of mind enough to know Tam did not want to talk about what had happened there, but she had a fleeting strong desire to turn Uncle around and beg Iris for help. She pushed down her feelings with great difficulty.

The road carried them around a bend in the river, and the lovely manor disappeared behind a screen of trees. Fiona struggled against melancholy. Yes, they were destitute now, but they didn't have to remain in that condition. The moment she saw the meadow ahead, she knew it must be the place Tam had in mind.

Uncle trotted in his eagerness to reach it, and Fiona and Tam gratefully dismounted once she halted the horse near the river's edge. She dropped Uncle's reins and approached the water cautiously, scanning the immediate area for signs of river dragons. Only blue-green dragonflies hovered over the surface of the river, scattering when she knelt on the bank and cupped her hands in the water. A fish leaped into the air mid-river and fell back with a splash. Frogs and some kind of insect sang nearby.

"This is a beautiful, peaceful place," Fiona said when Tam came near enough to hear her.

"Moor Point has many such places." He stared past the water, and Fiona wondered what he was thinking. She had to admit, she was thankful they could not speak mind-to-mind, like her parents could.

"How far do you think we'll travel today?" Fiona pushed to her feet and went to Tam's side.

"If we keep moving, we'll make it to Ravenford Village before nightfall." Tam bent down and picked up a small rock. As Fiona had seen Val do, Tam made the stone skip several times on top of the water before it fell in with a tiny splash.

"Then let's go." She grabbed his hand and led him back to the grazing horse. "Maybe we'll have a real bed tonight." That elicited a smile from him while they mounted Uncle and continued along the road.

With any luck, the village priest could marry them as soon as tonight! Fiona was well-pleased. Surely, she and Tam had put all their trials behind them.

* * *

The following day, Kieran and Fowler the tracker came upon a one-room house. No smoke rose from the chimney, and the door stood open.

"Hello!" Kieran called out. "Is anyone at home?" When there was no answer, he and Fowler dismounted and approached the structure. The tracker went down on one knee in front of the open door and studied the bare ground.

"There was a lot of blood spilled here recently." He rose and walked a few paces toward the nearby trees. "A body was dragged from here."

"Human?"

"That would be my guess, my lord. But did an animal kill him, or was he dead when he was taken away?" He continued to scan the ground.

Kieran's gut tightened. Fowler was certain Fiona and Tammeron had come this way. Had one or both of them met an untimely end? He stepped inside the small house to investigate.

There were no signs of a struggle inside, at least. The fire had burned itself out a day or two ago, and the iron pot had been emptied of its contents. The cot had recently been slept on, but nothing looked out of place. He'd noticed a barn nearby and went to search there next.

It was empty too, though a horse had been here a couple days earlier, by the state of the stall. No tack or saddle, so someone had taken it to ride. Kieran studied the hoofprints and determined it was a large animal, probably a heavy draft horse. That should make it easier to track.

When he returned to Fowler, the single-minded man was still examining the ground in front of the house's single door. Kieran waited until he finished.

"My opinion is that whoever died—and it was a single person—he or she was killed here and later dragged off by scavenger dragons." He finally met Kieran's gaze.

"Killed by another person then?" Kieran's heart lurched within his chest. Tammeron hadn't become violent again and killed Fiona, had he? God forbid!

"That seems the likeliest explanation, my lord." He nodded at the house. "What did you find?"

"Nothing that would help us, but there was a draft horse in the barn. It and its tack are missing. We should be able to follow its distinct footprints."

"Show me, my lord."

Kieran led Fowler to the barn, and he agreed the horse would be easy to track.

They mounted their horses and followed the large hoofprints until it became too dark to see and they had to stop again. Kieran's dreams that night were troubling, reflecting his grave fears for his daughter.

* * *

Val had anticipated the next week would be interminably long, but before he knew it, it was time for him and Reggie to fly to the Highlands and accompany Emma and Veynaria to the meeting place. The sky dawned clear, to his relief, for after one night of storm there had been rain showers nearly every day since. At least their flight would be a smooth one.

Emma and Veynaria were waiting for them and ready to leave, but Val slid down from Reggie's back anyway for the excuse to give Emma a hug and a kiss first.

You're looking well today. He pulled back with a grin. She'd arranged her dark hair into a braid over one shoulder and wore what looked like a jerkin over her tunic and riding skirt.

So are you. Emma gave him a pleased smile. "D'ye like me creation?" She gestured to the jerkin and then turned in a circle.

"I do like it. Warm, practical, and yet flattering." He chuckled with delight. "So, not only are you a midwife skilled at bringing babes into the world, you are a capable seamstress as well."

She shrugged, and a blush tinted her cheeks, making her even more lovely. "I dinna ken if I be capable or merely a fair hand, but Ma did teach me how tae sew."

Not just your hand, but all of you is fair, Emma MacRorie, especially your soul.

Now her blush darkened, but she hugged him fiercely. *And so be yours, Val d'Alden.*

He chuckled and took a step back, though he kept hold of her shoulders. "Though I'd rather stay here with you and continue with our mutual admiration, I suppose we ought to leave for the meeting, or we will be late."

"And that would nae be a good way tae begin, would it?"

He bit his lip and shook his head. "My brother might have second thoughts about putting me in charge of the lot." For an instant the thought came to him: *Would that be such a bad idea?* But he swiftly banished it, for he knew Dolan was counting on him to excel in this role.

Val clasped Emma's hand, and they walked over to the dragons. Emma climbed upon Veynaria with ease.

You two have been practicing. He mounted Reggie and grinned at Emma.

Why, so we have. 'Tis what ye expected, I hope?

Of course! I'm pleased to see you so comfortable with Veynaria already.

Emma patted the female dragon. *She and I be best friends already, right, friend Veynaria?*

I am pleased to have bonded with you, friend Emma. Veynaria snaked her long neck around to meet Emma's fond gaze. It warmed Val's heart to see them share the same special friendship he and Reggie had enjoyed for years.

Shall we go? Val spoke to Emma and both dragons.

Yes! came the answer from all three minds.

Reggie and Veynaria launched themselves into the air with such identical precision, it was as if they'd planned it all along.

*

Since they only had to fly straight across the northern border of the Highlands, it didn't take them long to reach their destination, which had finally been named Tuath Garrison. Val had been told *tuath* meant north in the old tongue, which Emma confirmed.

While they circled to land, Val noted that Dolan and Cephalorix had already arrived. Dolan and Kieran's brother Drystan, who commanded the garrison, stood at the steps of the hall, and both waved.

Val waved while Reggie descended directly in front of the steps, and Veynaria landed beside him. Though eager to greet his brother and Kieran's brother, Val waited until Emma dismounted so he could introduce her to Drystan.

"So this be our MacRorie cousin?" Drystan grinned at Emma. "Welcome tae Tuath."

"Glad I be tae finally meet you." Her eyes twinkled. "There be nae doubt ye are a MacLachlan."

"Aye, 'tis true. Our sainted ma did her best tae civilize him, but our da was one o'erpowering force o' nature." Drystan widened his eyes and bared his teeth, making Emma laugh.

"Och, aye, Lachlan MacLachlan were legendary 'twixt our clans." Emma gazed up at Val, and he winked at her.

Two dragons approached to land, and others appeared in the sky. Before a half hour passed, all had arrived. As soon as the final dragon riders dismounted, Cephalorix leaped into the air and called all the dragons to him. They spiraled away as a group and disappeared over the nearest mountain.

"Come inside, all o' ye, and make yourselves at home." Drystan welcomed them with open arms before turning to enter the hall beside Dolan. Val and Emma went next, followed by the rest of the riders.

Drystan had set up two trestle tables side-by-side so everyone could sit around them and be close enough to see and hear one another by the light of torches and candles. Dolan and Val sat in the middle on one side, and Emma sat beside Val. Caesg and Kentigern sat with their cousin, and young Sean Hendry sat on Dolan's other side. The remaining dragon riders spread around the tables, all with looks of anticipation.

"Welcome, Royal Dragon Couriers," Dolan said in a pleased voice. "I trust no one had trouble locating this garrison?"

"No, Sire," Hamelin de Grignon spoke up first. "But Frendatorix told me Cephalorix had contacted all the dragons to give them directions."

"Good." Dolan nodded pleasantly. "I felt sure Cephalorix would do that. But I hope you all are beginning to realize how vital it will be to know how to reach every important location in Levathia on your own. There may be times when Cephalorix is distracted and unable to send a timely message or directions to your dragon."

Val was encouraged to see most of the others nodding their agreement. "That is one reason we plan to meet weekly at first," he added, "to give all of you the opportunity to fly to these locations, one at a time."

Oriana, the young woman from the Southern Woodlands, raised her hand, and Val nodded at her.

"Pardon me, Sire, but is it acceptable if in between meetings those of us who live close to one another practice flying around the provinces to learn the location of villages and manors and other landmarks?"

Dolan indicated Val should answer.

"Of course it's acceptable, Oriana. Thank you for bringing up this subject." Val scanned the table. "The next few weeks are preparation and training for all future needs we can imagine right now." He indicated Dolan beside him. "This is a completely new venture, so we all need to be resilient and open to making changes if anything we are doing is not working.

"And that leads me to another subject." He pointed to Oriana and Norman from Southmoor. "I'd like you two to pair up and each become the first point of contact with the other, since you are geographically closest." Next he pointed to Erian of Moor Point and Fletcher of Westmoor. "The same for you two. Consider yourselves partners." With a grin, Val next pointed to Hamelin from Frankland and Sean of Northland, who coincidentally were the oldest and youngest riders. "You two will be a team, and you are the final team." He finished by pointing to Caesg and Kentigern of the Highlands.

"The one thing we never want any of you to feel is that you are alone. It is true that right now all of you except our riders from the Highlands are the only dragon rider in your entire province. We hope someday to add more, but the dragons are few in number at present."

"Hopefully there will be more dragonets by next year," Dolan said with a pleased smile. "Unfortunately, they will take time to mature enough to safely carry a rider."

"Until that time," Val pointed out, "your dragons can speak to one another at any time. And Cephalorix and Regnatorix have made it clear that all of them may contact one or both at any time. So in that way, you also have indirect contact with either of us, and with all of the other dragon riders."

He was glad to note the positive reaction everyone had to this news. Val had wondered if any of the riders were feeling isolated in their provincial castles, since most people would either be too awed to approach them, or would have no idea why they and their dragons were now living within those castles.

I have an idea. He glanced at Dolan, who raised his brows.

What is it?

Why don't we all fly together along the Mohorovian border so they can learn the locations of all the other garrisons?

Dolan grinned. *Don't you mean, why don't we make a spectacle of ourselves for those in the lonely outposts?*

Val barely held back a laugh, since the others weren't in on their private joke.

"Before you fly back to your provinces, let's practice flying as one large group and follow the border where the other garrisons are situated." He nodded to Oriana. "When we part from one another at the southernmost garrison, you'll have an advantage over the rest of us in that you won't have far to fly home."

"Why, thank you, Sire." Her smile was big enough to show her teeth, which Val returned.

"Sir Drystan, do you have any questions for us before we leave?" Val remembered to ask.

"Only one, Sire." He raised his brows in question. "Are ye not going tae eat before ye go?"

Val wanted to smack himself in the head. Beside him, Emma covered a laugh with her hand.

"I'd forgotten you offered to feed us, Sir Drystan." His cheeks grew warm, and this time Dolan chuckled.

I can't believe you forgot about eating, Val.

I can only blame it on the anticipation of making a spectacle, as you put it. To Drystan MacLachlan he said, "We are ready to eat, Sir Drystan. And we thank you."

Chapter 19

My son, if thine heart be wise, my heart shall rejoice, even mine.

When Fiona and Tam entered Ravenford Village, it was still afternoon and so the place bustled with activity. Sights and sounds and odors assaulted Fiona's senses, making her disoriented. They passed the blacksmith, who shaped a metal object with the ringing blows of his hammer, a goose girl struggled to keep her honking charges from wandering off, a squealing piglet darted around the feet of a goodwife purchasing colored thread from a merchant, a young man in homespun pushed a wheelbarrow full of manure, hawkers cried out the wares they had for sale. Above it all, the aroma of fresh bread wafted directly to Fiona's nostrils.

"Are you hungry?" She glanced back at Tam, who was studying everyone's face as they passed by.

"Yes." He pointed ahead. "Stop there at the sign of the boar."

Fiona pulled Uncle abreast with a sign hung over a wide door depicting a boar on a trencher with an apple in its mouth. The sign was so well-painted, it made Fiona's mouth water to imagine what good food might be served here. She was about to point out to Tam there was no place to tie up the horse when he slid down and held up a hand.

"Stay here and let me spy out the situation." Without waiting for her reply, he strode inside.

Well, of all things for him to do, Fiona did not expect this. She fumed for a few minutes, but when Tam did not return right away, she began to grow concerned about what happened.

As she had just decided to go look for him, Tam came out of the inn with a stern look on his face.

"What happened?" she asked, mirroring his frown.

"He is not here." Tam clenched his jaw.

"Who?"

"The man who wanted to hire me. He has gone to Mansfield Village." He pulled himself up behind her again.

"Is it too late?" Fiona's chest tightened. What would he do if it was too late for this opportunity?

"Not if we can reach him tonight." He gestured forward. "Let's go."

Fiona urged Uncle to a walk, the fastest she dared in this crowd. "How far to Mansfield?"

Tam glanced up at the sun. "Not before sunset, but soon afterward."

Fiona was glad Tam couldn't see the disappointment on her face. Her spirits drooped even more when they came near the church, and she could see the priest speaking to someone in front of the double doors. She didn't even ask, for she knew what his answer would be.

As they made their way down the road, the sun slowly sank in the west. Fiona's belly growled, and her mouth felt parched. Tam did not want to stop for anything or anyone.

The sun had gone behind the trees before they came to Mansfield Village. Again he studied the signs over the doors of the buildings.

"There." He pointed to the left side, where the doors of an inn stood wide open, and the sign proclaimed it The Golden Goose. How could it be any more welcoming?

Tam again directed her to wait for him, and he almost jumped off the horse in his eagerness to get inside. Fiona wasn't as comfortable waiting out front as she had been in the other village. For one thing, most of the villagers had gone home by this time, and the few that milled around looked less than savory. She did not like the way one of them stared at her.

After only a few minutes, Tam came out and took the reins from Fiona.

"Jump down, Fiona. We're staying the night here."

Though reluctant to leave the relative safety of Uncle's back, Fiona did so, following Tam while he led the horse to the stables in back. After settling him in the stall and removing his saddle and bridle, Tam found water and food for Uncle. Truly, her husband acted more animated this evening than he had in days. When he finished with Uncle, he took her hand.

"Come inside now. Our room should be ready." He wagged his brows at her with a grin. "We'll have a real bed tonight."

"I am looking forward to that!" Fiona smiled back, though her face fell at a new thought. "But I would hate to soil bedclothes by not bathing first."

"I'll find out if they offer a bath here."

"Please do." She wanted him to hold her hand, but he strode to the inn so quickly, she had trouble keeping up with him.

They entered The Golden Goose, and Fiona relaxed a bit. The main room was clean with a large fireplace and trestle tables and benches neatly laid out. The rooms were sure to be nice, too! And surely they would offer baths, though it would be at a price, and hopefully a price Fiona and Tam could afford.

Fiona then wondered if Tam was going to insist she sing for coins again.

The innkeeper's appearance was as neat as his establishment. No stained apron for him! And he assured Fiona a bath was included in the price of the room. In fact, he said, he would call for one to be drawn directly, before customers began to arrive for the evening meal. Then he promptly disappeared into the kitchen.

Fiona's enthusiasm dimmed when she remembered she had no spare change of clothing. Nothing clean to wear after washing herself. Tam must have noticed, for he leaned closer to whisper in her ear.

"What's the matter? I thought you were anxious to bathe?"

"These are all the clothes I have." She gestured to her dusty riding outfit.

"Leave that to me." He shooed her toward the kitchen and went out the door.

Fiona craned her neck to watch him until he vanished around the corner. Where was he going? Surely he wasn't going to spend the few coins they had on extra clothing?

But that's exactly what he did. Fiona was soaking in a wooden tub tucked in a corner of the kitchen when Tam appeared, pushing aside the privacy curtain and making her squeal.

"It's only me." He smiled down at her, making her feel self-conscious. Then he held up a green dress. "How do you like it?"

"It looks lovely. How did you pay for it?" She reached for the towel, but Tam tossed the dress over his shoulder and opened the towel for her.

"I had enough. Let me take care of such things." He wrapped the towel around her and pulled her close, leaning down to kiss her briefly. "I'll wait for you in the main room. After you dress yourself, we can eat an early supper. Then you can sing again, like you did yesterday. I've already spoken to a bard." He winked at her, hung the dress on a nail, and left her behind the curtain, still dripping water on the stone floor.

So, she would be singing for their supper again. With a sigh, she washed out her riding clothes in the tub and hung them over the side. Then she finished drying off and pulled on the green dress. It fit more snugly than she preferred, and the bodice was cut lower than she'd ever worn. Still, it was clean, and she was clean, and hopefully she wouldn't have to sing long so they could sleep in the real bed tonight.

When she entered the main room, Tam came to meet her, his eyes scanning her appreciatively.

"Yes, that will do very well." He took her hand and kissed it. "Shall we find a place to sit now?"

Fiona chose a table in a corner, from which they could see the rest of the room and the front door. She hated feeling so anxious, but the thought of singing in this revealing dress to a room full of strangers was almost more than she could accept. Fortunately, she didn't have to sing yet, and this inn's food had to be superior to the last one.

When a servant brought out trenchers and bowls piled high with meats and cheese, roasted potatoes, turnips, and bread, Fiona's mouth watered at the delightful aromas. She had to keep reminding herself to slow down and eat like a lady. But it was so good!

Once she and Tam had eaten every scrap, she sat back with her belly uncomfortably full and stifled a belch. Tam laughed at her before tipping back his head to empty his flagon of wine. How much had he consumed? She'd been so engrossed in her meal, she hadn't noticed if his vessel had been refilled. His personality seemed falsely cheerful, which she could only attribute to an excess of wine.

She had just decided to ask him about it when the bard entered the room, strumming on his lute. He was a young man with a cocky air, dressed in a gaudy green and yellow costume. Was that the reason Tam had chosen this dress? So she could match the bard?

The room had filled with patrons, and the young bard scanned the faces, taking their measure. At least, that's what it seemed to Fiona. Did he choose his songs based on who was in the audience?

Without warning, he played the opening bars of one of the songs from last night. A favorite in Moor Point, perhaps? Fiona hummed along while he sang, admiring his sure tenor voice. Though she thought her humming only audible to her and Tam, the bard slowly moved closer to their table. For a moment, Fiona considered stopping, but she kept going, defying him to find fault. She kept her harmony exactly in line with his chords, so there was no discordant note.

He stared at her while he sang the last verse, his head nodding in time with his strumming. On the final chord, Fiona hummed a descant note, and the bard raised his brows. Fiona could not tell if he approved or not, but the audience certainly did. They applauded enthusiastically while he made a showy bow.

"Thank you kindly. I am Allard, and I will be here all evening." He winked at Fiona. "I take requests, so please let me know what you'd like to hear tonight."

While the patrons murmured among themselves, Allard leaned against the table. "So," he said with a smirk. "Can you sing as well as you can hum?"

Fiona lifted her chin. "Yes. Better, even."

"Hmm." Allard glanced down at her dress for a moment, making Fiona wish for a shawl. "Come, stand with me, and we will find out." He strummed another set of opening chords, which Fiona recognized as a tragic old love ballad.

To her surprise and delight, their voices were superbly matched. In fact, Fiona could never remember singing with anyone better. Not even Papa, and she considered him the best singer she'd ever heard.

Until now.

That realization made her sad, for more than one reason. Now she had to admit someone sang better than Papa.

And she was no longer unattached, so there was no chance of getting to know this intriguing young man better.

Her gaze met Tam's in that moment, and he frowned. She would have to be careful to guard her thoughts, lest he read them in her face or eyes. The last thing she wanted was for him to think she was having second thoughts about marrying him.

She wasn't, was she?

Before she could answer herself, she had to concentrate on the song to follow Allard's final notes and sing the correct harmony. There must have been no lapse in her singing, though, for the crowd went wild, clapping and cheering for them.

"You do know how to sing," Allard said, leaning toward her. "In fact, you have an outstanding voice. Let's try another love song." He stared down at his long fingers on the strings and began a new tune.

Fiona had heard this one before, but she didn't know all the words. She concentrated fully on Allard, and so did not notice when Tam left the room.

* * *

It irritated Tam that the bard was flirting with Fiona, and that surprised him. It wasn't as if they were legally married. He still wasn't sure how long he wanted to keep her with him, but even so, he'd never thought of himself as a jealous lover. Wasn't jealousy related to a feeling of wanting sole possession of an item or a person? Tam shook his head. He certainly didn't want possession of the princess. She was too much trouble. But for the time they were together, he did not feel like sharing her with another man.

For now, Tam had to put aside his thoughts of Fiona and let her earn the evening's coins. He had his own coins to earn, as soon as possible, for his gaming debt loomed over his head like an executioner's blade.

He came to a cottage off the main road. The door and single window were shut for the night, but light from a candle or fireplace shone through the cracks in the boards, so he knocked.

A woman's voice called from within, "Who's there?"

"A friend of Folville," he answered as instructed, and the door creaked open.

A wizened older woman peered out and scanned Tam's tall frame. "Who're you?"

"My name is Tam, and I'm looking for Rodney Folville. I know he was to be either here or gone on to Cawthorne Village."

"He were here last night, but he left for Cawthorne this morning."

Tam nodded, satisfied. "Then I'll go there tomorrow. Thank you." He turned away and started back toward the inn.

"Wait," the woman said, and he stopped. "You aren't going to join his gang, are you?"

"What is it to you?" He cocked his head at her, wondering why she had asked that question.

"You seem like a young man from a good family, is all. I hate to see the likes o' you caught up in shady ventures." She shrugged.

"I am touched at your concern." Tam clutched his hands over his heart in a dramatic gesture, making her laugh.

"I doubt that." She shooed him away. "Just watch yourself."

"I know how to be careful." He walked away before she could continue the conversation.

When he came near to the inn again, he heard Fiona and the bard singing yet another song. They did sound very good together, so he hoped she would do even better than last night in tips. He did not feel like sitting inside the crowded room and watching her and the bard make eyes at one another, so Tam looked around to see if there was any other place to go in this village.

The door to the village church was still open, but Tam hurried past it. The last person he wanted to see was a priest. Farther down the lane, Tam came near to what appeared to be a brothel in a cottage. One of the women beckoned to him, but he ignored her. Not far from there, a small, rough-looking alehouse sat at the far end of the main road.

Tam paused before entering. He wanted another drink, but he did not want to be insensible after Fiona finished singing. They did have a proper bed at last, and he did not want to waste the opportunity. With a sigh, he turned back in the direction of the inn.

"You there, Longshanks," a rough voice called from the shadows. "Interested in a game of chance?"

"Maybe," Tam answered. "I need more details first."

"We play for keeps. Winner take all." The man grinned, revealing a gap between his front teeth.

Only for an instant was Tam tempted. The vivid memory of being cheated by Jevan and his friends was enough to make Tam want to avoid dice for the rest of his life.

"In that case, no thank you." Tam picked up his pace and left temptation behind.

Once he reached the inn, he waited until the current song ended before going inside and finding an empty seat. Then he spent the remainder of the evening sipping from a single flagon of ale while watching with growing irritation how much Fiona enjoyed the bard's attentions. By their final song, an idea came to Tam. Since she enjoyed flirting so much, Tam would encourage her to use that to her advantage and make even more coins by picking out individuals in the audience to flirt with. It could possibly garner more than she was making from her singing alone.

He smiled as he drained the last of the ale. Everyone in the crowded room clapped and cheered while Fiona and the bard bowed and coins rained down on them. Tam stood and slowly made his way through the press of bodies to Fiona's side. She did not notice him, since all her attention was for the bard.

"Oh, Allard, it wouldn't be fair for me to take it all," she was saying.

He handed her a heavy sack and cupped his hands around hers. "You have earned it. I have never played for such an enthusiastic crowd before. Word will spread, and I will be in greater demand than ever, thanks to you." He leaned forward and kissed her. "Are you sure you can't stay so we can sing together?"

Fiona glanced up and finally saw Tam. "I'm sure," she said to Allard. Then she returned her attention to him. "But I thank you. It was an enjoyable evening." She pulled away from the bard and came to slip her hand under Tam's arm, holding the bulging sack of coins with the other hand. "Shall we go to bed now?"

Tam nodded at Allard with a satisfied smirk, and then he and Fiona made their way to the guest room. After Tam shut the door behind them, he made sure it was locked.

"You certainly did enjoy yourself tonight." He couldn't help frowning, and Fiona narrowed her eyes.

"Why shouldn't I? Singing is one of my favorite things to do." She set the coins on the room's small table.

"I didn't mean the singing, Fiona." He pulled out the small chair at the table and sat down to count the coins.

"What did you mean, then?" She moved closer to him and rested a hand on his shoulder.

"I mean the flirting, the teasing, the kiss." He raised his brows. "I still can't believe you let him kiss you like that."

Fiona shrugged and walked away. "It didn't mean anything. We were just having fun so our songs would be fun for the people listening."

"It looked like something to me." Tam stacked the coins by tens.

She whirled around. "You aren't jealous, are you?" Now she came much closer, leaning down to kiss him. "I would never truly kiss anyone but you." When she deepened the kiss, he pulled her to his lap.

It gave him a feeling of power to know he could make Fiona forget about the bard, just as he'd been able to conquer whatever place Roland Campignon had once had in her heart.

* * *

Once the dragon "spectacle" had flown the length of the border, past the other five garrisons, all the dragons and their riders from the southern provinces left for home. Dolan and the dragon riders from the three northern provinces flew together with Val and Emma. When they all finally parted near the Keep, Val and Emma continued on to her cottage. They had just flown over the boundary of the Highlands when she sent him a somewhat timid message.

Can I ask ye, Val: would ye like tae meet my parents?

Today? He tried not to sound as shocked as he felt.

Why not now? I have written tae them about you, so they ken we are friends.

Only friends? He wanted to ask, but he feared what she might say. *Answer me truly, Emma: if they can see with their eyes my great affection for you, will their reaction cause you distress?*

Och, not at all! They be simple farmers, 'tis true, but though they ne'er have understood me desire tae be a midwife, leave the family homestead, and give up the chance o' being Rowdy's wife someday, I know they love me and always will.

Val stared across at Emma, his brows raised, though he doubted she could see the surprise on his face. *Rowdy? Who is that?* He could hear her mental laugh.

A distant cousin, o' course, whose land borders that o' me Da's, so Rowdy wants tae join those lands through marriage tae me.

Val let out the breath he'd been holding. *So your parents won't insist you marry him?*

They will nae insist I marry anyone. But they will most certainly be gobsmacked tae see me riding on a dragon!

Val chuckled at Emma's understated truth. He wanted to ask, but they were nearing MacRorie lands and an imminent descent, if she thought *he* would be acceptable to her parents. But then he might as well ask for her hand this very moment, and he was not prepared to do that.

There's Rowdy's homestead yonder, and me parents' is beyond the tree-topped hill.

Do you feel comfortable having Veynaria lead us to a landing site?

Aye, we be ready. Isn't that right, friend Veynaria?

We will lead you and Regnatorix. Follow me! The female dragon flapped her wings to gain a little altitude, and Reggie didn't hesitate to follow.

They circled the area in a gradual descent, which attracted the attention of neighboring clansmen. Val wondered if they would have a welcoming committee of curious folk, or *fawk* as Emma pronounced it. But when they landed in a fallow field not far from a rugged thatched roof house made of wattle and daub, only three people cautiously approached.

Emma dismounted first, eager to greet them. Val climbed down but didn't leave Reggie's side until Emma beckoned to him. While he strode closer, his nervousness returned, and he had to remember to smile.

Emma's father had a weather-worn face and more gray in his beard and hair than black. He was a tall, lean man, though still several inches shorter than Val. Her mother was more like Emma in appearance, though her face was lined with old sorrows. The third person had to be her younger brother, who was the only one of the three to eye Val with suspicion.

With a grin, Emma gestured to Val, as if her family couldn't already see him. "This be my friend Val. Val, this be my family."

"I am pleased to finally meet you all," he said as sincerely as he could. He really had wanted to meet them for a long time.

"Sassenach," Emma's brother muttered under his breath.

"What's that ye said, Cavan?" Emma frowned at him. "Say it loud enough tae hear or nae at all."

"What I want tae ken is, what are ye doing, riding upon yonder beasties as if they be nae more than an overgrown flying horse?" Her father's rough voice held a hint of humor, giving Val hope he could befriend the man in time.

"Well, sir," Val answered at Emma's mental encouragement. "In some ways they are large flying horses. They are our steeds because they have befriended us. And they have agreed to do so in order to form an order of Royal Dragon Couriers, at the request of King Dolan."

"I thought ye be a midwife now," Emma's mother spoke to her in a quiet voice, not much above a whisper. Was she shy or merely unused to speaking?

Emma's brother had no such compulsion. Before Emma could explain, he landed in the middle of the conversation.

"She be a midwife, Ma." Cavan glared at Val. "But this tattyboggle ha' bewitched her an' filled her heid with blather."

"Keep the heid now, son. Nae need tae be cruel." Emma's father held out his hand to Val. "I be Somerled MacRorie an' pleased tae meet a friend o' our lass."

Val gripped the man's strong hand gratefully. "I thank you, Somerled." He started to release his hand, but Emma's Da held it a moment longer, sizing him up with a discerning eye.

Finally, Somerled nodded with a crooked smile like Fiona's and Kieran's. "Aye, our lass be a good judge o' character."

"Da!" Cavan's face filled with anguish. Why was Emma's brother so distressed? Val soon found out when Somerled answered.

"When yer sis left us tae live in MacDonald lands, yer Ma and I knew 'twas likely she'd not live wi' us again." He gripped Cavan's shoulders, and the boy finally met his gaze. "Ye must accept that yer sis be a woman grown an' must make a life o' her own." Somerled's smile was melancholy. "'Tis the way o' this world, son."

Cavan sagged, all defiance drained from him. Emma came near and started to reach out for her brother, but he recoiled.

"Now, brother," Emma spoke gently, though a frown wrinkled her brow. "Ye ken ye canna hold onto the past. I'll e'er be yer sis, but ye ken both o' us must become adults. We canna stay wee bairns, no matter how much we wish for it." Now she smiled. "I miss ye too, an' I e'er will continue."

In answer, Cavan pulled away from their father and gave Emma a fierce hug. Val's sympathy for the boy increased, for he must love his sister very much and only hated that their relationship would never be the same again.

"Weel, come in the hoose, all o' ye." Emma's mother gazed at Val then. "You too, Val. I be Aingeal and also be glad our lass ha' found a right bonnie friend." She frowned a bit. "Though she didnae say how she met ye, Val. But ye can tell the tale whilst we sup inside." Then she grabbed Val's hand and pulled him inside the cottage. He had to bend down so as not to scrape his head on the low door frame.

Emma, what is a tattyboggle anyway? He glanced behind him, and Emma's eyes twinkled merrily.

Why, 'tis what we use tae scare off the crows from our crops.

A scarecrow? His eyes widened. Did he look that poorly?

Emma smothered a giggle with her hands. *Ye dinna look like a tattyboggle tae me.*

Then I suppose I should be grateful for that! He turned his attention to the family home.

Like Emma's even smaller house, this one was neat and tidy with a feeling of comfort and care though there were few possessions. Delicious aromas wafted from a kettle over the fire, making Val's mouth water.

"Mmm, something smells glorious, Aingeal." His feet propelled him closer to the cozy hearth.

"'Tis only me pottage, Val. I must finish wi' the oatcakes, an' then we can eat." When Aingeal smiled shyly at him, Val saw Emma reflected in her eyes.

"Is there anything I can do for you while we wait?" Val felt Cavan's gaze upon him, and it made him squirm.

"Aye, that ye can." Somerled popped his head in the doorway. "Come, Val."

Meeting Emma's dancing eyes with a nod, he ducked out the door. Cavan started to follow, but Somerled shook his head.

"Stay with yer Ma, son. We'll be only a bit."

The boy looked unhappy, but he obeyed his Da without argument.

Somerled led Val to the wood pile, within sight and hearing of the cottage. He picked up the ax and handed it to Val. "Would ye mind splittin' a few logs for the fire, lad?"

"Not at all." He smiled nervously at the man while he took the ax from his hand. The air between them felt charged, as if he was being tested by Emma's father.

Val had to set down the ax and remove his jerkin for easier movement. He was glad he'd worn a plain shirt underneath, though he knew eventually he'd have to tell Emma's family who he really was. For now, he hoped they would judge him for his character and not his position.

Thankful to Kieran for teaching him the knack of splitting wood long ago, as he was grateful to his Da for everything, Val set to work under Somerled's watchful eye. The first log took three strokes, but then he fell into the rhythm and split the rest in a single well-aimed blow. The pile of firewood grew rapidly, and Val thought he saw Somerled nod his approval. Perhaps he'd only imagined it, but he did so want the man's approval, if he was going to be his father-in-law in the near future.

"That be enough." Somerled took the ax from him. "We'll each take a load inside now." He gathered an armful of split wood, and Val did the same, after putting on his jerkin.

"I like ye, Val, though there be some mystery about ye, and I dinna like secrets." He stood facing Val, both holding their stacks of wood.

Val knew it was time to tell him. "Well then, I must be completely open with you, for I love your daughter and plan to marry her someday." He steeled his resolve, for he sensed Somerled would only respect surety of purpose and complete honesty. "My full name is Valerian d'Alden, and I am brother to the king. He has granted me the title Lord of the Sky, and I am the head of his new Royal Dragon Couriers."

Somerled had a startled look in his eyes, but it was soon replaced with something akin to relief. "Weel, then ye are nae lad but a royal laird. I dinna ken whether tae rejoice or weep for me dear lass."

Val shifted the heavy logs. "Pardon me, but why would you weep? I cherish Emma and want only to provide for her all the days of our life together."

Somerled nodded toward the cottage, and they walked over to stack the wood just outside the door. Then he beckoned for Val to follow him. They walked to the crest of the hill, from which Val could see the cottage, the barn, the sheep pens, and the fields of the family holding.

"This be our simple life, Val. 'Tis all Emma has e'er known. Ye are wantin' tae give her a far different life, an' I dinna ken what 'twill do tae her spirit." He met Val's gaze with his piercing eyes. "If ye be a prince, does that mean there be a chance ye could be king someday?"

Val almost blurted out, "Never." But something in Somerled's manner encouraged him to be more thoughtful in his response. "The chance is extremely small. My brother has two sons, so I would only become king if something happened to all three of them, which would be highly unlikely." His mouth went dry at the realization. "But yes, there is a chance."

"Does Emma ken this?"

"We have not discussed it." Val struggled to breathe normally. "I have not yet asked for her hand, but she knows how I feel about her."

"How do ye feel about my daughter, Val?" Though he was blunt, Val did not sense any hostility.

"From the first day I met her, I respected her intelligence and her quick wit, and I felt comfortable in her presence, so I could be myself and not merely a prince. We have developed a strong companionship, and we also discovered that we can speak mind-to-mind, like the great dragons. She could also speak to my dragon companion, which is why I encouraged her to be part of the dragon couriers."

"Ye can speak tae her mind? How does that work?" Somerled looked puzzled, not suspicious, which gave Val encouragement.

"We can hear one another's thoughts directed to each other. It's the voice of the mind, not the lips and tongue. It's also how we communicate with the dragons." Val realized he had never had to explain the process before.

"This be not a common thing then, tae speak tae the mind?"

"Not at all. My parents can speak to one another's minds, and so can my brother and his wife, but they must be in physical contact to hear the other's thoughts. Emma and I can speak without having to touch one another. As I understand, only my mother and my birth father could do that."

"I dinna understand. Who be yer parents, Val?"

He inhaled deeply. "My mother is a Healer of royal blood, Mercy, and she was first married to the Uncrowned King Valerian d'Alden, who sired me, though he was killed before I was born. Later she married Kieran MacLachlan, the man who raised me." He smiled. "Me Da, whose mother was a MacRorie."

Somerled nodded, as if he finally understood all the connections. He gave Val a smile, which felt like a great triumph.

"There be much tae like about ye, Val, and I can see it in me lass's eyes how much she adores ye. Me only concern 'twould be that she not be unhappy tae be pulled into a life above her station, that she ne'er feel adrift or forget who she truly be." He held out his hand, and Val gripped it again with great relief, for he knew this was Somerled's sign of approval.

"With all the resolve I have, and trusting in the grace of the Most High God, I pledge my life to your daughter's happiness. I know we are stronger together and will make a good team wherever life's journey takes us." Val wondered if what he'd meant as eloquent sounded awkward and bumbling.

"Then how can I stand in the way o' such resolve?" He clapped Val's shoulder with such strength in his corded muscles, Val had to shift his balance before he stumbled. "I give ye permission tae ask for me Emma's hand an' look forward tae the day I can call ye 'son.'"

"Thank you, Somerled." Warmth filled Val, and he felt he would burst with joy. "I look forward to the day I can call you Da."

They walked back to the cottage in comfortable silence.

Chapter 20

The robbery of the wicked shall destroy them; because they refuse to do judgment.

Tam and Fiona slept in after staying up so late. Tam only woke when Fiona wriggled close to him in the soft bed. He was tempted to wake her with kisses, but he didn't know when the innkeeper would knock and ask them to leave or pay for another day. Reluctantly he climbed out of bed and pulled on his clothes. He raked his fingers through his hair while watching Fiona smile in her sleep.

What was she thinking about? The bard? Or had he managed to help her forget how much she had enjoyed flirting with Allard? One thing Tam knew, he would not bring up the man to Fiona.

In fact, he would find another bard as soon as they reached Cawthorne Village. It wouldn't take long, no more than a couple of hours. Should he find lodging for them, or speak to Folville first? He supposed he'd have to secure employment before making any kind of plans.

The one complication to living in Cawthorne was that the village belonged to Sir Artemis Villeroy's lands. From his time serving Sir Artemis as his squire, Tam knew the knight did not frequent Cawthorne, which was the reason it harbored so many lawless people. But there was always the chance he might put in an appearance and encounter him or Fiona. What would he do then?

He would cross that bridge when he came to it. For now, he had to be certain his offer from Folville still stood.

Fiona stretched under the covers with a sigh and opened her eyes. She was very pleasant to look upon and to share a bed with. But Tam knew that, even if he was inclined to settle down with a wife and family, he couldn't imagine how they could remain together. Fiona was a member of the royal family. He was the son of a traitor knight raised by a provincial steward. While at the Keep, he'd been so focused on profiting by her, either by selling her jewels or through her family connections, he hadn't truly considered the impassable gulf between them.

"Good morning, husband." Her voice was sultry, making his resolve waver.

"Good morning, beautiful lady." Though everything in him wanted to go to her, he made himself stay where he was.

"Why are you dressed already?" She pushed out her lip in a pout.

"The day is no longer young, and we need to leave before the innkeeper charges us more for the room." He sat on the chair and pulled on his boots.

With a sigh, Fiona sat up, holding the covers in front of her body. "I forgot to wash my riding clothes."

Tam stood. "You'll have to wash them another time. Just brush off the dust." He unlocked the door. "Don't forget to bring your dress for tonight." Without looking back, he left the room.

The innkeeper was coming toward him. "Good morrow. Are you leaving?"

"Yes, as soon as my wife dresses, we will break our fast and press on to our destination." Tam pasted on a smile, hoping Fiona would hurry.

"I am sorry to hear that you are going. The guests are still talking about last night's performance. Your wife sings every bit as good as any bard." His eyes glinted. "She is bewitching."

"She certainly is." Tam wondered if he should wait for Fiona. The man wouldn't walk into the bedroom while she was unclothed, would he?

To his relief, the innkeeper turned and descended the stairs. Tam returned to the guest room and opened the door a crack. "Are you almost ready?"

Fiona appeared, wearing her riding clothes and boots. She'd slung her carry sack over her shoulder, and the fabric of the green dress was visible. "I am ready."

"Good. We'll eat something before we leave, since we've already paid for it."

It didn't take them long to eat and ready the horse. They were soon on the road leading southwest, and Tam's anticipation grew with each mile. This part of Moor Point was the most heavily populated, so they passed several riders, groups of riders, and wagons. Fiona began to hum one of the songs she'd sung last night.

"Thinking about that bard?" When he spoke, the words burst out in a surprisingly bitter tone.

"Not particularly," Fiona answered mildly. "I was thinking about some of the songs, though. Do you think they are the ones people from this province like most to hear?"

"Maybe. If I find a lute for you, could you play and sing them by yourself?" Tam calculated in his head how much he could afford to spend on a lute.

"Of course! I am a fast learner." She glanced over her shoulder with a satisfied smirk.

Tam both admired and resented her confidence, for that trait had never come easily to him.

They rode in silence for the rest of the way, for Cawthorne Village soon came into view. It was somewhat smaller than Ravenford, and much rougher in appearance, both the buildings and the people. Tam looked for the tavern where he'd met Folville for the first time last year.

There it was, the sign of the Black Raven. An ominous sign that hopefully did not portend disaster. He pointed to it.

"I must go in there before we do anything else, to find word about my employer."

Fiona turned the horse to cross the road and pulled up before the door. Tam slid down and met Fiona's gaze. "Wait here. This shouldn't take long."

He didn't wait for a reply, but straightened, gathered his courage, and entered the dark room. Blinking, he waited until his eyes adjusted to the gloom before navigating the obstacles of empty tables and benches. One man sat in a corner leaning over a mug, and a woman came toward Tam with a bored look on her worn face.

"I'm looking for Rodney Folville," Tam said before she could ask him what he wanted.

"He ain't here right now." Her voice was sullen. "If you ain't payin', you need to leave."

"When will he be back?" Tam had a sinking feeling in his gut that he was too late.

"How should I know? He don't tell me all his business." She glared at Tam. "Are you payin' or leavin'?"

"I'm leaving, as soon as you tell me where to find Folville." Tam made his voice as stern as he could. It had no effect upon the woman.

"I told you, he ain't here. He's gone on one of his hunts. Could be a week, so begone with you." She waved her hand as if Tam was a mere insect.

He turned away and clenched his fists. He was too late. What was he going to do now?

When he pushed open the door, the sunlight hurt his eyes. Fiona sat on the horse where he'd left her. The look she gave him was trusting and innocent, and he suddenly resented her seeing his humiliation.

"Well?" she asked. "What did he say?"

"He's not here." Tam made no move to mount the horse.

"What will we do now?" A hint of whining in her voice grated on his nerves.

"I don't know," he finally admitted.

"Are we going to stay here?" Fiona eyed the tavern with distaste.

"No." That much Tam knew for certain. "This is not a place that would appreciate your singing. We must find one that will." And with that much of a goal in mind, Tam pulled himself up behind Fiona.

He directed her to continue along the main road while Tam studied each place where a bard might venture. When he'd lived at the manor with Sir Artemis, Tam's only goal in coming to the village was to play games of chance and flirt with serving girls. He hadn't paid attention to whether there was music playing.

At the edge of Cawthorne stood a weather-beaten inn, little better than the Raven. But Tam wasn't certain they could reach the next village before dark, and he did not want to be on the road after night fell. He left Fiona with the horse again and went to find the innkeeper.

"No rooms," the man said irritably.

"What about the stables?" Tam was feeling desperate enough to sleep on hay again.

The innkeeper named an exorbitant sum, which Tam did not have. He bit back the retort on his lips and shook his head while he walked out the door.

"Not here either?" Fiona guessed.

Tam nodded and climbed up behind her. "We need to move as fast as this nag can carry us and hope we can make it to the next village before the sun sets."

"Why such a hurry?" she asked, turning the horse back to the road.

"Because I said so, that's why." Tam clenched his teeth.

"There's no need to be angry with me," she snapped.

"Just hurry!" Tam raised his voice, and Fiona slapped the reins. The horse lurched forward, and Tam tightened his grip around Fiona's waist while they cantered out of the village.

*

The shadows lengthened, and they still had not reached the next village. Tam was hungry and thirsty and growing more anxious by the mile. Surprisingly, Fiona had remained silent, though he could tell by her posture how angry she was.

The horse plodded along, tired and hungry too. The trees formed a canopy over the road, so it was difficult to tell what lay ahead, especially when the road curved. Tam kept his gaze on the road, hoping the village was just around the bend, and so he did not see the men emerge from the trees until they were upon them.

The horse whinnied while two men pulled Fiona off from the right, and at least two others pulled Tam off the other side. Fiona screamed, but Tam couldn't see what was happening, for someone put a hood over his head and dragged him off the road. His arms were gripped so tightly, he couldn't fight back if he wanted to.

Once they were far enough from the road, someone pushed Tam to the ground and sat on his back while another man bound his wrists and ankles together. Fiona shouted and thrashed nearby, but her voice was suddenly muffled. Had they gagged her?

Then a pole slid between Tam's bound hands and feet, and he was lifted off the ground like a trussed hog and carried further into the forest. Fear made his gut twist, and he was thankful they hadn't eaten since morning, or he would have been sick from the swaying motion.

Then he was dumped on a patch of bare dirt, the pole was pulled out, and immediately he struggled to a sitting position so he didn't feel so helpless. Low voices spoke together, but he couldn't make out their words. Without warning, the hood was pulled off his head, and he saw the outline of at least a dozen men by the dim light of a camp fire. One of the men approached him and turned his face toward the light.

"Tam?"

He was so startled, he couldn't answer right away.

"Y-yes. Who are you?"

"Folville. Can you not see 'tis me?" His voice was even deeper than Tam remembered. He peered at the shadowy face.

"I cannot see you clearly, but I know your voice, Rodney Folville." He jerked his head at the others. "Why did you attack us? We have nothing valuable but a horse."

"Oh, but there you are wrong," Folville said with a harsh laugh. "But first, why did you not contact me?"

"I tried, but the woman at the Raven said you weren't there. The inn was full, so we decided to go to Crickhollow Village for the night. I was planning to keep searching for you."

"You were planning to keep searching for me. I am touched, Tam, truly I am." The man's voice dripped with sarcasm, and Tam's fear increased. He knew Folville was a hard man, but he never expected to be treated like this. What was Folville capable of? Were he and Fiona about to find out?

"Is it too late to join you?" Tam's mouth was so dry, he could barely get the words out.

"Is it too late?" Folville was enjoying this, toying with him. "Well now, that depends."

"Depends on what?" Though now he was having second thoughts about joining this band of cutthroats, Tam was willing to say or do anything to save his life.

"It depends on how badly you want what I have to offer." Tam could detect the sneer in Folville's voice.

"What are you offering?" *My life, I hope.*

"You have two choices: you can swear your oath to me and live, or refuse, and we'll take you to the river just beyond those trees, tie you to a branch overhanging the water, and cut you enough to bleed, but not to death. We'd rather let the river dragons have their fun." He chuckled, and some of the others laughed too.

Tam had seen Folville bully others before, but he'd never imagined the man could be so merciless. "I'll swear your oath." Then an annoying twinge of conscience impelled him to consider Fiona. "What about her?" He nodded in the general direction where he'd heard Fiona struggling.

"She belongs to me, now." Folville grinned so wide, Tam saw his teeth in the firelight, making him look like a mad dog. "Join me, and I'll find you another woman."

Fiona squealed against her gag and started thrashing again. One of the men approached her.

"Keep your hands off the merchandise." Folville growled like a mad dog, too.

Merchandise? Was he planning to put Fiona in a brothel? He couldn't let that happen. Visions of King Dolan's wrath put more fear into him than Folville had.

"I'd rather not have another woman." Tam put all the sincerity he could muster into his voice. "You see, this is my wife, so I would appreciate it if you'd let her go, and then I will swear your oath."

"Your wife? Surely you don't expect me to believe that a lowly squire has gotten himself a wife?"

"I am no longer a squire, and the reason I arrived late to Cawthorne is because we were married and then had some bad luck on the way from the Keep." Bad luck kept following him, and it looked like Tam would never escape it.

"The Keep, eh? Don't tell me, you have married a noblewoman. Or a princess." Folville laughed again, but there was an edge to the sound. He walked over to Fiona and pulled off her hood but did not remove the gag. Even from this distance, Tam could see the fire reflected in her defiant eyes. She wasn't afraid; she was angry!

"Is it true? You are married to Tam?" After Fiona nodded, glaring, Folville returned to Tam and pulled a long knife from his belt. He crouched down beside him and held the blade to Tam's throat.

Tam stared into his eyes, though his heart threatened to leap from his chest. If he was going to die now, he wouldn't give this man the satisfaction of seeing his fear.

"It shouldn't matter to me that you two are married, but you see, I have to keep my reputation as one who cares about the lowly peasants." He frowned as if all his troubles were Tam's fault. "They would rise up against me and turn me in to Lord Dracen if I were to force a married woman into adultery." He glared at Tam before cutting through his bonds with the knife.

Tam rubbed his wrists to return circulation and shifted on the ground.

"I am probably making a mistake, but I will hear your oath of loyalty." Folville sheathed his knife and stood. "If I detect any falsehood, I'll slit your throat and make your wife a widow."

He would do it, of that Tam had no doubt. Glancing at Fiona, he knelt at Folville's feet and held up his hands in a token of submission. He kept his voice meek.

"Am I to say the usual oath of obedience?"

"No. I will say the words, and you will repeat them." Folville gripped Tam's joined hands tight enough to make him wince. "I, Tammeron d'Jean, do swear to Rodney Folville that I will obey every order given, no matter what, on pain of death."

Struggling not to react, Tam repeated the words and then waited for him to continue. When he didn't speak again, though his gaze bore into Tam as if *Seeing* his thoughts, Tam grew anxious. "Is there more?"

"There is more, but not words." Folville handed the knife to Tam, hilt first. "Kill your horse and then gut it. We're eating roasted horse tonight." He gestured to some of the others. "Build up the fire."

Tam pushed himself off the ground and stared at the knife. It wasn't his horse; this shouldn't be difficult.

But while he slowly walked to the tree where the animal had been tied, Tam realized the reason he'd been ordered to kill it. The horse represented the only way he and Fiona could escape this murderous group of thieves. Folville was testing him and making sure they were trapped into servitude.

Fiona's strangled cry unnerved him, and he had to still the shaking of his hand.

It was the hardest thing he'd ever done, to plunge the blade into the neck of the trusting horse. Much more difficult than killing the man at the isolated farmhouse, even though the motion was the same. And the copious amount of gushing warm blood.

* * *

Val enjoyed his meal with Emma's family. Pottage, as he discovered, was a stew made with mutton and several vegetables. He recognized carrots, parsnips, onions, cabbage, and what he suspected were turnips. With the fresh oatcakes, the food was filling and satisfying. Emma's mother looked pleased with he complimented her cooking skills.

Cavan was still sullen, but thankfully he did speak to Emma. Val resigned himself to the certainty that he would not quickly befriend his future brother-in-law. It might be a few years before the boy realized Val wasn't stealing his sister.

"Now," Somerled said while leaning back in his chair to smoke a pipe. "We'd like tae hear the story o' how you two met."

Val shared a look with Emma. There must have been panic on his face, because she sent him a mental caress.

I think 'twould be a better story if ye be the one tae begin it, since ye came tae me and nae the other way 'round.

You're probably right. You almost always are. He smiled and returned the caress. Then he straightened and looked at each of Emma's family in turn.

"I have a longer story to tell you someday of the time and the reason I came to be in MacDonald lands in the first place. But all I will tell you today is that Reggie—that's my dragon friend Regnatorix—and I were fleeing from a tribe of hostile people from the north, one of whom was trying to kill me. I had been their prisoner and was badly beaten, but Reggie rescued me. We thought we had plenty of time to work our way back to Levathia, but the northmen were traveling in their fast boats using a swift ocean current, following us." He smiled inwardly when he noticed Cavan listening intently.

"Why were they tryin' tae kill ye?" Aingeal frowned in concern. She clasped her hands in her lap, as if she were uncomfortable with idleness.

"They really wanted Reggie, the dragon, but he'd been injured, and I refused to tell them his location." He glanced at Somerled before continuing.

"Reggie flew all night over the water, and I could barely hold on because of pain and exhaustion and hunger. As soon as the sun rose, he saw land and headed straight for it.

"It turned out to be the coast of MacDonald lands near Emma's cottage in the village. I left Reggie on the beach to rest and went to find fresh water and food. Emma was out foraging and came upon me while I was drinking from a stream." He smiled at Emma. "I believe the Most High brought me to her. She gave me food and repaired my badly torn tunic before Reggie and I left to warn the MacDonald chieftain about the hostile men approaching."

"How did Emma repair yer tunic?" Somerled asked with a frown. "Did she sew it whilst ye were wearin' it? Or did ye have tae take it off?"

"I had tae take it off." It came to Val why Emma's father was concerned; he was picturing his daughter with a shirtless young man. "I wore my snow goat fur while Emma sewed the tunic."

"I taught her tae sew," Aingeal said with a proud look at Emma.

"A snow goat?" Somerled's brows raised. "What kind o' creature be a snow goat?"

"It's a large hairy beast that resembles a goat. There are herds of them in the far north, where the winter is so bitterly cold, their hair is long and thick and soft, to repel the snow and ice." Val wished he had the fur with him to show them. He'd make a point of bringing it sometime.

"How did ye get the beastie's fur?" Cavan asked eagerly. "Did ye kill one?"

"Aye," Val said, warming to his audience. "I killed several of them, in order to survive. Reggie and I ate the meat, and I used as much of the carcass as I could. Bones for needles and sinews for thread. With the fur I made clothing to stay warm."

"How did ye skin the beasties?" Somerled asked, puffing on his pipe.

"With my knife. It was the only tool I had brought with me." Val sat back, realizing for the first time how ill-prepared he had been for that journey. Truly the Most High had been with him every step of the way.

"Ye had quite the adventure, so ye did." Aingeal smiled at Val before turning to Emma. "Dinna let this one get away, lass."

Emma met Val's gaze with a new intensity. "I won't, Ma." *Val d'Alden, you be a most braw and bonnie man, an' I be proud tae know ye.*

I thank you, love. You mean the world to me.

Val's heart swelled to bursting.

*

They soon bade Emma's family farewell and flew back to her cottage. As was their custom, they sat on the bench outside her door. Val dreaded leaving her for another week. These partings were becoming more and more difficult.

He wasn't sure if it was those thoughts, or the good feelings he carried in his heart after spending time with her family, but Val decided he could no longer wait.

Going down on one knee, he faced Emma with a lump in his throat. He had to clear it before he could speak.

"Emma MacRorie, would you do me the very great honor of marrying me and sharing the rest of our lives together?"

Tears shimmered in her eyes, but she didn't answer right away, making Val's heart lurch. When she spoke, it was to ask a question he hadn't expected from her.

"Since ye be a prince, could there e'er be a time ye might become King o' Levathia?" She bit her lip, waiting anxiously for his answer.

Val thought carefully before answering. He reached out and gently cradled Emma's hand between his own.

"As I told your Da when he asked me the same question, the chance is very small that I would ever be called upon to be king, but yes, there is a chance. William is the heir, and if all goes well, once he marries and has a son, that child would become the next in line." He took a deep breath. "But were something to happen to Dolan and William before he came of an age to marry, God forbid, then Edward would reign. And if something happened to Edward before he had an heir, then—then the crown would fall to me."

Emma nodded. "'Tis as I reckoned." A tear spilled over her cheek, and Val's heart nearly stopped. Would she say no because of that very small possibility?

She smiled then, and his heart began to beat wildly. "Aye, m'love. I will marry ye, e'en with that fearsome chance o' responsibility hangin' o'er our heads, for I canna imagine me life without ye, an' I ken with all me heart we can face whate'er life throws at us, so long as we have the Most High and one another." More tears spilled over her cheeks, and Val reached up to tenderly wipe them away.

Emma grabbed his hands and kissed each one before throwing herself into his arms, nearly knocking him off balance. Laughing, he scooped her up and twirled her around until he was afraid he'd drop her because of his spinning head.

Val returned her to the door and gently set her on her feet. They held hands and gazed into one another's eyes.

"I did not plan to ask you today, so I have nothing to give you for a token."

"I dinna need a token. Ye have already given me your heart, an' ye have mine as well." Her eyes shimmered.

Then I will leave you with this to seal our betrothal until we can make formal vows. Val leaned down and kissed her soundly, pouring all the love he had for her into the gesture. When he finally and reluctantly pulled back, Emma gave him one of her lopsided grins.

That be the best token ye could e'er give me!

They laughed together and hugged one another fiercely. Parting had never been more difficult, but the promise of sweet days and nights to come gave Val's heart wings.

And when Reggie lifted them into the colorful sunset, Val waved until he could no longer see Emma. Then he raised his hands in exultation and shouted his thanks to the Most High.

Chapter 21

The way of the wicked is as darkness: they know not at what they stumble.

Fiona could not tear her gaze away from the horror of watching the death of the poor horse which had carried them here from the mountains. When Tam began to disembowel him, though, she had to shut her eyes. She couldn't afford to get sick with this filthy gag in her mouth.

Shutting out the sight of the nightmare all around her, Fiona at last understood how narrowly she had avoided being forced into a life of prostitution. Even though it didn't appear she would have to swear an oath to the horrid Folville, she'd have to make herself useful in other ways to avoid trouble for herself and for Tam.

At least, until she could find a way to contact Dolan and tell him what was going on here in Moor Point.

Had Tam known what kind of man Folville was? What kind of "employment" was being offered? Fiona shuddered, which only underscored the discomfort of the gag and her bound wrists and ankles. She and Tam were now enslaved to this criminal.

While Tam was preparing the horse's carcass for the group's evening meal, Folville himself approached her. The leer on his ugly face prompted her to give a false name when and if he asked it. Though he'd laughed at the idea that Tam had married a princess, Fiona wondered what Folville might do if he discovered who she was.

"Leave me," he ordered the man who'd been guarding her. "And whatever possessions you took from her."

Before he left, the guard tossed down her carry sack, which he'd already emptied in disgust at not finding anything of value. Fiona was perversely glad her jewels had been lost in the mountains.

Folville sat on the ground beside Fiona and picked up the carry sack. He pulled out the dress and held it up, nodding. Finally, he spoke to her.

"What is your name, *Lady* d'Jean." Laughing, he pulled the gag from her mouth, but she resisted the impulse to spit on him.

"Feena." She set her jaw, refusing to answer more than was absolutely necessary.

"What kind of name is that?" He gripped her chin and turned her head from side to side, studying her face.

"It's short for Josefina." She didn't inhale until he let go of her chin.

"You haven't been married long, since there are no marks on your pretty face." He leaned closer, tempting her to spit at him. "But I have no doubt your lord husband will have to take you in hand and curb that fiery temper I see in your eyes."

Fiona clenched her teeth to bite back a retort.

"Since I can't use you the way I first intended, you'll be a serving girl at the Raven." He narrowed his eyes. "Unless you have another way to earn your keep. Speak up now if you do."

"I sing."

Folville snorted. "Any fool can sing. Few sing well enough to make money."

"I can." Fiona lifted her chin, staring him down.

He rose and beckoned to one of the men before asking her, "Can you play a lute?"

"Yes, but not with my hands bound." She held them up, making him laugh again.

Too low for Fiona to hear, he ordered the man to do something and sent him away.

"If I cut you loose now, I think you're smart enough to know that if you try to run, you and your new husband will both be painfully executed. Am I right?" His voice was deceptively mild.

Fiona inclined her head. "I doubt not your intentions." After he cut the bonds on her wrists, she shook out her hands and then crossed her arms, still clenching her fists to return circulation.

She wasn't surprised when he left her ankles bound, but she was astonished when his errand boy returned with a lute. Fiona took it from him and examined it. The strings were intact and the wood sound, so she cradled it and strummed a chord. It made a pretty, if out of tune sound, so she adjusted the strings and tried again.

Without waiting for Folville's instructions, she began to sing the old sea chant Allard had taught her, for she remembered the chording was simple. Fiona also had an idea that kind of song would appeal to Folville and his cutthroats more than a love ballad. She was right.

Everyone but Tam stopped what he was doing to listen, so without a pause, Fiona finished the sea chant and began a new song, the ballad of a stable boy who rescued a merchant's daughter from a runaway horse. It was basically a love story but had more action than any other she knew. Besides, she reasoned, it wouldn't hurt for these criminals to hear about heroism from a commoner.

At the end of the second song, she was about to continue with a third one, but Folville stopped her.

"You've proven your point," he said in a stern voice. "You've distracted the men long enough." He took the lute and handed it back to its owner. "I'll get you another instrument, and you can begin singing tomorrow."

"At the Raven?" Fiona hadn't seen the inside, but the outside was a fair indicator of the types of rough characters who would frequent a tavern like that.

"Eventually. Tomorrow you'll sing at the River Dragon in Crickhollow." Folville picked up her dress with another leer. "Wearing this." Then he stuffed it into the carry sack before turning to leave.

"Are you going to free me?" Fiona boldly asked. When he turned back, she pointed to her ankles.

"I should wait until we leave in the morning." He shrugged and bent down to cut the bonds. "But I know you won't try to leave as long as you care about the health of your husband."

With a laugh, Folville walked away, leaving Fiona to massage her ankles so she could stand.

*

She didn't have the chance to speak to Tam all evening. Folville kept him busy cooking and then serving the meat. Fiona didn't want to eat any of it, but hunger won over principle. She wanted water to wash it down, but the cup she was given had sour ale. Though she was thirsty, she couldn't choke it all down.

At last the men who were not keeping watch bedded down around the fires. Fiona used the blanket she'd taken from the mountain cabin to claim a place apart from the men. Tam and Folville had disappeared, and she didn't know if or when Tam would return. With a sigh, she cushioned her head upon her hands and closed her eyes. Only the knowledge that Folville would punish anyone who touched her gave her any confidence she'd be allowed to sleep.

She startled awake when someone touched her shoulder. Expecting the worst, she tensed, ready to hit and kick with all her strength.

"It's me, Tam," he whispered in her ear, and she relaxed.

"Where did you go?" she whispered back, and he lay down beside her so they could better hear one another.

"Folville showed me where you and I will go in the morning. An inn called the River Dragon in the village of Crickhollow."

"Yes, he told me that's where I would sing tomorrow." She leaned closer, in case one of the men was listening. "Oh, Tam, what are we going to do?"

"For now, we do what Folville tells us."

"Why did you want to work for him? Did you know he was a criminal?" Fiona fought to keep her voice low.

"I knew he wasn't completely honest, but I had no idea he was so ruthless." He pulled her next to him and kissed her, but she didn't let him linger.

"Not here, Tam. We have no privacy. Will we have a room at the inn?"

He rolled to his back with a sigh. "Yes, but I don't know if I will get to stay the night with you."

"Why not?" Fiona scooted closer to him and propped her head on her elbow.

"I may have to ride out with some of the men tomorrow." Enough firelight glowed nearby that she could tell he closed his eyes.

"Then I will hope you won't have to go out, or that you'll return by the time I'm finished singing." Fiona smiled sadly when she heard his soft snore.

She lay beside him and attempted to return to sleep. It took a long while, for her mind would not be still.

Was Tam not the honest nobleman's son she'd believed him to be?

*

Birdsong woke her again at dawn. Some of the men were already stirring, but Tam still slept. Fiona sat up when she noticed Folville headed toward them. She gently shook Tam until he came awake.

"You two will walk to Crickhollow," Folville ordered. He handed Tam a coin. "Use this to pay for your room at the River Dragon. One of the men will bring you a horse mid-afternoon along with instructions on how to find us."

Fiona opened her mouth to ask a question, but Folville anticipated her.

"You will stay for two nights and sing for coins. I will make sure you have a lute before evening." He folded his arms and nodded. "Leave now. It is a several mile walk."

"What about food and water?" Fiona tried to keep the whining out of her voice.

Folville grunted. "A stream runs alongside the road, and there are berries this time of year." He waved a hand in dismissal and started to walk away. "When I turn around, I want you to be gone."

Hastily, Fiona folded the blanket and pulled on her boots. They would be sure to give her blisters by the time they reached the next village. Tam rubbed his eyes and headed for the road. Fiona scurried to keep up with his long legs.

She remained silent for the first little while. When they came upon a place where the creek had formed a pool, Tam hurried to it, and he and Fiona both dropped to their knees on the muddy bank and drank of the water. When Tam finally sat back on his heels, Fiona scanned the area around them and spoke in a low voice.

"Can we take advantage of this opportunity to sneak away? We might not have another extended time without supervision." Fiona imagined cutting through the woods, either making their way to Sir Aidan's manor or Castle Moor Point, whichever was closer.

"We are not without supervision," Tam said glumly. "We are being followed. This is a test of our loyalty, Fiona." He raised his gaze to hers. "If we don't do exactly as Folville says, he will kill us."

Fiona shivered, though the day was warm. She slung her sack over her shoulder and slowly rose.

"How long will we have to do exactly as he says, Tam?"

He stood beside her, though he made no move to touch her. "Until he has no more need of us. So we had better make ourselves invaluable to him."

*

The miles stretched on, and Fiona fell behind. Tam had to slow down several times to allow her to catch up. They found few berries growing near the road, though this stretch of road wasn't as heavily trafficked as yesterday.

Fiona's numbness at the reality of their situation soon changed into determination to find a way to contact her brother. If Dolan knew what was going on here in Moor Point, surely he would send mounted troops to wipe out Folville and his gang. She became so obsessed with the notion that there was a way out, she said nothing to Tam, and neglected to look for berries. All her thoughts were on devising a plan to escape.

The sun was almost directly overhead when they came to a sizeable village. The buildings here were in much better repair than the previous one, and the people looked somewhat happier. Fiona began to hope she could find an ally here.

The River Dragon was situated in the center of the village. Tam headed straight for it. Before he reached the door, Fiona ran despite the burning of her blisters and grabbed his arm.

"Can we afford to eat something here?" She looked up at him with pleading eyes.

Tam set his mouth with a grimness she hadn't seen before. "I don't know. We'll find out how much a room for two nights costs."

"I'll go with you." She tightened her grip on his arm, but he pulled away and shook his head.

"You need to stay out here. I'll call you in after I settle with the innkeeper on the room." Without a backward glance, Tam stepped inside, leaving her standing alone and forlorn.

Was he merely tired? Or was it something more ominous? Fiona hugged herself. Surely her exhaustion was causing her to see things that weren't really there, but Tam's eyes looked dead, without light or joy in the smallest measure.

She'd begun to pace when he finally opened the door and beckoned her inside. There were enough windows in the main room to give the place light and air, and one corner appeared the perfect place from which to entertain guests as a singer, even if something happened and her new lute never appeared.

Feeling better about her assignment as a bard, Fiona followed Tam up the stairs to the second floor. Perhaps after two nights of earning coins, Tam would return in better spirits, and they could make plans to find help and get away, before it was too late.

Tam dashed that hope the moment they entered the small guest room and he closed the door to face her. His despair was palpable.

"Fiona, there is something I must tell you, in case I don't return."

"What? Of course, you'll return! You're just going out with Folville's men, aren't you?" She came near and took his hands. He didn't pull away, but he didn't squeeze them either.

"I will probably have to break the law tonight, which means I will be forever trapped between two bad futures: either death by hanging at the constable's hand, or death by torture at Folville's order." He tried to back away, but Fiona wouldn't let him.

"There must be another way! Please, don't give up, Tam. We can endure this together." She threw her arms around his neck and tried to kiss him.

For a moment, he stiffened, but she did not back away. And when he gave in to her, even though his kisses were so fierce they felt more desperate than loving, Fiona assumed she had won a victory in the battle to keep his soul from belonging wholly to Folville.

*

They had fallen asleep but were awakened by a knock. Hastily dressing, they went to the door together. A man wearing a hooded cloak whom Fiona hadn't seen before stood in the hall holding a lute-shaped leather case. He handed it to her without a word and then beckoned to Tam. His cloak swirled around him while he turned to go, expecting Tam to follow.

With a gasp, Fiona clutched at Tam's hand and stared up into his eyes. There was so much she wanted to say, especially since this parting felt so permanent. But there was no time. She set down the lute and caught his face between her hands, kissing him soundly.

Then he hurried after the mysterious man, leaving Fiona alone. She waited until she could no longer hear his footsteps on the stairs before shutting the door. Then she rushed to the small window facing the road and caught a glimpse of two men on horseback galloping away.

Feeling lost, Fiona lay back on the bed and curled into a fetal position. It frightened her that she had such an overpowering feeling she would never see Tam again. That couldn't be right, could it? What would it profit Folville to send Tam into a deadly situation before he'd had a chance to earn his keep?

Her feeling had to be wrong. It just had to! Tam would return, and they would survive this bad luck together until an opportunity presented itself for them to escape.

Fiona sat up. That was her hope, and she would anchor herself by it. She reached for her carry sack and took out the dress Tam had bought her. She would do as he'd asked and flirt with the men in the audience. Perhaps if she could earn more coins than Folville expected, he would let her count that toward Tam's share of servitude. It wouldn't hurt to ask him when next she saw him.

Now that she had a plan, Fiona changed into the dress and took out the lute to practice until the time came to perform.

* * *

When Val and Reggie returned to the Keep, the dragon landed on the MacLachlan tower and let Val slide down before going to his newly constructed "cave" shelter beside the garden. It amused Val to watch his friend duck inside the narrow entrance, turn in a circle, and plop down with his head resting on his front legs. It reminded him so much of a favorite hound, he chuckled.

Rest well. You've earned it.

I know you will not rest for a while. I can still feel your joy radiating like sunbeams.

Val grinned so wide it made his face hurt. *I feel as if I could walk on the clouds right now.*

Reggie closed his eyes, but Val heard his mental laugh.

He took the steps two at a time descending to his family's rooms. When he entered the communal sitting room, his mother lay curled up on the window seat, asleep. She did not look comfortable, so he strode to her side. The sound of his boots awakened her, and she pushed herself up with a groan.

233

"Mother? Are you ill?" Val took her hand and sat beside her. She looked pale.

"I am well physically, but I am concerned about your father." Mercy met his gaze. "He has gone to find Fiona."

Now he frowned, remembering how he had reacted a few months ago when Dolan and the dragons had contacted him from a great distance. His brother had merely asked him to come home, and Val had reacted by running even further away. "What if she's not ready to be found?"

Mercy cocked her head, considering the question. "If that is so, then I hope and pray your father comes directly home. Safely."

Val patted her hand. "Father would not have gone if he hadn't had a plan." He shrugged. "Maybe his plan was merely to check on her, make sure she was well and cared for."

His mother nodded and then gazed up at him again. "Thank you, Son." She gave him a smile. "I'm sorry to trouble you, for you obviously have good news you wish to share."

Val let go of her hand and stood, unable to contain himself. He paced the length of the room and returned to face his mother. Before he spoke, he went down on one knee so she didn't have to crane her neck.

"I do have good news, and you are the first to hear." He beamed at her. "I have come from proposing to Emma, and she has accepted."

"Well, of course she has! I could tell how much she adores you. I wish you both all the joy in the world." Tears sparkled in Mercy's eyes.

Val leaned over and kissed her cheek. "Thank you, Mother. I know you already like Emma, but I am looking forward to my two favorite women getting to know one another better." He straightened. "I'm sorry Father isn't here, but hopefully he will return soon with good news about Fiona and Tam."

"I'm sure he will." But Mercy didn't sound sure, so Val reached down for her hands again. "Please don't be anxious. The Most High will watch after Fiona, like He took care of me, and she will be the better for her experiences." He smiled so she could feel his confidence, and she nodded.

"Thank you, my dear son." She kissed his hand and gave him a genuine smile this time.

"I love you, Mother." He squeezed her hands and released them. "I had better go tell Dolan now, or he will be hurt not being told right away." He chuckled. "Hopefully he will not begrudge my telling you first, though."

"Of course not." Mercy shooed him away. "Go on, then. I love you, too."

Val bowed and strode out the door. Even in the riding boots, his feet felt light as air all the way to the royal tower.

* * *

Kieran and Fowler tracked Fiona and Tam to a village in Moor Point. They discovered from a few of the townspeople that a young woman had passed through a few days ago, whom they remembered because she sang so beautifully. None of them knew if she had been alone, and none had seen her leave.

Since it had grown dark by that time, Kieran decided to stay in this village for the night and leave after the sun rose again, hopeful Fowler might pick up the horse's unusual hoofprints again and determine which way they'd gone.

He insisted Fowler sleep in one of the inn's rooms, but the tracker said he'd prefer to sleep in the stables, so Kieran didn't press him. As soon as the two of them had eaten a hot meal in the main room, Fowler left for the stables, and Kieran asked the innkeeper for writing implements.

"I only have what I use for the ledger," the man said apologetically, holding up a much-used scrap of parchment. "I can let ye have this."

"It will do. And I will pay you to give it to the next courier." Kieran then took the innkeeper's box of writing supplies to an empty table, scraped off the previous ink as best he could, and prepared one of the quill pens.

Mercy,

Followed Fiona through mountains and into Moor Point. Have not seen her yet but soon. Thank you for your letter. I am sorry, I love you, and I will tell you all when I return.

Yours, Kieran

He wanted to write more, much more, but the scrap was only so big. He hoped Mercy would read between the lines and understand how much he wanted to make things right.

After folding the parchment as best he could, Kieran used the innkeeper's wax and the seal on his ring so Mercy would recognize who it was from right away. Then he returned everything with instructions to deliver the message to Lady Mercy MacLachlan at the Keep, at which the innkeeper's eyes nearly bulged out of his head.

"Yes, sir, or should I say my lord?" Sweat beaded the man's forehead, and Kieran took pity on him.

"You dinna need tae call me either, friend." With a smile, Kieran counted out the price of the room and the courier's fee and an extra coin for the use of the writing tools. The innkeeper bowed.

"Thank you, sir, er, friend." He signaled a serving girl to bring more for Kieran to drink before leaving him alone at last.

Before the serving girl moved on, Kieran nodded. "I thank ye, and I was wondering if you were here the night a young lady, a stranger, sang with a bard?"

The girl nodded. "Yes, sir, I were."

"Did you hear anyone say her name?" Kieran stared into her tired eyes while she thought back. Then she shook her head.

"No, sir, I did not." Now she looked anxious to move on, so Kieran merely smiled.

"Thank you anyway." While he watched her scurry away, Kieran wondered if he looked like a grumpy old man to young girls now. There was a time, when he went by Finn MacRorie in his younger years, that young women looked at him quite differently. The thought made him blush.

No one ever warned him that growing older could be so . . . humbling.

* * *

Tam was given a cloak and a horse by Folville's man, and they rode in silence back to the camp from which he and Fiona had walked that morning. He'd been right; it was a test to see if they would obey instructions.

Folville himself was waiting, and as soon as Tam dismounted, the big man clapped him on the shoulder. Tam barely managed not to lose his balance.

"I knew you wouldn't run. You may be wet behind the ears, but I can almost always detect quality. You and your woman were born for this life." He grinned in a predatory way.

Tam clenched his jaw. "Will my wife be safe in Crickhollow?"

"Oh, yes." Folville gestured for Tam to join him at the fire. "One of my men is assigned to watch over her."

Tam tried not to reveal any anxiety in his face. Fiona would wait for him, wouldn't she, and not try to run?

Before he could say anything more, Folville took a stick and drew something in the dirt.

"Here is the road to from Cawthorne to Crickhollow, and here is our camp." He drew a circle close to the line. "If you travel back toward Cawthorne about a mile, you'll see a big yew tree with a large hollow in the trunk. Turn right and find the trail behind the yew. Follow the trail until you cross the river, and you'll come to the manor at Hogford Village."

"That's near Castle Moor Point, isn't it?" Tam pictured the map of Moor Point Sir Artemis had shown him many times.

Folville nodded. "Yes, it is. You were paying attention when you were Sir Artemis' squire." He drew a line perpendicular to the first one with the rough outline of a crenelated wall. "In the first house west of the fortified manor lives a leather merchant who has cheated many people, including myself. He needs to be relieved of his coins so we can distribute them to his victims."

"You want me to steal them?" Tam's eyes widened.

"Don't think of it as stealing; think of it as returning stolen coins to the rightful owners." He smiled, but it appeared more sinister than friendly to Tam.

"Am I to do this alone?" He'd never been to this village and was not familiar with the lay of the land.

"No, you will assist a man who will meet you at the river at sunset. He goes by Virgil, and he will know you as Thom." Folville's eyes narrowed. "In case you haven't figured it out, we do not use our real names. You only need refer to me as "Sir.""

"Yes, Sir." The familiar words tumbled off Tam's lips. He wondered briefly if Folville had once been a knight. If so, was his "distribution" of "stolen" funds the way he justified staying true to his oath of knighthood? "Is Virgil familiar with the layout of the grounds and house?"

"Intimately so, since he used to work for the merchant." Folville's grin was more of a smirk this time.

"Then I should leave now, to make sure I arrive at the river across from Hogford Manor before the sun sets." Tam stood, and Folville tossed aside the stick, almost meeting his height.

"This is why I chose you, Thom. I knew you would think ahead, unlike most of the men in my employ." He looked Tam over. "Be sure to keep that linen shirt under your jerkin. Light colors are a beacon in the smallest amount of light. Dark colors make you invisible in the night."

"Yes, Sir." Tam held back his nervousness in front of Folville. There would be plenty of time on the ride to release it with cleansing breaths. "Virgil and I will not fail to bring back the stolen coins."

"I know you will not fail me, because failure leads to severe disappointment, and I feel certain you would not want to disappoint me, eh, Thom?"

"No, Sir." Tam shook his head solemnly. He must always remember that Folville would never be his friend, and he could never afford to let down his guard around the man.

Without a backward glance, he gathered the reins of the borrowed horse, pulled himself up to the saddle, and rode off in search of the yew tree.

Chapter 22

Treasures of wickedness profit nothing.

When Fiona's stomach pinched with hunger, she decided it was time to go to the inn's main room. Whether or not there was a bard in town, she would play and sing as if there wasn't one. He or she could always join her later, as she had joined Allard. The thought put a smile on her face.

That was a good thing, too, because there were already patrons at the tables, waiting for their supper. Fiona strummed the lute and strolled among them, feeling the part of a bard.

Near the corner she'd chosen earlier sat a melancholy young man. Fiona was drawn to him, but she couldn't decide if he'd rather hear a frolicking tune to cheer him or a sad ballad to match his mood. Peering closer at his face, she decided he wasn't yet in the mood for a happy tune, and so she began with a tragic tale of love in a range that best suited her voice.

Though she tried to meet the other guests' eyes while singing, Fiona's attention most often returned to the sad young man. At first he seemed not to listen, but soon he was staring intently at her, as if the words spoke to his heart.

Before the final chord faded, those in the room applauded, all but the young man, who continued his uncomfortable stare. But he had straightened, and so Fiona felt triumphant. She expressed those feelings in the happier song which followed. By then servers arrived with the evening meal, and Fiona hardly faltered in her singing, though her belly was growling.

To her relief, a serving girl brought her a goblet of wine and a trencher with a small loaf of bread, a few slices of meat, and a hunk of cheese. She waited until after a third song, and then tore off a piece of the bread and folded it around the cheese, nearly swallowing the morsel whole. Then she washed it down with a long drink, ready to continue singing.

A few more people now sat at the tables, but Fiona did not see a man she could easily flirt with. So she played all the songs she had sung with Allard, and they were well-received here, too.

The earlier patrons had all left, including the young man, but more came to take their place. As the evening wore on, the guests became rougher, drank more, and were less inclined to listen politely and leave a coin in the lute case.

Between songs, Fiona noticed a man sitting in the opposite corner with his back to the wall. She couldn't see his face clearly in the shadows, but she could feel that he was staring at her, raising the hairs on the back of her neck. Even though there were still several people at the other tables, they were mostly drinking, laughing, and talking to one another, not paying attention to her singing.

She decided to sing one more song and then go to her guest room. It had grown late, and she was feeling weary. At the end of the song, only one man came forward to drop a small coin in her lute case. He nodded at her before leaving the inn.

Since no one else except the shadowy man was paying any attention to her, Fiona put the lute in the case, closed it, and made her way to the stairs. Glancing over her shoulder, she hurried to her room, unlocked the door, and rushed in. Then she locked the door from the inside and let out a sigh.

First, she set the lute case on the room's small table and thought about counting her earnings. But she yawned and decided to wait until morning. She climbed into the bed, still wearing her dress, since she had no nightdress. Maybe tomorrow she could buy one. With that thought to cheer her, Fiona closed her eyes and got comfortable under the covers.

She had almost fallen asleep when she heard a key in the lock and sat up with a gasp.

"Who is there?" she called out, hoping it was just another guest forgetting which room was his.

The door opened, and a man stepped inside, closing it behind him.

"What are you doing here? Leave at once, or I will scream." Little light came in the window, so all Fiona could see was the dark shape of the man.

"You don't want to be doing that," his deep voice said. "I'm from Folville. Your protector and his collector." There was a rumble from him that could have been a laugh.

"What do you mean?" She tossed aside the covers when she heard the lute case open. "Be careful with that! If you damage the lute, I won't be able to play tomorrow."

"With a voice like yours, you don't really need a lute, but I know how to be careful." The sound of tinkling coins made Fiona's heart sink.

Was he going to take all the coins for Folville?

"You can't take all of them," she protested. "How will I buy new clothes?"

"I left a few for you." He sounded amused, and Fiona was glad she couldn't see his face.

"How generous of you." She didn't hide her sarcasm. "Now you can leave."

But he came closer, making Fiona's heart race.

"I'll be sure and tell Folville what a good bard you are. He may want to send you to a bigger village." Another rumbling laugh, and then he swept out the door, leaving the room still and silent.

Fiona slipped out of the bed and locked the door again. This time she moved the small chair to the door and wedged it under the doorknob.

Satisfied, she crawled back in the bed, not only weary now but heartsick too.

"Oh, Tam," she whispered. "I hope you're faring better than I have this night."

* * *

Tam's weariness traveling the trail through the woods turned to anxiety when he and his mount finally reached the river. Since there was still at least half an hour before the sun set, he dismounted so he and the horse could drink their fill, and then he let the animal graze.

Though he was hungry enough to eat a fish raw, if he'd had a way to catch one, Tam looked instead for berries, knowing they wouldn't do much about the hunger gnawing at his belly. He found many of the water plants he and Fiona had eaten in the mountains, which he rinsed off before cramming the wet leaves in his mouth. They weren't very satisfying, but at least they helped take the edge off his hunger.

Before he had the chance to look for something else to eat, a movement caught his eye. A rider appeared across the river, so Tam knew it must be Folville's man. He took his horse's reins and walked toward the cloaked man.

"Are you Virgil?" he asked.

"Only if you are Thom," the man replied.

Tam nodded. "Should I leave my horse on this side of the river?"

"That would be safer for the horse and will make your getaway more sure."

Tam let go of the reins again. "I will go across downstream where the water is shallow."

"And I will do the same so I can leave my mount with yours." Virgil turned his horse, and Tam walked in the same direction until they met at the shallow ford.

Once Virgil joined him on his side of the river, Tam asked the pressing question: "How will we get into the merchant's house? Have you been inside before?"

"I worked for him in the past and am familiar with his house. We will have no trouble getting in and out. The trick will be finding where he keeps the great sums of money he has collected."

"Any idea where to look?" Tam frowned. Surely Folville wouldn't send them here if he wasn't sure they could find the money.

"I suspect he keeps it locked in his desk. We'll look there first. Do you have a knife?"

"Yes, why?"

"You might need it. Best to be prepared."

Tam's jaw clenched. There was only one reason he might need a knife, and that was to defend himself. He hoped he wouldn't need to draw the blade.

He followed Virgil in silence while they crossed the river and made a wide berth around the large fortified manor. Hogford Village would be nearby, and the merchant's house was supposed to be situated at its edge.

Virgil froze, and Tam did also. He saw nothing in the dark beneath the trees, but he heard something or someone approaching with a rustling of leaves. It made his skin crawl to imagine a man-at-arms from the manor had seen them from the tower and was coming to investigate.

Then Virgil pounced, and a small cry was abruptly silenced. Virgil stood and returned to stand close to Tam, keeping his voice low.

"An old hound, by the feel of his bony hide. Could be a stray, or could be from the manor. We must press on and be in place by the time the merchant retires."

Tam nodded. He assumed the dog had been killed, which he regretted, but if it had started baying, they would have had to abort their undertaking. Tam felt certain Folville would not accept any excuses for failure.

They continued even more carefully, pausing behind every large tree to scan the way ahead. Torchlight in the distance announced the village. No sound of celebration, so thankfully the villagers would be retiring soon, along with the merchant.

Virgil and Tam continued to move from tree to tree, stopping and listening. They finally came to a two-story whitewashed house, well-cared for with immaculate grounds planted with flowers, shrubbery, and many fruit trees. This was a prosperous merchant, indeed. Tam had seen much larger manors in worse repair.

They crouched behind a screen of flowering plants. Virgil leaned closer to whisper next to Tam's ear.

"I have seen no dog and no guard either. That speaks of an overly confident merchant who puts his trust in locks or in his own ability for self-defense."

"How will we enter a locked house?" Tam whispered back.

"Through the second story." Virgil pointed to a tall tree growing beside the house. "We will climb the tree and into that window. Then we will make our way to the first floor office and search there first."

"All right." Tam's heart began to pound faster. He'd done things of questionable legality in his life, but never outright robbery. What choice did he have, though? Refusing to participate would seal his fate, and Fiona's too.

They waited to make sure all in the house remained quiet, and then Tam crept behind Virgil to the large tree. The lowest branch was just within reach. Tam pulled himself up, staying just below Virgil while they climbed.

The window was not locked, so Virgil slowly opened the shutters and climbed in. After a few heartbeats, he appeared at the window again and gave Tam the all clear. Tam pulled himself up to the windowsill and swung his leg over the sill.

This room was a small bedroom, perhaps for a child who no longer lived at home or for guests. Tam pointed to a chest in the corner, and Virgil nodded. Better to search every possible location as they came upon it and know for sure.

No coins, only blankets and bolts of cloth. Tam lifted empty hands, and Virgil turned to exit the room. He peered in the door across the hall, which turned out to be a storeroom filled with the scent of leather. Both of them searched here, but they found no money. Only stacks and stacks of leather, some tanned and some rawhide.

There was only one more door, at the end of the hall, so Tam assumed that was the merchant's bedchamber. Virgil headed to an opening beside that door and made his way slowly down the stairs.

When one of the stairs creaked as Tam stepped onto it, he froze and listened. With his luck, the merchant was not a sound sleeper. But nothing happened, so Tam continued, careful to test each step, even if Virgil had already passed it with no hint of creaking.

By the time Tam reached the ground floor, Virgil had already entered a room in the corner, leaving the door ajar. Keeping all his senses alert, Tam followed.

This room had to be the merchant's office, for there was a writing desk and a large chest against the wall behind it. Virgil had opened it and was bent over, searching. When Tam came near, Virgil signaled him to stand at the door and keep watch.

Reluctantly, he did so, feeling exposed and nearly useless without a sword on his belt. Though he hadn't wanted to be a squire, he had enjoyed learning how to use a sword and considered himself better than average.

Tam jerked his head at the sound of clinking coins. The noise sounded loud in the silent house, and he braced himself for the sound of running footsteps on the stairs. To his surprise, no one came to investigate, and Tam had to rein in his impulse to go see what Virgil was doing.

At last, Virgil appeared in the doorway, carrying a bulging sack.

"Got it," he whispered, pointing toward the front door of the house.

With a frown, Tam started forward. Wouldn't this door open onto the road? Shouldn't they find a back way out? When he reached the door, he discovered it was not only locked but barred from the inside. There was no way they could lift that wood without making enough noise to wake even the soundest sleeper.

Virgil gripped Tam's shoulder, making him flinch.

"This way," he hissed, leading Tam back the way they'd come.

When they finally found the back door, it was barred, too. Tam's nervousness threatened to undo him. They were trapped!

"Can we go out a window?" Tam asked in a whisper.

Virgil shook his head. "They're locked, too. We'll have to go back up the stairs and out the window we came in."

So, they had to carry the bag of coins past the merchant's bedchamber and hope nothing bumped into the coins, shifting them.

They moved slowly and silently up the stairs, pausing to listen outside the bedchamber door. Tam imagined he heard soft snoring coming from within, and Virgil nodded. Continuing their careful tread, they entered the spare bedroom, and Tam closed the door behind them. He began to breathe easier.

Virgil handed the heavy sack to Tam. "I'm going to climb out to the tree, and then you hand it to me. Otherwise I might drop it."

Tam nodded and took the sack, careful not to jiggle it. Virgil swung his leg over the sill and leaned out to grab the nearest limb. He pulled himself onto it and held on with one hand, reaching back with the other. Tam braced against the sill and leaned out as far as he could, so Virgil could securely grasp the sack.

"Got it?" he asked and let go when Virgil nodded.

But Virgil wobbled on the branch and lost his grip. Rather than let go of the sack, he lost his balance altogether and fell out of the tree, landing with a loud thump. Tam heard noise out in the hallway and scrambled out of the window, climbing down as quickly as he could. He knelt beside Virgil, who wasn't moving, and shook him.

"Get up, we have to go!" But Virgil still didn't move, and Tam finally saw the unnatural angle his head made. Had he broken his neck?

Panicking now, Tam grabbed the sack, which miraculously had not burst open, and started running toward the trees.

"Stop, thief!" came a man's voice, and something *whooshed* past Tam's head.

Was the merchant shooting arrows in the dark?

Tam ran faster than he ever had, blindly dodging trees and brambles. He caught a glimpse of torchlight and hoped it was the manor house. Keeping the light on his left, he kept running in the direction he hoped was the river.

Then he heard dogs baying behind him. Though he had a stitch in his side, he pushed onward. He barely slowed in time to keep from falling into the water. There was no way to find the shallow crossing in time, so he walked into the river, holding the sack above his head while the water rushed past, deeper and deeper.

It came up to his neck but no higher, and now he wondered if river dragons hunted at night.

Struggling not to panic but to walk carefully along the uneven bottom, Tam reached the other side. He had to toss the sack onto the grassy bank and pull himself out of the water. His boots were full of water, so he pulled them off and emptied them.

The dogs were coming closer, and now there were shouts of men as well. Tam carried his sodden boots in one hand and the sack in the other and climbed up the bank. Behind him came the guttural roar of a river dragon, spurring him even more than the dogs.

He walked as quickly as he could, wondering how he was going to find the horses. When he'd gone some distance from the river, he risked a whistle. To his utter relief, there was an answering nicker ahead.

Tam released a sob when the two horses ambled to meet him. His fingers fumbled with the knot while he tied the sack of coins to the saddle of Virgil's horse. Then he secured his wet boots on his horse's saddle, gathered its reins, and pulled himself up with a groan. When he'd settled himself, he leaned over to grab the other horse's reins, and they set off down the path toward Folville's camp.

Once he could no longer hear the baying of the dogs, Tam slumped over in the saddle, shaking all over at his narrow escape. He wasn't out of danger yet, though. Would Folville understand that Virgil's death was an accident? Or would he blame Tam, even though he was bringing back all the money and both horses?

He shut his eyes, feeling more helpless than ever, like a leaf being carried downstream in a swift current. There did not seem to be a way to untangle all the predicaments he'd fallen into.

* * *

Val and Reggie flew beside Emma and Veynaria on their way to the Southern Woodlands for the weekly meeting of dragon riders. This time Dolan wasn't available to spend the day with them, so he had left Val completely in charge. He hadn't been anxious for most of the trip south, because he'd been enjoying his time with Emma, but now that they had almost reached the castle, Val's nervousness grew.

They landed within the castle yard, dismounted, and then Reggie and Veynaria flew over the wall to meet Neleisia, who was Oriana's dragon friend, in a large meadow within sight of the castle. Val and Emma greeted Oriana, and the three of them settled against the wall to wait for the others.

They had no time to talk, for the rest of the dragon riders arrived within five minutes. Val thought that very good timing, considering many of them had not been to the Southern Woodlands before.

Hamelin de Grignon of Frankland looked around after dismounting and asked Val where the king was. Val put all the confidence he had into his voice when he explained that Dolan had other obligations. He suspected Hamelin would be the one dragon rider who would have the most difficulty subordinating himself to one several years younger.

"Anyway," he added pleasantly, "my brother said it was past time I started fulfilling my obligation as Lord of the Sky. So, let's begin, shall we?" He smiled at Hamelin, knowing the young lord was usually easy-going. But it did not hurt to remind him that Val had duties bestowed upon him by his brother, the king.

"Your first solo flight, eh, Your Highness?" Fletcher Meverel quipped.

"Precisely," Val answered with a grin. He was grateful for the lifelong friendship he'd had with Fletcher, even before his sister had married Dolan. In fact, three of the nine dragon riders were already his friends, counting Emma and Sean Hendry. And Val was hopeful that he could develop a closer relationship with the others, too.

"First, let's each report anything new or noteworthy since our last meeting. Emma and I have something, but we'll wait until last to tell you." His cheeks grew warm, and Emma blushed as well.

"Since all o' us can figure out what that news be, why dinna ye tell us first, so we willna be distracted?" Caesg smirked, winking at Emma.

The others clamored for Val to tell them, all except Erian, who stood with his arms crossed and a sad smile on his face.

"All right!" Val held up his hands before clasping Emma's. He gazed into her eyes, and she sent him a mental caress. "I proposed marriage to Emma, and she has taken pity upon me and said yes."

They accepted everyone's congratulations with pleasure, and finally all the dragon riders were ready to conduct their business.

Once each had reported their problems and successes, Oriana suggested they fly together to learn all the major landmarks around the Southern Woodlands that she and Neleisia had learned from the air. It was such a good suggestion, Val decided they would fly such a "patrol" at each of the provinces during their weekly meetings.

After calling for their dragons and mounting, all ten lifted into the air and followed Oriana while she led them from the castle to several prominent villages, also pointing out major rivers. Then they flew along the coastline toward the place where the province bordered Mohorovia at the very edge of the sea.

What be that structure, Val? Emma asked. *It looks a bit like a wall made o' wood.*

It's the old Brethren village, where my mother used to live. It's deserted now. Val spoke to the dragons then. *Everyone, land inside the wooden palisade due north of here.*

The formation of dragons turned and gracefully came in to land within the old but still formidable wooden walls. Val had no memory of ever coming here before, but he'd heard the description often enough from his parents to be sure it was his mother's first home.

All the riders dismounted and looked around at the ruins. Val tried to imagine a thriving village, but it was difficult when little remained to mark the people who had once been here.

Oriana and Norman strode over to Val. Oriana's face glowed with an idea.

"Yes, what is it?" Val asked eagerly, catching her excitement.

"This would make a perfect place for the dragon riders to come and meet together, or even as a refuge or retreat." Oriana gestured around them. "The wall is still sound, and the grounds need only to be tended."

"A few sheep kept inside would be enough to keep the grass from taking over," Norman added. "And my brother could help me build a shelter large enough for several people to spend the night, if needed."

"I see this as a strategic location, if ever Levathia is invaded from the south again," Oriana added.

"It could be our southern dragon garrison," Fletcher said excitedly.

The others nodded and added their suggestions for improving the place.

"Does this mean we might also have a northern dragon garrison someday?" Sean wanted to know.

"That is an excellent idea," Val said. "You and Hamelin should scout out possible locations along the northern coast."

"We will." Sean looked to Hamelin, who nodded.

"Then it is agreed." Val made the proclamation, though he wondered if he should ask Dolan first. "I hereby declare this abandoned Brethren village will now be known as the Southern Dragon Garrison. Oriana and Norman will be in charge of its clean up and restoration, using any and all resources necessary." He nodded to the young riders. "And do not hesitate to ask any of us to help, too. We can each bring supplies and labor to help."

"I be sure Kentigern and I can find ye a few sheep tae keep the grass short," Caesg added. "'Tis transporting the beasties what might give us a wee problem."

"What do ye mean?" Kentigern balled his fists on his hips. "Uncle Nab be sure tae have a few runts tae give us. They willna be runts long once they come tae live here."

Oriana heartily agreed and then blushed when Kentigern grinned at her.

*

The dragon riders went their separate ways after that, and Val flew with Emma back to her cottage, well-satisfied with the day's accomplishments. As soon as the dragons landed, Val dismounted and went to catch Emma as she slid down from Veynaria's side. He kept hold of her, gazing into her beautiful, intelligent eyes.

"Ye ken ye do nae have tae do that." Her eyes sparkled. "Veynaria an' I have become bonnie partners."

"I do ken," Val said softly. "And I think *you* ken why I like to catch you." He leaned down and kissed her gently. She slipped her arms around his waist, and he wished he did not have to leave her.

Someday, love, her sweet voice whispered in his mind. *Someday soon.*

He touched his head to hers. *Though it's hard to wait, I pray each day for the Most High to bless our future life together, and that makes the waiting easier.*

Amen! She giggled, which made him laugh, and they sat on her bench for a little while, simply holding hands and talking over the day's events, as if they were already an old married couple.

Chapter 23

When the wicked rise, men hide themselves.

After a long and lonely night without Tam, Fiona's stomach awakened her with an urgent need to vomit. She barely made it to the chamber pot in time. Trembling, she wiped her mouth on the corner of the blanket and sat on the edge of the bed.

Why had that happened? She never got sick. Was it something she ate last night? No, because Mama always said if anything eaten was spoiled or poisoned, it would make symptoms known almost immediately.

Fiona massaged her temples at a sudden headache and lay carefully on her side. Since she wouldn't be expected to appear until this evening, it wouldn't hurt to stay in bed and sleep off whatever was infecting her. The big disadvantage to that was not eating, her pitcher of water was nearly empty, and she wouldn't have time to wash out her riding clothes, in the hopes she and Tam would be moving on tomorrow.

The queasiness returned, but this time she was able to keep from retching. She closed her eyes and decided to try to fall asleep. It did not take long for her to drift away.

*

Sometime later, there was a timid knock, loud enough to wake Fiona.

"Who is it?" she called out in a hoarse voice.

"I'm the chamber maid," a female voice answered.

With a groan, Fiona climbed down and opened the door. A kindly older woman frowned with concern.

"Are you ill, lass?" She stepped inside, still studying Fiona.

"I was, and I'm sorry about the mess, but I feel better now." She stifled a yawn.

The woman glanced down at the chamber pot and back at Fiona's face. A smile made her tired eyes sparkle.

"You're not ill; you're carrying a babe." The woman's smile widened. "Glory be! A new life will come into the world." She started to leave with the pot.

"Wait." Fiona blinked, hardly believing what she'd heard. The woman stopped and turned. "Did you say I was with child?"

She nodded. "Aye, that's what I said."

"How can you possibly know? I've been married less than a fortnight."

"I've had six of my own and helped bring others into the world. I can tell when a woman is expecting. Some have said I've been given special knowledge." The woman smiled again. "If you've been married longer than a week, you've had more than enough time, child." With a nod, she left the room.

Fiona stood frozen, stunned. It had never occurred to her she might become pregnant so soon. She had always assumed it might be difficult for her to get with child, since Mama and Joy had both talked about their difficulties.

Well, it didn't matter, did it? Apparently she *had* gotten pregnant right away. What would Tam think? Oh, what a disastrous time to have a baby growing inside her!

Her legs turned to jelly, and she had to sit in the room's only chair lest she fall on the hard floor. Oh, what was she going to *do*?

She covered her face with her hands and wept.

* * *

Tam reached Folville's camp before dawn. He could hardly climb down from the horse, he was so weary. Though most of the men were sleeping, Folville himself strode over. Even with only dim firelight, Tam could see the deep frown on the man's face.

"Where's Virgil?" he snapped.

"Dead. A stupid accident. He fell from a tree and broke his neck."
Tam squeezed his eyes shut at the last image of the man's face.

"And the money?" Folville turned his gaze to the horses, and Tam
limped to Virgil's horse, untying the sack.

"All here." He handed it over with great reluctance. There were
enough coins in this sack to pay off his gambling debt and start fresh.

"Come with me. I want you to tell me the whole story. Leave
nothing out." Folville walked away, and Tam struggled to keep up with
him. He was not used to walking barefooted.

When they sat beside the fire, Folville gave Tam a chunk of hard
bread and an almost empty wineskin, which he drained first. After
wiping his mouth, he began his account, occasionally nibbling on the
bread while Folville asked questions for more details.

Fortunately, he accepted Tam's version of Virgil's death. By the
time he finished the story, Tam was so sleepy he could barely keep his
eyes open. When he started yawning uncontrollably, Folville gestured
irritably to a blanket.

"Lay down and get some sleep. I'm going to count coins while
you dream of your pretty little wife." Folville chuckled and walked over
to a nearby wagon.

The last thing Tam remembered was an image of Fiona—lovely,
passionate Fiona.

*

Tam did not wake up until midday. Most of the men had gone,
but Folville and a couple others were loading the wagon. Tam pushed
himself off the ground and realized he was still barefooted. There was
no sign of his horse, so he stumbled over to the wagon.

"About time you woke up," Folville grumbled. "We need to leave
and make camp elsewhere. The merchant's dogs have somehow picked
up your trail."

For a moment, Tam wondered if they were planning to leave him
here and let the dogs find him. They would have woken him before
they left, wouldn't they?

"I waded across the river, so how could they pick up my scent?"
He raked his fingers through his hair.

"Some dogs are good hunters." Folville tightened a knot on the
rope holding down a tarp and stepped back. "So we are sending you
in a different direction to lead them away from our new camp." He
signaled one of the men, who brought Tam's horse. The boots were

still tied to the saddle, so he reached up and loosened them. Still damp, but he didn't want to ride barefooted again.

"How will I find you?" He struggled to pull on the boots and finally had to sit on the ground.

"Head toward Castle Moor Point." Folville tossed a handful of coins on the ground by Tam's foot. "Stay where you like as near the castle as you can, and after two days, take the road toward Port Town until you come to Knightsbridge. Wait at the Red Boar tavern until one of the men comes to fetch you." He stared at Tam so intently, the hairs rose on the back of his neck.

"What about my wife?" She was expecting him to return tonight, or at least by the morning.

"She will stay where she is tonight, and tomorrow I'll send someone to bring her to the new camp." For a moment his eyes gleamed, and Tam wondered what he *really* had planned for them.

*

Before he had twisted both feet into his damp boots, Folville and his men rode away. The wagon rattled when it hit a rut in the road, and then the sound faded away. Tam put the coins in his belt pouch and mounted his horse. He cocked his head. Was that the distant baying of dogs?

He slapped the reins and urged the horse toward the road. They went the opposite direction that Folville had taken, toward Castle Moor Point. Tam had been to the castle several times while he was with Sir Artemis, so he would not enter its walls. There might be a guard or, more likely, a servant girl who remembered him. The town outside the castle walls would be a good place to hide out for a couple of days. He might even find an opportunity to earn a few coins of his own in a game of chance.

When the road was straight, he kicked the horse into a canter, but for the curved sections, they slowed to a walk. Tam did not want to blunder into a bad situation. He felt exposed enough traveling alone, though Lord Dracen had worked hard to control highwaymen in the time Tam had lived here.

It was only cheating leather merchants who were no longer safe in their beds at night, thanks to Rodney Folville's vigilante justice.

Disgusted at his association with the man, Tam pondered why Folville would send him so near the seat of government for Moor Point. Was he hoping Tam would be caught doing something illegal?

Was he trying to rid himself of Tam? He was surely using Tam as bait to lead the merchant and his cursed dogs away from the new camp.

Well, if Folville was trying to eliminate Tam and take Fiona for himself, then, Tam reasoned, he was no longer obligated to do what Folville said. He would go to the castle's village because he wanted to, and he would find a way to earn his own wages, so he could pay off his debt and be free. If Folville wanted him dead, let him assume Tam was dead. He would not appear in two days, his man could tell him Tam must be dead, and he would never have to worry about Rodney Folville again.

Fiona could take care of herself. He had no obligation to her, legally. Though he would miss her sweet kisses, Tam knew he could find comfort elsewhere.

Now, all he had to do was disguise his appearance and come up with a new name.

* * *

Fiona finally ate something late afternoon, and her queasiness all but disappeared. She felt unclean in the dress she'd slept in, but she had tried to smooth out the wrinkles and comb her hair, at least. Before she took the lute out of the case, she pinched her cheeks to bring some color to her face. A serving girl brought her a goblet of water, which she sipped to keep her throat moist.

A few patrons had arrived for an early supper, and most of them she recognized from the evening before, so she went from table to table, speaking to them before asking for requests.

She had just settled onto a stool and was beginning a love ballad requested by one of the women, when a familiar voice joined in. Her fingers fumbled a chord at the sight of Allard entering the room. He held his lute but did not play it while he came closer with a smile in his eyes. Fiona managed to play the rest of the song without missing a note, though her gaze never left his face.

On the final chord, those at the tables burst into applause and cheers, and Allard took advantage of the commotion to plant a kiss on the corner of Fiona's mouth.

"What are you doing here?" she asked in a quiet voice.

"I could ask the same about you." He smiled and strummed the same chord Fiona ended on. "Let's tune our lutes and play together."

As soon as they were tuned, the requests for songs came without pause, and the room filled with patrons, becoming more and more crowded. After some time had passed, Fiona and Allard each took a turn singing solo while the other ate food provided by the beaming innkeeper. He offered Fiona wine, but after the chamber maid's pronouncement of her pregnancy, she asked for water instead.

The crowd never waned in their enthusiasm over Fiona and Allard's singing, but as the night turned toward midnight, Fiona felt herself wilting from exhaustion. She tried to excuse herself, but the patrons wouldn't have it. Not until she nearly dropped her lute and Allard had to catch her to prevent her falling off the stool did the audience finally accept that she could sing no more that night.

Allard packed her lute in its coin-heavy case, slipped the strap over his shoulder, and helped Fiona stand. She had to lean on him all the way up the stairs to her room and help her with the key. When he assisted her into the bed, she wanted to protest that she did not need that kind of help, but her eyes were so heavy, she fell asleep almost the instant her head touched the pillow.

The following morning, Fiona awakened to find a warm body beside her in the bed. Allard had spent the night! She sat up with a gasp, but he was sound asleep and didn't hear her. Then her stomach revolted again, and she scrambled for the chamber pot. When her stomach was empty and her mouth full of bile, she sank to her knees, completely spent.

At that moment, a key turned the lock and the door opened.

It was the same man from Folville who had taken her coins before. Fiona wanted to burst into tears!

The man stared at the sleeping Allard before addressing Fiona.

"I've come for your tips, but I also have bad news."

Fiona hugged herself. "What is the news?" She could hardly breathe.

"Your husband was killed last night. He fell from a tree and broke his neck." There was no emotion in the man's voice.

Tears filled her eyes. "Are you sure? Did you see him?"

The man shook his head. "No, but the man who was with him saw him fall and discovered he was dead." He went to Fiona's lute case and opened it. As before, he carefully removed the lute before pouring the coins into a leather pouch. Then he replaced the lute and closed the case before speaking again. "You have one hour to get ready to leave."

"Leave? Where will I go?" Fiona's voice was so strained, she could barely speak. *Tam! How can you be dead? We barely began our life together. You never even knew about our child.* Her tears came faster, threatening to undo her.

"Another man will come and take you to our new camp. Be ready in one hour." Then without a backward glance, he left.

Fiona could not weep. Though her knees were beginning to ache, she could only kneel there in shock while the tears streamed down her face and dripped onto the hard floor.

"Fiona?" Allard climbed out of the bed and came to kneel beside her. His hair stood up on one side, and his eyes were bleary, but the compassion in his voice broke her, and she covered her face, sobbing.

Allard moved closer and took her in his arms. Fiona clung to him as if he was the only one who could save her life. She cried and cried, soaking his linen shirt. And then three words penetrated her grief.

Save her life.

With a gasp, she pulled away so she could see his face.

"Allard," she said hoarsely. "Please, we must leave this place right away."

"You are in no condition to go anywhere right now. I will pay for another night in this room, so you can rest."

"Did you hear what that man just said?" Fiona was desperate to make him understand.

"What man?" Allard frowned.

"The man who took all my tips. The man my husband was working with. He said my husband was killed, and someone is coming to take me away in less than one hour." She grabbed Allard's shoulders. "Please! I have to get away from those people!"

Allard took her hands and cupped them between his own. "All right, it's all right, sweetings. We're bards; we can go anywhere. We make a perfect duet, and people all over Levathia will shower us with applause and food and drink and coins." He kissed her temple. "Come, bring your lute and whatever else you possess, and we will leave."

Fiona let him help her stand, and then she wiped her eyes and straightened. "Do you have a horse?"

"A horse?" He laughed. "No, no beast of burden. I travel everywhere on my own two feet." He glanced down at her bare feet. "I see you have two feet, too. So I hope you have adequate traveling shoes?"

She smiled in spite of the desperate circumstances. "I do, and I will change into my traveling clothes, if you'll wait downstairs."

He gave her a showman's bow. "Of course, my gentle lady." Then he quit the room.

As quickly as she could, Fiona changed into her riding clothes and pulled on her boots. She stuffed the tear-soaked dress into her carry sack, picked up her lute, and fled down the stairs. To her relief, Allard was waiting by the front door. He put a finger to his lips and beckoned her to come closer.

"There is a man waiting outside on horseback, watching the inn. I feel he is the one who wishes to take you against your will. We will have to slip out the back door." His eyes searched her face, and Fiona wondered what he was looking for. Courage? Resolve? She had plenty of that.

"Can we stay off the main roads? Do you know any back ways?" she whispered while slipping the carry sack across her chest so all she had to carry was the lute. It occurred to her that the lute did not belong to her, but since Folville's man had taken two nights' worth of tips, that was payment enough.

Allard nodded, smiling. "I know all the back ways. We will not be found, at least not on the roads." He held out his hand. "Come, my beautiful lady. It is time to take you to safety."

Though she had no idea what would happen if she went with him, Fiona feared what Folville would do too much to do otherwise. She took the bard's hand, and they went out the back door and disappeared into the woods with only their clothes and their lutes.

* * *

Kieran prodded the remains of an old campfire with the toe of his boot. Obviously several people, their horses, and a wagon had been here recently, but the horse Fiona had ridden into the camp had apparently not left camp, at least not alive. That made him frown.

"The trail has gone cold, my lord," Fowler spoke with the finality of a decree. He appeared disappointed with himself, so Kieran strode over and clapped the tracker on the shoulder.

"Not tae worry. They must be in Moor Point, so I will go tae consult with Lord Dracen." Kieran opened his belt pouch and removed several coins. "Here, with my thanks for your skills. I know I will call on you again someday."

Fowler's eyes widened. "My lord, this is too generous."

"Nonsense. You've earned it, along with the gratitude of the royal family." Kieran gave him a tired smile.

Fowler dipped his head. "Then, I thank you, my lord." He backed away to his horse and mounted. With a final nod, he was gone.

Kieran let out a sigh while he stared out at the familiar road. Somewhere nearby, his daughter was traveling with a scoundrel. He'd have to find her another way. After a final scan of the campsite to make sure he hadn't overlooked anything, he mounted Burdock and turned back toward Castle Moor Point.

Chapter 24

A wicked man hardeneth his face: but as for the upright, he directeth his way.

Fiona and Allard made it safely to Woodbridge Village, where they played for tips at a tavern until late into the night and then slept in a farmer's barn. Fiona would rather have slept in a real bed again, but she agreed with Allard that they were too close to the site of her disappearance, and Folville's men would be searching for her. Especially while they were on foot, it was too dangerous to stay in one place for more than a few hours.

Though the threat of being caught loomed over her head, Fiona found the situation strangely exciting. She missed Tam, but she was not as sad as she believed she should be, not while in the company of the charismatic Allard. His compelling voice, his wit, his flattery, and his affectionate kisses could make her almost forget her troubles. Almost.

She woke early again, vomiting. How long would she have this morning sickness? If only she had paid closer attention to things Mama mentioned regarding her pregnant patients. But who would have thought she would need to know about such matters so soon?

This time Allard did wake earlier than the day before, so they could steal away before the farmer discovered them. They quenched their thirst from a nearby stream, and Fiona found some berries for their breakfast.

The road was near enough they could hear travelers, especially those driving wagons or riding horseback. When Fiona heard the pounding of galloping hooves, she pulled Allard down behind the underbrush, for here the trees did not grow so close together and they might be visible from the road. Especially Allard wearing his bright colors.

Fiona waited until the sound completely faded away, and then counted to twenty before standing. Allard jumped up, chuckling. It made Fiona frown, wondering if he was taking the danger seriously.

"I don't think your pursuers will be traveling the main roads, especially at that speed." He gave her a patronizing smile. "The men who are looking for you are much more stealthy than that."

"I don't want to take any chances. I do not want them to find me!" To her bewilderment, she began sobbing, and Allard put his arm around her and gently guided her away from the road.

"There, there," he murmured. "You have suffered many trials of late, I fear. Let us go to a secluded place I know where you can rest without care."

Fiona's tears abated, but she let Allard lead her among the trees until they came to a lovely meadow of waving grasses and bobbing yellow flowers. A burbling stream was nearby, though Fiona could not see it beyond the tall grass. Birds sang in the trees, and under cover of shaggy oak trees, a doe and a fawn with fading spots searched the ground for acorns.

"This is beautiful," she murmured. "Why has no one built a house here in this perfect place?"

"Because this land belongs to the king, a preserve of sorts." Allard began humming a familiar tune, and then pulled out his lute, tuning it.

He strummed the opening chords of one of Fiona's favorite love ballads. Though she wanted to sing it in this lovely place, she wondered if any of Folville's men were near enough to hear.

"Please, Allard." She held up her hands. "I would love nothing more than to sing that song with you, but I fear we could be discovered out here."

He strummed a different chord then, changing it to make a sad sound. "I will stop for your sake, my lady, but we must sing this one when next we come upon an inn or tavern."

"I will gladly agree to that." Fiona offered him a sad smile, for her heart was heavy now. What had seemed an adventure earlier had become a race for survival.

"Come, let's drink some water, and you will feel better." Allard put away his lute and clasped her hand again.

They knelt at the brook and drank of the cold water, presumably from a spring, it was so pure. Then Allard lay back in the grass, staring at Fiona until she felt uncomfortable.

"What are you thinking?" he asked, patting the place beside him. She did not approach him right away.

"I am thinking that I should find a way to speak to Lord Dracen as soon as possible." After some hesitation, she sat down next to Allard, thankful he didn't try to touch her.

"What makes you think Lord Dracen would give you an audience? You are not from Moor Point, are you?" Allard sounded genuinely curious.

"I am not from Moor Point, but I have met Lord Dracen." Fiona had to be careful not to reveal too much to the bard. She trusted him to a point, but not with the knowledge of her true identity.

"My dear, Lord Dracen has met many people. Why would he remember you?" His gaze traveled over her before returning to her face. "Other than the fact you are an exceptionally beautiful young woman, that is."

Fiona's cheeks grew warm. "I think he would remember me," she said simply. She could not say anything else without him guessing she was more than a simple villager.

Allard rose to his knees and cupped her face. "Of course he would remember you, if he saw you." He kissed her lightly. "Why do you particularly want to speak with him?" His eyes were intent upon her.

"I want to tell him about Rodney Folville, about what happened to my husband." She dropped her gaze. "I want something done about those men before they hurt or kill someone else."

"Your loyalty is commendable, but your husband is no longer here to appreciate it, unfortunately." Allard's eyes filled with sympathy. "I am very sorry for your terrible loss. A widow as young as you does not need to be alone with her sorrow." He kissed away the tears that filled Fiona's eyes.

"Allard." Fiona sat back, away from his physical touch. His effect on her emotions was a bit frightening, and she needed to take control of the situation. "I like you, but I'm sorry. I am not looking for another husband right now."

He laughed, making her frown in confusion. "I am not looking for a wife, my dear. I do not plan to marry. But while we are traveling together, we can enjoy one another, can we not? Forget our troubles while drinking the ambrosia of love?"

Fiona pushed herself upright, swaying on her feet. "I am not looking for that kind of companionship, Allard. I enjoy singing and playing music with you, and I am grateful for your assistance, but I am not that kind of woman."

Even as she said the words, a chill gripped her. Tam had not legally been her husband, and now she was with child. That alone made her "that kind of woman," didn't it? What a hypocrite she had become!

Allard slowly rose. He stared at her a moment and then shrugged. "It will be as you say, my lady. I am happy to assist you in escaping those who wish to harm you, and I am also happy to keep singing and playing with you, sharing our tips." He smiled then as if her rejection had not affected him. "A wandering bard's life can be a lonely one, so I will take whatever kind of companionship you are willing to offer me."

His words and tone were so reasonable, Fiona felt badly for sounding so prideful when she really had no justification to act that way. None at all.

*

That evening they came to another village, one that was friendlier than the rest she had encountered in Moor Point. Fiona was relieved not to see anyone she would consider unsavory. The one small inn was clean and orderly and welcomed two traveling bards. When the innkeeper began serving food, those who patronized the place were farmers or merchants, and even a few fisherfolk, so they must be near the sea.

After several songs, Fiona was surprised when one of the men asked if they would sing "The Deed of Valerian." She realized she had never sung it in public before, though she'd heard Papa sing it many times. He'd written the epic ballad, in fact, for it was about his best friend, Mama's first husband, and the father of Dolan, Joy, and Val. None of that history was included, however, which was probably why this man requested it; the song itself was full of action and danger and heroism.

She leaned closer to Allard. "You should sing this one, and I'll play along and hum the harmony where appropriate."

Allard nodded, needing no further urging to bring the ballad to life. He really was an excellent bard, with the perfect blend of musical talent, a pleasant, compelling singing voice, and the kind of personality that drew in the listeners. While playing support to his lead, it surprised Fiona to realize that Allard was not very handsome at all, and yet it did not bother her in the least. She supposed it might make it easier in some ways to have good looks, but in his case, he did not need them, for he had other qualities in such abundance, even Fiona had overlooked his appearance.

When the song ended, the audience applauded more enthusiastically than for all the others they'd sung, and it gave Fiona an idea.

When Val had told the family about his experiences in the far north, he had joked with Papa about writing a ballad, but Fiona knew Papa never had. And why not? Val's adventure was sure to provoke the same reaction as the one about his father.

If Papa would not write a song about Val, then Fiona would. Val deserved his own ballad.

She couldn't wait to share the idea with Allard. Perhaps he had written songs before and could help her. The idea appealed to her so much, she had trouble concentrating on singing the rest of the evening.

All too soon, the audience drifted away, and Fiona realized how late it had become. The happy innkeeper gave them his best room and asked them to stay another day. The tips were not the most they had made, but the caliber of the audience more than made up for that, at least to Fiona. Not once had a drunken man tried to paw at her. Truly she had not noticed anyone in his cups here. What a blessing!

When they ascended the stairs, Fiona suddenly became weary and sad. What would her parents say, could they see her now? She hadn't bathed in days, had worn the same clothes without washing them, and was earning her keep by pretending to be a bard. Not only that, but she had lived with a man who was not her husband, lied to several people that he *was* her husband, and now was sharing a bed with another man, even though she was determined to keep this relationship strictly business.

And, worst of all, she was pregnant. If Tam still lived, they could have been married legally, so the child would not be illegitimate. Fiona looked up when Allard unlocked their door and gestured for her to go first. This room had two chairs, so she sank to one of them and leaned back her head with a sigh.

Allard sat in the other chair and began to pull off his long-toed leather shoes. They might appear gaudy, but Fiona was certain they were more comfortable to walk in than her riding boots.

"That went well, I think," he said softly. Then he looked up with a grin. "They always want me to sing 'The Deed of Valerian' when I am hereabouts, but with your harmony and your lovely, gracious presence beside me, the good people of Middleton Village applauded more appreciatively than any other audience for whom I've had the pleasure of performing." His eyes twinkled, making Fiona smile.

"I'm glad you had a better reception than usual. And I want to ask you something." She slowly straightened in the chair and jumped when Allard slid to his knees on the floor in front of her.

"Ask me anything, dear lady, except for my hand in marriage, and I am yours." He winked at her.

After she laughed, which surely was his intention, she studied him for a moment. "Do you ever write songs of your own?"

He barked a laugh. "Sorry, but I was not expecting that question." He pushed himself off the floor and returned to his chair. "To be sure, I have tried to write my own songs, but they are never as exciting when I sing them as they are in my imagination."

Fiona faltered. Perhaps she would not be able to write a ballad for her brother. Having an idea of how it should sound might not turn out as well as she hoped, either. But she continued anyway.

"Singing 'The Deed of Valerian' gave me the idea for another ballad. A similar heroic ballad about a young man I kno—have met. He told me the whole story in such detail that I'm sure I could remember it all."

Allard brushed at a few stains on his tunic. "I do know that telling a story and singing a ballad about it are two different talents. It's a matter of fitting the words to the musical tune. Do you have a tune in mind?"

Fiona hummed the one which had been in her head all evening. She was amazed she hadn't forgotten it, after the varied songs they had sung since then.

"That's a charming little tune." Allard repeated the melody while bobbing to the beat. "Any of the words yet?"

Fiona cleared her throat, feeling suddenly shy. But she started singing anyway. This was for her brother.

"Sometimes a brother will misunderstand, even when trying his best. This is a tale of adventure gone wrong that began with a friend's tragic death."

"Oh, that's a great beginning! That will draw in the listeners." Allard leaned closer, his whole face lit with interest, though he had to be as exhausted as she was.

While singing the verses she'd already written, the rest of the song came to her. The words and music were golden threads unrolling from a spindle and falling into place on a loom. It was very like a tapestry being woven by angelic hands, swift and sure. When she reached the end of the song, Fiona was no longer tired. She felt as triumphant as the final resonant chord.

Allard clapped, his face beaming. "My lady, that was magnificent! It has every mark of an enduring saga, from the simple yet moving melody to the rhythm and urgency of the words to the subject of the ballad, this Prince Val. Tell me, is he related to the one in 'The Deed of Valerian'?"

Fiona nodded. "He is named for his father but goes by Val."

"And how did you come by your information? Have you been to the Keep before?" There was no edge to Allard's voice, but Fiona was suddenly nervous. Had she said too much?

"Yes, I have been to the Keep. Those I spoke with there are quite interested in the royal family and like to talk about them." That sounded like it could be true, didn't it? Oh, how easy it was becoming to tell untruths! Fiona did not think that was a good thing.

"Once we begin singing your new song, even more people will talk about the royals, I am guessing." He became animated again. "But a title! Your wonderful song must have a title, so others may request it by name."

Fiona was taken aback. A title? What should she call Val's story? It wasn't a "deed" like his father had done, saving Levathia from monsters by renewing a covenant with the great dragons. Fiona supposed Val would call his time in the far north a journey more than an adventure.

"How about 'Prince Val's Journey'?" When she said it out loud, the title didn't sound right.

Allard shook his head. "If you want to use the word 'journey,' I would call it 'The Journey of Prince Val,' but even that doesn't do the song justice." He tapped his lips, deep in thought.

They spent several minutes coming up with words such as *voyage*, *adventure*, *flight*, and Fiona wanted to use *dragon* or *land of ice* in the title somehow. But Allard insisted it had to be simple, and so his was the title they decided on: "The Ballad of Prince Val."

"It's about a prince," he reasoned, "and audiences will note that the two names are similar, so they will want to hear it, no matter what." He grinned and patted her hand. "Let them be surprised while they're listening to the tale unfold. No hints in the title! No spoiling the pleasure by giving away the exciting bits too soon!"

Fiona nodded. He really did know what he was talking about. So, despite the very late hour, they sang the entire song together one more time, to make sure Fiona had it right. Allard certainly had a mind for memorization! Would she improve with practice?

*

They slept soundly, side-by-side in the bed but without cuddling or touching in any way. That suited Fiona just fine. Her short time with Tam had proved to her that she was not ready to be married, despite being sixteen. And when she was awakened by morning sickness again, she decided she was not ready for motherhood, either. Oh, what was she going to *do*?

All she knew for certain was that she did not want to go home until after she had recovered from the childbirth. Perhaps enough time would have passed that she and her parents could come to an understanding. What that would be, she couldn't yet imagine, but she had several months, at least, to ponder it.

Meanwhile, she and Allard could continue to travel, play and sing, and maybe write more songs. It was a life of freedom that appealed to her greatly.

Except she had to find a way to bathe more regularly.

*

The innkeeper was not anxious to see them go, but Allard promised they would return as soon as they could. Fiona was disappointed not to stay at least one more night. Allard was right, though; she was not out of danger yet.

They were given a ride in a wagon by a local farmer, and so they made good time as well as conserving their strength. That afternoon they came to a fishing village, and Fiona watched with interest as a tall-masted ship sailed into its small harbor. She found herself curious about where the ship was from, what kind of people were aboard, and what kind of cargo it carried.

"If you think that's interesting, wait 'til you see Port Town. There are always several ships, often Vandal dragon boats as well as ships from the Southern Isles and the northern provinces of Levathia." He walked with a spring in his step. Was he anticipating another hearty meal and a soft bed, like she was?

They came upon a weather-beaten inn with the sign of a Sea Dragon. Inside there were fishermen already eating, though it was only late afternoon. Thankfully none of them had been drinking long. One of them noticed Allard and held up his mug of ale.

"A bard! Sing us a sea shanty, bard!"

"A song, a song!" another cried. "And he's got a pretty lass with him."

Fiona started to duck her head, but Allard nudged her with his elbow. "Go on, smile at them. Their talk is bigger than they'll ever do." He winked at her. "This is evening for them, since they wake at the crack of doom."

The innkeeper, a stout younger man, was not as friendly as the one in the previous village, but he waved them over to a corner of the room and let them play. Fiona decided that most, if not all innkeepers had learned there was profit to be made if a bard came to perform in their establishment.

First, they played several sea songs for the fishermen. By that time other patrons were arriving, so Allard chose a wider variety of songs. As he had predicted, someone requested "The Deed of Valerian." Once he finished, with Fiona again providing harmony, he met her gaze and smirked.

"Shall we play your new song, my lady?" He wagged his brows, making her smile nervously.

"Do you really think these people would be interested?" She glanced around the room.

"There's only one way to find out, now isn't there?" And without waiting for her answer, he addressed the audience with a bow.

"I am Allard, and Feena here has written an exciting new song. You are privileged to be the first to hear 'The Ballad of Prince Val.'" He strummed the opening chord, and Fiona joined in.

To her amazement, everyone present grew quiet and listened intently, even the table of fishermen who had been laughing earlier. Fiona made sure to sing the words clearly, so the listeners would understand everything her brother had experienced and survived on his incredible journey with his dragon to the Land of Ice.

Before the final chord faded, the audience burst into applause and cheered. Fiona's cheeks grew warm when Allard indicated she should bow to acknowledge the crowd's acclaim. She had to admit to herself, it made her feel good to have written the song about her brother and for people to like it so well.

As the evening wore on, the innkeeper became more friendly to them, keeping them supplied with food and drink, and promising them a room when they finished. Fiona grew tired long before the audience was ready to leave. Her new song was requested three more times. Rather than tire of singing it, however, she was grateful for the chance to commit it to memory. She did like to hear Allard sing it, though; if Val were a singer, she imagined his voice would be as pleasant as the bard's.

*

After the patrons left, yawning but in good spirits, the innkeeper led them to their room. Fiona was so weary by that time, she tripped on one of the steps, dropping her lute. Allard managed to stop it before it tumbled all the way down. The moment they entered the room, Fiona set the case on the bed and opened it, fearing the worst. The coins inside had tumbled around, but thankfully not cracked the wood. A couple had fallen into the sound hole, and it took Fiona several anxious minutes to get them out without having to remove the strings.

Allard, meanwhile, was counting their coins, and he looked up with a tired but pleased smile. "We outdid ourselves tonight, my lady! In the morning we will find you a new outfit, fit for a bard, and new footwear for walking the back roads. How do you like that?"

"I like it very well." Fiona yawned, and her eyelids felt weighted down by stones. "We should try to sleep an hour or two, at least." She closed the lute case and set it on the floor beside the bed before climbing under the covers. "Goodnight, Allard."

He blew out the candle. "Goodnight, Feena."

*

It seemed as if no time had passed when a hand clamped over Fiona's mouth. She awakened and began thrashing in the bed, but her scream was only a noise in her throat. Allard heard it anyway.

"Stop!" he shouted, grabbing the strong arm that held Fiona down.

She felt rather than saw the stranger's other powerful arm strike Allard and knock him off the bed. Then the man tried to lift Fiona, but she flailed with her arms and kicked as hard as she could.

At least one of her kicks connected, for he dropped her, and she rolled over to Allard's side of the bed. He lay moaning on the floor. She shook him, willing him to wake up.

The looming hulk of the intruder strode around the bed and reached out for Fiona. Allard sat up, pulled something from the man's boot, and thrust upward. The man let out a strangled cry and grabbed Allard by the throat.

Fiona screamed then, as loudly as she could. Running footsteps came up the stairs. The door was flung open, and the innkeeper stepped in, carrying a lantern.

Now that she could see, Fiona began to beat on the man's arms. Allard was trying to push his hands away, but the man was too big. The innkeeper came closer and saw what was happening.

"Let him go!" But the man wasn't listening, so the innkeeper set down the lantern, picked up the nearest chair, and smashed it on the intruder's head.

Fiona ducked and covered her head, but the chair was a sturdy one. The man fell like a stone, on top of Allard. Fiona scrambled to his side, and the innkeeper joined her. Together they pushed the big man off the smaller bard.

"Allard? Are you all right?" He didn't answer, so Fiona felt his throat and let out a cry. His windpipe had been crushed! She leaned close. He wasn't breathing, so she opened his mouth and tried to breathe for him.

She could not push the air past the point of the crushing injury, no matter how hard she blew.

"No!" she wailed. If only she could Heal him!

She placed her hands on his throat again, hoping against hope that she *was* a Healer and her gift would finally appear when she desperately needed to save a life.

But nothing happened. She fell against his chest, weeping more for him than she had for Tam. How unfair that Allard should die like this, having his throat crushed, the source of his beautiful voice! *Folville*. This was surely one of *his* men. Fiona sat up, wiped her eyes, and glared at the intruder. By the lantern light, he lay sprawled on the floor, unconscious but probably not dead.

Unlike Allard, who would never sing again.

"I'm sorry about your man," the innkeeper said. "Do you know who this is?" He nudged the body with the toe of his shoe. "I've never seen him before."

"No, but I have an idea who sent him. Rodney Folville from Cawthorne Village. He murdered my husband."

The innkeeper nodded. "I'll get some rope and tie him up for the magistrate." He started to leave.

"Wait," Fiona called. "What about Allard?"

"I'll help you lay him out on the bed when I return. We can bury him in the morning." Then he left, leaving the lantern.

Bury him? Just like that? He was alive a little while ago, singing with the most beautiful voice Fiona had ever heard, and playing with the surest long fingers on his lute. And now he needed to be *buried*. All because *she* did not have the gift of Healing, like the rest of her family.

More tears poured down her cheeks. Now she was still being hunted, but she had lost her protector. She did not know where she was, precisely, or how far to the nearest help, which was Lord Dracen. Even so, Folville and his cutthroats could be anywhere between here and Castle Moor Point.

Then she thought of the boat in the harbor. Could she sneak aboard? Folville wouldn't expect her to do something like that, would he? How smart were these men he hired, anyway? And was there another man waiting for this one to help bring her captive to Folville?

Fiona stroked Allard's cheek. She had to get away; she couldn't even wait until after he was buried.

She would take his lute and play it, in his memory. She would live, because he couldn't. She would be a bard in his place, wherever she ended up, because she wasn't a Healer and couldn't save him.

With a sob, Fiona kissed his forehead, felt around for his lute case and the pouch he'd filled with their coins, snatched up her blanket, and fled the room before the innkeeper returned.

Chapter 25

The fear of man bringeth a snare:
but whoso putteth his trust in the Lord shall be safe.

When Fiona had descended the stairs, she heard the innkeeper coming from the back and hid behind a table until he started up the stairs. Then she crept toward the back door of the inn, opening it by the time he reached the guest room.

She made sure there was not another of Folville's men nearby, and then she followed the shadows while making her way to the wharf. There were a few drunken men along the way, but the hour was late enough that they had fallen into a stupor. In one case, the man was passed out on the grass.

Fiona was thankful to note that the wooden piers which jutted out into the water were cluttered with barrels and coils of heavy rope, affording her places to duck behind if someone approached. But it appeared everyone was asleep, and she made her way to the ship without being seen.

Because the ship was a large one, Fiona wasn't sure how she was going to climb aboard it. She crouched down between two barrels and studied it, but a rope ladder was folded over, out of reach. The others ropes she could see hung tantalizingly close, but even timing her attempts to grab one with the lapping waves that pushed the hull closer to the pier, she could not grasp it tightly enough to pull herself up. She had not considered the ropes would be slippery.

Next, she opened one of the barrels to see if there was room for her to stow inside, but it was full, so she assumed the others were also.

Squeezing in between the barrels, Fiona pondered what to do. If she were discovered here in the morning, what would the sailors do to her? Could she offer to pay for passage? Was that a legitimate way to get aboard? Oh, if only she had paid attention to how the world worked outside of the Keep!

Despite her desperate situation, the hour was late, and the sound of the waves lulled Fiona to sleep.

*

She came suddenly awake when she heard footsteps approaching, making the pier move beneath her. The sun had not yet risen, so she had concealing darkness for a little while longer, at least. Two men walked past her, and one of them barked an order to someone on the ship. Fiona peered around the edge of the barrels. Stifling a cry of excitement, a gangplank lowered from the ship and came to rest on the pier. The two men walked quickly up the narrow strip of wood.

Without thinking too much about what she was doing, Fiona pushed herself up, glanced around to make sure no one else was nearby, and hurried up the gangplank. She dropped down on the deck of the ship and, upon hearing voices approaching, ducked down behind a large coil of rope.

After those men passed her position, Fiona wondered where she could find a better hiding place, one that would conceal her once the sun rose. She raised up enough to scan the nearby area. There! Across the deck hung a small boat by several ropes. It was low enough that Fiona thought she could climb inside and remain unseen.

She looked both ways to make sure no one was nearby, and then she sprinted across the deck, pulled herself into the boat, and scooted beneath the wooden slats of one of the seats. Gazing above her, she could make out the ship's mast and had a vague notion that sailors would have to climb up the rope ladders attached to the mast when it was time to hoist the sails. If she remained underneath the slats, she should stay hidden to the sailors' eyes.

After a little while, the ship came alive with activity, and the rising sun began to lighten the sky. Fiona became aware of the hard wood she lay upon and how uncomfortable she was going to be. Her mouth was parched with thirst, and she was still weary from lack of sleep. This day promised to be a trial of patience and endurance, but as long as she avoided Folville's men, the discomfort would be worth it.

Heavy footsteps stopped beside the boat, and a deep voice called out several orders. A large sail was unfurled on the mast, snapping in the breeze, and the ship began to move away from the pier with creaking and a rocking motion. Thankfully the big man moved away, for the movement beneath her caused Fiona's stomach to be violently sick. She turned her head to vomit on the bottom of the small boat.

As the ship moved out to deeper water, the rocking became more pronounced, and Fiona continued to be sick, even though there was nothing left in her belly. She writhed beneath the slats in between dry heaves, more miserable than she'd ever been, but she didn't dare cry out lest she attract unwanted attention.

Finally, exhaustion overcame her, and she fell into a troubled slumber.

*

The next thing Fiona knew, strong hands were dragging her out from under the slats, and a man with large calloused hands tossed her over his massive shoulder. She couldn't see well enough to know what was happening, and she felt so ill, she didn't even care if he threw her over the side of the ship to be eaten by a sea dragon.

"What have you there?" another man asked.

"Stowaway, Captain. She's in a bad way."

"We're almost to Seaton. Make her someone else's problem." The captain sounded annoyed, and Fiona wondered in a hazy way where Seaton was.

She drifted off again and didn't regain awareness until she was abruptly dumped upon a hard wooden surface. Thankfully it wasn't moving. It did smell of fish, which made her stomach queasy again.

"You there! Find help for this woman; she's sick." Then the man strode away, leaving Fiona in a heap in the sunshine.

She cracked her eyes open, but couldn't see much of anything except a pair of boots coming toward her. Another man lifted her with a grunt and carried her away from the pier. There must have been a tree nearby, for he finally set her down on a patch of grass with shade overhead.

Fiona tried to sit up, but she had no strength to move. She closed her eyes and wondered if she was going to die.

After a little while, she heard another voice, a woman this time.

"Can you hear me?" A cool hand felt her forehead and then the back of her neck.

Fiona opened her eyes. "Yes," she whispered from a throat dry as dust and foul-tasting.

"Help me carry her to my house, Barnaby," the woman ordered in a firm yet pleasant voice.

"Sure thing, Elvina." Strong arms pulled her upright and scooped her up gently, supporting her head on his shoulder.

Fiona got her first glimpse of the woman. She was not young, but neither was she old. And though she was not pretty, there was a quiet dignity and calm about her that drew Fiona to her. Somehow, she knew she would be safe with this woman.

They came to a tidy house along a busy street, and Elvina opened the door, ushering Barnaby inside. He set Fiona down in a chair and stepped back. She gripped the arms of the chair and struggled to stay upright. Why did she feel so weak?

Elvina brought a cup and held it to Fiona's lips. "It's only water; sip it slowly."

Fiona did so. The blessed liquid cooled her tongue. And she was grateful to this woman for being so patient, not moving the cup until Fiona had drained it.

"More?" she rasped.

Elvina nodded. "In a little while I'll give you more. We must wait and make sure your body can accept it." She smiled sadly. "Seasickness can be deadly. I have seen it." With her free hand, she felt Fiona's forehead again. "Your skin is less clammy than before. That's good."

"Are you a Healer?" Fiona's voice sounded a little stronger.

Elvina shook her head. "Not a true one, but I have learned to grow and use herbs, and I also have learned by observation ways to help those who are ill."

"You sew up gashes, too, don't forget," Barnaby piped up. "And you know how to set broken bones." He grinned at Fiona, revealing a missing front tooth. "Elvina is our village healer, so don't let her tell you a fish story."

"I don't tell fish stories." By Elvina's smirk, Fiona could tell this was a friendly argument. Then the smirk was replaced by a concerned frown. "So, do you feel any nausea?"

Fiona shook her head. "Not even a little."

"Then you may have more water." She refilled the cup from a wooden bucket and held it to Fiona's mouth again.

This time, Fiona tried to help hold the cup, but her hands were still shaky enough that she let them drop to her lap. As before, Fiona drank all the water and wished for more.

"We'll wait a few more minutes before I give you a third cup." Elvina peered into Fiona's eyes. "It's best not to drink too much too quickly."

Fiona nodded. She had a vague memory of one of Mama's patients being severely dehydrated and trying to guzzle too much water. According to Mama, the man had narrowly averted death, and only because she and Papa had been nearby.

That made her remember Allard's terrible death, and how he could have been saved, if only she had Mama's gift. Elvina must have seen the sadness in her face, for she grasped Fiona's hand.

"Are you able to tell us your name?" she asked in a gentle voice.

Fiona glanced at Barnaby, who was still standing nearby, watching with interest. "Feena," she remembered to say. "Short for Josefina."

"My brothers and sister call me Vina, and now I'm grateful they don't pronounce it 'Veena.'" She chuckled in what sounded like fond remembrance. "I am glad to know you, Feena. You are in the village of Seaton, on the coast of Moor Point. Or did you know where you are?"

"I knew I was in Moor Point when I became a stowaway on the ship." Fiona closed her eyes. "I had no choice. The men who killed my husband are looking for me."

"They're looking for you?" Elvina frowned in alarm. "Surely they don't want to kill you, too?"

Thinking about Folville roused Fiona's anger. "I don't know for sure, but their leader captured us and forced my husband to swear servitude to him, for both of us. But all the money I made in tips, he sent someone to take from me, so between all that money and my husband's life, I consider my debt paid off." She knew she wore a frown, but she didn't try to hide it.

"Oh, dear. I am sorry you have had all that trouble and, most of all, have lost your husband so young." Elvina shared a look with Barnaby. "Do you know where your husband swore this oath?"

"All I know is, we were not far from Castle Moor Point, but I'm not familiar with this province." She wished again for a map, so she might see the villages where she and Tam had traveled, and later where she had gone with Allard.

"Our village is not far from the old castle ruins. It was the seat of government from the beginning of Moor Point until a few years before Barnaby and I were born. We are quite a distance from the present day Castle Moor Point."

"Are we the same age?" Barnaby spoke up. "I always forget how old we are."

"Are you brother and sister?" Fiona asked.

"Oh, no," Elvina answered. "We both have lived here all our lives, so we have become friends and allies."

"We could be permanent allies, if you'd only accept my proposal." Barnaby said the words so matter-of-factly, Fiona almost missed the wistful look in his eyes.

"Not possible, and you know it." Elvina's manner was not easy as it had been, and Fiona wished Barnaby would find somewhere else to be.

"I do know it." He nodded once, determined to be cheerful. "I'll make myself scarce before I wear out my welcome." With a smile, he tipped his hat to Fiona. "Good day, Feena." And then he was gone.

Elvina filled the water cup again. "Don't mind Barnaby. He has a good heart, and I do appreciate his friendship. But I do not plan to marry, you see." She brought the cup to Fiona. "I raised my brothers and sister when their Ma became sick. She was my stepmother and a kind soul."

"Where are your siblings?" Fiona asked after taking a long sip.

"Finn still lives with me, and Sylvia is married and lives nearby with her fisherman husband. And wonder of wonders, my brother Erian has found new employment in the most fantastical way, you would not believe it." She shook her head. "I still have trouble believing it, and I have seen them with my own eyes."

"Seen who?" Fiona disliked riddles, especially when she was too exhausted to follow along.

"I hope to introduce you to Erian and his new companion, a great dragon named Amadorix."

Fiona barely held in a gasp. Elvina's brother was one of the new dragon riders Val was talking about? Then if he did come to visit his sister, Fiona could get a message to Lord Dracen about Rodney Folville, couldn't she?

She wouldn't have to actually tell Lord Dracen where she was, would she? If he knew, then she felt certain he would tell Papa, and Papa would try to find her. There was no way she could return to the Keep expecting a child with no husband, but she would have to tell Papa the truth eventually. So perhaps she should write a letter to Papa also and ask Lord Dracen to deliver it to him.

"Feena? Are you feeling better? You drifted away from the conversation, but maybe you are simply exhausted and need to sleep the rest of the day?" She took Fiona's empty cup and set it beside the water bucket on a worktable.

"I'm sorry. I am very tired. I have not slept well for several days." Fiona gingerly rubbed her temples.

"Then come, let me help you to one of the guest beds." Elvina lifted Fiona and then supported her with a strong arm.

"You have more than one guest bed?" Fiona guessed.

Elvina nodded with a shy smile. "This was the house of a hospitable widow named Ardith. She passed it on to me just before she died two years ago, and I decided I wanted to continue her tradition of acting as an informal innkeeper."

They had arrived at the guest room. Though it was tiny, there was a bed with a handmade pillow and blanket, and Fiona had never thought a bed could look so inviting.

"Sleep as long as you need to, Feena." Elvina pulled back the blanket, but before Fiona could climb in, she held up a hand. "You'll feel better if you change out of your soiled clothes." She opened a trunk against the wall and took out a nightdress. "This might be a little long, but you are welcome to wear it."

Tears sprang to Fiona's eyes. "How can I ever thank you, Elvina?" She took the nightdress from her hand. The fabric was worn enough to be especially soft.

Elvina went to the door and turned before leaving. "The same way I did—by going forth and doing likewise." Then she shut the door, leaving Fiona to change and then sleep in comfort and peace.

* * *

While Elvina was preparing the evening meal, Barnaby returned before Finn did. She glanced over her shoulder. "Staying for supper, Barnaby?"

"If you have enough." He carried an armful of firewood, which he set beside the hearth. Then he perched on a nearby stool and watched her.

"I always do." She stirred the pot of soup. "What did you think of our visitor?"

"She looks familiar, but I know I've never met her before." He jerked his head toward the guest room. "She still asleep?"

"Yes, but I expect her to wake soon." She hung the spoon on a hook and turned to face him. "She does look familiar. I wonder if she is related to someone we've seen before, or used to know?"

"If she is, I expect we'll find out soon enough." He leaned over and picked a potato peeling off the dirt floor. "You going to let her stay?"

"As long as she needs to." Elvina shrugged. "She has obviously suffered a lot in the last little while."

That was an understatement if ever she heard one. When Erian stopped by next, she would ask him to keep an ear out for word about Feena's murdered husband. Elvina had an idea the poor girl would not completely heal until she was sure those who killed him were no longer after her.

* * *

Tam made his way toward Castle Moor Point by staying off the roads and even well-defined paths. He foraged for food, and there was plenty of fresh water, though his belly craved meat. When he came upon a patch of bleeding heart flowers, he had a memory of hearing that they could be used to lighten hair color.

He knew he couldn't do anything about his height, other than hunch down a little, but anything he could do to disguise his features might keep him from being discovered by Folville's men, or even Jevan and his friends, should they decide to search for him in Moor Point.

After crushing several handfuls of the bleeding heart flowers on a flat rock with a smaller one, Tam applied the tacky pulp to his hair and left it on for the rest of the day. While washing off his hands in the nearby stream, he saw a powder tree on the opposite side. He remembered as a boy climbing one such tree and being scolded because the powdery bark had stained his hands and clothing and did not wash off.

Slowly he rose and walked upstream to find a place to cross over without soaking his feet. Using a fallen tree and a partially submerged rock, he made his way to the opposite bank and backtracked to the tree. As he remembered, running his hands over the bark loosened the brown powder, which he used to rub on his hands, arms, face, and neck. Between the change in hair color and skin color and hunching down, maybe it would keep him from being recognized by anyone who wanted to harm him.

He walked alongside the stream in the direction of Castle Moor Point for a mile or so before stopping to get a drink of water. He washed off his hands, then cupped them to drink. He did this several times, checking his hands each time to make sure the brown stain had not come off. Then he washed his face and raked wet hands through his hair to remove all the dried pulp of the bleeding heart flowers. As soon as he came to a pool of still water, he hoped he would be able to see streaks of lighter color in his dark hair.

After walking another mile or more, Tam began to see glimpses of the road between the trees, and he knew he was very close to the castle. He would wait until the last possible minute to join the travelers on the road, for the more people and horses and wagons there were, the easier it would be for him to blend in and remain hidden from any of Folville's men who might be nearby.

When a farm wagon lumbered by, followed by several villagers on foot, Tam fell in behind them, keeping his shoulders hunched and his gaze lowered, as a peasant was supposed to do. He certainly looked the part with his torn, stained clothing and muddy boots.

Around the last bend in the road, the crenelated wall and towers of Castle Moor Point came into view, standing proudly above the height of the tall pine trees surrounding it. The village outside the wall was bustling this time of the afternoon, so Tam had no trouble slipping through the gates with the others.

Once the group was out of sight of the guards, Tam ducked down a side street, looking for a particular tavern he and Sir Artemis had visited once before about a year ago. Tam had listened to the conversations around them, so he knew it was a meeting place for those who played games of chance. He hoped the few coins remaining in his belt pouch would be enough to gain entry to one of the games. If only Fiona's jewels had not been lost in the mountains! But, he supposed, Folville's men would have taken them when they were first captured.

Then guilty thoughts intruded as he wondered how Fiona was faring without him. He shook his head, determined to smother his conscience. Fiona could take care of herself; she was not and never had been his concern. Not really. After all, they weren't even legally married.

He kept his pace slow to keep watch for the sign of the white dove and also to keep from colliding with the many people and animals going up and down the winding streets. Nearer the castle, they were paved with cobblestones, but on the outskirts, the streets were dirt, which Tam knew from experience became muddy mires after a heavy rain.

When he turned a corner, he spied the White Dove at the end of the street, which dead-ended at a section of the castle wall.

"'Ware below," sang a female voice above him, and Tam sidestepped before a pail of smelly slops landed on his head. It splashed hard enough that it splattered his boots and the legs of his trews, and he bit back a curse. Glancing up, the woman's head disappeared behind a shutter in a second story window.

Tam stomped the rest of the way to the tavern, hoping to shake off some of the droplets. The odor only underscored how far he had fallen. Surely his bad luck had to end sometime?

When he reached the door with the freshly painted sign, Tam stopped and pulled out the soiled handkerchief from his sleeve. He hesitated, but then reasoned he would not be a gentleman again, at least not right away, so no need to put on airs. The cloth with its embroidered edges would need to perform a much more mundane job, so he could have even a small chance at success tonight.

With a grimace, Tam used the handkerchief to wipe off the rottenness from his trews first and then his boots. Then he folded the cloth over the stain and tucked it back in his sleeve. Next chance he had, he would wash it, though he knew it would never look the same again.

* * *

Kieran decided to visit Sir Aidan and Lady Iris before going on to see Lord Dracen. There was always a chance Fiona had spoken to them, since she had obviously passed close by their manor house, and she and Iris had been friends for years. The day was mild, and Burdock was tired from their long journey, so it wouldn't hurt to let the horse rest at Aidan's before continuing on to the castle.

It had been many years since Kieran had spent much time in Moor Point, but the roads still looked familiar to him. The people he'd known had grown older, as he had, and his appearance had changed enough that there would be few, if any, who would recognize him.

He sighed. It was definitely true that a hard life could age a body more quickly. These years since Dolan became king had been hard in a completely different way than living the life of a laborer or a knight errant. Being the king's regent had been the beginning of his gray hairs, and then being a father to Val and later Fiona and Tristam had gradually completed the transformation of his hoary head.

The memory of his last goodbye with Valerian when his friend had begged him to take care of his family had faded somewhat, but not the solemn weight of that promise made during a time of desperation. Of course he hadn't begrudged his friend's desire that the one he trusted most be secured to take care of his pregnant wife and two bairns, when he knew the chances of his survival were so slim. One reason Kieran had made the promise, other than his love for Valerian and his family, was because he was convinced it would be him and not his closest friend who would die for the cause of taking back the throne from the usurpers.

If Valerian had lived to be king, he would have raised his own children, and Kieran would have never married, serving him as a knight just as he'd served King Orland. True, he never would have known the blessings of being a husband and father, but too often the weight of responsibility over the last seventeen years had crushed the joy out of him. He could feel the bitterness congealing in his bones, and it frightened him.

If only he and Mercy could have taken wee Val and moved to a small holding in MacLachlan lands, the children could have grown up to know hard but satisfying work, living off the land in peace and quiet, far from the crowded Keep and the pomp and luxury of being part of the royal family. Then Fiona might have been as grounded as—well, Emma MacRorie. And that would not have been a bad thing at all.

After all, Mercy herself had grown up in a simple village. Why could she not see that a simple life was what her younger children had needed and even craved unknowingly? Val had run away, he'd been so desperate for a different life. And now Fiona had heedlessly thrown out all her upbringing, the good as well as the bad. So far Tristam had seemed more content than the other two, but he was solitary by nature and spent most of his time studying or experimenting with herbs.

Kieran's ruminations came to an abrupt end when Sir Aidan's picturesque manor came into view, illuminated by the light of the late afternoon sun. Burdock's ears swiveled forward, and the horse picked up his pace.

"Smell your dinner, do ye, lad?" Kieran chuckled while they took the winding approach at a fast walk. He waved to the guard on the tower, who shouted down something Kieran couldn't make out. By the time he reached the gate, it had been opened, and Kieran rode through.

Aidan himself was in the yard to greet him. It made Kieran smile to see how happy the man was, especially after the tragedies he'd experienced in his life. He and Iris were certainly good for one another.

"Greetings, Lord Kieran." The knight approached and held Burdock's bridle while Kieran dismounted. "What an unexpected pleasure to see you here." He grasped Kieran's hand in greeting.

"'Twas unexpected for me to journey to Moor Point, certainly, but I did want to stop in while I was so close." He scanned the tidy yard and buildings of the estate. "Ye certainly have a well-kept manor here. I commend you."

"Thank you, my lord." After a groom arrived to take Kieran's horse, Aidan gestured toward the door. "Shall we go inside?"

Nodding, Kieran walked beside the knight, and they entered the house together. Kieran approved of the interior, which was as pleasing to the eye as the exterior. Footsteps sounded on the curving staircase, and Iris appeared, hurrying down to meet them.

"Lord Kieran!" The lady of the manor rushed toward him and Aidan and took her husband's arm. "How wonderful to see you here." She glanced behind him. "Did you bring anyone with you?"

"This time, I'm afraid I am alone." He shrugged. "But I am glad to see the two of you, for I am in Moor Point in search of Fiona and wondered if you had seen her?"

Iris' eyes widened. "Fiona is in Moor Point? I had no idea." She shared a glance with Aidan. "We have not seen her. Is anything wrong, Lord Kieran?"

Before Kieran could answer, Aidan held up his free hand.

"Why don't we make ourselves comfortable in the sitting room first. I suspect Lord Kieran has been traveling for some days and needs a chair and refreshments before we ask too many questions." Though he smiled, his eyes showed concern.

"Of course, I should have thought of that." Iris gazed adoringly at Aidan. "Please come this way, my lord." Then she led both men to the nearby sitting room.

Kieran took the offered seat and sank into it with a grateful sigh. "I have been in the saddle more days than I care to count." Aidan took the seat opposite, and after giving instructions to a servant, Iris sat in the chair beside Aidan. He reached over and took her hand before addressing Kieran.

"Now, Lord Kieran, please tell us what is going on, and how we may help."

Haltingly at first, he explained how Fiona had run away with Tammeron, and how he and Fowler had tracked them from place to place until they had run into a dead end in a deserted camp not far from the manor.

"But I want to continue searching and thought I'd see if Fiona had tried to contact you." He met Iris' gaze, and she shook her head.

"I'm sorry, Lord Kieran," she said. "I wish I could be of more help."

"You said there is a deserted camp near here." Aidan frowned with concern. "Who do you think they met in this camp?"

"Fowler could find nothing to identify them, nor any evidence to determine which direction Fiona and Tam were headed when they left." Kieran sagged in the chair. "It was as if the horse they had been riding disappeared."

Two servants appeared carrying trays of food and a wineskin. Iris directed them to set up a small table upon which they lay an assortment of meats, cheeses, and fruits. Kieran's mouth watered at the sight.

They spent the next several minutes filling their trenchers from the trays and cups from the wineskin.

"I'm sorry, my lord," Aidan said sympathetically. "I hope you will make our home yours while you are here in Moor Point, for as long as you need a base of operations."

Kieran smiled over the rim of his cup. "I thank you both. I plan to see Lord Dracen after I leave you—"

"Oh, my lord," Iris said earnestly. "I know Lord Dracen will want to know you're here, but please consider staying with us instead."

Kieran held back a chuckle at her eagerness to help him. He would not for the world offend her.

"I appreciate your hospitality, and I am happy to stay the night, but I feel I cannot commit to more than that 'til I speak with Lord Dracen."

They visited late into the evening, and finally Kieran had to beg their pardon so he could get a decent night's sleep. Yet another way he knew he was getting older.

*

That night, Kieran enjoyed the most comfortable bed he'd slept in for more than two weeks. Even longer than that, since he'd been sleeping apart from Mercy before he left the Keep. And as he lay back on the pillow and stared up at the canopy, he suddenly missed her, regretting his anger and resentment toward her more than ever. She hadn't been the cause of it, and she deserved to know the real source of that bitterness.

He resolved to write her a longer letter in the morning before he left for the castle. Perhaps it would be easier to share his true feelings with her using pen and ink than through spoken words, since he hadn't been able to say what was in his heart when they were face-to-face.

*

First thing after dressing for the day, Kieran asked a servant for writing implements. He stared at the blank sheet for several minutes, collecting his thoughts. How to begin?

He wrote, *My dear Mercy*, and paused again. It was important to him to say the correct words so there would be no misunderstanding. And yet, was that even possible?

With a sigh, he resumed writing.

At the root of our troubles is a deep discontent I have tried to push aside and ignore for the sake of duty. Now I realize that by doing so I have only succeeded in allowing the root of bitterness to fester and thrive in my heart, giving it permission to crowd out the love I feel for you and the children and the rest of the family.

I admit I have been too lenient with Fiona, but I have been too distant from everyone in the attempt to carry out my duties and responsibilities, no matter what the cost to myself. When I make a promise, I want to move heaven and earth to keep that promise, but I am beginning to realize that I have sacrificed too many important things at too high a cost on the altar of duty. The greatest cost has been the lack of time spent with our children to help them grow to maturity with a strong faith in the Most High.

Until I find Fiona, I remain at a loss to know best how to right all the wrongs, but I will continue to pray for strength to make the right choices from this day forward. I remember you and the children in my daily prayers and hope you will keep me in yours.

You can get word to me through either Lord Dracen or Sir Aidan. I will do my best to stay in contact with them both while I am in Moor Point.

Always, Kieran

When he set down the quill pen and read the words he'd just written, he wasn't completely satisfied. Yet what more could he add? He only hoped Mercy would see that this problem was far deeper than the discord between the two of them, though the loss of their mind speech was sure proof that their marital troubles were worse than Kieran had wanted to admit. It wasn't too late for them to reconcile, surely? He did desire to be reconciled, but changes would have to be made first, and change was never easy.

As soon as the ink dried, Kieran folded the letter and sealed it with his ring. For the first time in years, he studied the signet of his office as the king's Earl Marshall. There was no part of the design that was personal to him; the royal dragon dominated with a crown above and a sword below. Of course he'd been honored that Dolan had created the office specifically for him to continue at court, but Kieran's heart had never been content with the idea that he should live within the walls of the Keep for the rest of his life. He felt trapped, and on the worst days the Keep seemed a prison.

Tucking the letter inside his tunic, he rose from the desk and headed down the stairs.

*

When Kieran reached the manor's hall, Aidan and Iris were waiting for him. They fed Kieran more food than he should eat and sent for a courier to take his letter to the Keep. He promised to let the young couple know if he discovered Fiona's whereabouts and reluctantly rode a refreshed Burdock toward Castle Moor Point.

Though it was not far between the two places, there were fewer travelers on the road than Kieran would have expected. At a deserted bend canopied by interlocking branches, two hooded men rode out from the trees and blocked his path.

"What is this?" Kieran frowned at the men and wondered if there might be more of them out of sight. He was forcefully reminded of the roving bands of the unlawful regent's men causing terror during the brief reign of Mercy's brother years ago. His right hand was already resting on his thigh, close to his sword hilt, but he did not reach for it yet.

"We want to talk to you, old man," one of them said, jerking his chin. "Off the road, behind those trees." His voice sounded young, younger than Dolan at least.

Kieran shook his head. "Whatever you want to say to me, say it right here."

In unison, they pulled long knives from their belt sheaths. Kieran didn't move his hand, nor did he show any emotion.

"If you won't do as we say, then we'll toss your dead body in the brambles and take your fine horse." The speaker kicked his horse forward, and the other man turned his horse to come at Kieran from the other side.

Still Kieran waited, coiled to spring. The horses were on either side of him, and Burdock snorted.

"Get him!" The horses lunged forward, and Kieran gave Burdock his head.

Sensing danger, the trained war horse reared while Kieran drew his sword. Burdock turned as he came down beside the man who had spoken, and Kieran parried his knife thrust, twisting it out of his hand.

While the first man cursed and jumped down from the saddle to find his knife, Kieran pulled his stallion around to intercept the second man and block him from stabbing at Burdock. When he reversed the blade to throw it, Kieran instinctively sliced at the knife, knocking it away and cutting the man's hand to the bone. With a roar, he shoved the bleeding hand under his armpit and pulled another knife with his left hand.

Out of the corner of his eye, Kieran could see the first man running toward him and feared more for Burdock than himself. He signaled his horse to kick with his hind legs. Burdock spun around and struck the man with full force, knocking him to the ground. He did not get up.

The injured man was still mounted, though with his only free hand holding a knife, he could not direct his horse, and the animal shied away. With his knees, Kieran guided Burdock to the man's left side and disarmed him.

"Surrender in the name o' the king!" Kieran shouted. "Or I'll run ye through!"

The man held up his free hand, and Kieran ordered him to dismount, grabbing the horse's reins. He all but fell from the saddle, leaving a smear of blood.

Kieran spied a coil of rope on the saddle and reached over to pull it off.

"Sit on the ground," he snapped, and then slid down from Burdock. Sheathing his sword, he wrapped the rope around the man's upper arms and torso, knotting it behind his back as tightly as he could.

"Let me see the hand." He kept his voice severe to hide the tremor. His adrenaline hadn't run this high in a long time.

Using a cloth bandage from his saddlebag, he drew the edges of the slice together and tightly bound the hand. Since the castle was not far, he pulled out his sword again and ordered the man to walk. He took Burdock's reins and led the horse while he prodded the reluctant prisoner with his sword. In all that had happened in the last few minutes, the man's hood had not been pushed away from his face. Kieran decided to leave it that way, at least until they reached Lord Dracen.

They entered the village outside the castle walls to the stares of everyone they passed. When they finally came near the castle gates, one of the two guards strode toward him.

"What is this?" he asked with a frown.

"King's arrest. This man and his companion ambushed me on the road half a mile west of here. The other man lies on the road, probably dead, but I didn't check to make sure." He nodded at the prisoner. "Announce Lord Kieran MacLachlan to Lord Dracen."

The guard bobbed his head. "Yes, my lord. Come with me."

They entered the castle yard to more stares all the way to the steps. Word spread, and Lord Dracen met them there.

"Lord Kieran, what brings you to Moor Point?" Dracen balled his fists on his hips and stared at the hooded man.

Kieran finally pulled it back, revealing a sullen younger man. "This is not the reason I came to Moor Point, Lord Dracen, but I managed to collect a prisoner on the way here. One of two men who tried tae kill me."

Dracen peered closer at the man. "Sagar? Is that you?"

Sagar hung his head. "Yes, m'lord."

Dracen spoke to Kieran. "This man once had charge of my favorite hawk, until he and the hawk disappeared." His face darkened. "Where is the other man who attacked you?"

"Probably dead. If not, he will have two painful horseshoe-sized bruises."

"I see you have not lost your reflexes, my lord. I am glad to see that." Dracen gave him a grim smile. The Lord of Moor Point ordered guards to take the man to the dungeon and fetch the other one's body. Not until they were alone did he speak to Kieran again.

"Come, my good lord, and let us find a quiet place to talk. And something to drink."

Kieran nodded, suddenly thirsty. "That sounds good tae me."

He walked with Dracen up the stairs and into the castle. It wasn't far to Dracen's office, and he shut the door behind them to give them privacy. Dracen pulled a flask from a shelf and two cups. He poured them each a drink before gesturing for Kieran to sit across from him.

"I trust all is well at the Keep?" Dracen sipped from his cup while staring at Kieran.

"When I left the Keep more than a fortnight ago, all was well." Kieran grimaced. "Well, nearly all. My daughter Fiona has run away with Tammeron d'Jean, the son of the steward of Frankland." He then explained what little he knew and how their trail had gone cold in Moor Point, not far from Sir Aidan's manor.

"I hoped you would be able tae help me find whoever was in that camp, for it appeared a fairly large group of people had lived there. I also had a strong feeling while searching the clearing that Fiona is in trouble." Kieran's hands convulsed on the cup. Thank the Most High, he had not had any strong indications that Fiona was dead, but now that he'd been attacked on the road, the possibility had become more realistic.

"Of course," Dracen said without hesitation. "I'll lend you as many men as you want to keep searching for your daughter." His mouth tightened. "If I had a daughter go missing, I'd search the province with all the resources I had until I found her."

Kieran slumped in relief. "Thank you for understanding, my lord."

Dracen reached behind him and pulled a rolled-up parchment from a shelf. He pushed his cup aside and spread open what proved to be a detailed map of Moor Point. Kieran set his cup down and stood to better see the map.

"Can you show me the approximate location of this deserted camp?" Dracen stared at him patiently while Kieran studied the map to orientate himself.

He ran his finger down the road from the castle. "Right about— here." He stabbed at the place where the road ran through a forest. "It was not far from the road." An idea came to Kieran's head. "I wonder if the men who attacked me were from that camp?"

"Then they could be a company of bandits." Dracen's brows furrowed. "We try to find and arrest them, but it seems those kind of men are attracted to this province."

"There is a history of such roving criminals," Kieran agreed. "I know from my time traveling your roads, there are many ideal hiding places, especially in more remote areas near the moors."

"I don't remember you mentioning that before, my lord." Dracen stared down at the map as if seeing it for the first time.

Kieran shrugged. "I didn't have a reason to back then, nor was I thinking that those hiding places would be good for bandits. I was trying to avoid people altogether, the first time I learned my way around Moor Point."

Dracen looked up. "So you are talking about a time before the unlawful regency?"

"Yes, but only about a year before that time." He gave Dracen a lopsided smile. "It would have been the year before Sir Aidan was knighted."

"Hmm." Then Dracen chuckled.

"What is it, my lord?" Kieran couldn't imagine what he found humorous.

"We are growing old, my lord. That is all."

Kieran snorted. "That is quite enough, dinna ye think?"

Dracen nodded in agreement and rose from his seat. "The day is still young, so I believe 'tis time two old men rode out so you can show me where you found this deserted camp."

"Aye, I can do that." Kieran sketched a bow and gestured for Dracen to lead the way to the stables.

Chapter 26

Let another man praise thee, and not thine own mouth;
a stranger, and not thine own lips.

Fiona opened her eyes and started to panic. For a moment, she wasn't sure where she was. But then she remembered Elvina and her kindness, and Fiona let out a relieved breath while sitting up.

She had no idea how long she'd slept, but the bed had been so comfortable, and she obviously had needed the sleep. First she tidied the bedclothes and fluffed the pillow, and then she washed off her face in the basin on the room's small table. Now if she only had a comb, she could do something about the rat's nest that had once been her pretty hair. But her belongings were not in the room.

When she opened the door, no one was about, but a delicious scent wafted from the back of the house. Fiona followed it, her stomach pleading to taste whatever made that heavenly aroma. She found Elvina stirring a pot hanging over a fire. The slender woman turned and smiled.

"Do you feel rested, Feena?" She gestured to a nearby chair, and Fiona sat upon it.

"Yes, thank you. The bed is very comfortable." She pointed to the soup. "And that smells wonderful."

"It's my special fish soup. We will eat shortly." Elvina took a ladle from a hook and tasted the broth, nodding.

"I'm sorry to be a bother, but where did you put my carry sack and lute case?"

Edwina frowned in concern. "You had nothing on you when I was brought to help you."

Fiona jumped up from the chair. "Please, how do I get to the ship?"

"I'm sure it sailed on hours ago."

"No! I need my things! How can I get them back?"

Elvina shook her head. "I'm sorry, Feena, but that ship is surely a long way from here."

Dejected, Fiona sank back to the chair. How could Allard's lute be gone forever? She'd promised to play it in his memory. Now she had no way to earn a living as a bard, for she had nothing and no way to pay for another lute. What was she going to do?

In that moment when Fiona was feeling so despondent, two men entered the kitchen, both expected by Elvina, at least. One of them was the man who had helped her to Elvina's house, Barnaby. But the other was a young man, nearly her age, and he stared at Fiona with interest.

"Hello, Vina," the young man said. "Supper almost ready?"

"Yes, Finn." Elvina gestured to Fiona. "Meet our guest. Feena, this is my youngest brother, Finn."

He nodded at Fiona, his unruly curls bobbing. "Hello. What brings you to Seaton?"

Fiona didn't immediately answer, for she had no idea how to begin the tale. Barnaby spoke up.

"She'd gotten ill after stowing away on Dorrie's merchant ship. A couple o' the hands brought her ashore, and I was about when they asked for help." The big man smiled shyly at Fiona.

"That tub o' rotten planks would make any landlegger sick." Finn scowled so furiously, his face was distorted, and Fiona had to hold in a chuckle. He wagged his eyebrows at Fiona. "What'd you do, that you had to stow away on Dorrie's ship?"

Elvina picked up her broom and whacked her brother on the back of his legs. "Finn! What a question to ask our guest! If she wants you to know, she will tell you in her own good time."

Instead of being contrite, Finn laughed at Elvina. "And now our guest will think you beat me regularly."

Elvina propped the broom in a corner and pointed at the table. "Maybe I should beat you regularly, but it's probably too late to help you behave."

"Aye, too late," Barnaby said cheerfully. "He's a full-grown rascal now." He pulled one of the benches out from under the table and gestured for Fiona to be seated.

She did so with murmured thanks, and then Barnaby pulled out the other bench and sat across from her.

Once Finn helped Elvina bring the food to the table, he sat beside Barnaby, and Elvina took the place on Fiona's bench. Without a word, the three of them bowed their heads, so Fiona did likewise. To her surprise, Finn was the one who offered thanks.

"Most High God, we thank you for our lives and for this food. Amen."

Fiona realized with chagrin that she hadn't prayed once since leaving the Keep. She resolved to do better going forward.

The aroma of the soup in her bowl wafted around her, and gratefully it tasted as good as it smelled. Elvina had also made flat bread, which was piled high on a wooden platter. Both men snagged two pieces, and Elvina one, so Fiona began with one piece. When Elvina smeared something on hers from a crock, Fiona leaned closer.

"This is butter. Would you like some?" Elvina set down her knife and lifted the crock.

"Yes, please." Fiona wanted to ask where the butter came from, but she decided to try it first.

The butter was smooth and spread evenly. Fiona took a bite and chewed carefully. To her surprise, the bread was soft and the butter creamy and slightly sweet. A sound of appreciation escaped her lips.

"This is so good." She eyed the stack of remaining bread pieces and wondered if it would be greedy to take more. Elvina must have noticed her reluctance, for she took two more pieces and placed them beside Fiona's bowl. She nodded her thanks.

"Our best ewe has especially rich milk, which makes especially good butter." She met Fiona's gaze and smiled.

"You made the butter?" Fiona's brows raised. She had never before considered *how* butter was made. Then she felt her conscience pricked and knew she needed to be honest; she had never *cared* to find out where butter came from until now.

"Of course." Elvina held her gaze for a moment longer with a puzzled frown, and to Fiona it felt as if the woman could read her mind.

She would have to be more careful to guard her ignorance.

"You're not from around here, are you?" Finn asked.

Fiona shook her head, hoping that would be answer enough. It wasn't.

"Where are you from?" He leaned over the table as if eager for her answer.

Glancing sidelong at Elvina, she merely said, "From the north."

"The north?" Finn's eyes widened. "How did you get way down here?"

Fiona lowered her eyes. "It's a long story."

Finn pushed his bowl aside and planted his elbows on the table. "We have time to hear your story."

Before Fiona could panic or even think of what to say, Elvina intervened.

"Another time, Finn. Can't you see our guest is still exhausted from her ordeal?" Elvina paused when Finn drooped in disappointment. "Besides, you have to get up in a few short hours. You ought to get some sleep."

With a huff, Finn pushed himself from the table. "You're right, but I'm sure Fiona's tale is better than a fish story any day." He nodded to his sister. "Thanks for the supper." Then he gazed at Fiona one more time. "Right glad to have met you. I still hope to hear your story when you feel up to it."

Fiona relaxed her guard a bit and smiled at him. "It was nice to meet you too." That was polite without encouraging him, wasn't it?

When she didn't continue the conversation, Finn turned and strode away. Fiona looked to Elvina for an explanation.

"He works on a fishing boat, and they must leave in the middle of the night to reach the shoals by daybreak." Elvina patted Fiona's arm. "Don't let him push you where you don't wish to go. Finn can be over-eager sometimes."

"I'll say." Barnaby finally injected himself into the conversation. When he didn't continue, Fiona dared a question of her own.

"Is there a bard in this village?" She looked from Barnaby to Elvina and back again.

"As a matter of fact, there is one right now." Barnaby grinned at Fiona. "Why do you want to know?"

"I'd like to ask him—if it is a man—if he would like to learn a new song." Fiona felt her heart squeeze. "Since I no longer have a lute and can't sing it anymore."

"Why do you need a lute to sing a song?" Barnaby shrugged with a crooked smile. "I sing all the time, and I have no idea how to play a lute."

"People expect a bard to have a lute to accompany the voice," Fiona explained.

"You're a bard?" Elvina asked in surprise.

"I was learning how to be one from a man named Allard." Tears pricked Fiona's eyes. "But he was killed by one of the men who killed my husband."

Barnaby's mouth hung open. "Who was your husband, Feena?"

"His name was Tam." Tears leaked from Fiona's eyes. She knew they were for Allard, and not for Tam, which made her cry even harder.

Neither Elvina nor Barnaby said a word, and Fiona quickly pulled herself together.

"I'm sorry," she said.

Elvina patted her arm. "Don't apologize for honest grief, Feena." When Fiona met her gaze, the woman gently gripped her hand. "You can stay here as long as you like."

"Yes," Barnaby agreed, though it wasn't his house. "We will watch out for you and keep you safe from those murderers."

Finn poked his head around the doorway. "If they show up here in Seaton, they'll regret it." Then he stepped back into the room and grinned, making him look impish. "And if you ever don't feel safe here at the house, you can come out on the *Dolphin* with me."

"The dolphin?" Fiona cocked her head, trying to picture what one looked like. "Are they big enough to ride upon?"

Finn chuckled. "You can't ride a dolphin like a horse, but they are big and strong enough to let one pull you through the water. But my *Dolphin* is a fishing boat, the largest in Seaton."

"You own a fishing boat?" Now Fiona was even more puzzled. "You can't be much older than I am."

"I'm eighteen." He straightened and folded his arms. "Lord Dracen gave us the boat, and Captain Tolliver is the master until I finish my apprenticeship." His eyes brightened. "Less than two years, now."

"Lord Dracen gave you the boat." Fiona wanted to ask why, but she was reluctant to speak too freely of the lord of Moor Point, lest she give away that she actually knew him. And why.

"Aye." Finn puffed out his chest. "We know a man who is great friends with Lord Dracen."

"This man saved our family from ruin years ago," Elvina explained.

"How generous of him, and Lord Dracen, too." Fiona was glad for them, for Elvina especially was kind and hospitable and deserving of the lord's assistance. "And if you would, please tell me how to find the local bard. Allard helped me write the new song, and I need to teach it to a bard who can share it around."

"*You* wrote a song?" Finn appeared delighted. "Will you sing it to us?"

Fiona's face grew warm. "But I no longer have my lute."

"You only need your voice to sing," he pointed out.

Barnaby cleared his throat. "There is a bard at the Sea Biscuit tavern, for another night or two anyway." He pushed up from the table. "I'll just go on then and let him know you'd like to talk with him about a new song."

"Oh, would you?" Hope touched Fiona's heart.

"Of course I will." He winked at Fiona and then addressed Elvina. "Wonderful meal as always, Vina."

"Thank you, Barnaby." Elvina started to clear the table, and Fiona jumped up to help. Without looking at her young brother, she spoke again. "You ought to be in bed, Finn."

"Going now, Vina." Finn disappeared at the same time Barnaby left, leaving the two women alone.

"Please, let me help you clean up," Fiona asked Elvina. She had to pay her way, somehow.

"Not tonight, but I will need your help in the morning." Elvina patted a stool nearby. "Come, sit and talk to me while I tidy the kitchen. I've missed having another female to visit with since my sister got married and started her own household."

Fiona perched on the indicated stool. "How old is your sister?"

"She is twenty-one now, and I am twelve years older, so she has often felt like my daughter instead of my sister." Elvina started placing the dirty dishes in a basin of water.

"My only sister is twelve years older than me, too." Fiona was astonished to find two other sisters so far apart. Was it more common than she imagined? "Well, to be completely honest, she is my half-sister. We have the same mother, but not the same father."

"My sister and I are opposite: we have the same father but different mothers. How interesting." Elvina gazed at her in that piercing way again, and Fiona decided she'd best change the subject.

Thankfully, Elvina was eager to tell Fiona about the other villagers in Seaton, though Fiona would never keep all the names straight until she met them in person. She was most interested to hear about the fishing boats and the schedules they kept, such as Finn's boat going out early every morning in order to catch deep water fish. Other boats stayed closer to shore and worked to catch different kinds of fish and even crabs. Perhaps Fiona would get to see a crab up close. She had eaten the meat at Castle Moor Point before but had only seen a drawing of one. It had many legs and two large claws which appeared formidable weapons.

By the time Elvina had finished cleaning, Fiona felt so relaxed she began to yawn.

"You should go on to bed now. After a good night's rest, you'll feel yourself again in the morning." Elvina studied Fiona's face with a smile. Then her brows furrowed. "Are you sure we haven't met before?"

Fiona shook her head and stifled another yawn. "If we had, I would remember you. Thank you for being so kind to a stranger."

"You are very welcome, Feena. Sleep well, and I will see you when you wake." Elvina walked with Fiona to the guest room door, then nodded and continued down the hall to her room.

Fiona lay upon her bed and put her hands behind her head. She struggled to stay awake, thinking about everything Elvina had talked about. Someone was surely watching out for her by bringing her to this haven of rest. She thought to herself that she ought to thank the Most High, but she drifted off to sleep before she could form the words in her mind.

*

Birdsong outside her window woke Fiona the next morning. She lay still with her eyes closed to better hear the happy warbling, and then she tried humming a harmony with it, to which the bird replied with a series of chirps. Had she confused the poor thing?

She finally stretched and rose from the bed, feeling more refreshed than she had in a long time. Today she would insist that Elvina let her help around the house.

But when she entered the kitchen, a strange young man sat at Elvina's table, eating a bowl of porridge. He looked up at Fiona's approach.

"Well, hello there." His smile brightened his tired eyes. "You must be the singer."

"Singer?" Fiona looked to Elvina, who was kneading bread dough.

"At the tavern last night, Barnaby told me someone had written a new song. I'd like to hear it." He grinned and wiped his mouth with one of his wide embroidered sleeves. Since he wore one of the sleeveless tunics, a red one, which was also intricately embroidered, Fiona guessed he had to be a bard.

"I did write a song, but I no longer have a lute, and I want my song to be heard throughout the land." She straightened. "My name is Feena."

"And I am Noel." From his seat on the bench, he gave her an elaborate bow. At one time, Fiona would have called it a mocking bow, but after performing with Allard, she understood it was all part of the persona of being a bard. He gestured to the bench across from him, playing the host. "Please, be seated."

Fiona did so, and Elvina set a steaming bowl in front of her.

"Good morning, Feena." Elvina winked at her. "You must be a miracle worker, for I have never seen a bard awake at such an early hour before."

Noel pressed a hand to his chest, feigning shock. "You wound me, my lady hostess. The prospect of a new song being birthed into the world is an opportunity not to be missed, especially for something so trivial as sleep." He gestured to Fiona's bowl. "Go on, eat. Eat! You'll need your strength to teach me your song, but I confess I am not a patient man." He propped his chin in one hand and stared at her.

Fiona took a bite of porridge, but it almost stuck in her throat. She had to force herself to remain calm in the bard's presence. Though he looked nothing like Allard, he had the same kind of open, guileless demeanor and dry wit. For Allard's sake as well as Val's, Fiona determined to sing Val's song well so Noel would have no reason *not* to want to share it in other places.

She finished her porridge and drank half the cup of cool water Elvina handed her. Fiona now felt awake enough to do the song justice. She looked boldly at Noel.

"Should I just sing the song, then? I also have chords for the lute, though mine is lost forever." Would she ever stop grieving for that loss?

Noel reached down to his lute case and took out his fine instrument. Without a word, he handed it across the table, and Fiona took it reverently. She held it close and lightly strummed the strings, smiling at the sweet sound that would always remind her of Allard. Feeling shy, she looked up and found Elvina watching her.

"Go on," Elvina urged. "Pretend I'm not here." She turned away and began peeling potatoes.

Before she could lose her nerve, Fiona strummed the opening chords and sang her song about Val.

Noel listened intently, watching her hands play his lute. His concentration never wavered until she played the final chord with a flourish, and then he jumped to his feet, clapping with enthusiasm.

"What a marvelous song! People everywhere will love it! And I will love performing it." He reseated himself and put on a serious face. "Now, as soon as you are ready, please play and sing it again, so I will be able to commit the entire epic story to memory."

Fiona inhaled deeply to calm herself, for she knew once she finished singing Val's song a second time, she might never play a lute again, and it made her sad. What she didn't expect was how intently Noel listened, sometimes staring into her eyes so deeply, she had to look at the opposite wall. And on the last chord, before the echo had completely faded, Noel came around the table, took the lute from her, and sat beside her.

"Now I will play it to you. Please correct me if I heard anything incorrectly." And without missing a beat, he plunged right into the song.

Startled, Fiona worked at listening critically, but to her delight, the song accurately relayed Val's adventure, bringing out the beauties and the dangers he'd found in the far north and showcasing his heroism. Noel's voice was pleasing to listen to, though not as rich as Allard's had been. Oh, if only her friend could have lived to sing this song with her!

She was relieved when Noel finished without a wrong note or word. Now she could rest easy, knowing all of Levathia would eventually find out how brave and noble her brother was.

"So, how did I do?" The bard raised his brows, genuinely asking Fiona's opinion, so she nodded.

"Very well indeed. Thank you." She stared wistfully at the lute, and he noticed.

"I am sorry you lost your instrument." He cocked his head and winked. "You are welcome to travel with me and help me sing your magnificent ballad. Perhaps we can replace your lute eventually."

Fiona was tempted, but she shook her head. "Thank you, but I am content to stay here and let you share the song. Only please do not mention my name."

"Why ever not? The creator of such a masterpiece deserves to be credited." Noel strummed a triumphant chord.

"What is the name of your song, Feena?" Elvina came near and folded her hands. "It's an exciting story. Did you really write it yourself?"

Heat rose to Fiona's cheeks. "Yes, I did. It's called 'The Ballad of Prince Val.'"

"Prince Val?" Elvina's eyes widened. "Is he related to the prince in 'The Deed of Valerian'?"

"Yes, his son." She swallowed, hoping neither of them would deduce she personally knew Val, much less was related to him.

"You know, I met this Prince Val when he was just a baby." Elvina's gaze was distant, remembering. "That would have been about seventeen years ago." Her gaze drifted to Fiona again. "So is this ballad based on a true story?"

Fiona nodded. "Everything happened just the way the song tells it."

"And how, pray tell, do you know?" Noel was staring at her, too.

"I was at the Keep recently and heard the events related by a reliable person." Fiona ducked her head to hide her warm cheeks. "But please don't ask me who that person was. I'm not at liberty to say."

"Why were you at the Keep, Feena?" Elvina's voice was gentle, but there was something in it that made Fiona wonder if she had guessed the truth.

She avoided meeting Elvina's gaze. "My husband and I were there for the tournament."

"So you are no simple village maid." Noel sounded disappointed, for some reason.

"I am a destitute widow." She did meet his gaze. "I cannot say whether I am simple or not."

He strummed a sad chord. "I am sorry for the loss of your husband, but I am certain you are anything but simple, if you can write such a stirring ballad." Now he played the opening notes of her song. "Are you sure you cannot accompany me? Wouldn't you like to be a traveling bard?"

Fiona closed her eyes and dropped her head to her hands. She would have loved to be a bard, but it was not possible now. Not with Folville's men still searching for her and a baby to be born in a few months.

With a sigh she straightened. "I'm not sure where I belong now, but I know I cannot be a bard, traveling and performing in public. If you will share the song, I will be content." She forced a smile.

Noel stood and bowed to her before grasping her hand and pressing it to his lips. "Well then, if I cannot persuade you, I must leave you both. There are many places I must go and many people for whom I must sing your masterpiece." He gave her a sad smile. "I hope we meet again, Feena." Then he nodded to Elvina. "And thank you for the breakfast. Farewell."

He left the cottage, and they listened to him play and sing a marching song until he walked out of their hearing.

Elvina sat in Noel's place and took Fiona's hands. "You know you may stay here as long as you need to, Feena. I won't press you to share your secrets, but I hope you know I will hold anything you tell me in strictest confidence."

Fiona nodded. "I know. And I appreciate all you've done for me." She smiled shyly. "I am happy to stay here, as long as you will let me pay for my bed and meals by the labor of my hands."

Elvina chuckled. "All right. I confess, I could use the help, now that Finn is only home to eat and sleep."

"Good. Where shall we begin?" Fiona felt warm inside. It was good to find a friend and useful work to do.

Chapter 27

In the transgression of an evil man there is a snare.

Mercy was on her knees, pulling weeds with bare hands when a shadow blocked the sunlight, and she craned her neck to see what caused it.

Reggie was landing on the tower. As soon as his feet made contact with the stone, Val slid down the dragon's back. Mercy rose and brushed loose dirt from her hands. She frowned at the look on Val's face.

"What's wrong?" Had something happened to Fiona? Or Kieran?

"Hello, Mother." He gave her half a smile. "You're right; it's not good news. Lady Shannon MacNeil in the Southern Woodlands needs your help, so I've come to take you there."

"Is she ill?" Mercy started toward the stairs, and Val caught up with his long legs.

"Yes, but I don't have any more details, other than it came on suddenly."

Mercy hurried down to the family's common room. "If you'll let Tristam know, I'll get ready, but I want him to come with us." She gave him a tired smile. "And I'll need to let Dolan know."

Val nodded and gripped her hand. "I will."

Before Mercy could enter her bedchamber, a courier came to the open door and bowed.

"My lady, I have a message from Lord Kieran." He handed her a sealed letter, much larger than the small note she'd last received from him.

"Thank you." She looked to Val. "Do you have any coins on you?"

He took care of that, too, and Mercy thanked both young men before hurrying to her room.

First, she flung her carry sack upon the bed and quickly gathered everything she thought she might need. Then she broke the seal on Kieran's letter and opened the parchment, reading while she packed her medicinal supplies.

She had to read it through twice before she began to understand what he was saying. He hadn't found Fiona yet, and it sounded as if he meant to stay in Moor Point until he did. His resentment obviously ran deep and wasn't all directed at her. She had just been a convenient target for his frustration.

What tore her heart, though, was the lack of any warmth or affection in Kieran's words. In all the letters he'd ever written to her, there had never been anything to make her doubt his love for her.

Tears clouded her vision while she packed a change of clothing in a second carry sack. After she set it beside the first one, she sank to her knees and clasped her hands, begging the Most High to help her and Kieran come to an understanding so they might preserve their marriage and their family.

Then she wiped her eyes, pushed herself upright, and gathered her belongings to give to Val before going to speak to Dolan.

*

Dolan was surprised to see her but invited her into his sitting room and gestured to one of the overstuffed chairs.

"I'm scheduled to meet with Jambray in half an hour, but hopefully that will be all you need?" He raised his brows, inviting her to speak.

Mercy nodded and shifted to the edge of the chair. "Tristam and I are going to the Southern Woodlands. Lady Shannon MacNeil is ailing, and Nathan hopes we can do something for his mother. I just wanted you to know."

Dolan frowned. "If both of you are going, Lady Shannon must be very ill."

"Val did not have any details, but since it is so far, I'd rather take Tristam with me now in case both of us are needed, especially since we don't know when Kieran will return." Mercy's heart sank, wondering if he would *ever* return. He would, once he found Fiona. Wouldn't he?

"Have you heard from Kieran?" Dolan's frown deepened.

"Yes. Twice. He still hasn't found Fiona yet." She lowered her gaze, unwilling for her son to *See* how much Kieran's absence troubled her.

"Mother, is everything all right between you and Kieran?"

Without thinking, she looked up again and met Dolan's dark piercing eyes. "No, it is not. But I hope we can resolve our difficulties as soon as he returns."

Dolan leaned over and took her hand. "That is my hope as well." He kissed her hand and gave her a sad smile. "I don't like the thought that the two of you could be at odds about anything, but I suspect I know what has come between you. Or who." His jaw briefly tightened. "Meanwhile, I will be praying for reconciliation and for Lady Shannon's health."

"Thank you, Son." Mercy rose, and Dolan stood also, towering over her as his father once had. She slipped her arms around his waist to hug him, and he embraced her.

"Send word if you have need of anything in the Southern Woodlands." He kissed the top of her head, making her smile.

"I will. But I know we will be in good hands." She disliked leaving, not knowing how long they might be gone. But something occurred to her. "Now that there are dragon couriers who can transport people swiftly, you can always send for us if there is a medical emergency here that Romey can't handle alone." Mercy pulled away from Dolan with a sigh and headed to the door. She glanced back once, meeting his gaze with a nod, but no more words were necessary between them.

She raised a hand in farewell and hurried back to Val and Tristam.

* * *

Kieran sat at a corner table in one of the crowded taverns. He knew from his earlier search today that this town in the shadow of Castle Moor Point offered little chance of discovering any information about Fiona, but since he wasn't leaving until morning, he decided to seek out a traveling bard and ask if he'd heard of a new young woman bard in the area.

It really shouldn't surprise him that Fiona had been seen singing and playing for coins. The lass had a beautiful voice and was skilled in playing multiple instruments.

A brash young man dressed in a gaudy outfit and carrying a beautifully ornate lute stepped through the door of the tavern to scattered cheers. He bowed with a flourish, as if he expected all in the room to turn their attention to him. Kieran shook his head with a snort. These younger bards were all about appearance. True, some of them could sing and play very well, but he missed the days when the songs themselves were what captured the audience's attention, not the bard himself.

Kieran gave half his attention to the bard's singing, waiting for an opportunity to speak to him. The rest of the time he listened to the conversations around him and watched the door in case a familiar face entered.

One tall man ducked as he entered, and Kieran's hackles rose. He couldn't tell if he knew the man, since he wore a hood that shadowed his face, but Kieran had learned to trust his instincts. The tall one scanned the tables until he found what who he was looking for and strode to the opposite side of the room from Kieran.

Two men with unkempt beards sat at the table and looked up when the tall man approached. They did not invite him to sit down but did speak to him briefly, and one made gestures with his hands as if he were giving directions. The tall one nodded, and his hood slipped back from his face. Kieran gasped.

It was Tammeron d'Jean!

The young man pulled up his hood and headed back to the door. Kieran stood while draining his cup, took a coin from his hidden belt pouch, and thanked the innkeeper before setting out to intercept Tammeron.

* * *

Tam walked through the streets of the crowded village, forgetting to duck his head in his eagerness to find the gamblers' meeting place. He felt lucky tonight and was anxious to recoup some of what he had lost in the last few weeks.

He turned off the main way to a side street, and someone slammed him into the wall of the nearest building.

"What—" His words were cut off by a sword pointed at his throat. The hooded man pinning him to the wall was shorter than he was by two hands, yet he could feel the strength and anger radiating from him. One of Folville's? How had he been found out?

Then the man shrugged back his hood. It was Lord Kieran! Tam didn't dare swallow. He was wishing this was Folville's man, after all.

"Where is my daughter?" Kieran said through gritted teeth.

"I don't know. It has been several days since I saw her." Then he added as an afterthought, "my lord."

"Why are you here and not with her?" Kieran's eyes flashed with so much fury, Tam thought they would burst into flames.

"It's a long story—" Tam flinched when the sword tip pressed tighter. A warm trickle of blood dripped down his neck.

"Tammeron d'Jean, as the king's officer, I am placing you under arrest."

"On what charge?" Tam's heartbeat raced while he pretended bravado. "You can't arrest me for running away with Fiona."

"No," Kieran admitted. "But only me great desire tae go tae heaven someday prevents me from taking off your bloody head right here in the street." He shuddered and continued in a steadier voice. "You are being arrested for assault of a royal prince."

Tam's eyes widened. *Edward.* He should have known that stuffing the tiresome page in the wardrobe would return to haunt him, even though it was nothing worse than often happened to pages, especially uppity ones.

He did not resist when Lord Kieran sheathed his sword and gripped Tam's arm to walk him toward the castle. Even with his shorter stature and advanced age, Fiona's father had a well-earned reputation for being strong and agile and deadly with a sword.

Tam wanted to pull up his hood to cover his face. Most people paid no attention to them, but a few stared at him in particular, wondering what was happening.

They did not slow their pace until they reached the castle gate. The guard signaled them to halt with a halberd.

"What be your business at this late hour?" The big man had a deep voice.

"Lord Kieran MacLachlan, a guest of Lord Dracen." He jerked his chin at Tam. "I have a prisoner."

The guard straightened and lowered his weapon. "Aye, my lord. Proceed."

Then Lord Kieran was marching Tam across the yard. The few people about stared at the odd pair. When they reached the steps, it hit Tam like a blow that he was in serious trouble. This was a different matter altogether than the trouble he'd had with Jevan and Folville; this was an offense against the royal family.

Would he *hang* for what he'd done to Edward?

* * *

Fiona's days quickly fell into a rhythm while she stayed with Elvina. Washing, sewing, preparing meals, sweeping, and helping with the livestock. To her surprise, Fiona enjoyed the satisfaction of completing each chore and worked at doing them to the best of her ability. She found she enjoyed working with the animals most of all. All her life she'd been good with horses, so she used her ability to calm a horse by singing or humming to Elvina's sheep, pigs, and chickens.

On the fourth day, Elvina announced that her brother Erian would be eating with them that evening. Elvina had obvious pride in Erian, who had been chosen by the dragons to be a courier. When Fiona learned he lived at Castle Moor Point, she decided to write her father a letter and ask Erian to deliver it. For a dragon it shouldn't take long to reach the Keep from Moor Point.

Upon discovering Elvina had no writing implements, Fiona's disappointment must have been obvious, for the resourceful woman was able to borrow pen, ink, and parchment from the magistrate. Grateful, Fiona sat at the table and wrote the letter while Elvina went out to tend her garden.

Dear Papa,

First of all, I want you to know I am well and safe and have need of nothing, except forgiveness from you and Mama and Tristam, if you are able. I am so sorry for causing all of you grief by my foolish actions in running away with Tam.

She paused and lifted the pen so the ink wouldn't smear. How much should she tell Papa? Squeezing her eyes shut, Fiona suddenly wished he was here so she could tell him in person, even knowing how angry and disappointed he would be in her. And he had every reason, for she had acted foolishly and was now suffering the consequences for her rash decision.

Her free hand went to her belly, imagining the tiny life growing inside. It was time now to be completely truthful, no matter how painful that truth was, for her and for Papa.

Taking a deep breath, she continued.

Our intention was to be married in a church. We did say our vows to one another before God, but I know in my heart we were not legally married, and now he is dead and I am carrying his child. My hostess does not know who I really am, and I do not plan to tell her. Meanwhile I am working hard to earn my keep, and when I see you again it is my intention to be the hard-working, unselfish daughter you deserve, and loving all my family with my whole heart, something you have always done and taught me to do.

Until that day, I keep you ever in my heart with love and hope.

She hesitated, wanting to add the words "and prayers," but she realized she had all but forgotten the Most High after everything that had happened. She knew without a doubt He would not approve of some of the things she had done. Until she had the chance to make things right, she'd best not promise any prayers. So Fiona simply signed her name, stoppered the ink, and cleaned off the pen.

Then she realized she had no wax or seal to keep the letter from being read by others. But Elvina had many candles and had promised to show her how to make them. Fiona found a remnant of a taper that still had some wick left and lit it by the embers of the cooking fire. She folded the letter and then dripped the wax as neatly as she could to seal it. Before it hardened, she pressed her thumb to flatten out a lump.

Fiona smiled at the thumbprint clearly outlined in the wax. She might not have a signet ring, but she had personalized this letter, after all.

In a little while, she would meet Elvina's dragon-riding brother and could ask him to deliver this letter. Then she frowned. How could she keep Erian from connecting her with her father? Even if she had another piece of parchment, it would be wasteful to address this one to Lord Kieran MacLachlan and an outer one to Lord Dracen.

The wax with her thumbprint had hardened, so she turned the folded parchment over and addressed it to *Lord Dracen Woodville, Castle Moor Point, KM.* That way, even if Lord Dracen opened and read the letter, he would realize it wasn't directed to him. How many people with the initials "KM" could there be who were personally acquainted with Moor Point's Lord?

Fiona was confident Lord Dracen would make sure her father received the letter. And if she asked Erian not to reveal her name or location, he would honor her request, wouldn't he?

She would just have to hope that Elvina's brother was a man of honor.

* * *

Beside Kieran, Tammeron stomped up the castle steps. Another guard met them at the double doors, admitting them after Kieran explained the matter in greater detail. While the guard went to inform Lord Dracen, Kieran opened the door to the empty hall and led the sullen Tammeron inside. It wasn't long before Lord Dracen arrived, glaring at Tammeron. Only then did a hint of worry appear on the young man's face.

"Who is this? Another highwayman?" Dracen's frown deepened, making him appear like an angel of doom.

"I dinna know if he is a highwayman, my lord." Indeed, Kieran hadn't even considered that Tammeron might have joined them, which would explain why Fowler tracked the horse to the deserted campsite. "I do know he is wanted for assault of a royal. A very young royal."

Kieran went to stand beside Dracen so they could provide a united front to Tammeron and hopefully impress upon the young man the seriousness of the charge against him.

"I did not assault Prince Edward, my lords." The arrogant look had returned to his face. "I did not hurt him; I only wished to keep him from telling Lord Henry that I was leaving."

"Did ye not strike him on the jaw? I saw the prince's bruise, and he claims ye knocked him unconscious." Kieran glared at Tammeron. To him, the greater crime was what he'd done to Fiona, but he made himself concentrate on the legal charge of assaulting a royal prince.

"My lords, haven't you ever been knocked out? It only hurts one's pride."

"Men have died from such a blow," Dracen pointed out in a grave voice.

"And the prince is but a child, and ye are much bigger and stronger than he," Kieran added.

Tammeron had no response for that, but neither did he appear particularly contrite.

"I think a few nights in the dungeon while we wait to find out what King Dolan wishes to do with him will be beneficial." Dracen beckoned to the guards. "And may God have mercy on your soul."

While guards led Tammeron away, Kieran let out a sigh. Though he would rather not see or speak with him again, he knew he'd have to question him in more detail about Fiona's whereabouts.

*

He could not wait until morning, not even to give Tammeron a night alone with his thoughts and his conscience in the dungeon. Lord Dracen offered to accompany him, but Kieran felt Tammeron might be more forthcoming if he went alone.

A guard led him to the last cell, where Tammeron sat on the stone floor with his long legs stretched out and his head drooping down to his chest. Was he asleep?

The guard banged on the bars, and Tammeron's head snapped up. When he saw Kieran, his eyes widened, and he scrambled to stand. He straightened his tunic before approaching the bars. Kieran was not surprised to note that even being locked in a dungeon had not humbled the young man.

"Come to gloat over your prisoner, Lord Kieran?" he said with false bravado. Kieran could hear the tremor in his voice.

"Why should I gloat that the son o' me old friend has fallen so far as tae deserve time in the dungeon?" Kieran kept his voice hard.

Tammeron's eyes narrowed. "And did your 'old friend' ever tell you that I am not his son? That my real father was Mortimer d'Evrow?"

"He didna need tae tell me; I already knew." He glared at Tammeron. "And I know Slade and your lady mother did their best tae raise ye tae be a far better man than the likes o' Mortimer d'Evrow."

For a moment, doubt and a hint of regret showed in Tammeron's face. But then he hardened his stance and returned Kieran's glare. "They lied to me. There is no one I can trust."

"And yet, my daughter trusted *you* enough tae leave her family and her friends and run away with you. What do ye have tae say about that?" Kieran crossed his arms.

"She knew what she was doing," he muttered, hanging his head.

As fast as a serpent's strike, Kieran lunged forward, reached through the bars, and gripped Tammeron's tunic, pulling him up against the bars. "How dare ye treat the life o' a young woman as a plaything tae be discarded when she's no longer convenient! I should have beheaded you in the street whilst I had the opportunity!" He lowered his voice. "Where is my daughter?"

Tammeron struggled to pull away, but Kieran held him fast. Finally he sagged in defeat. "The last time I saw her she was at the River Dragon in Crickhollow Village. She was singing for tips."

Kieran nodded and released him. "Ye should think very hard about your future, young d'Jean, for I dinna think King Dolan will be as forgiving as I am." Then he turned and strode away, unable to bear the sight of him any longer.

*

After bidding Lord Dracen farewell, Kieran took the fastest route to Crickhollow Village. In several places he left the road when he heard the sound of multiple horses approaching, but none of the groups appeared suspicious. Still, best to be cautious when he was traveling alone.

Sometime in mid-afternoon, a shadow overhead caught his eye, and he looked up, spotting a dragon with a rider on its back. Moor Point's new dragon courier, perhaps? He'd been so focused on Fiona's disappearance since the day the dragons chose their riders, he hadn't even learned the names of those now under the oversight of the Lord of the Sky.

A smile came to his lips, the first in many days. Val had always been a true son to him, even though he hadn't sired him, and he couldn't be more proud of him. Then the smile faded. Had Val ever doubted his love, as Tammeron obviously doubted Slade's love for him? What was the difference between the two young men, both born after their sires' deaths? The biggest difference, of course, was that Val's father had been a godly, noble man and Tammeron's a traitor, but Kieran had never believed that blood was more important than upbringing.

Or hadn't he?

There was a stream nearby, so he dismounted and led Burdock to it. While the horse drank his fill, Kieran cupped some water upstream and quenched his thirst. A nagging worry grew louder and louder, and he could no longer push it aside.

Had he counted on blood to develop Fiona's character over upbringing? Had guilt over his many absences led him to spoil the lass when she'd needed a stronger hand than either of the boys had?

He slumped to the grassy bank and dropped his head to his hands.

"God Most High, forgive me, for I have sinned. Please, dinna let it be too late for Fiona, nor for Mercy and me. Please, have mercy on us all."

He wept then, and it was a blessed release of all the strong emotions he'd tried to ignore for too long. When his tears were spent, he washed off his face and pushed himself upright. The air was cleaner and the sun brighter. Burdock finished chewing the grass in his mouth and snorted, making Kieran laugh.

"Sorry, old man, I dinna mean tae carry on so." He took Burdock's reins and pulled himself up to the saddle. "Let's try tae reach Crickhollow before dark, shall we?"

Refreshed, horse and rider returned to the road and cantered for the next little while.

Chapter 28

A man that hath friends must shew himself friendly.

Fiona hummed while she helped Elvina finish preparations for the evening meal. Barnaby arrived first, followed by Finn. It struck Fiona that not long ago she would have gone out of her way to flirt with Elvina's youngest brother. But even though he was appealing in his way, she found that she no longer desired that kind of attention from a young man. It was not the path to real, abiding love, and after the way she'd behaved with Tam, she was not sure she'd ever find that kind of love now.

But Elvina appeared to be content, never having married. True, Barnaby would marry her in a trice if she were willing. Apparently Elvina preferred to have his friendship and nothing more. Fiona would offer Finn her friendship without sending him the wrong message by flirting.

The two men hovered about until Elvina sent them to the table. They had just taken their places when a third man entered the cottage. He was older than Finn, though he resembled his younger brother. To Fiona's surprise, Erian had deep sadness in his eyes. What had happened to cause it, and why hadn't Elvina told her?

"Erian! So glad you could join us tonight." Elvina gave her brother a hug, and he smiled at her. "Meet our guest, Feena."

Erian gave Fiona his attention with a polite nod. "I'm glad to make your acquaintance, Feena." His voice was soothing, the way Fiona talked to animals. And though he was not tall, he held himself erect, as a soldier would. There was more to this man than she would have guessed.

"And I am glad to finally meet the brother of Elvina and Finn." Fiona fought the urge to curtsy and gave Erian a smile instead. "I hear you ride a dragon. Did you bring it with you?"

"I am a dragon rider," he said proudly. "Amadorix brought me here from Castle Moor Point, but he is resting in the barn."

"The barn?" Fiona pictured all the flammable materials inside a typical barn. "How can a dragon fit inside a barn?"

Erian chuckled. "I suppose calling the shelter a barn is too great a compliment. The structure is more like a lean-to."

"A very *large* lean-to," Finn added, laughing.

"I can imagine," Fiona agreed. "I look forward to meeting Amadorix." She sat beside Erian, as Elvina indicated.

Then it made her wonder if Elvina had any design in doing so. She wouldn't try to match her with Erian, would she? Elvina started passing bowls of shellfish and vegetables around the table.

"Are you not afraid of dragons, Feena?" Erian seemed surprised.

"Not at all. Though they have a fearsome appearance, they are noble and good." Fiona took the bowl of vegetables from Finn and scooped some out onto her wooden trencher before passing it along to Erian.

For several minutes, the four of them focused on eating Elvina's well-cooked meal with a minimum of family banter. As soon as Erian ate his last bite, he spoke to Fiona again.

"Have you been around dragons before? You seem to know something about them." He pushed his bowl to the side, shaking his head when Elvina offered more.

Fiona shrugged and tried to appear nonchalant. "I've seen them, surely, but I have never ridden one, as you have." There. Would that direct the conversation back to Erian?

"Where did you see dragons?" He was persistent.

Fiona glanced at Elvina before answering. "I was recently at the Keep during the tournament with my husband." She stared down at her food, hoping Erian would talk about something else.

"Is your husband here, too?" Erian snagged another piece of Elvina's warm bread.

Fiona hesitated, so Elvina answered for her.

"Feena's husband was murdered, and she is staying here." Elvina gave her a sad smile.

Erian's brows raised. "Murdered? Have you told Lord Dracen about this?"

Fiona shook her head. "I did not dare try to go to the castle. Folville and his men would surely find me."

"Folville? Is that the name of the murderer, then?" Erian dropped his half-eaten bread to his trencher, all business now.

"No, he is the leader. One of his men, or at least one of them," Fiona amended, "did the deed." Again it struck her as odd that she felt so emotionless about Tam's death, but not Allard's. "Another man killed the bard I was escaping with."

"*Two* murders?" Erian frowned and rose from the bench. "I feel I must tell Lord Dracen right away. He may know of this Folville, and I know he will want to arrest him before he can harm anyone else."

"If you please." Fiona rose also. "I have a letter I would like you to deliver to Lord Dracen, but please do not tell him my name or location."

Erian stared at her, as if weighing her words. Then he grimaced. "I can ask Lord Dracen to honor your request, but if he orders me to bring you to him for questioning, I will have to obey him."

Fiona let out a sigh. She was not a princess here and could not order anyone to do anything. She had to get this letter to Papa. Though she would hate to leave Elvina, she was willing to keep running if she had to. "I understand. Thank you, Erian." Then she hurried to her room to fetch the letter.

When she picked up the sealed parchment, her hand trembled. Sending this with Erian might be her undoing, but it was her own fault for blurting out Folville's name. Erian was right about one thing: Folville and his men needed to be arrested for their crimes to protect innocent people. If she hadn't answered Erian's questions, Lord Dracen might never discover what those evil men were doing in his province.

Slowly she returned to the main room, where the others stood around the table. All four looked at her when she entered and handed over the letter to Erian. He looked down at the name she'd written on the front.

"Do you know Lord Dracen, Feena?" His gaze bore into hers again, making her uncomfortable.

"I have met him," she admitted. *Please, don't ask me anything more.*

Erian nodded, as if acknowledging her silent request. Then he turned to Elvina and kissed his sister's cheek.

"Thank you for the meal, Vina. I'm sure I'll return soon. The day after tomorrow, all the dragon riders are to fly over Moor Point, to give the others a chance to learn the location of villages and important landmarks." He grinned at her then. "If you happen to look outside at the right time, you may see us flying together. It's quite a sight."

"It sounds like a marvelous thing to see." Elvina shared a look with Fiona. "Perhaps we should work outside that day. There are plenty of chores to keep us busy."

Fiona smiled at her enthusiasm. "I would be happy to see the dragon riders." Val would be among them!

Erian gave Finn a rough hug and clasped hands with Barnaby. Then he nodded at Fiona and left them. For a moment, Fiona was tempted to follow and see where Erian kept his dragon, but she wanted to help Elvina clean up the kitchen. Perhaps she'd ask him to show her next time he visited.

As soon as Finn retired and Barnaby went home, Elvina asked what Fiona thought about her dragon-riding brother.

"He is very pleasant, though I sensed a sadness about him." Fiona wiped off the largest serving dish.

Elvina took the dish from her and returned it to its place on a shelf. "About a year ago, he lost his wife and young daughter to a fever. It happened so fast, there was no time to send for a physician. Until he was chosen to be a dragon courier, I was afraid that grief would haunt him all his days. But now he has a new purpose and a dragon to speak mind-to-mind with." Elvina sighed. "Having that dragon bond with him has helped bring him back to life. But I hope someday he will marry again and have children." She looked sidelong at Fiona.

"I am sorry he had to experience such a loss, and I hope he will find happiness again." *But not with me.* Fiona would not say those words aloud, for she would never intentionally hurt Elvina. She did hope the woman wasn't trying to push Erian and her together, though.

"Thank you." Elvina's soft voice was full of emotion, and Fiona was glad they had finished cleaning up so she could leave her new friend alone with her thoughts.

Hers would not be still after she shut the door to her guest room. She wondered if she had done the right thing, writing to Papa. Perhaps she should have waited until closer to time to deliver her child. But the words had begged to be written; Fiona's conscience burned within her, and she wanted to make things right more than postponing any potential discomfort that was sure to find her in the future.

* * *

After Tristam and his mother arrived at the castle in the Southern Woodlands, he carefully dismounted Reggie and left Val to help their mother down. Val only stayed long enough to greet Lord Rudyard, and then he and his dragon departed. Mother, of course, wanted to see Lady Shannon right away.

The elderly woman received them in her sitting room while propped in an overstuffed chair with many pillows.

"Come in, both of you. I'm so glad you are here." Lady Shannon shifted with a grimace, and Mercy hurried to her side.

"Where does it hurt?" Mercy asked.

"My back is the worst, but now sharp pains are traveling from there, through the hips, and down the legs. But sometimes my legs feel so numb I am afraid to walk lest I take a bad fall." She sighed. "I am sorry to be such a bother."

"You are no bother, dear Shannon." Mercy leaned over and kissed her friend's cheek.

While he helped his mother gently turn Lady Shannon to her side so they could examine her back, Tristam pictured all the bones and muscles of the back and legs, preparing for what he would shortly *See*.

Because their patient was a woman, Mercy led the Healing by placing her hands on Lady Shannon's lower back, and Tristam added his on top before closing his eyes. He felt the Healing power come to his mother's hands, and he immediately added his, bringing a sharp image of the elderly woman's bones to his mind's eye.

Mother, do you See *how inflamed are the joints of her lower back?*

Yes, I do. That alone could be pinching the nerves and causing her pain and numbness.

It could but—he shifted his hands atop hers to better *See* the individual vertebrae. *Do you see those bone spurs? They look wicked sharp.*

Oh, I do now. Thank you for catching that. Let's take care of those first, and then the inflammation.

I agree. That should reduce the pain and the numbness.

Working together as they had for hundreds of patients over the years, Tristam and Mercy dissolved the spurs and calmed the inflamed joints. With a sigh, he lifted his hands while they released the Healing power and opened his eyes. Then they helped Lady Shannon turn back to settle into her chair again. She clearly had easier movement and no longer groaned in pain.

"My dears, what did you do so quickly to banish my pain?" She moved her legs with a beaming smile. "What a blessed relief! How can I ever thank you?"

Mercy patted the woman's hand. "We are happy to be of help to you."

At that moment, Tristam's stomach growled, loud enough for both women to notice. Lady Shannon chuckled.

"Well, I see how I can repay you, young Tristam. I never knew a young man who wasn't hungry. Run down to the kitchen and tell my cook to feed you whatever you wish." When he hesitated, she urged him. "Go on; I know you're hungry, lad."

Sheepishly, Tristam met his mother's gaze, and she nodded.

"Thank you, Lady Shannon." He dipped his head and left the room.

Since he hadn't been in the Southern Woodlands often, he got turned around and had to ask for directions. As he neared the kitchen, however, the aroma of roasting meat led him the rest of the way, making his mouth water.

To his surprise, he found a familiar face in the kitchen. Oswald Cornwall, Sir Nathan's squire, was sitting at a small table in the corner, finishing a large bowl of stew and a hunk of bread.

"Hello, Tris," he said around a mouthful of bread. "Did you come with your lady mother?" He gestured for him to take the other seat, which he did.

"Yes, we came to Heal Lady Shannon. She sent me here to find something to eat." He stared at the bread with longing, and Oswald gestured with his spoon to one of the kitchen workers.

"Bring another bowl of stew for my friend the Healer." He held up his bowl. "And more for me while you're at it."

The young man hurried to comply, and Tristam gratefully dipped his hunk of bread in the steaming broth.

"Is this your meal break, then?" he asked Oswald to be polite.

The squire nodded. After he finished chewing he added, "I heard Prince Val and Regnatorix announce the arrival of the Healers, so I guessed you might have come also."

Tristam started to ask Oswald how he heard Val and Reggie, but then he remembered Oswald had been one of the candidates for dragon rider who had not been chosen. Since he could hear the dragons, Val had explained that he would still be part of the Royal Dragon Couriers because of his ability to send and receive messages for Lord Rudyard.

Was he very disappointed not to be riding a dragon?

He soon learned the answer to that question, for Oriana entered the kitchen. Slight of build, she wore a sturdy split riding skirt and leather vest over her long-sleeved shirt. She smiled when she noticed Tristam.

"Hello," she said in a soft voice, including both young men. She cocked her head at Tristam. "Do I know you?"

"He's Lord Tristam, a Healer," Oswald said with a scowl. "A laundress should address a lord with greater respect."

Tristam held up his hands. "No need to scold her, Ozzy. She would never have guessed who I am, and anyway, I don't require special treatment from a dragon rider." He added a slight emphasis on the last two words to remind Oswald he knew who and what Oriana was now, no matter that a short while ago she'd been a laundress.

"I am pleased to meet you, Lord Tristam." Oriana dipped her head before stiffly addressing Oswald. "Sir Nathan is looking for you. He's coming from the stables, and he doesn't look happy."

The annoyance on Oswald's face changed instantly to nervousness, and he scampered from the kitchen, looking more like a page than a senior squire in that moment. Tristam held back a smile.

Oriana served herself from the cauldron of stew over the fire, speaking over her shoulder to Tristam. "Would you like some more, my lord?"

"Yes, please, but I can serve myself." He rose from the table with his empty bowl, which Oriana exchanged for her full one. Not until then did he notice she wore her brown hair in a single braid that fell to her waist.

"I'll fill your bowl if you'll place mine on the table." She smiled shyly and ladled stew into his bowl. Then she grabbed a loaf of bread from a tray and came to sit across from Tristam. She tore the loaf in two and offered half to him, which he took with a nod of thanks.

After eating in silence for a few bites, Oriana broke the silence. "So, you are a Healer, my lord? Have you been one long?" She watched him while chewing a bite of bread.

Tristam nodded, swallowing before speaking. "Since I was four, so for ten years."

"You're fourteen?" Oriana studied his face. "I would have guessed you were older than I am. I'm sixteen."

With a shrug, Tristam fought the urge to duck his head and hide the warmth that crept up his neck.

"Everyone says that. Mother thinks it's because I never had a childhood, so I grew up quickly." Then he swallowed. Why was he being so open with this young woman he'd only just met?

Oriana sopped up the juices with the last of her bread before replying. "I can understand that, my lord. My father died in an accident when I was only three, and my mother nearly died birthing my brother a few months later. She was left an invalid, so my brother was given to my aunt to raise, and I started work in the laundry very young to keep us fed."

Tristam straightened. "An invalid? Why did you not apply to Lord Rudyard to send for my parents to Heal your mother?"

Oriana sat back with a frown. "Who are your parents, my lord?"

"Kieran and Mercy MacLachlan." He had a sinking feeling the moment he said their names.

Oriana jumped up and started to leave the kitchen, but Tristam reached out and caught her hand.

"Wait. Please wait, Oriana." He kept his voice as gentle as possible, and she slowly turned to face him. "Did they try to Heal your mother, then?"

She nodded, and tears welled in her eyes. "They said they could not reach her, that she had given up and was trapped inside her mind." She wiped her eyes. "Mother stays alive only because I feed her. Her muscles are completely useless after all these years."

"Do you have somewhere you must be right now?" He let go of her hand, and she didn't run off.

"Not until late this afternoon. Why?" The look she gave him was part suspicion, part hope.

"Take me to her. Let me examine her and see if there's anything more to be done." He slowly rose so as not to startle her.

Oriana took a step back. "Please, don't give me any false hope."

"I won't. I just want to see her for myself." Tristam saw the moment she relented.

"Follow me, then." And she pivoted and strode from the kitchen.

Tristam hurried to keep up with her. They crossed the castle yard to a row of thatched huts along the inside wall. Though Tristam wasn't much taller than Oriana, he still had to duck to enter the low doorway. The single room was simply furnished with a table and chair, two cots, a wooden trunk, and cooking utensils hung by the fireplace.

In the cot nearest the fireplace lay a sleeping woman with limp brown hair and pasty skin. Tristam approached her without hesitation and knelt at her head.

"Will you kneel across from me, in case she wakes up and startles to see a stranger touching her?"

Oriana nodded and copied Tristam's posture.

"What is her name?" he thought to ask while rolling up his sleeves.

"Felicity." She lifted her chin with a grim smile. "No one ever asks."

"I have learned that the name of the patient is the most important thing for a Healer to know. How else can I try to reach her?" He broke eye contact with Oriana and took a deep breath before lightly placing his hands atop Felicity's head. Then he closed his eyes and called on the Healing power.

To his great sadness, the poor woman was barely alive, as if she had a wasting disease that began in the mind and spread throughout her body. Indeed, Tristam was shocked she had held on for thirteen years.

Felicity. My name is Tristam. I want to help you. Please, let me help you. Your daughter Oriana needs you.

Nothing happened right away, but then a small stirring came from inside her. Tristam gently reached out to touch the spark of life, imagining he was blowing on a tiny ember to encourage it to glow brighter.

No, came the feeble answer. *Let me go.*

I cannot do that. You have the gift of life from the Most High God. Your life is precious, and your daughter loves you dearly.

Felicity's eyelids fluttered, and Oriana gasped.

Daughter? Love?

Yes, Felicity. Oriana your daughter loves you and wants you to get well.

The woman's mouth formed an "O" and finally whispered, "Oriana?"

"I am here, Mother." Oriana picked up her hand and pressed it to her lips. "I have been with you the whole time. I will never leave you."

While Felicity stared into her daughter's eyes, Tristam took the opportunity to examine her as best he could without moving his hands from her head. A general profound weakness, which was to be expected, but he felt certain that if her spirit could be restored, the body would follow. So he sent a surge of the Healing power through the woman's veins to strengthen her heart. The only true Healing for her wasted muscles was very slow, gradual use, and that required determination on the part of the patient.

So as unobtrusively as he could, Tristam sent a little determination before releasing his hands and sitting back. He let out a sigh, more exhausted than he would have guessed. But he had helped Mother Heal Lady Shannon not long before.

That gave him an idea. He stumbled as he rose to his feet.

"I'll return as quickly as I can," he promised Oriana. She mouthed "thank you" while he quietly left the cottage.

Tristam returned to the castle and made his way up to Lady Shannon's room. He was glad to see that Mother was still with her.

"Tristam?" she said with a frown, rising when he entered. "What happened? You're very pale."

"I used some Healing power on a very ill woman, the mother of the new dragon rider, Oriana. I was wondering—" He paused, for he had a thought he might be stepping out of bounds with the Lady of the Southern Woodlands. "Lady Shannon, I was wondering if there was a chair similar to yours that a feeble woman might use to help her sit upright and regain her strength?"

Shannon looked down at her overstuffed chair as if seeing it for the first time. "A feeble woman, eh, young Tristam?" She chuckled and winked at Mercy. "I suppose that's what I have been for far too long." Then she pointed across the room. "I have not been able to sit in that chair for years. Not sure why I've kept it, for guests never sit so far away." She smiled at Tristam. "Find two of the guards to carry it for you wherever you need it, and it's yours."

"Thank you, Lady Shannon." Tristam's grin nearly split his face, and he went to find the nearest strapping guards to carry the chair down the spiral stairs and into the castle yard.

Tristam led the way to Oriana's and Felicity's cottage, knocking first to give them the opportunity to ready themselves. When Oriana opened the door, she smiled at Tristam with a puzzled frown, and then she saw the two guards carrying the chair. She immediately knew what it was for, and directed the men to place it near the fire.

"Do ye want that we should move the lady to the chair, my lord?" asked one of the guards in a gruff voice.

"Yes, please," Tristam said after getting a nod from Oriana.

Far more gently than Tristam would have expected from them, the men lifted Felicity and settled her in the chair. Oriana rolled up two blankets and placed them on either side of her mother's head while the guards hovered near the doorway until they were sure all was well.

"Thank you so much," she said in her sweet voice, making them smile as they left the cottage.

Then she faced Tristam. "How can I ever thank you, my lord?"

"By calling me Tristam and not 'my lord.'" He shrugged before turning his attention to Felicity.

She was exhausted by the change of position, but her eyes were open, watching him.

"How do you like your new chair, Felicity?" He used his most cheerful voice.

"Yes," she whispered, and her eyes twinkled briefly.

"That was a smile, Mother!" Oriana leaned over and kissed Felicity's cheek. "It will be so much easier for you to eat, and you can better see what is going on."

"Yes," Felicity whispered again, and a tear tracked down her cheek.

"I will come back to see you before I must return to the Keep," Tristam promised. He took one of her limp hands between both of his and smiled when he felt her try to squeeze. "That's right, Felicity. Keep moving those muscles, and they will return to life, as you have." He patted her hand and headed to the door. "Farewell for now."

Oriana followed him outside. "How can we ever thank you, Tristam?"

"You already have." He nodded at the cottage. "Who looks in on your mother while you are off delivering messages?"

"My aunt has been helping." Oriana gazed down at her feet.

"But not enough to help your mother regain her strength." When she shook her head, Tristam knew Lord Rudyard would be able to recommend someone who could come daily and stay as long as necessary. "Don't worry, Oriana; I'll take care of it."

With a spring his step, Tristam strode across the castle yard. It had been a good day of Healing, and he had made two new friends.

Chapter 29

Better is a neighbour that is near than a brother far off.

Kieran paid for stabling for Burdock before entering the River
Dragon Inn, the place where Tammeron said he'd last seen
Fiona. There were no rooms available, but Kieran didn't mind
sleeping in the stall with Burdock if he had to. First, he paid for a meal
and sat in a corner of the crowded common room, waiting to speak
with the bard, if one showed up to play. He did discover a handful of
regular customers, and one remembered hearing Fiona singing a while
back.

"Lovely girl with the voice o' an angel," the old man said with a
toothy smile. "Better 'n the bard, if ye want to know the truth." He
chuckled and went back to his ale.

Finally the bard arrived, another young one wearing an outrageous
costume. Kieran couldn't look at him for long, the colors were so
garish. His voice was pleasant enough, and the crowd was pleased at
his selections.

Toward the end of the evening, he strummed a chord and spoke
brightly.

"Thank you for staying to listen to a poor traveling bard. In my
travels I came upon a new epic ballad, which I will share with you
tonight. It tells such a fantastical tale, 'tis hard to believe it could be
true, yet I am told from a reliable source that everything happened as

the ballad describes." He bent over his lute, and Kieran's ears perked up.

At first he was listening so intently to the new melody and chords, he didn't realize whose story he was hearing. And then it came to him: Val! This was his adventure last year, put to music by a skilled songwriter. Had Val told the story to a bard, as Kieran had shared Valerian's story with another bard many years ago?

Once the song ended, the bard stood to receive the crowd's applause and announced the name of the song as "The Ballad of Prince Val."

Who had written it? Kieran had to know. He waited until most of the people had left and then went forward to toss a coin into the bard's lute case.

"Thank you, kind sir." Up close, the bard's eyes were bleary, his ornate costume worn from long use. Kieran glanced around to make sure no one was within hearing.

"That last song, where did you learn it?" He kept his voice friendly.

"From a bard named Noel." The man placed his lute on top of the coins and shut the leather case. "Did you like it?"

"Very much, especially since I know the subject of the ballad and have heard him tell the story. The song captures the adventure admirably." Kieran smiled at the bard's surprise.

"You know Prince Val?" He picked up his case and held it under his arm.

"All his life. Tell me, where might I find this Noel? I would dearly love to share the details of Prince Val's adventure with him."

The bard looked more closely at Kieran then, his eyes narrowed with suspicion. "Why are you so interested in finding Noel?"

"It's as I said: I know Prince Val. I'm his stepfather. I know a thing or two about writing songs, as well. 'The Deed of Valerian'?" He raised his brows, and the bard's eyes widened.

"No." He seemed to realize Kieran was not joking. "Truly? You wrote that song, oldtimer?"

Kieran chuckled. "I suppose I must look like an oldtimer to you, but I was there for the events in Valerian's song, and I raised his son after his untimely death." His mirth faded. "Please, I must speak to this Noel and find out who shared the story with him. The future of a young life could be at stake."

The bard nodded. "When we parted yesterday, he was headed for Woodbridge Village. If he only stays one night, then I would check the next village. He prefers traveling among the villages closer to the coast." His face screwed up in disgust. "Imagine, he *likes* to eat fish!"

Kieran laughed again and bade the bard a good night.

*

Early the next morning, Kieran awakened to find himself in a stall with Burdock. His dreams had been so intense, he'd forgotten where he was. After brushing off straw and saddling the patient horse, they headed south to find the bard named Noel.

By noon they reached Woodbridge Village, and Kieran remembered why it had been given that name. A lovely wooden bridge had been built over the river here, and Burdock's hooves tripped along it, echoing below. Kieran scanned the tidy buildings along the scenic waterway with appreciation. He had only been here once before, but it had been a peaceful place, the kind that seemed especially idyllic to him now.

He spotted an inn and went there first to inquire about the bard. If Noel was not here, there was no need to spend the night when he had time to press on to the next village. Kieran fastened Burdock's reins to an obliging post out front and entered the nearly empty common room. At the sound of his steps on the wooden floor, the innkeeper peered in from a doorway opposite the entrance.

"May I help you?"

"I'm looking for a bard named Noel. I was told he came this way." Kieran smiled so as not to appear a grumpy old man.

The innkeeper nodded. "He did, and he left early this morning. Not sure which way he was headed, but he oft plays in Middletown and Wycliff."

"Those be south o' here?" Kieran tried to picture the map in his head.

"Aye." The man grinned, as if he'd been waiting for an opportunity to speak to a Highlander. "Anything else? Food? Ale?"

"I thank ye, but I must press on tae Middletown. I only hope tae stay in this fine establishment someday soon. Good day." He admired the cleanliness of the place on his way out. Even the sign above the door was freshly painted, and window boxes overflowed with bright yellow and red flowers.

While he continued south, Kieran's opinion of the elusive Noel grew lower. Why wouldn't the bard want to stay in Woodbridge as long as he could?

* * *

Fiona was looking forward to spending the day out of doors, especially since all the dragon riders were supposed to be flying over Moor Point, and she might catch a glimpse of Val. Since Erian was the courier assigned to Moor Point, would he be leading them? And if so, wouldn't he try to fly over his sister's cottage if at all possible?

She helped Elvina gather all the wash to do first, so it would have time to dry in the sun. Then they would care for the animals and work in the garden. The sky was clear and the breeze warm for early fall. Of course, Seaton was far south of the Keep and so the weather was warmer at every season.

Not until they had finished the washing and were hanging the dripping garments and sheets did Elvina venture a question.

"Feena, do you not have family who would take you in, now that your husband has died?" The way she asked the question, Fiona wondered if it was a hint for her to leave, and her eyes filled with tears.

"I'll go if you want me to." To her distress, she burst into sobs, and Elvina dropped what she was holding in her basket and hurried to Fiona's side.

"I'm sorry if you thought I was asking you to leave, because I'm not." She reached out and held Fiona close, rubbing her back. "I am glad you're here, but I can't help but wonder if you have family elsewhere who would be worried about you. I know I would be worried, if you were my sister or my daughter."

Fiona shook her head until she was able to control her emotions. Why did she cry so easily now? Did it have something to do with expecting a child? Once again, she wished she'd paid closer attention to such matters.

"I can't tell my family where I am. Not yet." She wiped her eyes and pulled away from Elvina. "You see, Tam and I ran away, because I knew they would not approve of our marriage." She let out a sigh. "I thought I knew what I was doing. I was a fool." With a groan, she covered her face. "I'm not ready to face them."

"I understand." Elvina patted her shoulder. "I won't press you to contact them." She waited until Fiona looked up at her. "And I meant what I said; you can stay as long as you need to."

"Thank you," Fiona whispered.

They finished the laundry and hurried to feed the protesting animals.

*

The sun was near its zenith, and they were busy weeding the garden when the light suddenly dimmed. Fiona looked up with a gasp to see a close formation of ten dragons skimming the treetops overhead. So near! It was impossible to see which rider was Val from this angle, though one of the dragons looked a little smaller and bluer than the others. Wasn't that Reggie?

She stood and wiped her hands while they passed over, grinning at the beautiful sight they made together. And then her grin faded when the dragons made a wide turn and headed back toward Elvina's house. They weren't going to *land*, were they?

With a gasp, Fiona panicked, racing back to the house to hide in her room. Elvina intercepted her at the door.

"Feena? I thought you weren't afraid of dragons?" She peered into her face with concern.

"It looks like they are coming here, and I'd rather not meet them up close. The riders, I mean." Fiona knew the excuse was lame, but she truly hadn't thought the dragon riders would come to the cottage. She simply could not let Val know she was here! "Please, let me wait in the guest room until they leave." She must have sounded desperate, for Elvina nodded sadly.

As soon as Fiona shut herself in her room, she heard voices coming from the direction of the meadow. Closing her eyes, Fiona listened intently for Val's voice, but the ones speaking were other young men. Elvina wasn't planning on feeding all of them, was she? Fiona would feel terrible if she left all the serving to Elvina!

But then she heard Barnaby's cheerful voice and the general hubbub of a large crowd. Had all the village come out to see the dragon riders? Fiona covered her head with her pillow. If only she dared make herself known to Val!

A long time passed with none of the voices coming closer or into the cottage. At least, it seemed like hours to Fiona in her awkward position upon the guest bed. When at last she heard exclamations of excitement from the villagers, Fiona hurried to the window and peered out. She caught a glimpse of multiple dragons lifting into the air and continuing north.

Letting out a breath that was part disappointment and part relief, Fiona sagged against the window frame until she heard Elvina enter the cottage.

"Feena?" she called. "They're all gone. You can come out now."

Embarrassed now that the danger of discovery had passed, Fiona opened her door and joined Elvina in the kitchen.

"I'm sorry, Elvina. When it looked as if you might have to feed ten hungry dragon riders all by yourself, I felt terribly guilty. You didn't, did you?" She waited expectantly for Elvina to answer.

"No, I didn't, though I was prepared to." Elvina shook her head with a smile. "Barnaby had already stirred up the village, and many brought food for the riders." Her eyes twinkled. "You should have seen Amadorix—that's Erian's dragon—taste one of Goodwife Esther's brambleberry tarts! Some of the lads had been placing bets, and it was too tart even for a dragon!"

Fiona would have liked to see that! And to meet the other dragon riders. And especially, to see Val again. "Some of the riders are female, aren't they?" Emma was supposed to have tried out, but Fiona had run away before she'd learned whether Emma was chosen.

"Yes, three of them are young women; the other seven are men, although one is very young still, no more than twelve or thirteen, I would guess." Elvina placed two bowls on the table. "Come, sit and eat before we finish weeding."

Fiona ate two bowls of Elvina's tasty stew before returning outside in the pleasant afternoon sun. The two of them finished pulling all the weeds before the sun touched the horizon and it was time to ready supper for Finn.

* * *

Val followed Erian's lead on their flight across Moor Point. The young man enjoyed pointing out landmarks through an amused Amadorix, notably the castle ruins jutting into the sea at the far southwest corner of Levathia, the swamps, and the villages along the coastline and beside rivers. Though Moor Point was the smallest of the seven provinces, it had quite a varied landscape, and Val hoped to explore it more thoroughly someday.

Erian, of course, wanted to stop in his own village, and the villagers had certainly been welcoming and obliging. None of them were the least bit apprehensive about seeing ten dragons up close!

They'd brought enough food to feed a hundred dragon riders, and Val had to decline much more than he was able to eat.

They did act as if they had experience with dragons, e'en before Amadorix became a frequent visitor. Emma gave Val a mental caress, and he turned to meet her gaze where she flew upon Veynaria's back.

I remember Erian mentioning his village had sheltered Dorricia after she had been badly burned many years ago. He chuckled. *I believe they must have sheltered Kieran, too, for he'd been riding on Dorricia, and both were flamed.*

They were flamed? How frightful! Do ye ken what happened?

Not from personal experience, since I was but a babe in arms, but Dolan and my parents and another lord at the Keep, Drew Campignon, were trying to rescue Joy from an evil man and the dragon he had controlled with poison.

Och, a right wee fankle, that was! Since I ken your brother an' your Mum an' Da an' Dorricia are alive and well, I assume this Lord Drew be alive and well, too?

Yes, he is, thankfully. And the man who kidnapped Joy, I am told, was executed by the dragons. Val grimaced at the image he'd always pictured of that event.

Executed by the dragons! Did they burn him, then?

Yes. He fell silent, for he had just remembered the reason Cephalorix and Dorricia and Mathairia had asked Dolan's permission to carry out the execution. That man had been responsible for the deaths of all the other great dragons. He had nearly completed his goal of eradicating them from the world! Val shuddered at the thought, and Emma sent another caress.

The Most High didnae let him succeed. Think o' that and be glad, love.

Val met Emma's gaze again. *Trust you to hear me even when I'm not trying to be heard.* He smiled so she would know he was glad she had. *Thank you, love.*

Before he could say more, Castle Moor Point came into view, and the dragons practiced their close formation landing in the castle yard. One man leading a panicking horse had to scramble to get out of the way of the downdraft of many wings. Val realized the landing had been too close for safety and immediately thought of a way to prevent that from happening in the future. He slid down from Reggie's side and strode to meet Erian.

"Did you see the man having trouble leading a horse out of the way of our landing?" He pointed toward the stables, where the man and his mount disappeared from view.

"I did, my lord." Erian grimaced. "Obviously, I need to more strongly impress upon the guard here how to safely interact in the presence of dragons."

Val held back a smile at the young man's seriousness, for this was a serious business. "In future, when the entire flight will be landing in formation, the resident dragon rider should ride ahead and clear the way."

Erian nodded, pleased. "That should solve the problem, my lord. Admirably."

Lord Dracen came out to meet them.

"A fine show of strength, Your Highness." He clasped hands with Val. "We are pleased to have the services of the loyal Erian and Amadorix here at Castle Moor Point and want to reassure you of our pledge to help the Royal Dragon Couriers in any possible way." Dracen's gaze traveled over the other dragons and their riders.

"Thank you, Lord Dracen. We count ourselves blessed indeed to have Erian and Amadorix among the couriers." Val inclined his head to them. "But, before we continue on to the border and complete our passage over Moor Point, is there anything we can do for you today?"

Dracen tightened his jaw. "There is a problem that ten dragons and their riders could solve much more quickly than a small army on foot or horseback could alone, Your Highness." He met Erian's gaze, who nodded. "A gang of cutthroats has been robbing and murdering innocent people. They think they have outsmarted us because they are so good at hiding out in the forests, but my best tracker has found their most recent camp and can lead you to it, if you are willing to help capture these men from the air."

"It's not a matter of being unwilling to help stop a gang of cutthroats, Lord Dracen, but how many are there? And will the dragons be able to capture them without too much risk to themselves and their riders? Will we have support from your men on the ground?" Val's gut tightened. Not all of the riders were armed with any weapon larger than a belt knife. Erian, Fletcher, and Hamelin were the only ones who wore their swords.

"Actually, Sire, it was my intention to send my men to flush out the criminals, but if you and the dragon riders could fly above and watch from the air for any who escape the ground troops, I would be in your debt." Dracen waited hopefully.

Val beckoned the other dragon riders to come closer, for not all of them had heard the conversation. While Lord Dracen laid out to the riders his plan of attack and the proposed role of the dragons and their riders, Val explained it to the dragons. He wanted them to know the risks before he had to decide whether this action was within the scope of what the Royal Dragon Couriers could be called upon to do in the service of any provincial lord.

This was not what he and Dolan had ever foreseen, after all, but Dolan had put complete faith and trust in Val's judgment to decide these matters. The royal couriers were meant to transport messages and people. Yet they were not being asked to flame at criminals nor harm them in any way, but to transport them, if necessary. Val smiled at a long ago memory of the terror that could be instilled in lawbreakers when coming up close and personal with a roaring dragon.

And I am much older now and more ferocious than I was when the Keep was under attack, Reggie reminded him. *I think we should help to stop these men from hurting anyone else.*

One by one the other dragons agreed.

"Lord Dracen, it is unanimous among the dragons that they choose to help." Val scanned the faces of the dragon riders and found them all in agreement as well. "All of us riders, too."

Dracen looked relieved. "Come then and speak to my scout while I give the men orders to head for the outlaws' camp."

*

In less than an hour, the mounted men and the dragon riders converged on the hidden camp. Val had the dragons spread out in a loose circle over the dense trees, so that each one only had to watch one small section for escaping men. It was, he decided, good practice in making tight circle patrols.

Yelling and the clash of weapons could be heard beneath the canopy, and Val kept watching his and Reggie's area. Even though he was expecting it to happen, when a man came running out from under the trees, trying to mount a horse while on the run, Val was startled.

Do you see him? he asked Reggie.

Yes. Do I pick up the man or both man and horse?

Just the man. Val tightened his grip on Reggie's back ridge, preparing for the dive.

But then a second man followed the first on foot, running even faster. The first man had finally mounted the horse, though it must have scented the dragons, for it shied and whinnied in fear, and the man fought to control it. The second man reached up and yanked the first from the saddle, pulling him down with such force that the first man did not get up. While the second man struggled to pull up to the saddle, Val leaned into Reggie's steep dive.

At the moment the dragon snatched up the man by the arms, the horse screamed in terror and finally galloped away, riderless. Val could not see the man Reggie had caught, but he clearly heard his stream of angry curses all the way back to Castle Moor Point. Guards were waiting to take Reggie's captive, and Lord Dracen strode closer.

"Rodney Folville. I thought you were dead." Dracen glared at the big man. "Are you the ringleader, then?"

Folville clamped his jaw and refused to answer. Before the guards led him away, he turned a murderous look upon Val and Reggie. No fear in that one, which made him especially dangerous.

Dracen must have realized that too, for he gave instructions for Folville to be chained hand and foot in a solitary cell.

Now more dragons were landing, each with another prisoner, but to Val's relief, there were a few dragons without such a burden, including Emma. Did that mean the action was over?

Yes, Reggie told him. *Amadorix says Lord Dracen's men captured or killed all the others.*

Good. Val checked the position of the sun. It was nearly time for all the dragon riders to disperse to their home provinces. They would have to finish flying over Moor Point on the next rotation, for the following week it was Fletcher Meverel's turn to lead the dragon riders over Westmoor.

Lord Dracen's heartfelt thanks to all the couriers had to be cut short, but Val was sure he would understand. After bidding Dracen and Erian farewell, Val and the others went aloft, and Reggie gave instructions to meet at Castle Westmoor in one week's time.

Then Val and Reggie flew with Emma and Veynaria to Emma's village, arriving as the sun was beginning to set.

Me dear Val, ye dinna have tae come all the way here after such a long day, for I know 'tis a long way yet tae return tae the Keep. Emma dismounted and encouraged Veynaria to eat and drink something to replenish her strength.

I know I don't have to, but I want to. Val had dismounted also and came to take Emma's hand. "After all, it's nearly the only time we have to spend a few minutes alone." They sat together on the bench by her cottage's front door.

Val was too tired to say much, but he never minded if all they did was sit holding hands. The last orange rays of the sunset lit up the western sky, making him smile. One day closer to the end of Emma's apprenticeship, and one evening closer to their wedding day, when they would no longer have to be separated for days at a time.

"Only a fortnight 'til I be a full-fledged midwife." Emma squeezed Val's hand.

"Not long at all, now." Val brought her hand to his lips. "I'm proud of you Emma, for working so hard at midwifery while still doing your part with the dragon couriers."

She shrugged, and he could imagine her face growing warm. "I sometimes canna believe all that has happened since I first met you. Are ye sure ye are real, Val? Perhaps 'tis all a pleasant dream."

"I am as real as you are. And if this is but a pleasant dream, then I hope I never wake up." He let go of her hand and gently cupped her cheek, leaning down to kiss her.

Emma slipped her arms around his waist, and he held her close with his cheek against the top of her head. If only they could be married in two weeks! But he knew she and her mother wanted to plan a proper wedding, and Val was not going to spoil any of their plans.

As he felt weariness settle over him, Val kissed Emma's head and reluctantly stood up.

"I'd better return to the Keep now. Reggie and I will come for you next week, same time."

"Veynaria and I will be ready. The Most High watch over ye 'til then." She stretched up to kiss him once more, and Val felt a twinge of actual pain when he finally had to let go and leave with Reggie.

Even though she couldn't see him in the dark, he waved until Reggie flew over the hills and away from her presence.

Chapter 30

The glory of young men is their strength;
and the beauty of old men is the grey head.

Fiona was helping Elvina wash up after dinner when Erian burst into the kitchen, startling them both.

"Erian!" Elvina brushed at the soapy water that had splashed on her dress. "What has gotten into you? I don't expect you to knock, but you don't need to scare us half to death either."

With a chuckle, he kissed her cheek. "Sorry, Sis, but I have good news for Feena and couldn't wait to share it."

Fiona met his gaze with anticipation. She wiped her trembling hands on her apron, and he came closer.

"You no longer have to fear the men who killed your husband, for they have all been taken into custody at Castle Moor Point." He smiled grimly.

Fiona felt for the stool behind her and sat upon it. "Folville too?"

Erian nodded. "Yes. He will hang for his crimes. And I don't believe Lord Dracen will require you to be questioned, either."

She frowned, not sure Erian could be right about that. "Lord Dracen won't want my testimony at the trial?"

"There are so many witnesses against those men, they won't all be needed." Erian straightened with confidence. "I heard Lord Dracen say so myself when he spoke with Prince Val."

"Prince Val?" Fiona blurted out the words without thinking and then tried to pretend she hadn't said them.

Erian chuckled. "Yes, Feena. The prince is Lord of the Sky and head of the Royal Dragon Couriers, so he was present when us dragon riders helped capture the gang of criminals."

"You helped capture them?" Fiona's eyes widened, trying to imagine it.

"It was much more satisfying than I could have believed possible when Amadorix dove down and snatched one of the men right out of the saddle." He grinned at both women.

"With his teeth?" Elvina's eyes widened in horror.

"Oh, no, Vina. Amadorix used his front claws. He was fairly gentle about setting the man down in the castle yard, too. Not much blood at all."

"Not *much* blood," Elvina muttered, finishing the dishes.

Fiona turned her attention back to drying them, but the image of dragons and their riders chasing Folville and his men greatly appealed to her. Had they been frightened out of their wits by the great dragons? She certainly hoped so!

She only wished she could see Val for herself and speak to him. But she just couldn't. Not yet.

* * *

When Kieran arrived at Middleton that evening, there was one room left at the inn, so he paid for it and stabling for Burdock. The bard was another young man, but he wore a much plainer costume. Could this be the elusive Noel?

Kieran took a seat at one of the crowded tables and enjoyed the fresh fish and shellfish while listening to the bard's singing. Kieran learned from one of his table mates that it was not Noel, after all. This Clive had a good voice and played unerringly on his lute. Most refreshing to Kieran was his lack of self-conceit. True, not all bards had that air about them, but enough of them did that they irritated Kieran more and more. Was he truly becoming a curmudgeon, after all?

Shaking his head, he reflected that there were many things about himself he did not like. He prayed it was not too late to change them, for his own sake as well as for those around him.

Meanwhile, Kieran thoroughly enjoyed Clive's performance. He listened more closely when the young bard sang "The Deed of

Valerian" and "The Ballad of Prince Val" one after the other. Had he learned the new song from Noel or from the actual songwriter?

He had to wait until the end of the evening to find out. Kieran held back until everyone else had left, and then he dropped a coin onto the bard's substantial pile.

"Thank you," Clive said wearily and bent down to pick up his lute case.

"That new ballad about Prince Val," Kieran blurted out. "Did Noel teach it to you?"

Clive blinked with a smile. "Why, yes he did. Do you know him?"

Kieran shrugged. "I have not had the pleasure of meeting him yet, but I have been told he learned the song from a person with firsthand knowledge, and I very much wish to find the songwriter."

"Well, then, I can help you a little there, for Noel said the songwriter lived in Seaton, though he was not at liberty to give the person's name." Clive placed his lute in the case and carefully shut it.

"Seaton, eh? Not far from here, as I recall." Kieran knew he would need to head west and travel all the way to the coast.

"An easy two-day journey, assuming you have a horse?" Clive's voice sounded hopeful.

"I do, and he's strong enough to ride double, if ye were wanting tae head that way, too." Kieran would consider it a blessing and no burden to travel with a bard as easygoing as Clive seemed to be.

"I am headed that way." Clive grinned, revealing straight teeth. "And I would be obliged to you. Riding for two days would save my feet and my shoes. In fact, I plan to visit the fine cobbler there in Seaton so he can repair mine." Clive turned up one foot to show Kieran that the sole of his leather shoe was worn through.

"Aye, looks like 'tis time tae visit the cobbler, all right." Kieran held out his hand. For all of two seconds he considered introducing himself as Finn MacRorie, but he put away that vanity. "I'm Kieran."

"Clive." The bard gripped his hand. "Do you have a room here?"

"Aye. You?"

Clive nodded. "This innkeeper is always generous when I pass through."

"Then I'll meet ye back here in the morning to break our fast and leave after?" Kieran raised his brows, wondering if the young man would want to sleep in.

"I'll be ready. I'm off to bed right now." And with a yawn, Clive shuffled off.

While Kieran climbed the stairs to his room, it struck him that this bard was young enough to be his son. He might not have been born when Kieran had traveled Moor Point as Finn MacRorie. The thought sobered him and made him feel even older.

Well, I canna do anything about getting older, he thought as he shut and locked his door. *But I can choose whether tae be pleasant about it. No more curmudgeonly behavior, old man.*

With a chuckle, Kieran was soon asleep.

*

The following morning, he quickly readied himself and made his way down to the common room. Clive arrived at the same time, nodding to Kieran. They ate their simple breakfast in companionable silence.

Kieran had just finished and was about to stand when a courier entered and spoke to the innkeeper, who pointed at Kieran.

"That's him, sitting there."

The courier came to Kieran and bowed. "My lord, Lord Dracen received this after you left Castle Moor Point and sent me to find you, as the message had instructions to forward it to you." He held out a piece of folded parchment.

Kieran took it from him and pressed a coin into his gloved hand. "I thank you for your pains."

"Good day, my lord." The courier bowed again and exited the inn, leaving Kieran to ponder the mysterious message.

There was no seal pressed into the wax, except a fingerprint, which he only noticed by turning it toward the firelight. Clive spoke up then.

"Sir, I perceive you are too important a person to transport a lowly bard like myself, so I'll just be on my way. Thank you all the same." Clive dipped his head and started to rise, but Kieran held up a hand.

"I am definitely not too important tae spare a talented young man's feet." He gave the bard a crooked smile. "You are doing me a favor, Clive. I find I dinna like traveling alone." When he glanced down at the parchment, Clive rose from the table.

"In that case, my lord, I thank you. I'll let you read your letter in privacy while I settle my account with the innkeeper." He bowed and left the room.

Kieran broke the seal on the letter and opened it. His heart lurched when he saw it was from Fiona.

She sounded well, but the stark truth on the page hit him like a bludgeon. As he'd feared, she was with child without benefit of marriage, and oddly, believed Tam dead.

But she did sound genuinely remorseful, so perhaps the experience had humbled her.

Who was her "hostess" and would the woman turn her out once her pregnancy could no longer be concealed? Kieran's thoughts leaped ahead with his desire to protect and shelter his daughter. If he could find a quiet place, out of the public eye, would she be willing to go with him? Would she allow him to be her protector so she wouldn't feel the need to work so hard to provide for herself?

Anticipating that he would find her soon and be able to offer such protection, Kieran asked the innkeeper for ink and parchment and quickly wrote a letter to Dougal MacLachlan with a request he'd been wanting to ask for many years. Now it was time to attend to his family's needs. Their true needs, not the ones he had convinced himself were adequate to sustain them while he put the kingdom's demands ahead of his own children.

While the ink dried, Kieran read the request twice to make sure it was clearly worded. It was, and Kieran nodded, satisfied. He sealed the wax with his signet ring and wrote: *Lord Dougal MacLachlan, Castle MacLachlan.*

Then he paid the courier fee, thanked the innkeeper, and strode out to the stables, feeling the shedding of multiple burdens with each step.

* * *

The morning of their third day in the Southern Woodlands, Mercy received a message from Oriana, the province's dragon rider and Tristam's new friend. Val was planning to fetch them later in the day so he could return them to the Keep.

"Already?" Tristam said when Mercy relayed the message.

Mercy cocked her head at her son, studying his face. "I thought you'd be glad to return to the Keep so quickly."

He shrugged, and a blush came to his downy cheeks. "I do need to get back to my studies."

"But?" She tried to coax him into saying what he was obviously holding back from her.

Tristam shrugged again. "I've been helping Oriana learn to read and write. But I suppose there's someone else here who can continue with her. She's a fast learner."

"Oriana didn't already know how to read and write?" Mercy had a strong memory of her first husband teaching her those skills, for which she would ever be grateful. She'd been about Tristam's age then.

He shook his head. "She was a laundress before she became a dragon rider. I guess she wouldn't have had the opportunity to learn."

"No, I don't suppose she would have." Mercy bit her lip. "Would you like to continue teaching Oriana? I need to return to the Keep, but I'd be willing to ask Lord Rudyard if you could stay longer."

Tristam let out a sigh. "I suppose I ought to return with you. But before Val comes, I want to find another tutor for Oriana."

"What about Oswald Cornwall? Isn't he part of the Royal Dragon Couriers, even though he doesn't ride a dragon?" Mercy felt certain Oswald would be able to teach Oriana how to read and write.

"He would not be a good choice for Oriana's tutor." Tristam sounded adamant. "But I will ask Lady Shannon. She would know who to ask."

"Yes, she would." Mercy smiled at her youngest son, pleased he was being so sociable here.

"I'll request to see her now. I won't be long." He strode from the room, leaving Mercy pleased at how decisive he'd been in the last little while. Usually that only happened in matters of Healing.

How quickly children grew from being completely dependent to independence. Too quickly.

*

Mercy was packed and ready when Val arrived. Tristam returned minutes later, reporting that Lady Shannon herself agreed to continue Oriana's lessons. Mercy didn't ask, but she hoped Tristam had had a chance to say goodbye to Oriana and her mother. He'd grown close to both of them in a very short time, and Mercy couldn't help but wonder if that friendship would continue.

The three of them made their way to the tower, where Reggie waited patiently. Lord Rudyard met them there, thankful again for their help.

"Come any time, all o' ye," he said with a grin. "Ye are always welcome here."

"Thank you, my lord," Mercy said with a curtsy.

Then Val mounted first, followed by Mercy and finally Tristam. Mercy always wondered if it was a strain for Reggie to carry three of them, but the dragon never complained. Though he would always be smaller than his siblings, he had grown strong in the last few years, and his blue scales had a healthy glow.

Because he carried three, Reggie found it much easier to take off from the height of the tower, rather than leaping into the air from the castle yard. He caught an updraft, and Mercy glanced down at the receding castle in the midst of the dense forest of the Southern Woodlands.

It was a pleasant flight, and the fall day was calm and clear, as near to perfect as could be. Mercy had time to think about Kieran. Would she find a letter from him waiting for her at the Keep?

Chapter 31

Train up a child in the way he should go:
and when he is old, he will not depart from it.

Fiona kneaded the bread dough while Elvina was gathering eggs. She'd forgotten how much she used to like making bread in the Keep's kitchen. Her hands fell into a rhythm, and she began to hum a tune. After several notes, she realized which song she was humming, and so she sang softly in time with her kneading. Could the baby hear her in the womb?

"Come, little lambkin, come and play.
Let us run and jump all day.
'Til the sun moves through the sky,
And the time for bed is nigh."

With a pang in her chest, Fiona had a sudden vivid memory of Papa singing that song to her while he held her in his strong arms. How safe and loved she had always felt with him! She hadn't realized how much she'd missed him, until this moment.

And something else she remembered him telling her on more than one occasion suddenly had new meaning.

"Ye are me bonny lass, Fiona, and I love ye with all me 'eart. But ye have a far greater Father in heaven. He gave ye an imperfect Da like me tae show how much more that true Father loves ye and wants tae give ye good an' perfect gifts."

Fiona shaped the loaves and covered them with a cloth to let them rest. She stepped outside to wipe off the remains of flour on her hands, thinking of Papa's words.

He and Mama had taught her so many things, like honesty, patience, determination, and loyalty. How she'd drifted away from their ideals! And oh, how she'd ignored her conscience and forgotten the faith she'd once had.

Tears dripped to her cheeks, and she wiped them away. All the tears in the world would not undo what had been done. Was there a way to return to her family? Would they take her back, after all she had done?

Fiona strode toward the henhouse, where Elvina had just finished gathering the eggs.

"Can you tell me which direction is the village church?" She tried to stand calmly, though she knew Elvina was too perceptive not to see her inner turmoil.

With a smile, Elvina shifted the basket on her arm to steady it and pointed. "The trees are hiding the steeple, but if you follow the road north, past the blacksmith, you'll come to Seaton's church."

Fiona swallowed. "If the bread finishes rising before I return, will you please put it in the oven?"

"Of course." Elvina studied her again. "Stay as long as you need; I'll take care of the bread."

"Thank you," Fiona breathed. Then she lifted her skirts and hurried to the road. Once she reached it, she slowed her pace, though she did glance back. Elvina was still standing there, watching her.

When her cheeks grew warm, Fiona turned and set herself to walk directly to the church.

* * *

Kieran and Clive rode along the familiar coastal road, nearing their destination after the pleasant two-day journey. Now that they were almost to Seaton, Kieran pondered the song Clive had sung in the previous villages. Who else but Fiona would have known all the details in that epic ballad about Val? Clive had assured him Noel learned the song in Seaton. But if Fiona was the songwriter, how had the lass made her way all the way down to the tip of Moor Point without a horse?

Then the town came into view, and memories assaulted Kieran, as fresh as if they'd happened yesterday and not close to twenty years ago.

"The cobbler is in the first building on the right as we enter Seaton," Clive said with a sigh.

"I know ye will be glad tae repair those shoes." Kieran's voice sounded gruff. This return to Seaton held more emotion than he had reckoned with.

He spied the sign of the shoe and pulled up Burdock to let Clive slide down. The bard reached up to grip Kieran's hand.

"I can never thank you enough for sparing my feet." The young man grinned.

"No thanks necessary." Kieran tried to smile back. "If ye discover the identity of the songwriter, though, I would appreciate it if ye would let me know."

"Where are you staying?"

Kieran shrugged. "I dinna know yet."

Clive pointed down the road. "I'll be at the Salty Dog tonight."

"Then I'll find ye there." Kieran didn't move, reluctant to part with his new young friend.

Clive gave Kieran a jaunty wave and disappeared into the cobbler's shop.

With a sigh, Kieran continued into town. He nodded at the villagers he passed, but they barely acknowledged him. And why would they? The first time he'd arrived, going by the alias Finn MacRorie, he had been a young man. He'd only stayed a few days, but his encounter with Elvina and her desperately poor family had changed their lives forever.

The second time he'd been in Seaton, he had received a near-fatal burning by a rogue dragon, and Mercy had found a way to Heal him. In Widow Ardith's cottage, he remembered, which was located just off this main road. Perhaps he should begin his search for the song maker there.

He recognized the cottage as he approached. Freshly whitewashed, thatch in good repair. But did Ardith still live here?

Kieran halted Burdock and dismounted. His gut roiled from the swirling memories. He gathered his resolve and knocked on the door.

It wasn't Widow Ardith who answered his knock.

"Elvina?" She was older too, of course, but she had developed a serenity about her that put him at ease, despite the circumstances that had brought him here. Now he felt wretched for not returning to Seaton sooner to personally check on her well-being. Instead, he'd relied both on Mercy to send the occasional letter and Lord Dracen to make sure the family was cared for.

Elvina no longer appeared to need anyone to "care for" her now. She narrowed her eyes before pressing her hand to her heart with a gasp.

"Finn MacRorie? Is it really you?"

"Aye, 'tis me. How are ye faring?" He cringed at how banal that sounded.

"Well. We are all well. Erian is a dragon courier, Sylvia is married to a hard-working fisherman in the village, and Finn lives with me still. He's become a fisherman, too." She looked behind him. "Are you alone? Where is your lady wife? And your children?"

Kieran's neck felt hot, and he loosened his collar. "Mercy is at the Keep. And Tristam. They are well." At least, they were well according to the last letter he'd received. He'd been gone from home more than a month. Closer to two, now. He wasn't even sure what day it was. "Does Widow Ardith still live here?"

Elvina shook her head. "No, she passed on more than two years ago. She left the cottage to me, and I have tried to keep it up as she did." There was mingled pride and sorrow in her tone.

"I'm sorry tae hear that. She was a gracious woman, and I know ye must miss her still." Kieran's gaze traveled over the tidy appearance of the place. "She left her cottage in capable hands." Had Elvina ever written to tell him about Ardith? He had a vague recollection of her sharing some kind of news, but he could not remember any details. Now he was utterly ashamed he had neglected to maintain the friendships he'd once had here in Seaton.

"What can I do for you, Finn?" Now Elvina seemed less comfortable with his presence. He had interrupted her busy day, after all.

He held up his hands. "Nothing but information, and then I'll not trouble you further. I'm searching for a bard who came through here recently."

"Still on the King's business then?" she asked with a sad smile.

347

"Not this time." He gave her a crooked smile. "I be on my own business."

"I would ask you to come in, but I am alone at the moment. My guest has gone to the village church, but if you are hungry or thirsty, I'll be happy to get you whatever you need."

Kieran shook his head. "Lord Dracen made sure I was well-provisioned, but I thank you." He backed away from the door. "I will go now and ask at the taverns."

"Will you at least come join us for the evening meal? My brother Finn will be home by then." Elvina smiled. "Your namesake, of a sort."

Kieran nodded. "I would be pleased tae join you, and tae meet young Finn."

"And he would be pleased to meet you at last."

"At last?" Kieran blinked, trying to remember if he had ever seen the lad since he was a babe.

"All his life he's known about the legendary Finn MacRorie." Elvina lost some of her composure and blushed.

"Oh, dear." Kieran felt deflated and suddenly very, very old.

"Why do you say that?" She sounded concerned.

He gestured to himself. "Well, as ye can see, I am nothing like that young MacRorie fellow. I'm an old man now, Elvina."

"Nonsense." She frowned, and Kieran wondered if she was changing her mind. "Your hair is no longer dark, but you still have strength and vitality." Her voice trailed off, and her cheeks reddened again.

He held back a chuckle. "'Tis very kind o' you, but ye dinna need tae appeal tae me vanity." A sigh escaped him. "I have learned on this journey that 'tis no hiding the fact I am old." Then he straightened and gave her a lopsided smile. "I canna do anything about that, but I am working on not being a grouchy old curmudgeon."

"Curmudgeon?" Elvina frowned. "I do not know that word."

"Bad-tempered. Resentful. Difficult and stubborn." Kieran took a deep breath. "Bitter."

"Ah, now I see." She looked even more puzzled. "But what do you have to be bitter about, Finn?"

Indeed, what *did* he have to be bitter about? Perhaps he'd let his disappointments congeal into bitterness because he had fallen out of the habit of counting his blessings.

"I have become an old fool, Elvina. I didna voice my concerns tae the king when I had the opportunity. I knew what he wanted me tae do, and I suppose I had been in the habit of doing what he wanted for so long, I couldna ask him tae let me do what was best for my family." He shut his eyes, embarrassed at his stark admission to a woman he had barely known many years ago. "I'm sorry; please forgive me."

"You don't need to be sorry for being honest, do you?" She cocked her head.

"But I should not have burdened you with my troubles, especially concerning the king." He took a step back.

"Finn." The tone of Elvina's voice stopped him. "Isn't that what friends do, share their burdens? The least I can do is give you a listening ear, after the burdens you shouldered for my family."

A smile came to Kieran's lips, and he gave Elvina a courtly bow. "I thank ye for your friendship, Elvina. Ye have become a wise woman, and your words are balm tae a troubled soul." When he straightened and met her gaze, she returned the smile. "I'll try tae return in time for supper."

She nodded and stepped back into her cottage. "Until then, I hope your search is successful." The door slowly closed, but Kieran felt her gaze upon him until he heard the quiet *thud* of the door shutting.

With more optimism than he'd felt in some time, Kieran mounted Burdock and directed him toward the town's wharf.

* * *

Fiona entered the village church with trepidation. It had been many weeks since she'd been inside a church, much less prayed to the Most High. But she knew she had to confess her transgressions before even attempting to restore the feeble faith she'd once had. Was it too late to make things right with God?

The church appeared to be empty. Two candles burned on the simple altar, so she walked to the front and dropped to her knees on the hard stone. Clasping her hands upon the altar rail, she focused on the flame nearest her.

God Most High, my faith has never been what it ought to have been. My parents and Val and Joy, and Dolan and Tristam as well, all have faith and confidence in You. They've all taught me by deed and word to do more than claim an empty shell of faith. If I am going to put my trust in You, I want to do it wholeheartedly. Anything less would be worse than a hypocrite.

Fiona lowered her head to her hands. *I thought I was so clever to come up with the scheme to say our wedding vows directly to You on the mountain. I was lying to myself, to Tam, and to You. We never should have run away together. It was all my fault for being so brazen with Tam.*

Her eyes leaked tears, and she let them flow onto her hands. *Please, forgive me. I could have prevented Tam's death and the coming of a fatherless child into the world, if I had shown restraint and good sense before stealing that kiss with Tam.*

She waited until her tears stopped, and then wiped her eyes and stared at the candle again.

I don't deserve Your love and mercy, but I am grateful for them. If it is possible, please let me see my family again so I can tell them how sorry I am.

Then she sank back on her heels and placed her hands upon her barely rounded belly. *And please watch over this innocent child. I want to do what is best for him or her, for the poor babe did nothing wrong and doesn't deserve to be called that ugly name—bastard.*

Fiona remained in that uncomfortable position for a little longer, until a hint of peace began to grow within her heart. Then she rose with new resolve to do better going forward, not only to grow in wisdom but to put the needs of others above her own selfish whims.

With a smile on her tear-streaked face, she left the church to return to Elvina's house.

* * *

Kieran checked in every tavern near the wharf. The few men about remembered Noel but could not tell Kieran anything about the songwriter. The last one he visited was the Salty Dog, where he found Clive eating an early supper of fish stew. Or perhaps it was only a late midday meal. What time was it anyway?

"Hello, Clive," he said while seating himself across from the bard. "Are your shoes repaired?"

"Greetings, friend Kieran." Clive grinned and picked up the clay bowl to drain it. "Aye, the cobbler did his usual expert work. Even stopped what he was doing to fix my shoes right away, once he saw how bad they were." Then he set down the empty bowl and gestured to the loaf between them. "Care for some bread?"

Kieran shook his head, though the bread looked freshly baked. "No, thank you. I have an invitation to supper, so I'd best arrive with an appetite."

"All right, then." Clive tore the loaf in half and proceeded to devour one of the large hunks. In between bites he asked, "Any luck finding the writer of the song about Prince Val?"

"Not yet." Kieran folded his hands on the table. "But I feel sure the songwriter is here somewhere." He nodded to Clive's lute case. "How long are ye staying in Seaton?"

"One night, maybe two, depending on how many successful fishermen show up this evening." He made a comical face, and Kieran laughed.

"Or how many coins you earn?"

Clive shrugged. "That, too." He picked at the other half of the loaf. "I've been curious about you, since you are a lord, but you seem like a regular fellow." He leaned on his elbows and stared at Kieran. "I am now even more curious. Can you tell me *why* you want to find the one who wrote that song?"

Kieran bit his lip. How much should he tell the young man?

As he studied Clive's honest face, Kieran decided to share more details than he normally would have.

"Believe it or not, I was once a young man. At seventeen I became squire tae Prince Valerian—"

"You don't mean the one in 'The Deed of Valerian'?" Clive's eyes widened.

"Aye, the prince who later became the Uncrowned King. Before he died, he asked me tae take care o' his family, including his unborn son, who is now Prince Val—"

Clive gasped. "The one in the new song!"

Kieran nodded. "And since he is me adopted son, I am anxious to meet the one who wrote the song about him." He took a deep breath. "Or confirm that 'tis one I know well."

"Then I hope you discover him soon. And—" Clive stared earnestly at Kieran. "I hope we meet again, my lord. Truly I do."

Kieran rose from the table with a smile. "Oh, I feel certain we will, lad." He held out his hand, and Clive gripped it.

Then Kieran left for Elvina's.

* * *

Fiona hummed while helping Elvina prepare supper. Finn had already arrived and was washing up, for Elvina had said that an old family friend would join them. Only a few days ago, Fiona would have been anxious about meeting a stranger. But thanks to the dragon

351

couriers, she no longer needed to worry about Rodney Folville or his henchmen. Now, in the familiar comfort of this cottage, with both Elvina and Finn present, Fiona could be friendly to the unknown person without fear.

Almost the moment Finn entered the common room with his curly hair still damp and his face bright and clean, a knock sounded at the door.

"Will you get that, Finn?" Elvina gestured with her ladle.

He strode to the door and opened it wide.

"Come in, sir, and welcome to our home." Finn dipped in a little bow to the stranger.

Fiona glanced over, but Finn blocked her view, so she turned away to collect the bread basket.

"Thank ye, lad. Ye must be Finn, though ye be much taller than when I saw ye last."

At the sound of Papa's voice, Fiona gasped and whirled around. It *was* him!

"Papa?" She set down the basket and wiped her hands on her apron, suddenly shy.

"Fiona?" He started toward her, and the look on his face told her all she needed to know.

She rushed into his arms, crying happy tears. It felt so good to hug him again! She melted against him while the tears streamed down her face. It wasn't until hers abated that she realized he was crying too. When he kissed her head, she pulled back to see his face, though she did not let go of him.

"Did you get my letter?" Her gut clenched, wondering what he was thinking.

"Aye, lass," he said in a hoarse voice.

Fiona let out the breath she'd been holding. Papa was not angry, only relieved.

"Fiona?" Finn piped up, startling her. She'd forgotten for a little while that there were others in the room. "Your name isn't Josefina?"

She bit her lip and shook her head. "I'm sorry for not telling you." Fiona included Elvina in her reply. "I had told Folville my name was Josefina, hoping he wouldn't discover who I really was." Her face grew warm. "Will you ever forgive me?"

"Well, sure," Finn said, his brows still furrowed. He gestured to Papa. "So, Finn MacRorie is your father?"

"Finn MacRorie?" Fiona met Papa's gaze, and he shrugged. "I've heard that name before. That was you?"

Elvina chuckled when Finn put his hands on his hips and spoke to Papa.

"Aren't you Finn MacRorie?" His tone was almost pleading.

Papa loosened his collar with his free hand. The other still held Fiona close. "Well, lad, I did go by that name years ago, but I actually be Kieran MacLachlan, and this be my daughter Fiona."

Finn shook his head before throwing up his hands. "Does anyone in your family go by their real name?"

Fiona and Papa laughed then, and all their tears dried up. Papa answered Finn's question.

"All o' them do." He squeezed Fiona's shoulder and kissed her head again. "Only me daughter and I use an alias, and only while in Moor Point, it appears."

Elvina came closer. "I knew you looked familiar, but I did not even consider you might be his daughter." She looked from Fiona to Papa and back. "You have his eyes."

"She takes after her mother in beauty," Papa said proudly. "They have the same hair."

"Does your mother sing and play too?" Elvina asked.

Fiona shook her head. "She has other gifts." She tightened her embrace. "Papa taught me to sing and play the lute."

"You wrote Val's song, didn't you?" His voice was rough with emotion.

"Yes," she whispered. "I wanted to honor him. Has he heard it? What does he think about it?"

Papa quirked a smile. "I dinna know if he's heard it yet. But ye know your brother; he's sure tae be quite embarrassed by the attention 'twill bring him."

"So the prince in the song you wrote is your brother?" Finn blinked and spoke to Papa before Fiona could answer. "Then he is your son?"

"My stepson, though he feels like me flesh and blood. Fiona does have a full brother, two years younger. His name is Tristam."

Finn's eyes widened. "If your brother is a prince, does that make you a princess?"

Fiona shook her head. "Val's father was a prince, but mine is a lord, so my title is Lady."

With a sigh, Finn closed his eyes as if praying for patience. "It sounds complicated."

"Maybe a little bit," Fiona admitted.

"Well come and sit down," Elvina urged them. "We can continue this conversation while we eat."

"Thank you, Elvina," Papa said, "for taking care o' me lass."

"You are very welcome." Elvina met Papa's gaze so intently, Fiona wondered what hidden message had passed between them.

*

After a supper extended by animated conversation, Finn excused himself to get to bed, and Elvina insisted on cleaning up.

"You and your father should go out to the bench," she said quietly. "I'm sure you have much to talk about."

"Yes, thank you." Then Fiona took Papa's hand and led him out behind the cottage. The moon had risen, giving them enough light to keep from stumbling. The chickens were shut in the henhouse for the night, and the other animals had quieted down as well.

Fiona sat on the bench, and Papa sat beside her.

"I'm so sorry for behaving like a complete fool. I've made so many mistakes. I hope you and Mama and Tristam can forgive me."

"Oh, love, ye are not the only one who has made mistakes. O' course I forgive you. I'm certain your mother and Tristam will, too." His brows furrowed. "But what about the babe? Do ye know when it will be born?"

She shook her head. "I never paid attention to those matters, so I don't know how to figure the birth date." She placed her hands on her belly, a gesture becoming more and more familiar. "I think the babe must be almost two months old by now."

Kieran nodded. "Aye, that sounds close." His voice hardened. "Does Tam know?"

Fiona let out a sigh. "He never knew." Then something occurred to her. "Did you know he was dead?"

"What makes ye think he's dead, lass?"

"Why, one of Rodney Folville's men told me, just before I had to run away." A chill came over her. "He's not still alive, is he?"

"Aye, I've seen him." There was no warmth in his voice. "He is arrested and is waiting in Lord Dracen's dungeon until he's taken tae the Keep for trial."

"Arrested? Trial?" Fiona's head started spinning, and she leaned against Papa. "How is Tam still alive?"

"Folville's man must have lied tae ye." Papa forced himself to relax, and his voice softened. "Tammeron has been arrested because he assaulted Edward."

Fiona's hands went to her mouth. That was a serious charge. "What kind of assault?"

Papa looked down at his hands. "He apparently knocked your nephew senseless, tied him up, and locked him in a wardrobe."

With a gasp, Fiona placed her hand on Papa's arm. "When did this happen?"

"The night you two left the Keep." He covered her hand with his own.

Fiona shook her head. Tam had not mentioned Edward, but he must have done this to the boy immediately before coming to her room! "I had no idea," she murmured before tightening her grip on Papa's arm. "Is Edward all right?"

"Aye, but he's mad as a wet hen and is insisting Tammeron be punished."

Fiona could believe that about her spiteful nephew. "I'm glad Edward wasn't hurt, and I'm glad Tam isn't dead, but it was a terrible mistake to run away with him. I know that now."

Papa squirmed a little on the bench. "E'en so, you will have tae make the marriage legal, whether he is convicted or not."

Her breath caught. "But, I don't love him anymore. I know what he is now." He had known Folville was breaking the king's law when he accepted employment with him, even before they were so roughly treated.

"Doesn't matter." Papa turned a little to better see her in the dim light. "Much as it pains me tae say it, ye must marry Tammeron d'Jean so the child willna be illegitimate."

Fiona's heart sank, and she felt sick. If Tam was a criminal now, why did she have to marry him?

"Please, don't make me marry him, Papa." Then she would truly be *trapped* with Tam for the rest of her life.

"I'm thinking o' the child now, Fiona, and ye should, too. An illegitimate child, especially a male, grows up tae be the closest thing tae an outcast in our society. Ye canna do that tae your son or daughter."

Son or daughter. The words made the upcoming birth suddenly *real.* She was going to have a baby, and the father of her child was still alive and still not legally married to her.

"I wish it were not so, love, but there oft be consequences tae our actions which change the entire course o' our lives. We should always put our trust in the Most High, for He is able tae bring good out o' evil situations." He reached over and gently cupped Fiona's cheek. "I'm sorry, dearest one, more than you can know, but you and Tammeron must marry tae give the child a proper name and place in the world. All our wishes must be set aside, for the sake of the babe you carry."

"But what if he doesn't want to marry me?" Fiona had visions of Papa holding a sword at Tam's throat and dragging him to the priest. "Will you force him?"

Papa didn't answer right away. "Perhaps," he said thoughtfully, "perhaps Edward will agree not to insist on punishment, as long as Tammeron agrees to willingly marry you and make the child legitimate."

Fiona shivered, and Papa put his arm around her, pulling her close. This joyful reunion had not gone as she'd imagined. True, Papa still loved her and had forgiven her. He had even spoken to her, not as a child, but as one adult to another, though his stark words pained her to the core.

But she had never in her wildest imaginings thought Tam could be alive. Though Papa was right about putting the child's needs above her own, her heart filled with dread when she contemplated a binding, legal marriage to Tam, now that she knew what his true character was.

* * *

Kieran hadn't wanted to impose on Elvina any more than necessary, but she had insisted he stay the night. With both Fiona and her brother Finn in the cottage, there was no appearance of impropriety, she'd said with an embarrassed smile.

Refusing to allow Elvina to make up a guest bed for him when he wasn't planning to stay long, Kieran had slept on a pallet in front of the fire, cozier than he'd been since leaving the Keep. He hadn't been able to fall asleep right away, though, for all his thoughts were of Mercy. Should he send her a message, letting her know that Fiona was safe? For he did not want to tell her about his plan to live in the Highlands in a letter; that was news best told face-to-face.

What would she think about his decision? Would that be the final straw to sever their marriage bond irrevocably? Or would it be, as he fervently hoped, their chance to begin anew, away from the pressures of living at the Keep and all the responsibilities that entailed upon both of them?

Moving to the peace and solitude of the Highlands could even help Fiona and Tammeron become their best selves, possibly even growing to have a true marriage bond of hearts and minds. Kieran felt his face grow warm. It would help if he and Mercy set the example of a happy marriage, wouldn't it?

Please, God Most High, let us rekindle our love, even if it be Your will we ne'er speak mind-to-mind again. I want to be the husband Mercy deserves, the father Fiona and Tristam need. Please, let it not be too late.

He turned on his side and stared at the smoldering embers. With a smile, he recalled the days he and Mercy had spent here when Widow Ardith was alive. Painful, to be sure, while Mercy Healed and then helped him recover from the terrible burns he'd received. But during that time their bond had deepened. Kieran felt sure it could again, as surely as this fire would reignite if only he added fuel and stirred the embers.

That's what he would do—add the love and attention he had neglected to give Mercy and stir the embers of affection into a healthy flame once more.

*

In the morning, he was awakened by stirrings nearby and sat up. Elvina was preparing breakfast and noticed him.

"Good morning, Finn. I hope you slept well?" She stirred the pot once and then turned to face him.

"Aye, like a babe in swaddling." He pushed himself off the floor and started to fold the blankets.

"No need to do that." Elvina started forward, but Kieran held up a hand.

"Now, Elvina, I be not a paying guest that ye should wait upon me." He gestured to the steaming pot. "You have taken care o' me daughter, and ye are feeding me. 'Tis a wee thing for me tae pick up after myself." Out of habit, he winked at her.

Blushing, Elvina nodded. "Fair enough, Finn." Then she frowned at him. "I suppose I should call you Kieran, for that is your name."

He shook his head, placing the pillow on top of the stack of blankets. "I dinna mind if ye call me Finn." Then he grinned. "Though it might be confusing when your brother is about."

Elvina covered her mouth with her hand, trying not to laugh.

"What is it?" Kieran said, attempting to discern her thoughts.

"I suppose you wouldn't want me calling you 'Old Finn' would you?"

Kieran laughed, realizing just a day or two ago, it would have troubled him very much. "Not at all, Elvina. 'Old Finn' will do very well."

Fiona came upon them while they were laughing about the name, giving Kieran a puzzled frown.

"What is it, Papa?" When he didn't answer, she turned to Elvina. "Vina? What is so funny?"

"You see, I have known your father as 'Finn' since I was a girl. Even after I learned his real name, I simply could not think of him by any other." Elvina chuckled. "But he has come up with a way to keep us from confusing him with my brother." She met his gaze. "I shall now call him Old Finn."

Fiona started to speak, but Kieran came near and hugged her. "And what a fine name tae call an old man, for that is what I be." He grinned again, feeling younger than he had in years.

As soon as they sat down to eat, someone knocked at the door.

"Come," Elvina called out.

The door opened timidly, and Clive peered in.

"Pardon me," he said, "but I've been looking for Kieran MacLachlan." His eyes brightened when he met Kieran's gaze.

Kieran sent Elvina a silent question, and she nodded.

"Come in, Clive, and join us while we break our fast." He gestured to Finn's empty seat.

"Good morrow to all of you." The young bard shyly dipped his head. "I am Clive."

Elvina set another trencher in front of Clive. "I'm Elvina."

"And this is my daughter Fiona." Kieran's heart swelled with gratitude that she truly was safe and sound.

"Pleased to meet you both." Clive pulled his lute case off his shoulder and set it on the floor.

"You're a bard?" Fiona said with interest.

"I am," he replied humbly.

To Kieran's relief, there was nothing in his manner that revealed an inclination to flirt with Fiona.

Then Elvina asked Kieran to bless the food before they began eating.

After wolfing down his portion, Clive asked Kieran, "Have you had any luck finding the song maker?"

Kieran swallowed the bite he'd just taken before answering. "I have, and she was who I'd suspected."

"She?" Clive's eyes widened.

"Aye." Kieran indicated Fiona. "She is me daughter, after all. I taught her everything I know."

Fiona gave him a sweet smile before speaking to Clive. "Papa is too humble. He is an excellent singer, musician, and dancer. And he writes songs, too. Did you know he wrote 'The Deed of Valerian'?"

Clive's eyes widened. "Is that so? Why did you not tell me?"

Kieran shrugged, glad it was just the four of them. "It never came up."

"Are you finished eating?" Clive rose and bent to retrieve his lute case. "I would love to hear both of you sing."

"Not quite." He looked down at the remains of his meal, but he was suddenly no longer hungry. "But I would like for you and Fiona tae teach me Val's ballad, so I can commit it tae memory."

So he and Fiona quickly finished, much to Elvina's amusement. While she cleaned up after the meal, Clive played and encouraged Fiona and Kieran to sing "The Deed of Valerian" first to warm up their voices. It felt so good to sing with his daughter again, Kieran's self-consciousness swiftly vanished.

To his surprise, by the end of the song, not only was Elvina listening with interest, but a familiar man stood beside her.

"Barnaby?" he asked quietly, in case he was mistaken.

"Yes, it's me, Finn MacRorie. But you keep on singing. Pay no attention to us." The man grinned with such good nature, Kieran did not even mind that their audience had doubled in size.

"What shall we sing next, Papa?" Fiona's eyes shone brightly.

"I'd *really* like tae learn the words and chords to 'The Ballad of Prince Val.'" Kieran gave her a pitiful look, making her laugh.

"Come on, Clive, we have to teach him now, or he will never stop begging." Fiona's fond gaze never left Kieran's face, making his heart leap. Just a few short weeks ago she would have rolled her eyes at him and given the amiable Clive all her attention.

Since Kieran had heard the song several times now, he remembered most of the words. They sang it three times in a row. The first time, Kieran focused on the words, and the second he watched Clive's fingering for the chords while continuing to sing.

"Would you like to try playing it now?" Clive held out his lute, and Kieran didn't hesitate to take it.

His hands went automatically to their positions, even though he hadn't played in several months. After only a moment's hesitation, he strummed the opening chord, and this time Fiona sang with Clive while he concentrated on the accompaniment. Kieran couldn't help but note how well the two blended their voices together, as if they'd been singing together always.

With the last chord still ringing in the air, many people started clapping. Kieran's head jerked up. They had attracted quite a crowd, some inside Elvina's cottage, and others crowding the doorway.

Clive's eyes lit up. "We should go outside and play and sing some more."

"Yes, let's." Fiona's eagerness drew Kieran along with them.

For a full two hours, they took turns playing and singing a variety of songs, from local favorites to a few Highland ballads Kieran had taught Fiona. The audience, who appeared to include most of the villagers, requested "The Deed of Valerian" and "The Ballad of Prince Val" several times before they finished their impromptu concert. Clive, of course, had set out his lute case, and it contained a large quantity of coins.

After finishing a lively song with three-part harmony, Clive announced in typical bard fashion that, regretfully, they had to stop so he could make his way to the Salty Dog. He tried to share his coins with Kieran and Fiona, but they insisted he take them all. He waved to them all the way down the road, followed by a few of the fisherfolk who had come in early on their boats.

"Oh, Papa, that was so much fun." Fiona slipped her arms around his waist and hugged him.

"Aye, I enjoyed that very much." He held her close and kissed her head. "You wrote an exceptional song about Val."

"Allard help me a little," she confessed while they went inside, leaving Elvina in conversation with a few neighbors.

"Who is Allard?" Kieran tried to hold back his alarm.

"He was a bard I met and traveled with for a short while. He shared his coins with me." Fiona's voice sounded sad, and they sat at the empty table together.

"Was this after you thought Tammeron was dead?" He frowned despite himself.

"I met him before, but he was with me when Folville's man came, so we ran away together."

A knife stabbed Kieran's heart. Had he been wrong about Fiona's change of heart? "How long were the two o' you together?"

Fiona didn't answer right away. "Three or four days? I'm not certain." Then her eyes widened. "Oh, Papa, we traveled together, but we were not intimate." Her cheeks reddened. "Not that he didn't want to, but I was firm with him." She looked wistful. "I felt more grief at his death than I had upon hearing about Tam."

Perversely, Kieran was grateful the man was dead and no longer a temptation for Fiona. "I'm sorry he died, love, truly I am."

"It was horrible." Tears welled up in Fiona's eyes. "One of Folville's men found us and tried to take me by force. Allard stopped him, but he was killed." She shuddered. "I kept his lute, but I lost it on a ship."

"A ship? When were you on a ship?" Apparently a lot had happened to her in a very short time.

Before she could answer, Elvina came inside, along with Finn, who had returned after a long day on his fishing boat.

Fiona squeezed his hand. "I'll tell you later. I promise."

"I'm holding ye tae that promise, love."

Chapter 32

In the fear of the LORD is strong confidence:
and his children shall have a place of refuge.

Mercy tossed and turned, unable to get comfortable. It was impossible to sleep in this big bed all alone. She sat up, her heart racing. What if Kieran never returned? And if he did, what if he no longer wished to be married to her?

Had she pushed him away? Was it her fault they could no longer speak mind-to-mind?

With a groan, she slid down from the bed and went to the wardrobe. By the dim glow of moonlight through the window, she opened it and felt for Kieran's dressing gown, which he rarely wore. She held it to her face, inhaling the faintest scent of him, before pulling it on over her nightdress. Then she took her cloak off the peg and wrapped it around herself. Lastly, she slid her feet into a pair of worn slippers.

Slowly, so as not to stub her toes, Mercy left the bedchamber and glided through the dark and empty common room. How much life there used to be here, when the four of them ate meals together and spent the occasional evening in one another's company, even if each was reading and rarely spoke. At least they'd been *together*.

With tears burning her eyes, Mercy fled down the tower steps and made her way to the Keep's chapel. The guards she passed were startled but said nothing. After all, she had wandered the castle at night before, usually going to check on a patient.

This time, however, her heart was too heavy to do aught but spend time with the Most High God in prayer.

She entered the empty chapel and went straight to the front bench. After seating herself, she covered her face with her hands, but she had trouble praying coherently. The Most High would understand what she wanted to say, wouldn't He?

"Please," she whispered. "Please don't let our family break apart. Help me, for I don't know what to do." She rocked herself on the bench, holding back her sobs, though tears leaked through her fingers.

Time passed, though Mercy didn't know how long she sat there. Once her tears dried up, she wiped her nose and glanced to the alcove on her left. It had been a year since she'd visited Valerian's effigy, after Val had run away and she felt she needed to talk to his departed father.

But Fiona was Kieran's child. Would it be awkward to mention her? Kieran had been Valerian's closest friend, though. They'd been more like brothers.

Slowly Mercy rose and walked the few steps to the effigy of her long-departed husband. It was both strange and comforting to talk to his carved image atop his tomb, as if he could really hear her.

Valerian, I miss your gentle wisdom and your loving kindness. She reached over and cupped her hand around his stone hands. *I can't believe you've been gone so many years, but Val will be eighteen soon, so I know it's been that long. Dolan and Joy will turn thirty shortly afterward. How incredible that time moves so swiftly!*

She shut her eyes. *But that's not why I'm speaking to you now, in the middle of the night. I'm ashamed to admit this, but Kieran and I have drifted apart. We let our disagreements over our daughter drive a wedge between us, so that we've lost our mind speech.* Mercy gripped the cold stone more tightly. *I want to save our marriage, and I have been wondering what you and I might have done in a similar situation.*

What would they have done? She opened her eyes and stared at the indistinct image of Valerian's serene face in the candlelight. They had had their disagreements, and Mercy remembered being angry with him on more than one occasion. But they'd always resolved those problems swiftly, not let them fester as she and Kieran had done the last few years. Their bitterness over Fiona had grown strong roots and taken on a life of its own. Could that be overcome? Or was it already too late?

With a sob, Mercy folded her hands atop the effigy and bent over until her forehead rested on her hands.

Oh, please, let it not be too late. Please, help me see what I must do to save our marriage.

Her troubled mind could not utter any more words than these, but she was convinced the Most High knew the situation better than she ever could. Certainly, He knew her heart—and Kieran's—and what was best for them both.

Though her desire to make things right had strengthened with Kieran's absence, he had been gone almost two months. In that time, she had only received two letters from him. Was he still searching for Fiona? Or had he grown comfortable with his taste of freedom and no longer wished to return?

Mercy sagged against the stone, fighting despair. She did not expect any kind of direct answer, and so she wasn't disappointed.

But then, to her astonishment, she felt the sensation of hands upon her head, and a feeling of peace enveloped her. She didn't dare move while she savored the love and encouragement that accompanied it.

When the "hands" lifted, and Mercy no longer sensed the otherworldly presence, she straightened and let go of the effigy's hands.

"Thank you," she whispered before leaving the chapel and heading back to her room.

It wasn't until she entered her bedchamber that she realized she had no way of knowing whether the hands she had felt had been the Most High's, or Valerian's.

It does not matter, she realized with a smile. *The Most High knew what I needed and provided. That's all I really need to know.*

After she climbed into the bed, she swiftly fell into a deep, dreamless slumber.

* * *

Fiona was eating the midday meal with Papa and Elvina the following day when they received an unexpected visitor.

"Erian?" Elvina rose and hurried around the table. "Is something the matter?"

But he was staring at Papa.

"Finn MacRorie? Is it you, then?"

When Fiona turned to Papa, he was smiling, to her surprise.

"Aye, Sir Rascal. 'Tis been a few years since we saw one another." He pushed himself up from the table and went to greet the dragon courier.

"I thought I saw you at Castle Moor Point about a fortnight ago, but I never had a chance to speak with you." Erian's face relaxed, and he pulled out a letter from his courier bag. "This urgent message came from the Highlands more than a day ago, but it took me this long to track you down. You travel like a bard." He glanced down at the letter. "Kieran MacLachlan *is* your real name, isn't it?"

"Aye." He held out his hand, and Erian handed him the letter. When Papa saw the seal, he opened it eagerly and scanned the message. "How did this answer come so quickly? I only sent it five days ago."

Erian grinned then. "That shows the level of efficiency already reached by the Royal Dragon Couriers."

"But I sent it to the Highlands by horse." Papa gestured to the letter.

"It went first to Castle Moor Point, so Lord Dracen must have seen it was from you and sent me and Amadorix to deliver it to the MacLachlan. Then Lord Dougal had me wait for the reply to bring it back to Moor Point, but Lord Dracen could only tell me the last place he knew you might be, else you might have gotten it yesterday." Erian looked from Papa to Fiona to Elvina. "How long have you been here?"

"I just arrived the day before yesterday." Papa folded the letter and tucked it inside his tunic.

"Fiona here," Elvina said, indicating her, "whom we knew as Feena, is Finn's daughter." She beamed, making Erian startle.

"Daughter?" He stared closely at Fiona's face and then slowly shook his head. "I should have noticed you have the same eyes." He spoke to his sister. "Had you noticed that?"

Elvina looked sheepish. "Barnaby and I both agreed she looked familiar, but I did not make the connection." She smiled at Fiona. "Not at all."

"What does Dougal say, Papa?" Fiona had stayed seated on the bench through the entire interchange, and she kept hoping everyone would resume their seats.

He sat down again and took Fiona's hand. "He has agreed to my request. A minor lord had recently died with no heir, so he wants tae give the manor to us." Fiona's gut roiled. Her life was about to change again, yet she was reluctant to leave Elvina. Papa must have noticed. "Ye dinna have tae leave right away, love. I must go speak with your Mum and Dolan before any firm plans can be made."

"You're leaving now?" Her voice sounded panicked, but Papa appeared resolved.

"Aye. From here 'twill take several days tae ride tae the Keep. I canna in good conscience stay longer, now that I have heard from Dougal." When he started to rise, Fiona tightened her grip on his hand.

"You need to go to the Keep?" Erian said. "Amadorix and I can fly you there in a fraction of the time. We could even wait for you to bring you back, if necessary."

Papa slowly rose, and Fiona stood beside him, not letting go.

"I would be grateful for your assistance, Erian." He glanced at Fiona and then Elvina. "Is it all right if Fiona stays here a while longer?"

"Of course it is. She may stay as long as she needs." Elvina moved closer to Fiona, as if ready to physically remove her from Papa. "Your horse is happy in the barn, and I will ask Finn to help care for him until you return."

"Thank you." He embraced Fiona then, and she hugged him tightly, unwilling to be parted from him. "I will come back for you as soon as I can." He kissed her head and stepped back, leaving Fiona bereft.

While he gathered his carry sack, Elvina slipped her arm around Fiona's shoulders. Fiona held onto her friend's waist for support while they followed Papa and Erian outside to the waiting dragon.

Erian mounted first, and Papa scrambled up behind him.

"I love you, Papa," Fiona called out. "Please, hurry back."

"Dinna worry, I will." He gave her a little wave and smiled. "I love you, too."

With a mighty downstroke, Amadorix launched into the air. Fiona and Elvina did not move until the great dragon became a speck in the sky, hidden by the high clouds.

* * *

Mercy was writing Kieran a letter at her desk when she heard footsteps on the stairs. She gasped, for she knew they had to be *his* steps. Quickly she wiped off the quill pen and stoppered the ink before rising from her chair.

When she turned, the door opened, and he peered inside. At the sight of his tousled head, Mercy's heart fluttered, and tears sprang to her eyes. His shimmered as well, and he stepped inside, shutting the door behind him.

She hesitated, feeling shy. He slowly came closer, and so she met him halfway.

"I've missed you." Her voice was hoarse.

"And I you."

She swallowed. "Are you back to stay?"

When he shook his head, Mercy thought the floor would open and swallow her. A whimper escaped her throat. But then he spoke.

"I came tae tell you that I have found Fiona. She is living with Elvina, and she is with child."

"With child?" Mercy's knees wobbled. Kieran must have noticed, for he came close and supported her to the nearest chair. Once she was seated, he went down on one knee beside her, gazing into her eyes.

"She has suffered much, but she has grown much as well." He took her hand. "I have spoken with Dougal, and he has offered me a holding in a peaceful part of MacLachlan lands. Fiona has agreed to move there for her confinement, out o' the public eye. I plan tae join her." He pulled a letter from his tunic and handed it to her.

Mercy opened it with trembling hands.

Uncle Kieran,

To answer your question, yes, of course you must move to MacLachlan lands. An elderly minor lord, a distant cousin of ours, has recently died without an heir. I was pondering what to do with the land and house, which is a large cottage or a small manor in good repair, only two miles east of Castle MacLachlan. It is now yours, dear uncle, and Beatrice and I rejoice to know you will soon be our neighbors.

Affectionately,
Dougal

Mercy did not know what to say. Kieran didn't act as if he wanted nothing to do with her, but he wasn't coming home; he was moving to the Highlands. He must have seen her confusion, for he continued.

"I kept me promise tae Valerian. I have taken care o' his children. All three are grown now and nae longer need me as they once did."

His green eyes brightened with resolve. "Now 'tis time for me tae do what is best for my children, and what they need is peace and quiet, fresh air and sunshine, and satisfying work with their hands, the way I was brought up." He gently gripped her nearest hand and stared into her eyes.

"So, you're leaving the Keep? And you want to take Tristam, too?" Mercy's throat tightened when he nodded. *Do you want me to stay here? I don't think I can bear to be apart from all of you.* But he didn't react to her thoughts.

"Dinna worry, I will let Dolan know first." He continued to stare at her. "So ye still canna hear me in your mind?"

She shook her head, feeling profoundly sad at the loss of their mind speech. Could they ever reestablish the link?

Mercy squeezed Kieran's hand and straightened with resolve. "I don't know if we can ever speak mind-to-mind again, but I know we can begin anew and grow our love into a flourishing marriage again. Wherever you and Fiona and Tristam are, that is where I want to be."

"You would leave the Keep? Truly?" Hope lit his face, erasing the stress of years.

"Of course I will." She threw her arms around his neck, and he pulled her upright to better embrace her.

They stood together, savoring the hug. Mercy had feared they never would embrace again. She pulled back first with a shy smile.

"I'm all out of practice at anything more."

"So am I." He swept a stray hair from her eye. "But I be willing tae keep trying." He leaned down and lightly brushed her lips. "You have me heart, Mercy. You always have and you always will."

"And you have mine, Kieran MacLachlan, always." It felt as if they'd just said their marriage vows again.

So Mercy took Kieran's face between her hands and kissed him soundly to seal the bargain.

* * *

Kieran took the steps two at a time leading up to the royal suite. His heart pounded in anticipation, for he imagined Dolan would not be happy about this decision. He was just so immensely grateful that Mercy was happy about it, he caught himself humming as he strode to the door of the king's suite and knocked.

Christopher Decourt answered, and his eyes widened when he met Kieran's gaze.

"My lord! His Majesty will be pleased to see you again. Please, come in." The page stepped back and gestured for Kieran to enter the sitting room.

Dolan looked up from the letter he was writing at his desk, and his face went from serious to pleased in a moment. He set down the pen without wiping off the ink and rose to greet Kieran.

"You are a welcome diversion indeed." Dolan clasped Kieran's hand and then embraced him. "When did you get back?"

"Only an hour or so ago." Kieran gave Dolan a nervous smile. "I saw your mother first."

"Ah, of course. That's as it should be." Dolan gestured to the chairs in front of the fireplace. "Come, have a seat and tell me about your journey. Did you find Fiona?" There was genuine concern in his voice.

"Yes, I did." Kieran let Dolan sit first before choosing the chair beside his. "She is well and living with a kind woman in Moor Point."

"I am glad she is well. Does she plan to return to the Keep?" Before Kieran could answer, Dolan spoke again. "Did you know Tammeron d'Jean was brought here from Moor Point? He is in the dungeon."

"I knew he would end up here eventually, but I left Castle Moor Point after he was arrested and have not returned, so yours is the first news I've had of him." Kieran's voice hardened. "Ye haven't had his trial already, have ye?"

Dolan shook his head. "I'm waiting for Lord Henry to bring Edward, so Tammeron can face his accuser."

Kieran almost blurted out that Fiona should testify also, but he had presence of mind to weigh his words before speaking. It would be challenge enough to force Tammeron to marry Fiona, at sword point if necessary, no matter what the sentence turned out to be. So he simply nodded.

"Have Slade and Aleia been told their son is here?" He dreaded having to face his old friend, afraid their friendship might be forever strained after the terrible mess their children had gotten themselves into.

Dolan nodded. "They arrived yesterday evening, and I believe they met with him earlier today."

"A sad business." Kieran's nervous guts made a gurgling sound.

"Indeed." Dolan stared at Kieran with a frown. "Is something more bothering you?"

Kieran shifted in the chair. "As a matter o' fact, there is a wee matter I must discuss with you." He had to consciously leave off the 'Sire.'

"By all means, tell me." Dolan gripped the arms of his chair as if prepared for bad news.

"Do ye remember when you and Joy had your twentieth birthday and ye no longer needed a Regency Council?" Kieran realized with a start that the twins would turn thirty on their next birthday. Had it really been *ten* years?

"As if it were yesterday." Dolan frowned a little. "Sometimes it feels like yesterday, but other times, as if a lifetime has already been lived since that day." He grew silent, patiently waiting.

"Before your twentieth birthday, I had been contemplating moving tae the Highlands with Mercy and the younger children. Did I e'er tell you that?" A fresh wave of remorse came over him at the thought of how different things might have been for Fiona had they lived there for the last ten years.

"No. This is the first I have heard of it." Dolan's frown deepened. "Why did you never tell me?"

"Because you are my king, and I felt compelled to obey your wishes that I remain here." Kieran dropped his head, unable to meet the stern gaze.

"I am your king," Dolan agreed, "but you are also my father. I consider that relationship much more important."

Kieran's breath caught. He slowly raised his head. Dolan had never said that before. He had to clear his throat before speaking again.

"It has been an honor tae have that relationship with you, and an absolute joy tae watch you become such a magnificent king, husband, and father." Tears burned his eyes. Truly, he had no regrets on Dolan's account.

"Thank you," Dolan said simply, reaching over to grip Kieran's shoulder, and through the contact Kieran could feel his affection. "So, you want to move to the Highlands?"

Kieran nodded. "Aye." Again, he had to consciously omit the honorific.

"Are you homesick, after all these years?" Dolan frowned in confusion, and then his eyes widened. "This is because of Fiona, isn't it? You want to remove her from the Keep's temptations?"

Kieran shrugged. "Ten years ago, I was homesick and fervently wished for a quiet life. Now, I want that still, but you're right; Fiona is a big part o' this decision." He let out a sigh. "I canna help but think, had I taken the lass away from temptation—meaning the way her status as your sister resulted in a cadre of fawning young men—she might have grown up thinking less o' herself. She could benefit from living a simpler country life with daily chores." A smile came unbidden at the changes he had already seen in Fiona, which he attributed in part to the quiet and productive life she was living with Elvina.

"But you are all my family, and I wish to provide for you, always." Dolan seemed distressed, which Kieran had not anticipated. He'd only thought Dolan might be angry or at least disappointed not to have Kieran nearby in case he needed something official from him at any time of the day or night.

"Ye have always been generous with us, e'en giving us the new tower whilst your family stayed in the old one." Kieran slid from the chair and went down on one knee. He felt compelled to show his gratitude to his son and king. "Now that there are several dragon couriers, the distance willna be a limiting factor in our move; we can fly back at a moment's notice, whene'er ye have need o' us."

Dolan's distress increased. "Please do not kneel to me." He rose from his chair, urging Kieran to rise also. Then he embraced Kieran with a fierceness that startled him. "Of course I don't want you and Mother to leave the Keep." He pulled back with tears in his eyes. "It will be lonely here without you."

"Lonely?" Kieran chuckled while wiping his eyes. "In this bustling place?" But he knew what Dolan meant, for he would miss the daily interaction with Dolan and Rhianna and the grandchildren.

"I would never want you to stay here against your will. I hope you know that." Dolan's serious gaze bore into Kieran, and he wondered if the king was *Seeing* his thoughts. He would know, wouldn't he? Ah, but since he and Mercy had lost their mind speech, perhaps he would no longer know when a Seer was reading his mind.

"Aye, I do know that, and I hope ye will forgive me for the bitterness o' spirit I let grow inside me the last few years." He shook his head grimly. "I wanted tae blame your sister's headstrong behavior on everyone and everything else but where the blame truly lies: with my unwillingness tae be a strict parent when she needed it most, and ultimately, with her own poor choices o'er the years."

"Truly, being a parent can be the most difficult job in the world." Dolan grimaced. "Each child is different from the others, a unique personality. It's not easy to let them make mistakes, but they must learn that choices have consequences. And then we must follow through with those consequences, which I have not always done with Edward." He gripped Kieran's shoulder again. "I think you and I have had similar challenges, so I will be the last person to cast stones at you."

They gazed at one another in unspoken sympathy and understanding, until finally Kieran brought up what he needed to know and dreaded to hear.

"So, when we move, do ye want that I should resign as your Earl Marshall?" Kieran bit his lip in anticipation of the change that was fast approaching.

"Never." Dolan shook his head emphatically. "That office and title belong to you for life, no matter where you happen to be living."

"Thank you," Kieran said simply. Though he'd been prepared to be demoted back to Sir Kieran, he had to confess, it would have been a grief to lose what had been entrusted to him.

"How soon will you leave?" Dolan folded his hands, deceptively calm.

"Not immediately," Kieran assured him. "I want tae bring Fiona here first, and then inspect the manor house in the Highlands, to see what needs repairing before we can move in."

"That is sensible, regarding the manor house," Dolan agreed. "And of course you want to bring Fiona back as soon as possible. Mother must be anxious to see her."

"Aye." Kieran paused, reluctant to tell Dolan, but he had to.

"What is it?" Dolan's mouth tightened.

"Do ye already have an idea what Tammeron d'Jean's punishment will be?" Kieran swallowed, for he had to hold back his own desire to see him punished severely.

"How can I, until he is brought before me to make his defense?" Dolan's piercing gaze made Kieran squirm. "Is there more to this situation than I already know?"

Kieran nodded. "Fiona is with child, and she and Tammeron are not married. They must marry, of course, for the sake of the babe tae be born."

"And you plan to force him, if he is unwilling?" Instead of anger, Kieran heard only concern in Dolan's voice.

"Aye. At the point o' me sword, if necessary." Kieran's own anger flared, and he had to banish the image of Tammeron's sneering unconcern about Fiona. If he had resisted arrest, Kieran could have in good conscience ended his life and spared Fiona having to marry the rogue. But he shook his head, berating himself. The best thing for Tammeron d'Jean would be to accept responsibility for what he'd done and become a better man.

That, he thought ruefully, *is what Valerian would have said*. His gaze returned to Dolan. *And what his son is probably thinking at this moment.*

"Let us hope, then, that the young man has profitably spent his time in the dungeon, and is not only willing but eager to make amends where both Fiona and Edward are concerned." Dolan's tone was that of a royal pronouncement, so Kieran inclined his head.

"Aye, 'twould be best for all concerned if he did." Kieran let out a sigh of resignation.

"As for the matter of you and your family moving to the Highlands?" Dolan gave Kieran a sad smile. "Of course I give you my permission, on one condition."

"What is that?" Kieran wisely asked, instead of immediately agreeing.

"That you come to visit often, for you will be sorely missed."

Kieran grinned. "That is one condition I can heartily agree to."

With another fond embrace, Kieran left the king's suite. His heart swelled with hope for the future, and he couldn't wait to make all the necessary arrangements for the move.

Chapter 33

A friend loveth at all times, and a brother is born for adversity.

Val and Reggie flew alongside Erian and Amadorix on the way to Moor Point. Mother sat behind him, and Kieran rode with Erian. Tristam had stayed behind at the Keep, seemingly not as eager to see Fiona as the rest of them. But Val knew his brother well enough to know he had been just as concerned about their wayward sister, in his own quiet way.

The sky was clear and cold over the Dragon's Backbone, thankfully with very little wind. Once they passed beyond the mountains, the air grew warmer with a breeze from the west. Soon Val spied the edge of the sea, and his anticipation to see Fiona grew, though mingled with a bit of dread. How much had she changed in the last two months? Kieran was convinced she had grown for the better, but the fact remained she was expecting a child without a legal husband, and that complicated her situation.

Erian took the lead on the final approach to his home village of Seaton. The two dragons landed in a grassy field within sight of the main road, and Val slid down from Reggie's back. He stood by while his mother dismounted, and the four of them left the dragons to rest in the sun while they walked to a nearby cottage.

"Your sister's name is Elvina?" Val asked to make sure. He had to admit to himself that he was nervous about this meeting.

374

"Yes, my lord. She is my older sister." Erian glanced over at him.

"Elvina was your age when I first met her, Val," Mercy said thoughtfully. "You were just a babe then. And Erian still a child." She reached out to take Kieran's hand. "How has so much time passed? It honestly does not feel so long ago."

"Though the days be long, the years be short." Kieran kissed her hand, making Val smile and think of Emma.

By the time they reached the cottage door, Val was impatient enough to want to burst in unannounced. Erian stepped forward and knocked before slowly opening the door.

"Elvina? Finn MacRorie, or rather Lord Kieran and I have returned with two guests."

"Come in, all of you," came a pleasant voice.

Val started to enter, but caught himself and waited for his parents to go first.

"Mama!" Fiona's voice rang out, joyful, and Val caught a glimpse of her when she rushed into Mercy's arms.

He waited until they parted, and then Fiona met his gaze.

"Val! You came!" She let go of their mother and hurried toward him with outstretched arms.

He embraced her tenderly, aware that she carried a child, and so did not want to squeeze too tightly. Fiona had no compunction, however, and for a moment Val thought she might crack his ribs.

"I missed you," she murmured against his chest.

"I missed you, too." He waited until she looked up at him. "How long have you been here?"

Fiona turned to Elvina, drawing Val's gaze. He did remember the woman from the day the dragon riders had flown over Moor Point. She had made sure all of them were well fed. But he hadn't seen Fiona that day, and he pointed that out to her.

"I was too ashamed to show myself to you," she admitted. "I have been here more than a month, but I don't know exactly how long."

"It doesn't matter," Val assured her. "I'm just relieved you are well and safe." He spoke to Elvina then. "Thank you for taking care of my sister."

"Yes, we are so grateful for all you've done for Fiona," Mercy said in a voice filled with emotion. "How can we ever repay you?"

Elvina approached Mercy and took her hands. "You know what your husband did for our family, my lady. There is no question of repayment." She smiled at each of them in turn. "Besides, Fiona has been such a great help to me, I'm going to miss her." Her gaze rested on Fiona. "Terribly."

To Val's surprise, Fiona stepped away from him and covered her face while she burst into sobs. Distressed, he met his mother's gaze. She nodded at him.

"Elvina, may we please speak to Fiona privately for a few minutes?"

"Of course. I'll go gather the eggs." She started to leave, but Mercy hugged her first.

"Thank you." Then she waited until Elvina left the cottage before leading a distraught Fiona to the table, where the two of them sat together on one of the benches.

Val and Kieran took the bench across from them and waited for Mercy to speak first.

"Your father says you are carrying Tammeron d'Jean's child?" She slowly rubbed Fiona's back. Val didn't know if Mother used her Healing power, but Fiona soon calmed down and nodded.

"I was a fool, Mama." Her voice was subdued. "We said vows to the Most High on top of a mountain, intending to find a priest as soon as possible to ensure it was a legal marriage." She sighed. "At least, that was *my* intention. I don't know if it was Tam's." Then Fiona glanced at Val, but she didn't hold his gaze. "When I was told that Tam was dead, I confess I was relieved. It was a terrible mistake for me to run away with him, and I'm sorry."

Val could hear the sincerity in Fiona's voice, and he disliked what their parents would bring up next—the fact that she would have to marry Tam, whether she wanted to or not. But they didn't have to mention it first.

"I know I must legally marry Tam, for the sake of the baby." Fiona paused to wipe her eyes. "But I dread seeing him again and having to bind myself to him." The tears continued to flow down her cheeks. "How could I have ever believed myself in love with him?"

While Mercy held Fiona close, Val thought back to a time he'd witnessed Tam flirting with a serving girl. He could be charming when he wanted. Even the most sensible young woman might find herself yielding to his beguiling professions of undying love. And Fiona, Val was grieved to admit, had not always acted in the most sensible way.

The four of them discussed details of returning Fiona to the Keep under cover of darkness, and how they might approach Tam, who was in the dungeon. They soon decided to leave tomorrow afternoon so as to arrive at the Keep after the sun had set. Kieran would first inform the bishop of the situation before going to speak with Tam.

It was not the greatest plan, in Val's opinion, but it was the best they could come up with in such a short time. Mercy left the cottage to find Elvina and explain what they would do, so Val reached across the table and grasped Fiona's hand.

She looked up with a grateful smile, but Val could not think of anything to say that might encourage her. The situation was so awkward and full of heartache, he merely lifted Fiona's hand to his lips to let her know he still loved her.

And then it came to him what he needed to do.

"Fiona," he said, glancing at Kieran. "I want to talk to Tam first, before you do anything else. He and I used to be friends. I think I can convince him to do the right thing so he doesn't feel like he's being pushed into a corner."

"How would you do that?" Fiona's voice was strained.

"Assuming he still has a conscience, I want to remind him of it by appealing to the earnest and dutiful boy I once knew." Val shrugged sheepishly. "I know he must be inside the grown Tam somewhere."

Kieran's jaw tightened, and for a moment Val thought he might be annoyed with the suggestion. But he nodded and let out a sigh. "'Tis an excellent plan, Son. I only hope ye can persuade him tae marry your sister for the right reasons." Then he frowned, making him look fiercely protective. "Though I will nae have any qualms at all about forcing him at sword point, if that becomes necessary."

*

Elvina, of course, insisted they all spend the night in the cottage. Though she had few real beds, she had blankets and sleeping furs, enough to make a cozy nest for each of them. Fiona prepared the evening meal while Mercy helped Elvina make up the pallets. When Finn came home after a long day of fishing, he was delighted to welcome the rest of Fiona's family. Over supper, he urged Kieran to tell the entire story of his journey to find Fiona.

Val stayed quiet, unable to join in the banter. All he could think about was Tammeron d'Jean, and how he might approach him once he and Erian flew Fiona, Mercy, and Kieran back to the Keep tomorrow.

That night he had trouble sleeping, thinking of all the possible reactions Tam might have. Sleep only came once Val prayed to the Most High and gave Him the burden.

Erian joined them for breakfast, after which Fiona said a tearful goodbye to Elvina. Mercy and Kieran thanked the woman profusely, and then the dragons lifted into the sky. They first flew to Castle Moor Point to confer with Lord Dracen, and after eating the midday meal with him headed north, leaving Moor Point behind.

A few hours later, the Keep came into view. Val had scarcely dismounted and helped Fiona down from Reggie's back, when he kissed his sister, thanked Erian for his help, and made his way to the royal tower.

*

Val descended the stairs leading to the dungeon. With each step the way became more and more oppressive. Had Tam spent his time here in contemplation? Was he willing to turn his life around? To make amends? Was he at all sorry for what he'd done, both to Fiona and to Edward?

The keeper unlocked the entrance and bowed when Val entered. Then the man led him to the last cell. Tam sat on the floor with his long legs stretched out, his head bowed.

"Open the cell," Val said as quietly as he could and still sound commanding.

"But, Your Highness—"

"I want you to open it. I must see the prisoner's face clearly."

"Aye, Your Highness."

While the keeper unlocked the door, Tam slowly raised his head. He was hardly recognizable. His hair was long and tangled, his eyes bleary with dark circles underneath. When he recognized Val, his eyes widened.

"What are you doing here, Your Highness?" he said in a raspy voice.

"I've come to talk to you, Tam, as an old friend." Val spoke then to the keeper. "You may leave us."

The man frowned, obviously reluctant, but he dipped his head and backed away into the shadows. Val entered the cell but stood just inside the doorway. He expected Tam to stand and face him, but he remained slumped on the floor against the back wall.

"I have nothing to say." Tam sounded resigned, not angry as Val had expected.

"Nothing? Are you sure about that?" Val allowed his own anger into the words, and it worked. Tam straightened and stared up at him.

"What do you mean?" Tam's eyes narrowed.

"When did you last speak to my sister, Fiona?" Val kept his voice curt.

"I don't know. A fortnight? A month?" His stare pierced Val. "Why do you want to know?"

"Only to confirm that you did not already know, which would make your leaving her a much greater transgression." Val balled his fists on his hips. "She carries your child."

Tam pushed himself off the floor and stared at Val with his mouth open. "My child?" He shook his head. "Are you sure?"

Val nodded. "My mother examined her, and Fiona is most certainly with child." Now he glared at the shaken Tam. "My question to you is, what are you going to do about it?"

"Do?" Tam remained silent, thinking. Was he contemplating how to rectify the situation? Or how to escape the consequences of his actions?

"When a man has created an innocent child outside the bonds of matrimony, the only noble remedy is to marry the mother." Though Val did not believe Tam was acting like a man, he still hoped, for Fiona's sake, that he could learn to be one.

"If I do, will the king be lenient with me?" Tam looked like a trapped animal, and Val fervently wished he would not bite the hand of the one who was trying to free him from his trap.

"It is possible he would, if he knew you had sincerely repented of the deed. Have you?"

Tam recoiled. "Which deed?"

"The one to which the accusation is directed, namely, that you assaulted Prince Edward." To his surprise, Val sounded just like Dolan, and Tam responded as if he had.

"I confess I did assault the little—" Tam bit back whatever word he'd been about to say. "I did hit the prince, Your Highness. I regret doing so, very much." He bowed his head. "I submit myself to the king's judgment, hoping for mercy."

"You know my brother is a Seer, Tam. He will know whether you are sincere."

Tam jerked up his head. "King Dolan will *See* my honest regret." Though his voice was defiant, his eyes revealed his fear.

"Then I will plead for you, provided you agree to marry Fiona." Val did not move from his stern posture. He was glad of it when Tam didn't answer right away.

Finally, he spoke, though misery lined his face. "I will marry her, Your Highness, and thank you in advance for standing up for me."

Val could not honestly say, "You are welcome," so he merely nodded. "I will leave you now and hope to see you again tomorrow."

Tam shut his eyes and lowered his head, and Val left the dungeon without a backward glance. He felt even more unsettled than he had before speaking with Tam, but what more could he have done to encourage him to make things right for Fiona's sake?

Chapter 34

By wisdom kings reign, and princes decree justice.

Fiona sat on a bench against the wall of the throne room between her parents. Dolan had not yet entered with Edward, but there were others present to witness the proceedings. Val stood nearby speaking with Bishop Ignatius, Lord Jambray, and Uncle Drew, who occasionally glanced her way. Rhianna and William sat on a bench against the opposite wall speaking quietly to one another. There were a few others, but Fiona only knew them by sight. Except for Tam's parents, who sat apart as if they had exiled themselves in shame. Both Slade and Aleia appeared diminished in their grief. What could Fiona say, if ever she had the chance to speak with them?

Then the door to the spiral staircase opened, and Dolan, his page and squire, and Edward exited. Dolan wore his full regalia as well as a frown. Edward had also dressed in royal attire, probably to remind Tam that he had not assaulted a mere page, but a prince of the royal house of Levathia.

Everyone present rose and bowed to the king. Then he seated himself on the throne and beckoned Edward stand at his right hand. With a rustling noise like wind, the others took their seats, and Fiona sat again with her parents.

At an unspoken signal, the doors opened, and two guards escorted the tall prisoner, his hands bound with a rope. Fiona held in a gasp at Tam's altered appearance. His hair had grown shaggy and unkempt, his clothing was soiled, and he hunched as if he'd been beaten. Pity warred with revulsion while she studied him. He did not look in her direction, but when he raised his head to meet Dolan's gaze, Fiona was able to see the despair in his eyes.

How had she ever believed herself in love with him?

"Tammeron d'Jean, step forward," Dolan commanded.

Tam did so and dropped to his knees at Dolan's feet. Fiona could tell her brother was *Seeing* Tam's thoughts. Though she was grateful not to have that ability, she did wonder what Tam was thinking in that moment.

"Do you understand why we have arrested and imprisoned you?" Dolan's voice was severe, making Fiona cringe.

Tam answered in a shaky voice. "Yes, Your Majesty. I treated Prince Edward abominably ill and deserve whatever punishment Your Majesty imposes." He dropped his head, and tears came to Fiona's eyes. Tam sounded sincerely humble and repentant. How would Dolan answer?

In the pregnant pause, Fiona turned her attention to Edward. He stood straight and proud beside his father and could not quite hide his smirk of satisfaction. A chill gripped Fiona's belly when she realized Edward would not be satisfied with anything less than the harshest punishment for Tam.

"We have *Seen* your heart, Tammeron, and know that you are truly sorry for what you did in anger. Though we are inclined to spare your life, yet we must impose a suitable punishment due to the gravity of the offense." Dolan gripped the arms of his throne, and Fiona noticed the tightness of his jaw.

"Father—" Edward began, but Dolan held up a hand to silence him.

At that moment, to everyone's surprise, Val stepped forward and went down on one knee beside Tam.

"Your Majesty." He inclined his head. "Pardon me, but I would ask a boon, for the sake of our sister."

Dolan glanced at Fiona and nodded before addressing Val. "Rise, Prince Valerian, and ask your boon of me."

Val gracefully rose to his full height and bowed. "For Lady Fiona's sake, I ask that you grant Tammeron leave to marry her before he finishes his sentence. And then, when he is released, allow him to go to her in the Highlands, where she will be living a quiet country life, out of the public eye."

Fiona held her breath, awaiting Dolan's answer. Would his pride allow him to make this concession for the sake of the innocent babe she carried?

Dolan turned his head to gaze at Fiona, and she shrank back from his piercing eyes. To her surprise, his face softened, and he nodded.

"Prince Valerian, I will grant your petition for the prisoner. His life is spared, and he will be granted leave to marry our sister." He smiled at Fiona. A grim one, to be sure, but a smile nevertheless!

"After the completion of three months in the dungeon, Tammeron d'Jean will be freed to reunite with Lady Fiona in the Highlands." Dolan glanced at Tam's parents then.

"But, Father—" Edward's high voice was strident, and Dolan snapped his head around to give the boy his royal glare. Thankfully, it was enough to silence him again.

"Lord Steward." Dolan addressed Drew, who came forward with a bow. "Appoint someone to help young d'Jean prepare for his marriage in the morning. The ceremony will be held in the chapel with only family members present."

"Will Lord Bennet and Lady Joy be in attendance, Your Majesty?" Drew asked.

Dolan and Val stared at one another, so Fiona assumed they were speaking mind-to-mind.

"Prince Valerian will fly on Regnatorix to Frankland and fetch Lady Joy for the ceremony," Dolan said in a more relaxed voice. He glanced at Fiona again, but this time it didn't make her cringe.

"I would like to stand up with Tammeron," Val said, making Tam glance up at him from his kneeling position.

"So be it." Dolan nodded at Val before addressing all in the room. "Judgment is pronounced, and justice is served. You are dismissed." He then leaned down and spoke in Edward's ear. Fiona could only tell that Edward was still disgruntled. When Dolan finished, the young prince stormed from the throne room.

With a grim look, Dolan slowly rose from the throne, staring in the direction Edward had gone. Then he shook his head, and to Fiona's surprise, walked straight toward her. She timidly stood to meet him.

"Fiona," he said quietly, "I am very glad you are safe." He took her hands. When had he ever done that before? Then he led her to a corner of the room, out of hearing of the rest.

"Val assures me you now regret your hasty actions in eloping with Tammeron." He squeezed her hand. "I am sorry for the reason you must marry him now, for I had hoped you would marry someone more noble, like Roland Campignon."

Fiona's eyes widened. She had truly never thought Dolan cared a whit about her. Had she been wrong this entire time?

"However, I did *See* his heart, and Tammeron still has a conscience and genuine regret for the poor choices he has made. I pray it is enough to begin to build a life together, so your marriage becomes a real chance for happiness." He smiled sadly, but there was love in his eyes directed at her. "You are strong and strong-willed, Fiona. I believe you can bring out the best in Tammeron. I am certain you can both grow to love one another."

"T-thank you." Fiona swallowed the emotion that suddenly rose into her throat. "I am so sorry I brought shame to you and all the family. That was never my intention."

"I know," he answered simply before gathering her in an embrace. "I love you, little sister."

Startled by his unexpected words and gesture, it took Fiona a moment to reply.

"I love you, brother," she said hoarsely before gratefully returning the hug.

* * *

Val walked with Tam from the room in which he'd bathed and dressed in a formal blue tunic. A guard walked ahead of them, and two came behind. Fiona's bridegroom was still the king's prisoner, after all.

Despite the circumstances, Tam seemed more than just resigned to marry Fiona; he had spoken to Val a little about what he wanted to do after completing his sentence.

"I never thought I would like to be a farmer, but I have wondered if I could learn enough about sheep to raise a flock. The Highlands would be an ideal place for it." He'd had a faraway look in his eyes, as if imagining the solitude and the peace he could find there.

Could Tam be successful in such a simple life? And could he and Fiona find contentment together? Maybe even a growing love and appreciation for one another? Surely they could bond over their coming child? Val fervently hoped so.

They entered the chapel then and made their way to the altar, where Bishop Ignatius was speaking with Dolan and Kieran. Tristam sat on the front bench with William, Robard, Edward, and Matilda. Since Mercy and Joy and Rhianna were not present, Val decided they were accompanying Fiona and would bring her shortly.

"Are you ready to meet your bride, young Tammeron?" Though Bishop Ignatius was now elderly, he still had a strong voice and hardly stooped at all.

"I am, Your Grace." Tam bowed to Dolan. "Thank you, Your Majesty." And then he turned to Kieran, to Val's surprise.

"I know I am not who you would have chosen for your daughter, my lord, but I am resolved to make the best of this situation and the opportunity His Majesty has given to Fiona and me." Tam did not look away from Kieran's piercing gaze.

"I canna lie, lad; I did nae want you anywhere near her, but 'twas her choice tae run away with you then, and 'tis her choice tae marry you now. So I am expecting you tae be a man and treat her as your parents taught you." He stopped talking when Slade and Aleia entered the chapel.

"I plan to do so, Lord Kieran." Tam glanced in the direction of his parents, but he did not appear glad to see them.

Before anyone else could speak, Mercy and Rhianna appeared at the door.

"The bride has arrived," Mercy announced with a tight smile while she and Rhianna glided down the aisle to meet them.

"Then let us take our places." Dolan held out his arm for Rhianna, and Kieran did the same for Mercy. Everyone found a seat, except Val and Tam, who stood beside the bishop.

Tam's face drained of color, so Val reached out to grip his shoulder.

"Everything will work out. You'll see."

Tam jerked his head, obviously nervous. "That is my hope."

Monks in the gallery began to sing an anthem for the bride, and Val watched the door. In a few moments, Fiona and Joy appeared, bringing a smile to his lips. Both his sisters were beautiful but somber as they walked down the aisle, not one in front of the other as he'd seen before, but arm-in-arm. Was it because of their close relationship?

Was Fiona in need of physical support? Or was it for the emotional support Joy would be able to give her through her gift?

Then it occurred to Val that Kieran had not walked his own daughter down the aisle to meet her husband. Had it been his idea, or Fiona's? Was it Father's way to protest this marriage? Suddenly, Val's stomach roiled.

When Fiona and Joy reached the altar, Joy kissed Fiona's cheek and stepped back to Dolan's other side, clasping his hand.

Alone, Fiona took her place beside Tam. They did not hold hands or even look at one another, that Val could tell. It wasn't until Bishop Ignatius directed them that they clasped their right hands together, and he wrapped a stole around them.

Finally, while repeating their vows, they faced each other. Val listened carefully, but he did not hear any resignation in their voices. If anything, both sounded determined to keep their promises.

When it was time for the ring, Val handed a small gold band to Tam. Kieran had given it to him, saying it had belonged to Fiona's namesake, Kieran's mother. If he was willing to part with such a precious heirloom, then why hadn't he walked with Fiona down the aisle?

His contemplation was cut short by the need to bow his head while Bishop Ignatius prayed for the newly married couple. And then they were pronounced husband and wife, and Tam leaned down to briefly touch his lips to Fiona's. They faced their small audience of witnesses, and Val saw a tear sparkle in Fiona's eye. It made him sad that she and Tam could not wholeheartedly celebrate this union the way he and Emma planned to celebrate theirs.

But Fiona and Tam had both promised to do their best, to work at making this marriage successful. That was much more than anyone could have hoped for, just a few days ago.

* * *

Tam sat on the edge of the narrow bed in his new prison cell located in one of the Keep's towers. Unlike the dungeon, he had a narrow window to let in light and air, and he even had a small desk and chair with parchment and ink and quill pens, presumably so he could write to Fiona.

The events of the last two days had an unreal quality to them, now that he was alone again. Prince Val had stood up for him, both to petition the king on his behalf and also during the marriage ceremony.

Why had he done that? Unlike most of Tam's associates, Val appeared to have no ulterior motive for doing so, other than a genuine concern for his sister's happiness.

His sister.

Tam slowly stood and paced the small room, more spacious than the cell in the dungeon, at least. He and Fiona were legally married now, though they had been parted shortly after the ceremony. They were not likely to see one another again until his three-month sentence had been completed.

But Dolan had changed his mind about Tam remaining in the dungeon and given him this nicer cage. Might he also shorten the sentence, if Tam remained a model prisoner? And how could he prove his trustworthiness? By writing regularly to his wife? Perhaps even a written thank you to both the king and Prince Val?

Tam pulled out the chair and sat upon it. Since he had no knife, he wondered how he was going to prepare a quill. But when he examined them, he noted they had already been cut. He chose one, opened the pot of ink, and took the top sheet of parchment.

Dear Fiona, he wrote as neatly as he could. But then he put down the quill. Where to begin?

She had put her life in his hands when she agreed to leave the Keep with him. She had trusted him, and he had abandoned her. True, he had not known she was carrying his child. But would it have made a difference then? Tam cringed when he realized he would have left her anyway.

But that was in the past. He had a chance to start afresh, even saddled with a wife and child he hadn't expected to have. Living with them in the remote Highlands was far, far better than looking over his shoulder the rest of his life, wondering who might want to hurt him over a gambling debt.

At the sound of a key turning in the lock, Tam turned his head but did not rise. The door slowly opened. Expecting a guard, Tam was startled to see Prince Edward enter and lock the door behind him.

"Your Highness?" he said with a frown. "What are you doing here?"

"I've come to talk to you," Edward said in his most imperious voice.

"What about?" Tam tried to hold back his annoyance.

"I did not say I came to talk *with* you. You are a blight upon the royal family. Father should not have allowed you to marry my aunt, no matter what the circumstance." The boy's eyes narrowed, and a chill went down Tam's spine. He'd seen that look before, in Folville's eyes.

"Well, the king did allow it, and even you cannot gainsay the word of the king." Tam realized after the words left his mouth that he should not provoke Edward, no matter how vexing he was.

Edward took a step closer. "You have one choice left. You will leave the Keep and disappear." His hands clenched into fists.

"I can't leave; I'm a prisoner." Tam stared at the young prince.

"You *can* leave because I will provide a horse for you and a cloak to hide you." Edward smirked, and Tam wanted nothing more than to knock it from his face.

He crossed his arms. "I'm not running away this time." With a glower of his own, he stared down the arrogant prince. "Your father pardoned me, Your Highness. His is the final word in the kingdom, not yours." Then, because he couldn't stand to look at the boy, he turned and picked up the quill again. "I must ask you to leave now. I am writing a letter to Fiona."

Holding the pen poised over the parchment, Tam listened to Edward's angry breaths, but thankfully the prince did not speak again. After a few minutes, the door opened, and the key turned in the lock. Tam let out a shaky sigh and did begin to write, haltingly at first until the words began to flow.

Before he reached the end of the sheet of parchment, the key turned again, and he gritted his teeth. Had Edward returned?

But it was a guard bringing his evening meal on a tray, along with a flask of water. Tam thanked him and set the tray on the desk, pushing aside the letter. In the act of placing the stopper in the inkwell, however, something compelled him to add his closing and signature before eating.

The food was better than he'd had in a long time. A piece of roasted venison, potatoes, and a hunk of bread and cheese. Tam gratefully finished every bite before washing it down with the water, still cool from the Keep's well.

As he set down the flask, his hand began to tremble violently. Then his throat tightened. His heart pounded frantically in his chest. The room had become unbearably warm, and Tam suddenly had trouble breathing. He pushed himself up from the chair, gasping for breath.

Mother, Father, please forgive me—

He tried to make his feet move toward the door, but his muscles went limp, and he fell, hitting his head on the corner of the desk.

Darkness covered him like a shroud, and he knew no more.

Chapter 35

He that covereth a transgression seeketh love.

For once, Kieran woke before Mercy and bounded out of bed. Today he and his family would begin their move to the Highlands. He quivered with excitement, and he only wished he could hurry the sun's rise so they could leave sooner.

He had just changed into his clothes and pulled on his boots, when a frantic knock sounded at the door. Wondering who might have fallen ill, Kieran strode to the door and opened it.

"Drew?" His friend was obviously distressed. "What is wrong?" Kieran started to ask Drew to come in, but he beckoned to Kieran instead.

"I see you are already dressed. Good. Come with me." Drew glanced at the other doors leading to Fiona's and Tristam's bedchambers. "I can't tell you here." Then, before Kieran could ask more questions, Drew spun on his heel and headed to the stairwell.

Kieran followed, puzzled at Drew's behavior. "Can ye not give me a wee hint?"

Drew just hurried to the base of the stairs and led Kieran out to the hallway. "It's better I show you than tell you, so you'll know what to do next."

With his mind sprouting possible scenarios, Kieran hurried to keep up with Drew's strides. They came to another stairwell, which Drew entered. While Kieran followed him up, he felt cold dread. This was the tower where Tammeron d'Jean had been moved after he and Fiona exchanged vows yesterday.

At the top of the stairwell, Drew took a large key off a hook beside the heavy wooden door and inserted it in the lock. The door opened slowly, and Drew indicated Kieran should enter first.

The rays of the rising sun slanted through the narrow window, illuminating the few pieces of furniture. On the floor between the bed and the desk lay the still form of his son-in-law, and Kieran went to examine him.

He was dead, and had been for several hours. When Kieran turned Tammeron's head, he discovered dried blood on one side. It appeared he had fallen against the sharp edge of the desk and hit his temple hard enough that it had killed him. What an unlucky accident!

Kieran sat back on his heels, disturbed. True, he hadn't wanted Fiona to marry the rogue, but he would not have wished for this to happen to him now. He swallowed, feeling a pang of guilt. His dislike of Tammeron hadn't manifested itself in a fatal accident, had it?

No, of course not; he was being superstitious. But it was true that he was not entirely displeased.

Please forgive me, God Most High. I should have prayed for this wayward young man's soul instead of ruing the necessity of his marrying my daughter. I pray now he made his soul right with You.

With sigh, Kieran stood and faced Drew. "I see why ye didna tell me outright."

Drew nodded, clearly distressed. "I dread having to bring the news to Slade and Aleia."

Kieran's heart sank. He knew how devastated he would be, had Tammeron been his son. "I think they should come and see for themselves, as painful as 'twill be for them, or they will have trouble accepting the truth."

Drew's jaw tightened. "I think you're right. I'll go to them myself. Will you tell Fiona?"

"Aye, of course. Go on, and I'll lock the door when I leave."

With a jerk of his head, Drew quit the room.

Kieran gazed once more at Tammeron before he slowly turned. Out of the corner of his eye, he saw a piece of parchment on the desk beside a pot of ink and a quill pen. Tammeron had penned something before he died.

Dear Fiona, the letter began. Without reading more, Kieran picked it up and took it with him. He grimly shut the door, turned the key in the lock and hung it on the peg.

* * *

Fiona awakened when someone knocked on the door. She could make out Papa's voice, but not who had come for him. Then the door shut, and their footsteps faded.

Though she'd hoped to sleep a little longer, she was awake now and might as well rise and dress for the journey on horseback to the Highlands. Or would Papa want her to ride in the wagon with their belongings? It wouldn't hurt the baby for her to ride Firestorm, would it?

After yawning, Fiona splashed cold water on her face. She'd had trouble sleeping, thinking about what she and Tam had done yesterday. How different from the "vows" they'd exchanged on top of the mountain. Then it had seemed exhilarating, but yesterday was a sobering reminder that their thoughtless decision to run away had produced life-changing consequences. Her damp hands went to her belly.

Could she and Tam bring up this child when they were still children themselves? They would have to find a way, wouldn't they? As soon as she and her family settled in their new home in the Highlands, Fiona would make the effort to write to Tam. Perhaps it would be easier to accept that she was his wife if she could put her thoughts and hopes and even fears down on parchment to share with him. Might he even write her back?

When she finished putting on her riding clothes, she made sure her bags were packed and then entered the common room to see if Mama or Tristam were awake yet. She could hear them stirring, and she was about to knock on Mama's door to see if she needed help when Papa entered, grim-faced.

"Papa?" She rushed over to grip his hands. "What's wrong?"

He gathered her into an embrace. "Come tae the tower and I'll tell ye all."

With a shiver of dread, Fiona followed him up the stairs to the open air. Papa paused long enough to take her hand before leading her to the bench in the middle of Mama's garden. The early morning air held a chill that made her wish she'd paused to put on her cloak.

They sat close together on the bench. When Fiona shivered, Papa put his arm around her and pulled her close.

"'Tis no other way but tae be blunt, I fear. I'm sorry, love, but Tammeron is dead."

Fiona stiffened while a tangle of emotions bubbled up inside her: surprise, disbelief, and guilt that, just like before, when she'd been told he was dead, she felt no sadness. Perhaps that was unfair, though; she was sad Tam had not turned out to be the shining hero she had hoped for. Yet, she was grieved more for his sake than for hers.

"What happened?" she finally asked.

Papa cocked his head to meet her gaze. "An unfortunate accident. He must have tripped and fallen in just the wrong place tae hit his head against the corner of the desk." With a sigh, Papa pulled out a folded piece of parchment from inside his tunic. "He had written this tae you."

Fiona took the letter and unfolded it. While she read Tam's words, her guilt increased more and more. If he'd been sincere, and there was no reason to doubt that he had been, then it made his death a real tragedy instead of a relief.

Dear Fiona, I know you are probably feeling as uneasy as I am about our forced marriage, so there is something I should have said to you earlier that I need to tell you now. I am sorry for all the ways I mistreated you and did not show you the respect you deserve. I hope you can forgive me someday. It is my desire to prove my change of heart by my actions, not just words. As we both know, it is too easy to lie to ourselves and to each other. From now on, I want there to be only truth between us, even if it hurts.

This child we have created deserves to have a father and a mother, a real family. I don't know how to do that, but our parents were good examples, so I think maybe we can learn how to be a family, too. I am willing to learn how to be a husband and father, both, and I hope you will be patient with me and give me a chance to show you my sincerity.

Until we meet again, I remain yours, Tam

"Oh, Papa," she choked out, and tears streamed down her face. "Until the moment we said our vows yesterday, I wished that he *had* died so I would not have to marry him. Is it my fault he's dead?"

"No, no." Papa held her close again, rocking her gently. "If anyone be at fault, 'tis me. But truly, 'tis no one's fault. A senseless, tragic accident, is all." He let her cry herself out before speaking again. But first, he pulled back so they could see one another's faces.

"Did you love him, Fiona?" He brushed away the tears on her cheeks with his thumbs.

"I thought I did, but now I realize it was only desire, not real love, like you and Mama have, and Dolan and Rhianna. And Joy and Bennet." She shrugged, embarrassed to confess that particular truth to her father. "But I was prepared to try to love him, and I think he was prepared to do the same." With a sigh, she folded the letter to keep from seeing Tam's handwriting. She couldn't bear to look at it right now, but she decided to save it. Someday his son or daughter might want to read these heartfelt words from his own hand.

Something occurred to her then. "Will he be buried at Frankland?"

Papa nodded. "I'm sure Slade and Aleia will wish to take his body back there for burial. They should be with him now."

"I would like to see him before we leave, to say goodbye, if I may." Fiona's cheeks warmed.

"Then come, let's tell your mother and Tristam, and I'll arrange it." Papa helped her stand.

*

Less than an hour later, Papa led Fiona to the tower room where Tam had been taken not long after they said their vows in the chapel. Her heart beat faster at the sound of voices coming from the room. She had hoped to have a few minutes alone with Tam's body.

Papa knocked on the partially open door, and Slade bade him come in. Fiona sidled in behind Papa. As she suspected, the other voice had been Aleia's. Tam's mother knelt beside the low bed where his body lay, combing his unruly curls with tears shimmering in her eyes. Aleia looked up and met Fiona's gaze.

Though Fiona's gut tightened, she made herself go to her mother-in-law. Fiona knelt beside Aleia, and after a moment's hesitation, they awkwardly embraced.

"I am so sorry," Fiona whispered in her ear.

Overcome, Aleia could only nod. When she let go, she stared at Fiona, searching her face as if for answers, though she did not ask a single question. Finally she pulled away and gracefully rose.

"We will leave you for a few minutes, so you can tell him goodbye." Leaning down, Aleia lightly kissed Fiona's cheek and then hurried from the room with Slade and Papa.

As soon as they shut the door, Fiona gave the still form all her attention.

Lying there with his eyes closed, he appeared to be asleep, not dead. Even though Fiona had seen dead bodies before, Tam's appearance surprised her. An image came into her mind of leaning down to kiss his full lips and waking him. But he would not wake again.

She placed her hands on her belly. "I am sorry you won't get to meet your child, Tam. I didn't want this to happen to you, at least, not after we made our vows yesterday." Tears pricked her eyes. "Thank you for the letter. Now I will ever think of you with fondness and regret, not resentment."

Fiona reached out to touch his cheek. It was cold and so, so still. With a sob, she shut her eyes and bowed her head. She would never know if they could have learned to love one another, but she chose to believe they would have. For the child's sake, she wanted a legacy of good to pass on about the father he or she would never meet. With all the influence she had to shape the future, she would prevent the child knowing about the sins of the father to avoid feeling tainted by them.

"I will do that for you, Tam," she promised. Then she pushed herself upright, gazing down at his face a final time to burn a remembrance of him upon her heart. It was both for the child, and to help *her* remember the terrible cost of their foolishness so it would never happen again.

Chapter 36

Hope deferred maketh the heart sick:
but when the desire cometh, it is a tree of life.

By the end of the first week in November, Kieran and his family arrived in MacLachlan lands. He had sent word to Dougal not to expect them at the castle right away, but he promised they would visit after they had settled in. Since Kieran rode in the lead, he spied the manor first.

"There it be! We're home!" He turned to grin, first at Tristam, who rode beside him, and then at Mercy, Fiona, and Oleta in the wagon. All four smiled back, caught up in his enthusiasm. It was difficult to keep from urging his horse to a gallop to reach the house sooner.

The road followed the contour of the hills, so it was another half hour before they pulled up in front of the large wooden door. Kieran slid down from the saddle and hurried to the wagon to help the women down. Mercy studied the thatched roof, the closed shutters over each window, and the two chimneys.

"It's bigger than I imagined." Her voice was neutral.

"That will nae be a problem, will it?" He must have sounded anxious, for she moved closer and laid a hand on his arm in reassurance.

"No, love. It's a beautiful house and well situated on this hillside." She turned her head and smiled. "It's quiet and peaceful out here."

"Aye," he said with a happy sigh, making her laugh and lean over to kiss him.

"Can we go inside now, Papa?" Tristam frowned, and Kieran wondered if his son would feel isolated here, after living at the Keep.

"Aye, let's go." Kieran started to grasp Mercy's hand, and then remembered an old tradition.

"Kieran?" she asked when he didn't move.

"Wait here, all o' ye." Without pausing for them to answer, he opened the door and hurried to the windows to open all the shutters, letting in as much natural light as possible. To his relief, Dougal had indeed asked someone to clean the place thoroughly. Then he hurried back out the door, staring at Mercy.

"My gracious lady, 'tis an old Highland custom tae carry the bride across the threshold o' her new home." His heart warmed, just to see her here in this place and to know they were *home*.

"But we have been married too many years for you to call me your bride," Mercy pointed out.

"Does nae matter. You'll always be my bonnie bride." He scooped her into his arms and struggled to carry her into the house, grateful the doorway was a bit wider than for most Highland homes. With a groan, he set her down. Mercy was still slender, but his aging back was protesting. Or maybe 'twas just his old wounds reminding him to slow down. To make up for not carrying her all the way to their new bedchamber, he kissed Mercy soundly.

"Welcome tae your new home, dearest o' me heart." Then he took her hand and showed her all the rooms, from the spacious hall, to the kitchen, to the study, guest room, bedchambers for each of the children and Oleta, and finally, their private bedchamber at the rear of the manor. A large canopied bed awaited, ready for her to prepare with their linens and pillows. The window faced southeast, and the distant mountains were visible, since the day was unusually clear and mild for November.

Mercy met his gaze with a smile, her eyes sparkling, before she abruptly exited the bedchamber and returned to the hall. Kieran followed, wondering what she was thinking, and whether he should be alarmed that she hadn't said anything, good or bad. He stood in the passageway, watching her study the walls and ceiling of the great hall, until the others returned from examining their new rooms.

"What d'ye think, love?" Kieran hadn't moved from the low doorway, his heart filled with anxious hope.

Mercy glanced at Fiona and Tristam before giving him her full attention. "It's lovely, even better than I hoped. There's room for gatherings and space for privacy, and the land is full of possibilities. We can grow a large garden and keep chickens for eggs. But there's just one concern."

Kieran's brows furrowed when she didn't continue. "What?"

Mercy smiled at Fiona. "I have not had to prepare meals for a long time. But if Fiona will instruct me, then perhaps I can relearn the skills?"

Fiona rushed into Mercy's embrace. "Of course, Mama. Elvina taught me many valuable things." She pulled back and gazed into Mercy's eyes with tears shimmering. "We can do this together."

Before Mercy could reply, someone knocked on the door and immediately pushed it open.

"Hello? Can we help with anything?" It was Val, and Emma stepped in behind him. Each of them carried a large covered basket.

"We brought ye a meal prepared by me Ma," Emma said shyly. "Your first meal in your new home."

"That is very kind of you and your mother." Mercy embraced Emma.

Fiona came forward with a shy smile. "So, you're Emma."

Val gasped. "I'm sorry, Sis, I forgot you two haven't met yet. Fiona MacLachlan, this is Emma MacRorie. Emma, my sister Fiona."

Both young women smiled brightly, as if recognizing a kindred spirit. Fiona reached over to take Val's basket and lifted the cover, but whatever was inside was cloth-wrapped.

"I can't wait to see what you've brought," she said with a contented sigh. "I'm so happy to meet you at last."

"Tris," Val said brightly, grinning at Emma. "Come, help me unload the wagon." They went outside together.

"I'll help the lads." Kieran winked at Mercy and then followed them.

* * *

Mercy watched Kieran until he disappeared through the front door. Then she turned to Fiona. "Where should we begin?"

"Let's take this food to the kitchen." Fiona's face and posture were completely at ease. "We ought to put that room together first, since we'll be spending a lot of time there."

Mercy paused before following, letting the two younger women lead the way. She *would* be spending much time in the kitchen now, wouldn't she? It had been many years since she'd had to prepare daily meals. In fact, not since she was younger than Fiona and used to cook for her father and young brother.

That was more than *thirty* years ago! Could she remember how to do it?

Of course she could. She wouldn't have to do it alone; she had a capable daughter.

That thought warmed her heart as she entered the kitchen.

Fiona and Emma were unpacking the baskets, chatting away as if they were best friends. Mercy found herself hoping that would be the case, for both their sakes.

"Mmm, this bread smells delicious." Fiona opened a cloth-wrapped loaf and leaned close, shutting her eyes with a pleased smile.

"Ma usually makes flat bread, but she baked these wee loaves in the village oven early this morn." Emma grinned at Mercy. "She was up long before the rest o' us. Before all o' the animals, even."

"Did you and Val spend the night with your family?" Mercy wondered how close Emma's family lived and how difficult it might be to visit them.

"Aye, so we could help pack the food for transport by dragon." Emma laughed. "Ma was concerned the dragons would drop sommat, but I assured her they knew tae be careful."

"I'm sure they did." Mercy heard Kieran and the boys bringing in crates of linens and clothing and personal items. Dougal had assured them they needn't bring any furniture or kitchen implements. From a cursory glance around the kitchen, Mercy supposed he was right.

It wasn't long before the seven of them sat around their new table, holding hands while Kieran blessed the meal provided by Emma's mother. When she opened her eyes, Mercy had to blink away happy tears at the sight of her dear husband, their three younger children, soon-to-be daughter-in-law, and the precious Oleta all together in this new home.

Though once again she was a stranger in a new province, Mercy felt certain Kieran had made the right decision for their family. And in the same way she had learned to thrive after other moves in her life, Mercy was determined to make the best of this one also.

* * *

It took the weeks between their move and winter feast to discover the best rhythm for their lives in the manor. With the help of two young men from the MacLachlan castle, Kieran and Tristam made a few repairs to the barn, paddock, and henhouse before purchasing sheep and chickens. They borrowed a team of oxen from a nearby farmer to prepare the ground in two fields for later planting, and Mercy began a garden behind the house for winter vegetables and herbs. The work was hard but satisfying. Although Tristam struggled at first, occasionally remarking that he had little time for his studies, the hours outside and the unaccustomed exercise strengthened him.

Mercy and Fiona spent hours together daily, and Kieran was thrilled at the contentment he saw in Fiona, especially when they sang and played together almost every evening. They befriended their neighbors from the nearest farms as well as the villagers down the road from the manor, inviting them weekly to share an evening meal on the grounds, weather-permitting, with songs and dancing.

Mercy especially enjoyed these evenings and her opportunity to socialize. Kieran had been concerned she would feel lonely out here, but as long as she could spend time with the neighbors, she seemed happy.

"Are ye happy, love?" he asked her one evening when they climbed into their bed, the curtains closed against the chill of early December in the Highlands.

"Aye, my bonny husband." She leaned over and kissed him. When she pulled back, her smile faded. "The only thing I miss about living at the Keep is the grandchildren. And their parents."

Kieran stroked her hair and then slid his arm around her, drawing her to him. "I miss them, too. Dinna forget, you'll be traveling tae the Keep when Rhianna's time tae deliver grows near."

Mercy nodded and snuggled closer. "And we'll meet Emma's family at last when they come for winter feast."

"And the two o' you Mums can plan a spring wedding tae your hearts' content. That will bring all the family here tae celebrate, will it not?" He kissed her head, and she turned to meet his gaze.

"Yes," she whispered. "Much to anticipate. And meanwhile, we have letters and dragon couriers to deliver them in a timely manner."

Mercy's smile returned, and Kieran let her know how much he loved and appreciated her by keeping her warm in every way.

* * *

The day before winter feast, Val and Emma flew above her family's wagon while they traveled from MacRorie lands to his parents' manor house in neighboring MacLachlan lands. Though he was certain the families would get along splendidly, he felt unaccountably nervous.

Dinna worry, love. Emma sent a mental caress. *All will be well.* From Veynaria's back, Emma blew him a kiss, making him smile.

I'm sorry if I have spoiled your joy with my worry. He returned the mental caress. *I guess I am anxious for our families to become close to each other.*

If they're meant tae be friends, they will be, was her sensible reply.

As we were meant to be? The question made Val wonder yet again if the Most High had indeed brought them together. What else could explain how he'd managed to encounter her at just the right place along the isolated northern coast of MacDonald lands?

Aye, exactly so. Then Emma's attention was taken by Veynaria's gentle turn so they could circle back to her family's steadily moving wagon. The brown draft horse pulling it was more spirited than any work horse Val had ever seen, as if it knew how important the destination was to the humans in its care. Val had no need to signal Reggie, for the dragon mirrored Veynaria's turn, tracing a graceful arc in the sky.

While they were turning, Val spied the manor on a nearby hill. *Almost there!*

He urged Reggie to circle the house, which had been his prearranged signal for Somerled, to let Emma's father know he was near his destination. Val suspected Somerled didn't really need a signal to know where to go, but his future father-in-law seemed eager to learn more about the dragons and their capabilities.

After circling twice and waving at Kieran and Tristam, Val asked Reggie to land in the field opposite the sheep pens, so as not to panic the beasts. Veynaria landed soon afterward, and Val and Emma dismounted and walked hand-in-hand the short distance to the house. By the time they reached the entrance, the wagon came into view, and Kieran and Tristam had reached the house.

Mercy and Fiona came outside then. After a round of hugs, the six of them waited expectantly to greet Emma's family.

Somerled pulled up the draft horse and set the brake on the wagon. Then he stepped down, helped Aingeal out, and waited for Cavan before the three MacRories stood facing the MacLachlans. Val and Emma stepped forward to make the introductions. As they'd hoped, Kieran and Somerled greeted one another like old friends, and Mercy and Aingeal embraced warmly.

"'Tis good tae have ye and yer family in the Highlands, my lord," Somerled said.

"Och, ye dinna need tae call me lord, for this be not a court, but 'tis God's country." Kieran grinned and then became sober. "Truly, knowledge o' the land and yer good common sense be worth more than all the titles and honors a king can bestow."

"Weel then, Kieran. I can call ye cousin, if ye prefer." Emma's father grinned wider than Val had yet seen.

"Come inside, all o' ye," Kieran said with an expansive gesture. "Our home be yours, and we have a good supper prepared tae welcome ye, though it pales in comparison tae what we'll have for winter feast on the morrow." Then he spoke to Somerled again. "Let's put your horse in the paddock so he can graze while we eat."

The two fathers unhitched the draft horse while the rest of them made their way into the manor house. Tristam, Val was glad to note, had been uncharacteristically outgoing while walking with Cavan. Apparently the two had found a common interest in plants and were discussing the weather like old experienced farmers.

I've ne'er seen Cavan so friendly with a stranger, Emma remarked.

Nor have I seen Tristam do the same. His brother gestured to one side of the table, obviously seating himself beside Emma's brother.

Perhaps they will become fast friends? She smiled up at him with a twinkle in her eye.

We can always hope. One can never have too many friends. Val leaned over to kiss Emma's head before they took their places at the table.

Emma and Fiona had apparently worked out the seating arrangement, for they sat together, and Oleta sat between Fiona and Mercy, at Mercy's insistence. After Kieran said the blessing, everyone filled their trenchers, while conversation continued between bites. It warmed Val to his toes that their families were getting along so well, just as he'd hoped.

It wasn't until the end of the meal that Mercy and Aingeal began a discussion of the upcoming marriage celebration. How he wished it could be tomorrow, while just the immediate families were together. But Val knew Dolan and Joy and so many others would be hurt if they weren't allowed to share in the happiness of the day.

When his mother mentioned the first of May, it was all he could do not to protest. That was more than *four* months from now! How could he and Emma wait that long?

It was Somerled who spoke up for the couple, though he had another motive than Val's.

"I must remind ye both that once March comes, we will be too busy with planting and lambing tae think about a wedding." Then he looked a bit abashed for speaking up so frankly.

"Is there much snow in February?" Mercy asked.

"Aye," Kieran and Somerled said together. "But it does nae snow as much here as nearer the mountains," Kieran added. Emma's father nodded his agreement.

"'Tis more snow toward the beginning o' the month than near its end," Somerled pointed out.

"How many o' your family plan tae be at the wedding?" Aingeal looked from Mercy to Kieran and finally Val, who answered.

"My brother and sister and their families, which would be eight." He met his mother's gaze. "Would Uncle Drew and Auntie Gwen come also, do you think?"

"I'm sure they would not want to miss it." Her eyes twinkled.

"The only problem," Val began with a frown, "is that I can think of several who might wish to attend—including all the dragon riders—but where would we put all those people?"

Mercy and Aingeal looked at one another with their mouths open.

"I always assumed our Emma would marry in the wee village kirk." Aingeal appeared distressed. "But our home be small, too small for a large number o' guests."

"If we had the wedding here, would your village priest be willing to travel to perform the ceremony for Emma's sake?" Mercy asked, ever the peacemaker.

"When is Rhianna's child to be born?" Fiona added yet another complication.

"She is due the end of March," Mercy said.

"Is it safe for her to travel so near to her time?" Fiona asked, placing a hand on her own belly.

Emma reached over and grasped Val's hand. *Please, let us not be married at the Keep.*

Val met her troubled gaze. *We will not be married at the Keep. If we have to deny any witnesses other than our immediate families, so be it.* He kissed her hand while in his grasp before addressing them all.

"Mother, Da, Somerled, and Aingeal, it does not matter to Emma and me if we have two witnesses or more. We do not wish to burden any of you, but we would rather not wait until next summer to be wed." *Do you have anything to add, love?*

Aye. Emma cleared her throat. "I would like tae propose that we have families only tae be our witnesses, and be married on the last day o' February, so Val can easily remember his birth is the first day and our anniversary the last." She suppressed a laugh before continuing, though some of the others chuckled.

"And, if ye be willing, Ma, tae have the wedding elsewhere than our village kirk, and if ye be willing, Mercy, tae let it be here so our loved ones can better stay warm and out o' the weather, a MacLachlan village kirk would suit us just as well." She slipped her arm in Val's.

Both mothers had tears in their eyes, and both nodded with fond smiles.

"Any objections?" Val asked, just to be sure. There were none. *And I would remember our anniversary, no matter what the date was, you know.*

O' course I ken. She squeezed his arm.

Two months and a handful of days. Val sighed. Hopefully time would fly as swiftly as a dragon's flight.

Chapter 37

Be thou ravished always with her love.

The winter passed slowly for Val. Even celebrating his eighteen birthday with his family and Emma's family, and a week later celebrating Dolan and Joy's thirtieth birthday at the Keep with all his family, did not make the days march any faster. Though he enjoyed his time with his older siblings, he was anxious to return to Emma. She had missed the gathering because one of her patients went into labor that morning. Val was curious if a new little person now shared the king's birthday.

And he wanted to report his family's reactions to his and Emma's request.

"I think Rhianna is actually relieved not to feel obligated to travel to the Highlands so near to her time," he said while they sat together in her parents' cozy cottage.

"But your brother the king will come tae stand up with you?" She stared up into his eyes with the same longing he felt for her.

"Yes, he will come alone." Val smirked. "Except for Cephalorix, of course."

"'Tis quite an impressive escort." Emma grinned so wide, the corners of her eyes crinkled, making her irresistible. He leaned down and kissed her lightly. "What about Joy?" she asked when their lips parted.

"Hamelin will bring her on Frendatorix and visit with Kentigern until Joy is ready to return to Frankland."

"And her husband and son be not disappointed tae be left out?" Emma bit her lip with an anxious frown, not knowing Bennet and Rob as well as he did.

"Believe me, they will be almost as relieved as Rhianna not to have to travel north in February for a wedding." He squeezed her hand. "They will be happy to congratulate us when next we see them."

Emma let out a sigh. *Then our wedding will be a wee one. I confess, I be right glad.*

So am I, love. So am I.

* * *

Fiona helped Mercy prepare for the wedding in their village's church and also the small feast to be held in the manor house afterward, leaving Aingeal free to sew her daughter's wedding dress. Joy as well as Emma's family planned to arrive two days early, so there would be many hands. Fiona hoped there weren't going to be *too* many hands! But it would be a relief to have help with cooking and the gathering and arranging of greenery for decorations.

She did wonder if there was going to be music and dancing at their small private gathering. If Papa would allow her to use his lute, Fiona could provide music all evening.

Then, on the afternoon before the family was to arrive at the manor, Papa returned from the village in higher spirits than usual. He slipped in the door with a grin, holding it closed behind him until Fiona and Mama turned to look at him through the kitchen entrance.

"What is it, love?" Mercy asked, wiping her hands on her apron and going to greet him with a kiss. "You look like you've swallowed all the joy in the world."

He laughed at that and beckoned to Fiona. "Ye will ne'er guess who I found in the village, so I will show you." He waited until Fiona came near with growing curiosity before pushing open the door.

"Clive?" Fiona clasped her hands. The quiet bard she'd met at Elvina's stepped inside and dipped his head to Fiona and then Mercy.

"Yes, my lady, it is I. Or, as I should say while I'm in the Highlands, aye, 'tis me." He gave Fiona a genuine smile.

"How did you get here all the way from Moor Point?" It had taken hours to fly on a dragon. How many days would one have to travel by foot or by horse?

Clive shrugged, his face darkening with embarrassment. It was such an atypical bardic reaction, that Fiona smothered a laugh. "I happened to mention to Erian one night that I had always wanted to see the Highlands and learn their songs. He offered to fly me as far as the Keep, so it wasn't too long a journey from there." His shyness vanished while he pulled his lute around from his back. "I've been traveling through a few of the clan lands since then and have many songs committed to memory. Would you like to hear one I played at a wedding only a fortnight ago?"

"Of course!" Fiona glanced at Mercy. "I need to get back to my bread dough, but you can sit at the table and entertain us while we work."

So Clive played and sang several songs he thought might be appropriate for the upcoming wedding celebration. After eating supper with them, he and Papa played and sang together. Fiona joined them, usually harmonizing, and the enjoyable evening made her realize how much she missed her brief time as a traveling bard.

When she felt a tiny movement within her, Fiona placed her hands on her belly. Could the baby hear the music? If so, she should sing to the child every day. Her gaze returned to the amiable Clive, and Fiona envied his freedom. There was no way she could be a bard, and that was that. At least she would have opportunities to sing and even play while living here. Fiona was already convinced that Highlanders were born with music pulsing in their blood, so often did they want to sing and play and dance. No wonder Papa was so good at all three!

*

Late the following morning, Joy arrived on the back of an unfamiliar dragon. The rider was Hamelin, who'd once been Bennet's heir and was now Frankland's dragon courier. He didn't linger, merely helped Joy down from Frendatorix's back, delivered letters from Bennet and Slade, and took to the air.

Joy hugged Mercy and Kieran at the door, but waited until she came inside to embrace Fiona. When Joy stared wistfully at Fiona's belly, she took her sister's hand and let her feel the baby move.

With a sigh, Joy leaned closer and kissed Fiona's cheek. "Did you know, even before Bennet and I married, I dreamed of having ten or twelve children?" She smiled, but Fiona could see the pain in her eyes. "It was not the Most High's will, and I am grateful for Robard." She stared down at her hand still resting upon Fiona's belly and closed her eyes, her smile widening. "Truly, a child is one of the most precious gifts in the world."

"If you had had a daughter, what would you have named her?" Fiona grasped Joy's hand the moment she lifted it.

"I wanted to name her after a flower, nothing grand like Rhianna has chosen. Did you know she and Dolan plan to name their second daughter Rosamund?" Joy shook her head. "What a name for a babe! I plan to call her Rose or maybe Rosie."

"A flower," Fiona mused. "I never gave it much thought, but Iris is named after a flower."

"Yes, and there are many other flower names: Lily, Daisy, Violet, Pansy, Petunia—"

"Petunia?" Fiona's eyes widened. "Please tell me you would not name an innocent child Petunia?"

Joy giggled. "Well, probably not. That sounds more peculiar spoken aloud than written."

Fiona's gaze traveled to the greenery she and Mama had been collecting. "How about Holly? Ivy? I suppose those are not really flowers."

"They are pretty names," Joy agreed. "Also Lilac, Primrose, Aster, Laurel, Calla, Bryony—"

Fiona felt the baby squirm. "What's that last one?"

"Bryony. It's a small star-shaped flower that grows on a vine."

"I have never heard Mother or Tristam mention it." Her voice softened. "Bryony."

Not long afterward, Val and Emma arrived. To Fiona's surprise, Emma's mother and brother rode behind her on Veynaria, and Emma's father rode with Val on the somewhat smaller Regnatorix. Once everyone dismounted, the enthusiasm of Emma's family for their first dragon ride was so keen, only Papa could understand their broadened Highland accents.

*

The morning of the wedding dawned cold but with no sign of snow or freezing rain. Fiona woke before Joy and Emma, who were sharing her big bed, both for warmth and because all the other beds were full.

Emma sat up on the other side of Joy, her grin visible in the dimly lit room.

"You aren't excited, are you?" Fiona teased.

Emma tossed back the cover and bounded out of bed. "Excited? O' course not. Why should I be excited?" She twirled on the rug, barefooted, her arms thrown out in excess of joy. When Emma stopped and hugged herself, a pang of sorrow squeezed Fiona's heart. She loved Emma and was happy for her and Val, but Fiona's relationship to her brother would forever change, and it made her a little sad.

Not as sad as the realization she herself had thrown away her opportunity for happiness such as Emma's. But for her sake, and for Val's, Fiona was determined to put on a happy face for them and hope a portion of their joy might spill over to her.

It was a little tricky for everyone to break their fast without the bride and groom seeing one another. Dolan, thankfully, arrived on Cephalorix before they'd finished eating.

"What brings you here so early, brother?" Val stood and went to greet him. "Why are you dressed so formally?"

Dolan frowned for a moment, until he realized Val was teasing him. He glanced over at Fiona in the kitchen doorway and winked. "Oh, I don't know what got into me. I woke before the sun and had an overpowering urge to join my family for breakfast." He looked over Val's shoulder. "Did you save some for me?"

Emma's parents and brother sat with Mercy and Kieran and Tristam at the table. The three MacRories were wide-eyed watching their almost son-in-law bantering with the king. When Dolan sat with them, he was able to put them at ease. It helped that Val and Kieran were there, too.

Soon the ladies retired to Fiona's room to help dress the bride and themselves too, while the men did the same elsewhere in the house. It wasn't difficult to make Emma look like a princess. The blue dress her mother had sewn was a simple design with long, flowing sleeves. Aingeal had painstakingly embroidered the edge of the scooped neckline and the edges of the sleeves, and had added a long embellished belt wrapped twice around her waist.

"I wore this belt when I married yer Da," she said quietly with tears in her eyes. "I saved it all these years for ye tae wear at your wedding."

"'Tis bonnie, Ma, what ye added tae the belt and the dress. I feel the love in every stitch o' it." Tears welled in Emma's eyes.

"Och, dinna cry now, lass. Ye dinna want yer groom tae think ye've changed yer mind." Aingeal's smile concealed her own sorrow at how her relationship with her daughter would change. Fiona wondered that she recognized it so clearly.

At the sound of the church bell, the tender moment ended, and with a bustle of happy chatter, the ladies bundled up in their cloaks and made their way to the front door, where Somerled, wearing a kilt like Papa, waited with his wagon. Someone had tied ribbons on his draft horse's bridle.

"The groom an' the rest o' them have gone tae the kirk and await the bride." His smile mirrored Aingeal's, and Fiona's heart lurched in empathy.

Somerled helped the five women into the wagon and drove the short distance to the church door. Then he set the brake, hitched the horse to a post, and handed them down, Emma last.

"Dinna forget tae put yer right foot forward, love," he said in a husky voice.

"I willna forget, Da." Emma smiled up at her father, giving Fiona a lump in her own throat.

"What does that mean?" Fiona asked when Emma glanced her way.

"Just a bit for luck." She smiled and lifted her right foot. "I'm tae always step out first with me right foot today." Then she lifted her modest bouquet of greenery. Fiona saw a hint of purple that hadn't been there yesterday. "Same reason Ma dried some thistles last fall, tae add tae me bouquet for luck."

Somerled nodded and tucked Emma's hand under his arm. Then they entered the church.

With Emma and her parents hanging back out of Val's sight, Tristam came forward to escort his mother and sisters to the front. Kieran stood to let them sit on the front bench, and Val winked from his place before the altar with Dolan and the priest from the MacRorie village, assisted by the MacLachlan priest. Fiona's brother wore a tunic similar to Dolan's rather than a kilt. His hair was pulled back in a queue, and he looked so handsome, Fiona's heart swelled with pride. She was glad to note the singers in the gallery, though she didn't know where they'd come from. Was there a monastery nearby? She'd have to find out later.

410

Cavan sat alone on the opposite bench, appearing grieved. Surely he realized what a wonderful brother-in-law he would have? But Fiona supposed he loved his sister and was going to miss her as much as their parents would. It made Fiona realize how *much* she had hurt her family when she'd run away with Tam. How could she have been so thoughtless?

Once the anthem for the bride began, Fiona turned and watched Emma glide down the aisle between her parents. The bride's face was radiant, watching Val, but her parents were sober, understanding as Emma could not yet know what a momentous change was being wrought this day. Change that Fiona fervently hoped would be all to the better for each soul in this church.

When the three reached the front, Aingeal and then Somerled kissed their daughter and handed her over to Val, who met their gaze and nodded solemnly.

That made Fiona feel better, that Val was taking this marriage far more seriously than she had taken hers to Tam. She realized her attention was wandering when the MacRorie priest asked Val and Emma to face one another. Then he had them clasp right hands, which he bound with a strip of embroidered cloth. He said a few words, which Fiona could not understand, and then the couple exchanged their vows loud enough to be heard.

"I, Valerian, in the name of the Most High, by the life that courses in my blood, and by the purity of the love in my heart, take thee, Emma, to my hand, my heart, and my spirit, to be my chosen one to walk beside me all the days of my life. I pledge thee my faithfulness and will wholly love thee above all others 'til death parts us." The love in his eyes for Emma was so palpable, it made Fiona tear up.

"I, Emma, in the name o' the Most High, by the life that courses in my blood, and by the purity o' the love in my heart, take thee, Valerian, tae me hand, me heart, and me spirit, tae be my chosen one tae walk beside me all the days o' me life. I pledge thee my faithfulness an' will wholly love thee above all others 'til death parts us."

Then Dolan handed the priest two rings, which he blessed before untying Val and Emma's hands so they could exchange the rings. Fiona fingered the ring on her left hand that Tam had given her during that brief ceremony. She wasn't sure why she still wore it, except she felt strongly the need to prove her baby legitimate, especially in this new place.

When it was time to kiss the bride, Fiona couldn't help but smile when Val's lips lingered on Emma's. It was not what she had expected from her usually shy older brother. Even Dolan raised his brows in surprise. That made a different thought appear in Fiona's head: This simple little church had probably never had so many noble people inside its four walls as it did on Val and Emma's wedding day.

That was followed by another thought: *Noble is more than rank. Noble is the essence of a person.* By that definition, the church was *filled* with noble people on this blessed day.

* * *

Joy sat beside Dolan at the small banquet in Mama and Kieran's manor house. It was so different from her own wedding banquet, and yet it was as near to perfect as it could be. Except for missing Bennet and Robard, Rhianna and her brood, Joy could not imagine how the day could have turned out any better. Even Emma's parents seemed to have grown comfortable with Val and his family. Joy could not be happier for her young brother.

After the meal ended, Dolan stood and cleared his throat. "I will forego a long speech, for my brother's sake, but I just want to say how pleased our family is to welcome Emma, and you also, Somerled, Aingeal, Cavan. A marriage is more than a union of individuals, after all. We also marry the family.

"As an *old* married man now—" he made a face, and Joy knew it was because of their recent milestone birthday— "I can tell you that life is far better lived with a loving spouse beside you. May your lives together always be joyous, through good times and bad, and may you be fruitful and prosperous all your days and live to see old age together." He lifted his goblet, and everyone else did likewise.

"One more thing before I sit down and be quiet for a change: Val and Emma, it is my great pleasure to be able to gift you with a manor house of your own—with a very large barn—near the border of the Highlands, due north of the Keep. There you will have your privacy, but not live far from either family, for we all hope you will desire to keep in close contact with us, as we wish to do with you." He grinned, which made Joy smile, for her brother rarely had occasion to be so relaxed and happy.

Then Dolan resumed his seat and reached over to squeeze Joy's hand. She squeezed back and kept hold of it when Val met his gaze.

"I hardly know what to say, other than thank you. In truth, we hadn't yet decided where to make our permanent home, but if it's the manor I'm thinking of, it is well situated. I don't remember it having a large barn, though." He frowned in puzzlement.

"It was there a week ago," Dolan said with a smirk. "I hired several carpenters to build a sturdy shelter big enough for two dragons."

"Ah!" Val shared a knowing look with Emma. "Then we thank you double."

"It's furnished as well," Dolan continued, wagging his brows. "So you can fly there tonight, if you wish."

"Tonight?" Val stared at Dolan for a little while before turning to Emma. "What do you think, love?"

She nodded. "I would like tae see our new home, but I had rather have music and dancing with our families first." Emma spoke to Dolan then. "I thank ye, Sire, for your generosity."

"You are both very welcome." Then Dolan put on a serious face. "But please, call me Dolan when just the family is together."

Emma's cheeks reddened. "As ye wish, brother. Dolan." She gave him a winning smile.

"Aye, that's more like it!" Dolan even managed to roll the R, making the others chuckle.

At a nod from Kieran, the young bard Clive tuned his lute and began a love ballad while Joy helped Mercy, Fiona, and Oleta clear the table. Aingeal insisted on helping, too, but she wouldn't allow Emma to get up from her seat.

As soon as they finished in the kitchen, Clive was ready for the next song. He played the opening chords of a Highland dance. Joy turned her head when Dolan called her name.

"Yes?" She smiled up at her twin.

"May I have this dance, my lady?" He gave her a little bow.

"Why of course, kind sir." She took his hand, and he led her to their places between the parents of the bride and groom.

With Val and Emma leading, the four couples danced in an intricate weaving pattern. Joy was glad once again that Kieran had taught her several of these kinds of dances. He was obviously comfortable in his element here.

When the final chords ended, everyone begged Clive to let them catch their breath before the next one. Instead, he chose a slow, simple dance. Dolan leaned down.

"Why don't you dance this one with Tristam, and I'll partner Fiona."

Joy nodded. "Good idea."

While Dolan approached Fiona, Joy went to sit beside Tristam. He and Cavan were having a discussion, and he didn't look at her for several minutes. Finally, he turned his head, and his eyes widened.

"Hello, Joy."

"Hello, Tris. Care to dance this one with me?" The song had just begun, but Joy knew it was easy to insert oneself into the slow-moving circle.

"Uh, sure?" He gestured to Cavan. "I'll return shortly, and we can finish talking about this."

"I willna be moving from here," Cavan said with a shrug.

Joy didn't speak again until they had positioned themselves and were moving with the flow of the other couples.

"So, how are you liking this new home?"

Tristam looked around, as if searching for an answer. "I did not think I would like it, because it is so very different from the Keep. But I am growing more comfortable, and I think it will suit us all very well."

"I see you have a friend." Joy nodded at Cavan. "He looks close to your age."

Tristam nodded, stiff and uncomfortable. Joy held back a smile at how serious her youngest brother tended to be. She hoped, as did the rest of their family, that he would find a way to "loosen up," as Kieran put it.

Joy tried again to engage Tristam in conversation.

"I think you've grown taller since you moved here. Are you taller than Papa now?"

"No, of course not." Tristam tried to pull away from Joy's hands, but she wouldn't let him go. Since they were touching, she called on her Healing power to flow into him, calming him. "I might be a little taller now," he confessed, "but I don't want Papa to ever feel short."

"I meant no offense, Tris." Joy glanced over at Kieran, dancing with their mother. Both their faces were radiant. "Kieran MacLachlan is the biggest man I know, in every way that truly matters."

The glowing smile that spread across Tristam's face warmed Joy's heart.

* * *

414

Fiona could not have said why the thought of dancing with Dolan made her uneasy. But he was the king, so how could she refuse without appearing petty, or worse? Holding back a sigh, she glanced over at Clive, wishing she could rather sit beside him with Papa's lute and sing. She made herself smile up at her brother while the dance began. Since it was a simple one, neither she nor Dolan had to concentrate on their steps.

"Are you well, Fiona?" he asked with raised brows, expecting an answer.

"I am well, thank you," was her formal reply. "How is Rhianna?"

"Ready to have the baby." His fond smile was for Rhianna, surely?

"I pray the birth is as easy as possible, and she is safely delivered of your daughter." Fiona lowered her gaze, wondering if the conversation was now at an end.

"Thank you, sister." Dolan cleared his throat, and Fiona looked up at him again.

"Yes?" She made herself hold his gaze.

"I also pray for your birth to be as easy as possible, and—"

Fiona could scarcely believe it, but the king of all Levathia appeared . . .uneasy.

"What is the matter?" *What have I done now?*

"I feel a great need to apologize for the uncharitable thoughts I once had concerning you. We all have made our share of mistakes and deserve to be forgiven. The past ought to stay in the past so as not to hinder us in the present." He stopped then, in the middle of the dancing circle, and grasped both of Fiona's hands. "Can you ever forgive me?"

At first Fiona could not make her mouth form words. Surely this was a dream?

"Of course I forgive you, Dolan. You had every right to be angry or at least disappointed in me and my inexcusable behavior. I have been angry and disappointed in myself." She swallowed the lump in her throat and hoped fervently to continue maturing and making better decisions.

"Even so," Dolan continued softly, "you are my sister, and though we are separated by many years and differing responsibilities, I do care what happens to you, and I pray the Most High will bless you in the coming days and months." He lifted one of her hands and kissed it.

"And I want you to feel comfortable enough to contact me, should you ever need me."

Fiona's gaze softened toward her oft-stern sibling. "Thank you, Dolan. I care about you, too." She felt her cheeks grow hot, but she said the words anyway. "I thought you did not truly care what happened to me, but I understand better how much responsibility you have for all your many subjects and how little time being king allows you to do all that you'd like to do for others, even those in your own family."

Dolan smiled warmly then, and Fiona felt a small connection grow between them, an unexpected meeting of minds.

"That is insightful of you, and very true." He guided them back to the circle of dancers. "I must say, I am looking forward to being an uncle again. Did you know, your daughter will be the cousin closest in age to my daughter?"

Fiona shook her head in wonder. "I had not considered that." She returned his smile.

"It is my hope that our girls will be good friends, as Will and Rob have become."

"That is my hope as well." A chill went down Fiona's spine when she considered the prospect of her daughter becoming friends with the new princess would not have been possible, had she not legally married Tam that fateful day.

And yet, there would still be a gulf between the two girls. Dolan's family lived in the Keep, and his new daughter would be a princess, while Fiona's family lived a very different life in the Highlands now, so hers would be a farmer's granddaughter. Dolan's daughter would have two loving parents. Fiona's had no father. True, she would have grandparents, aunts, uncles, and cousins, but not having a father would leave a vast emptiness in her life. Even if Fiona talked about Tam in the most glowing terms, how could anything replace being raised by a loving father, as she had?

And then the words of Tam's letter came to her so forcibly, Fiona feared they would hurt her head as well as her heart: *This child we have created deserves to have a father and a mother, a real family.*

Her gaze traveled to Joy, dancing nearby with Tristam. Like Dolan, Joy lived a very public life of service and responsibility. What was it Papa once said? A duke was only one step below a king in the weight of duty toward their subjects. Dolan and Bennet led much more influential lives than Fiona ever would. No wonder William and Robard had grown to be as close as brothers. Their families understood one another because they shared most of life's experiences, as well as their grave responsibilities.

Fiona's life was not only freer and simpler, but she was a widow. Her place in society was now uncomfortably strange, since she was expected to wear black or at least drab colors for an entire year. How could her daughter and Dolan's *ever* have the opportunity to be close friends? If it was Joy and not Rhianna soon having a baby girl, then a friendship would be certain to blossom, for Fiona had always felt close to Joy. In some ways, she had never felt closer to her sister....

At least she could be grateful for the new understanding she had with Dolan. Today was a good day, indeed.

* * *

Look at our parents, love. Emma nodded to the side, and Val turned his head. While dancing close together, Somerled and Aingeal beamed at one another, and Kieran and Mercy had the same loving look on their faces.

They look happy. Val smiled at the two couples before returning all his attention to his beautiful bride. *I hope we will be as happy, when we grow old together.*

O' course we will, Val d'Alden. Emma's eyes sparkled. *They brought us up with love and taught us how tae love in word and deed.*

You are a wise woman, Emma d'Alden. He leaned down and tenderly kissed her.

Not yet, I'm not, but 'tis my hope tae be a wise woman someday.

My love, I am so blessed to hold your heart and will do all I can to show you every day how much I love you. You not only have wisdom, you already resemble the worthy woman in the Holy Writ.

Her eyes twinkled. *As long as I be your woman.*

Always, love. My heart belongs to you. Forever. Val gave Emma a mental caress, smiling when she snuggled close with a sigh.

Be it nearly time for us tae see our new home? She gazed up at him with a twinkle in her eyes.

He nodded. *This song is almost over, and then we can call our dragons to fly us there. I'll even carry you over the threshold.*

Emma beamed. "I will hold ye tae that promise, *mo leannan*."

"Mo what?" Val's eyes widened.

"It means *my lover* or *my sweetheart* in the old tongue."

Ah, then I shall promise you whatever you desire, mo leannan.

* * *

"They get along so well together." Mercy sighed, and Kieran looked down, relieved when he saw her smile.

"Aye, Val and Emma are very well matched. I predict they will be blissfully happy all their days." He grinned when she met his gaze.

Not as happy as we are, surely. Mercy's smile was so serene, he leaned over and kissed her.

And then he realized she had not opened her mouth when he'd heard her voice so clearly.

Mercy? Can ye hear me, love?

Her eyes widened. *Yes, I can. I can!* She threw her arms around his neck, and he twirled her around, oblivious to the beat of the song.

All that mattered was their hearts once again beat as one.

Epilogue

A gift is as a precious stone in the eyes of him that hath it.

Three months to the day after Val and Emma married, Fiona was awakened by uncomfortable twinges, much sharper than any she'd felt before. When the sensation passed, she turned and tried to get comfortable in the bed so she could fall back to sleep. But the pains came again a few minutes later, and she sat up. Could it be time for the child to be born?

Fiona carefully slid down from the bed and waddled to the door. She peered out, but no one was yet awake. Should she knock on Mama's door? Mama wouldn't mind, surely?

The next pain was sharper, and that decided her. She knocked softly.

Mercy opened the door in moments. "Fiona?"

She nodded. "I think I'm going to have the baby."

Wide awake now, Mercy placed her hands on Fiona's abdomen, and the Healing glow appeared bright in the darkness. "Yes, the baby is ready to be born. I will let Cephalorix know so he can send word to Emma and Joy."

As had been decided months earlier, Emma soon arrived on Veynaria, and Hamelin and Frendatorix brought Joy from Frankland not long after.

Though the three of them had never worked together to deliver a child, Emma, Mercy, and Joy were so in tune with one another, Fiona felt safe and well-cared for.

By late afternoon, Emma told Fiona Val had arrived and was keeping Kieran and Tristam company.

"Please tell him thank you and give him my love." Then Fiona had to concentrate on the next contraction. The pains were coming closer and harder. Only Joy's Healing gift kept Fiona from despair. No wonder childbirth was called *labor*; this was hard work indeed!

"The head be in position, Fiona," Emma said with excitement in her voice. "When next the pain begins, ye will feel a strong urge tae push. Do so!"

Pain like nothing Fiona had ever felt before gripped her. If not for Joy's encouragement, Fiona would have recoiled, held back. She pushed once, twice, and the third time the baby slipped into the world with a lusty cry.

"Is she—"

"Aye, your daughter is whole and healthy." Emma grinned briefly at her.

Bryony. Fiona lay back, gasping, while Mercy took charge of the babe and Emma worked at something, but Fiona was too exhausted to care what it was. If Tam had lived . . .but he was gone forever. This child deserved to have two parents who loved her, who desperately wanted her.

Fiona had prayed since the wedding for the strength to make the best decision for the baby. She thought she had already made that decision, but it was confirmed, as if by heaven, when Mercy handed the swaddled newborn to Joy so she could help Emma.

Joy looked so *right* holding that baby in her arms. The adoring, wistful gaze she gave the little one melted Fiona's heart, knowing her beloved sister could never have another of her own, though she desperately wanted more children.

And so, when Joy tried to hand the precious bundle to Fiona, she did not look at the babe, but stared into her sister's eyes with all the love and determination she possessed.

"I want you to have her. Meet your daughter, Bryony."

Joy's eyes widened. "But, Fiona—"

"Please, Joy. This child needs a mother *and* a father, and you need her. Please, say you will be her mother?" For a moment, Fiona feared Joy would refuse.

When Joy stared down at Bryony again, the glow in her eyes lit the room.

"Bryony," she said softly. Then she looked up at Fiona with tears spilling onto her cheeks. "What a wondrous and precious gift, dearest sister!" Joy leaned over to kiss her forehead before pressing her cheek against Fiona's. "You know I will love her with all my heart."

"I know you will." Fiona lay back, exhausted but pleased. "Bryony is in the very best hands."

Neither Mercy nor Emma had dry eyes. Mercy wiped her hands before smoothing back Fiona's sweaty hair with a tender caress. Together they watched Joy carry the child to a nearby chair and gingerly sit upon it, never taking her gaze from the baby's face.

"My dearest girl," Mercy said softly while clasping Fiona's hand. "Are you sure this is what you want to do?"

Fiona nodded. "I prayed harder than I ever have, Mama." She hissed when the afterbirth pain struck and gripped her mother's hand. "It's what Bryony deserves," she said through gritted teeth. When the pain subsided, she added in a whisper that only Mercy could hear, "I wasn't ready to be a wife or a mother."

Mercy nodded gravely. Surely she knew in her heart Fiona was right? She stroked Fiona's face again and smiled. "I believe that is the greatest act of love I have ever witnessed."

"All my life, you and Papa have taught me to love. I'm sorry it took so long for me to finally learn the lesson." Fiona smiled back, weary but oh, so pleased. Her gaze drifted back to Joy and Bryony again.

What she had anticipated might feel like emptiness had instead filled her entire being with radiant joy and peace.

THE END.

Cast of Characters

Fiona's Gift begins August 1185

At the Keep:
King Dolan d'Alden, 29 (page Christopher Decourt)
Queen Rhianna d'Alden, 28
Prince William Orland d'Alden, 10
Prince Edward d'Alden, 8 (page to Lord Henry Cornwall)
Princess Matilda d'Alden, 5

Lord Earl Marshall Kieran MacLachlan, 49
Lady Mercy MacLachlan, 46
Prince Valerian (Val) d'Alden, 17
Lady Fiona MacLachlan, 16
Lord Tristam MacLachlan, 14

Lord High Steward Drew Campignon, 47
Lady Gwendolyn Campignon, 46
Cory Campignon, 19
Roland Campignon, 18 (squire to Sir Thomas Cornwall)

Lord High Constable Jambray Decourt, 49
Lady Robena Decourt, 33
Evander, 15 (squire to Sir Henry Cornwall)
Christopher, 12 (page to King Dolan)

Lord High Chancellor Tavis Richmund, 49
Lady Arella Richmund, 37
Captain Hodor
Parkin
Conrad
Darby

At Frankland:
Duke Bennet d'Ardelane, 42
Lady Joy d'Ardelane, 29
Robard d'Ardelane, 9

Slade d'Jean, 45 Steward of Frankland
Aleia d'Jean, 33
Tammeron d'Jean, 17 (squire to Lord Henry Cornwall)
Arthur d'Jean, 14 (squire to Bennet)
Jessa d'Jean, 9
Lord Hamelin de Grignon, 27
Sir Aubrey Durandal, 25

At Westmoor:
Lord Nowles Meverel
Lady Shamina Meverel
Sir Alfred Meverel, 26
Bardalf Meverel, 23 (a merchant)
Griffin Meverel, 18 (squire to Lord Dracen)
Fletcher Meverel, 16 (was to be squire to King Dolan)
Sir Edelbert, 37 (Steward of Westmoor in his invalid uncle's place)

At Moor Point:
Lord Dracen Woodville, 51 (squire Griffin Meverel)
Lady Dulcinea Woodville, 33
Bryce Woodville, 12 (page to Sir Aidan)
Paisley, 10
Sigurd, 1

Sir Aidan Fitzhugh, 37
Lady Iris Fitzhugh, 21

Sir Artemis Villeroy, 27
Squire Weston Cornwall, 19
Rodney Folville
Virgil
Allard
Noel
Clive

Elvina
Erian
Finn
Barnaby

At Southmoor:
Lord Pascar Gowen, 27
Lady Eleanor Gowen, 21
Rodney Gowen, 3

Norman, 17, falconer's apprentice

Lord Henry Cornwall, 49
Lady Helena Cornwall, 43
Sir Henry Cornwall, 27
Lady Luella Cornwall, 25
Sir Thomas Cornwall, 25 (squire Roland Campignon)
Lady Lidia Cornwall
Weston Cornwall, 19 (squire to Sir Artemis Villeroy)
Oswald Cornwall, 17 (squire to Sir Nathan MacNeil)
Lady d'Evrow
Serene (Mercy's old friend)
Jevan, 20 (Serene's youngest son)

At the Southern Woodlands:
Lord Rudyard MacNeil, 61
Lady Shannon MacNeil, 59
Sir Nathan MacNeil, 31 (squire Oswald Cornwall)
Lady Rowena MacNeil, 26

Oriana, 16, a laundress
Felicity, her invalid mother
Arnulf, her brother, a stable hand

At Northland:
Lord Geren Wyldwood (Guardian of Northland)
Minor Lord Sean Hendry, 12
Lord Hugh Blythe

Lady Caitlin Blythe

At the Highlands:
Lord Dougal MacLachlan, 37
Lady Beatrice MacLachlan, 35
Angus MacLachlan, 15 (squire to Tarran)
Maisie MacLachlan, 12

Lady Moira MacLachlan, 59
Kerren MacLachlan, 18
Sir Tarran Campignon, 23 (squire Angus MacLachlan)
Lady Merry Campignon, 18

Sir Drystan MacLachlan, commander of Tuath Garrison
Jillian MacLachlan
Mhairi MacLachlan

Somerled MacRorie
Aingeal MacRorie
Emma MacRorie
Cavan MacRorie
Kentigern MacRorie
Caesg MacRorie

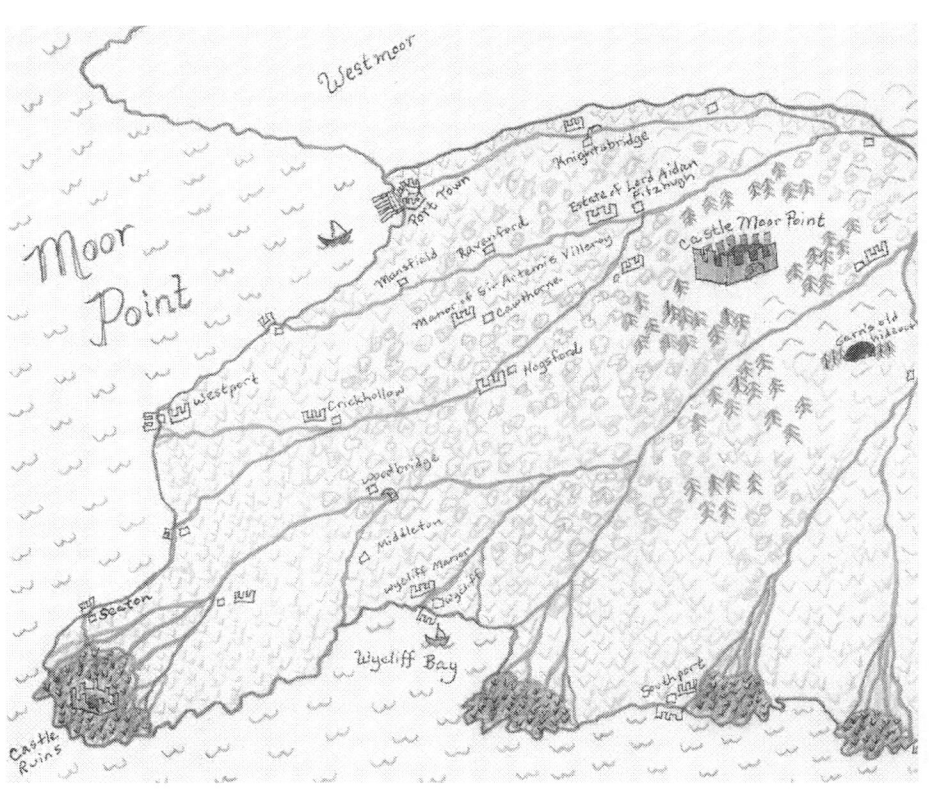

Made in the USA
Middletown, DE
06 September 2022

72122233R00257